Faculty of Physicians and Surgeons of Glasgow

Minute Book 1

Faculty of Physicians and Surgeons of Glasgow

Minute Book 1

ISBN/EAN: 9783741197604

Manufactured in Europe, USA, Canada, Australia, Japa

Cover: Foto ©Andreas Hilbeck / pixelio.de

Manufactured and distributed by brebook publishing software (www.brebook.com)

Faculty of Physicians and Surgeons of Glasgow

Minute Book 1

That gras it is known to us that ther wa
ane band lost at the fire of ane 100 ttb
ondew to us be Gabriell thomsoune in
longsyd these ar therfor testifieg yt the
foirsd Gabriell hes compleitly payed the
sd 100 ttb & anual rent wh iswas 5 ttb therfor vpon the
12 day of november 1654 to dainell
Broune collector for the sd year

Fallowes ane short abrigment
of the gift granted to the
chirurgianes of glasgow by the
deceast King James in the
year 1599.—

1 They have power to call summond and
convein w^tin the brughe of glasgow or
any other brughe w^tin the Schyrefdomes
of Lanerk, dumbritaine, Renfrew, Tyall,
Carrick, Air & Cunyng hame befor them
vsing or professing the airt of chirurgianes
to reeamein them vpon ther literature
knowledge & practice and if fund worthie
to admit them & grant testimoniall
according to ther airt & knowledge that
they sall reereise therafter receive ther
oathes & authoriso them ac accordis,
and to discharge them to use any
farder nor they gave knowledge of on
passing ther capacitie.—

2 That those eitit report testimoniall of
the ministers and elders or magistts of
they dwell of ther lyf & conversatione
ohi eaier contumaxe being laufie eitit

to be unlawit in 40 lib toties quoties half
to the judges & the rest to be disponit
upon at the visitauris pleasour, and
for payt to have bres on the ptie
or magrates wher the contumax dwellis
charge them to poynd gif fond in 24
houris under the paine of horning and
the ptie not having geir to incarcerat
them whill cautione be fund that the
contumax appear gn the visitour
appoyntes gevand tryeall of ther
qualificatiouns.—

3 That the visitour visit rarire murdered
or poysoned personne tains away
extraordinarilie and to report to the
magrates as the fact is.—

4 That the visitour and his bretherin may
mak statutis for the weill of the subjectis
anent the sds airtes & using therof——
faithfullie & the brekers to be punished
and unlawit according to the fault.—

5 Non to exerceis wtin the sds boundis
wtout are testimoniall of ane famous
universitie gr medicin is taught or at

leist of his malies or his spous cheiff mediciner
and in caice of failyie to discharge &
inhibit them throughe exercring theroff
under the paine of 40 lib to be
distribuit as aforsd ay and gff they
bring sufficient testimoniallis as sd is.—

6 Sextlie.— That no mannier of persoune sell
any drugis wt in the citie of glasgow
except the same be sightit be the saidis
visitouris under the paine of confiscatoune
of the druges.—

7 Sevintlie.— That non sell rattoune poysone
or senuck or sublimer under the paine
of ane hundrethe merkes except onlie
apothecaires wha sall be bund to tak
cautoune of the buiers for cost skaithe
& damage.—

8 Eightlie.— That the facultie convein everie first
mononday of ilk mouthe at som conveniene
place to visite & give counsall to poor
disrased folkes gratis.—

9 Lastlie.— Ther is granted to the facultie
imunitie & exemptioune from all
wappingshawingis, raidis, oistis, bearing

of armour, watching, warding, stenting, taxationis
passing on assyisse, inquisitis, justice
courtes, Shreff or burrow courtes in
actiones criminall or civill notwithstanding
of the actis lawes & constitutiones
therof except in giving their counsall
in materis appertenning to the saidis
artes — Ordaining all provestes, baillies
Shreffes, stewartes, baillies of regalities
& otheris ministeris of justice wt in
the sds boundis & ther reputis To
assist, fortifie concurre & defend the
sds visitouris and ther posteritie
processouris of the forsds artes and
putt the sds actis maid & to be
maid to executioune And that
lres be grantit to charge them to
that effect wt in 24 houris nixt
after they be chargit therto — Givin
under the privie seall at halyrud hous
the penult day of Novr 1599 and of the
kings regne the 33 year
                    Per Signaturam manuum
                S D N Regis nec non

Litera Magis Petri Low

Chirurgii et Magri
Ro: Hamiltonne,
professoris medicinae

maucibus dominorum ducis
Lennucios, thesaurii ac
secretarii dicte domini
regis subscriptum.—

fallowes the names of the facultie sett
downe the 7 of Marche 1655.—
　　　　burgeses
1 Johne Hall Visitor
2 Mr Jo: Crichtonne
3 Mr James hamiltoune
4 Mr And grahame
5 daniell browne
6 James Frank. Geo Lockhart
7 Androe Muir dead
8 Thomas Lockhart
9 Johne dow Ro: houstonne
10 Wm Soutter Mr Ch Muat
11 James Thomsone
12 Ro: Stanes Jo hall barbor
13 Wm Clydisdaill And Ralstoun
14 Morthon george dead Jo: Hallfoirt

v 15 James Scot dead Ruelie Hall
v 16 James Lies — James Wir
17 Johne Lies
18 Ard bogle
19 Adame grorge dead
20 James braidwood
v 21 Androe Millar 20 S
22 Jon Liddell
23 James Mowatt
Mr David Sherp
Andro Elphistonne
Mr Jon Muir
James Wilsonne
Iver M'neill
James frank younger
Ja Watt
Johne Robiesone
Adame Graye

Strangers licentiat

Johne Hoe in Kilbarchen 1654	20 S
Wm Wallace in paisley 1654	20 S
Jon Patersoune in paisleye 1652	20 S
Jon Millar in Kilmarnock 1654	12 S yir

Ro͞t Sargonshill [1654] in Air	30 S
Thomas Chisholme [1654] in Air	30 S
Johne Reid in Air / 35 [1654]	16 S
James Tobias [1655] in Air	30 S
Johne Tod in dean	12 S
Allan Kirkwood at the grein end brigs	30 S
Iver M'neill	30 S
Ro͞t Muir in gorballis yearlie	16 S
Mr Tho Younge 59	30 S
Jo͞n Forster 59	30 S
Jo͞r Mathiesonne M: 1654	20 S
Tho Robiesonne M: 59	20 S – 0 – 0
Wm Flemyng M 59	20 S – 0 – 0
Mr Alexr Dunlop M 59	30 S
Gilbert Andrews M 59	30 S
Adam Patersonne in paisley 1662 yearlie	1 lib
Jo͞n Ewing in paisley 1662	30 S
Androe browne in hamiltonne admitit	
1662 in Septer yearlie	30 S
Johne Reibing in dumbartane	20 S
Mathow Millar 1668 to pay yearlie	20 S
Thomas Start yearlie	20 S
Gilbert Wilson in straven	20 S
Peter Boill	20 S

A burges sone at his admissioune to be
a frie manis to pay 20 lib
& if a prenteis wt a frie man he is to
pay 30 lib for his admissioune
if a stranger enter frieman he is to pay
100 Merks but non to be admitit till they
be first burges

p: Prenteisis in the third page

Auires over other menes heordis ff 3

b: Admissioune of barbouris f 3
Quarter comptes f 6. 36
Statuts bookit f 7
Statut anent those calumniates their
brother f 8. 12. 25 _
Non of the crafts moneye id out consent f 8
Clerkes fie : f 36 _

Die tertio Junii Millesimo
Sexcentesimo secundo.-

The 9th day w^m in the Blackfreir Kirk
of Glasgow In presence of Sr George
Elphistoune of Blaithwood knyght Provest,
James Forret, Johne Andersoune, Will
Andersoune, Baillies therof, Compeirt
Mr Peter Low, and Mr Rot Hamiltoune wha
product ane gift of our Soveragne lord
anent ther libertie w^t the provest & baillies
autoritie interponit thereto as the samyn
at lenth beires & ward convention w^t
y^r breithren videlicet Adam Fleming
Mr Rot Allasone, William Sparg, Thomas
Thomsoune, Johne dorie and the
samyn being red the s^d Mr Peter and
Mr Rot was content of ther awne consents
notw^tstanding of thet nomination of
gift y^t ilk yeir ance at Mickelmes
the samyn shall be lytit amongst the
Brethrine, and wha be maist vootts
bris elected ~~deacon~~ to remaine visitor
for ane yeir y^r efter & so furth yearlie

in all tymes coming And also is content
yt the forsds persons brethren of craft
presentlye admittit by them shale have
power and liberties to use ther craft
and calling as free as themselfs after ther
finentayes & that they shall not visit
any of the forsds brethren patients being
on cair wtout ther anne consents &
the patients first had and obtained
therto — 9th brethren being present consents
to concure asist and had hand to,
And therefter the sd Mr Rot present
Visitor whill Michalmese be consent of
the brethren hes elected Rot Herbertsone
Notar Clark to them, wha hes given
his oath of fideliti and also creat George
Burnell officier qwill Michelmes & hes
given his oath & the sd brethren to
~~coteine~~ convaine all such tymes as shall
be apoyntit being warned be the officier
under the paines conteined in the
ordinance to be set downe theramentt,
the brethren hes putly given ther oathes
and ordained the rest and Johne Mall

to be convened & y[t] they shall concur and
assist y[e] w[t] uthers as becomes.—

   Sic Subscribitur R[o]
    Herbertson Notarius.—

die 17 Junii 1602

The q[lk] day compeirit Mr R[o] Hamilltoune
Visitor & the Brethren w[t] his anne Sone
and ther elicit thir persons under
wrytine to be q[r]ter mrasters q[ll]
Michellmesse nixt to com viz Mr Peter
dow William Spany Mr W[m] Allasone, Adam
Fleming wha geve ther oathes as afresd
And therefter they w[t] on consent statute
and ordaine y[t] give any therof doc
convine w[t] the Visitor for setting doune
of any good order shall be sufficient.—
Also give any of yame or uthers of the
brethren being wernd personally to any
conventions & wilt compeirance sall pay
ten shilling of penaltie w[t] out ane resonable
excuse to be aplayed to such uses as
the Visitor & his Masters shall think

expedient—

die 22 Junii 1602

The qlk day Mr Rōt Hamiltone Visitor, Mr
Peter Lou, William Spang, Adam Fleming,
Mr Rōt Allason qrter maister conveined in
the sd Mr Rōt aine dwelling house wt
the rest of the Brethren. The qlk day in
respect yt Thomas thomsone having given
his oath at his entrie to beir burdine
wt the rest of the brethren & discharging
of his dewtie he being synsein desired to
compeir wt them to ther assistance in
doing ther leasome busines severall tymes
hes most wrongeously contemptouslie disobayed
Therfor they ordaine him to tyne whatsoever
libertie he hes be yin & to tak in his
Barsones, as also John Hall & uthers.
to be dischargit sick lyk & to that effect
requeists the provost & baillies to interpon
ther autoritie therto.—

And als condischende to give up the particular persons names that any way vsurps any libertie and privilage of ye brethren to the provist and Boullies requisting yame to cause them to convine and to find catier for abistinance conforme to his magisties Comissions & the autoritie of the toune interponit thereto.—

Eodem die

Being convined as ad is they heve condischendit & be thir presents condischende that give any persone being qualiyed does enter being a burges son shall pay for his admission fortie pund, & give any Burges sone be prentise is in the toune is a fre man of the sd calling enters fre man shall pay threttie pundes for his admission, & a stranger that coms to enter freiman sall pay — 66. lib — 13 — 4 & non of the above named persons to be admitted till they produce ther Burges ticket befor the deacon and grter masteres according to the act of the gildrie.—

Eodem die

14

Act for fre mens sons.

It is condischendit that all fre men sons of the sd calling ether being prenteis to ther parents or to other fre men in any place shall enter paying only 20 lb

Act anent the admission of prenteisis & Booking.

The sd day ordaines that all prenteises to be entred shall remaine no shorter space nor seven yeares & the last two therof for meat and fee and at his entrie shall pay five pund to the craft and to the clark — 1 lib — 13 — 4 give he be ane extraordinar on, & give he be a burges son to pay — 2 lib to the boy & to the clark — 1 lib 6 s 8 & to the officer — 12 s. And yt ilk

Act for reexamination of prenteises.

prentise shall be reexamined after the first three yeares compleating upon his airt of craft & to pay 5 lib for the dinner at that tyme & to every reexaminator 20 s & to the clark 6 s 8 at the day of reexamination & the visitor to admonise the reexaminators upon they shall reexamine to be wrytten and at the 5 yeares and to be reexaminat lykwise & to pay alyk.
And at the seven yeares end when he passes

master to be reexaminat upon the holl
particulars of his airt, & the definitions
causses signes accidents & cures of all
desrises perteaning to his airt wt the
composition of nature & fit medicaments
as shall be requisit payand at the tyme
for ane denner ten pund & to the reexaminat
and others as is aforsd.—

Eodem die

Act for taking of ewes of others hands.—

It is statute and ordained that non of ye
brethrein tak ane patient out of ane others
hand untill the tyme yt the sd brother be
fully satisfied for his paines & yt at the
visitores sight & qrtermastres under the paine
of paying to to the box 40 lb unforgiuen
and the foir named acts we ratifie &
aproue & sines the sd act wt our hands
that it may heive the force of ane decreit.—

Eodem die

Act for admission of Barbors

It is statute and ordained that barbors
being a pendecle of chirurgerie shall pay
at ther admission forties punds scots &
ilk yeir twentie shilling to the pin
and   to midle nor any

thing furder belonging to chirurgerie under
the paine of five pund toties quoties &
shall pay to the clark of the calling
for his buiking thretties shilling scotts &
to the oficer tuel shilling

       sic subscribitur
        Ro: herbisoun -

die penultimo Septembris -
1602 -

Visitor
Hamiltonne

The 9th day the brethren of the chirurgians
convening in the hie Kirk all in on votte
presentlie hes electit & chosen Mr Ro:
hamiltonne Visitor for the yeir to com
all Michellmese niest & hes given his
oath of fidelitie as afferis And thereafter
they hen chossen thir persons qrtermasters for ys year to com viz Mr
peter low, William Spang and Mr Ro:
Allasone who hes given ther oathes as
afferis & ws power wt any two to
convene wt the visitor in tyme coming

       sic subscribitur

Ro: herbeson

Eodem die

Officer hall

Thereftir they hes electit & chosen Johne
Hall officer for this yeir to com ghill
Michellmas & hes given his oath of
fidelitie as afoiris..

Admission Hall & Spang

The 9th day William Spang younger and
Johne hall ar admittit fre men wt
the reft of the Brethren after due tryall
and reexamination who hes given ther
oathes of fidelitie as afoiris

die penultimo Septembris
anno 1603..

Visitor hamiltoune

The 9th day the holl Brethren of the
airt of chirurgeons being convenit wt in
the new Kirk of glasgow hes electit &
be thir presentis elects Mr Ro: hamiltoune
Visitor for ane year to com vy Michellmes
wha hes given his oath for dew administration
therin & yrester they hes chosen thir
persounis to be quhr masters for the sd

18

yeir viz Mr Peter Low, William Spang, Mr
Rbt. Allason & hes given ther oathes And
also hes electit Johne Craige Notar to be
ther Clark

Officer for yt yeir
Johne Hall

die 22 Septembris 1604

Visitor
hamiltoune

The qlk day the holl brethren of the
airt of chirurgerie being convenit for
in the hye Kirk of Glasgow, hes
electit & at this prits elects Mr Rbt
Hamiltoune Visitor whill Michelmes
1605 who geve his oath for dew administration
therein & ther efter they have chosen
ther persons (viz) Mr Peter Low, William
Spang Mr Rbt Allason qrter maisters who
hes given ther oathes & hes continuell
Jou: craige notar ther clark.—

5

The qlk day Thomas Read is admittet
free man & hes given his oath.—

freiman
Read

Officer
for yr yeir to com

Thomas Read.

The sd day Mr Rot hamilltoun producit
ye letter of gild grantit to yame be his
magistie under the privie seall at
hallyrud house the penult of november
1599 Togither wt the ratificatioun yrof
be the provest ballies & counsell upon
the 10 of feberuarii 1600.

die 23 of maii 1605.
The glk day in presence of Mr Rot
Hamilltoun present Visitor being convenit
wt his wholl brethrin In consideratioun
yt George berrell hes beine ane old
bruges sone, & for the somme of ten
punds money to be payed to the
common boxe of the craft Therefore they
have admittet the said George freman
wt them wt libertie to him to proces the
airt of Barborie wt simple wounds in
the flesh wt Comision he medle wt na
farder wt on speciall consent to the
brethren & deacon for the tyme & the

st George hes given his oath.-

& is officer fra this Michelmas nixt whill
Michelmas 1605.-

die 21 Septembris 1606.-

The gfk day the brethren hes electit Wm
Spang deacon for this yeir to com wha
hes given his oath & hes electit Mr
Rot Hamilltonne, Mr Peter Low, Mr Rot
Allasonne qrtermasters who in lyke
maner hes given ther oathes.-

Visitor
Spang

die 22 Septembris 1607.-

The gfk day the brethren being convined
hes electit Mr Rot Hamilltonne deacon
for this yeir to com & hes given his oath
& hes electit Mr Peter Low, Wm Spang, Mr
Rot Allason qrtermasters gha hes given
ther oathes.-   Officer
                    George Birrell

Visitor
Hamilltonne

die 22 of September 1608

The gfk day Mr Rot Hamilltonne is electit

Visitor
Hamilltonne

deacon for this yeir to com & hes given h
oath & hes electit Mr Peter Low, Wm Spang,
Mr Rot Allason glater masters wha hes
given ther oathes.—

(6)

die 22 of September 1609.

Visitor
Hamilltoune

The gfR day Mr Rot Hamilltoune is electit
Visitor for this yeir to come & hes given h...
oath & hes electit Mr Peter Low, Wm Spang
& Mr Rot Allasoune gater masters wha hes
given ther oathes.—

die 22 of September 1610.—

Visitor
Hamilltoune

The gfR day Mr Rot Hamilltoune is electit
Visitor for this yeir to com & hes given
his oath.—

Act anent
the gater comptis.

The sd day It is statute that the Visitor
in tymes coming be him self if he be
present and in case of his absence the
officer to be apoyntit be him shcall gaterly
four tymes in the yeir collect ttu gater
comptis, & if not the Visitor shall pay
tha samne himself for relief of tha

rest of his Brethren..

fre man Read

The glk day James Read is admittit fre man wt the rest of the brethren and hes given his oath..

& is chosen officer for ys yeir..

fre man duncan

The glk day James duncan is admittit fre man wt tho rest of the Brethren & hes given his oath..

dic 22 Septemb: 1611..

Visitor Allason

The glk day Mr Rot Allasoune is chosen Visitor for ane yeir to com wha hes given his oath.-

Quartermasters

Mr Rot Hamiltoun. Jon Hall..

die the 23 of Januarii 1612..

The glk day Mr Rot Allasoune present Visitor grants him presentlie to have received the Letters of gift from Mr Rot Hamiltoune last Visitor grantit be his majestie under his hynes privie seall of the Libertie

of the airt of chirurgeri w~ are set doune
be the provest Bailies and counsell of
Glasgow · ratifying ye sds Letters w~ the
burgs Letters of publicat theiroff raisit upon
the samyng together w~ his Buik of the
Acts & Statutes of the sd airt of chirurgeri,
glk Letters the sd Mr Rot Allason oblesses
him to mak patent & furth coming to
ye sd Mr Rot Hamilltoune & deliver the
samne to him gn necessarly he shall
have to do w~ them in putting the same
to execution against all contraveiners theroff
so long as the sd Mr Rot Allason remaines
Visitor & hes the same in his kiping
as Visitor.—

       Sic Subscribitur MRobert Allason..
           w~ my hand..

      die the 28 of Januarii 1612..
The glk day Andro Mill is content to
abyd ane tryall of his qualification in
the airt of chirurgeri at any day as
the Visitor & his brethren shall dpoynt
him to yt effect And is com in ther

(margin left, upper) Act anent the gift..

(margin left, middle) (F)

(margin left, lower) Tryall Mill

wills y^t he shall pay for his admission
as ane brother of craft..

The sd day Rot Archibald is in lyk
maner to abyd ane tryalls of his airt
when he shall be chargit to that yeet-
be the Visitor & in lyke maner is com
in the will of the Visitor & brethren
y^t he shall for his admission..

The 9th day Mr Rot Allason Visitor acompained
w^t the hole brethren of craft setter
doune thir statuts fallowing which shall
be obayed in all tymes coming..
Imprimis Conforme to ther Letters of Gift
& priviladge grantit to them be his
Majestie ilk first day of the mounth
they visit ye puire (Gratis) gife they
heue Intelligence of the pur Sick creature
is & be requirit to that yeet..

As also that the deacon or on of thie
q[uar]termasters teach upon medicine chirurgerie
or apothecarie the nature of herbs droges
& such lyk as shall be thogh[t] expedient

by the brethrene of the sd vocation..

3 Breaus ther ar sundrie who sells drogs
wt in this brugh and hes not sufficient
drogs that ilk quter of yeir once the
Visitor wt his masters visit the sufficiensie
therof conforme to tte article conteined
in Bur charter..

4 ffourthly for helping of the poores necessiti
and incresc of ther airt and tread to
be ane help to the common boxe + common
chairges yt ilk Brother of craft give 2
penies of ilk 20 lib that they shall
win of frei yeir, for any euir that comes
to them ilk month once to pay the
saming according to condischendances..

(8) 5 That wt all dilgences that they be ane
common Boxe maid wt tuo locks + keis
to keip the fre money that comes to
the common afaires wt ye Buik + Charter
+ uther ther evidences + yt the keis of
the sd boxe remaine in keiping of tuo
of the qutermasters In all tyme
coming:-

Apud Glasgow die nono
mensis Maii anno domini 1612..

The qlk day Andro Mills is fund qualifit
to proces the airt of chirurgeris & sic
uthers of the airt of medicine as he
has knolage of, be Mr Rot Allasone pnt
Visitor & his qtermasters & has given on
sufficient tryl thereintill, & therfor they
have admittit the sd Andro fre man
wt them who hes given his oath for
dew administration therintill as becomes
& hes payit of upset to the relive of the
common chairges of the calling of chirurgerie
20 lib money besyd the banket or denner
to the visitor & brethren..

die subscribtin
Craige Clark..

Apud glasgow die 22 Sept 1612..

The qlk day the holl Brethren of the airt
of chirurgerie being convenied all in on
voce hes electit Mr Rot Allason to be
ther Visitor for the yeir to come wha
hes given his oath for discharging his

fre man
Mills

Visitor
Allason

dentie thereintill _

Act against any brother to abuse ane other

The sd day the sd Visitor w' consent of his sd brethren of craft Condischends y' giue any member of the sd calling blasph' any brother of his craft ether publicklie or privatlie or utherwise or misuses any of them in word or deid du y' ease tryall takin + prouin against him be witness shall pay 4 lib to the calling + giue the brother scandalised satisfaction at the deacon sight + masters, Otherwise to be dischairged to use his calling totics quoties _

Act that no Visitor giue any of the crafts money w'out consent

The sd day it is statute that no Visitor shall depurse any money in any thing concerning the afaires of the craft w'out consent of two or three of his brethren of craft, utherwise no allowance to be giuen to him therof _

M' of Craft. M' Rot Hamiltoune
don Hall _ Thomas Thomsoun _

Apud glasgow vigesimo nono die
Mensis Septembris 1613..

Visitor Hall The 9th day the haill brethren of the
airt of chirurgerie being convained they
all in on voce hene electit Johne Hall
(9) ther Visitor for this niset yeir to com.
who hes giuen his oathe of fidelitie for
dischargeing of his druties faithfully yrint-
The sd day the Visitor wt consent of
his brethren of craft hene electit + chosen
for his masters of craft..
Mr Rot Hamiltoune
Mr Rot Allasone
James duncane..

die 24 of September 1614

Visitor The 9th day be pluralitie of votts of his
Hall brethren of craft is chosen visitor for ys
et certificatione yeir to com wha hes giuen his oath for
dew administration therintall, and in
caice he use not his diligence in convga
the brethren qrterly four tyms in the
yeir (viz) hallowmes, candelmes, beltan,
+ lambes + warne them to yr effect

he shall pay 5 lib to the box of the craft.
the sd day it is ordanit that yf any
brother of the craft be warned to conveine
ather personally or at his dwelling house
he bring wt in the toune & conveines not
shall pay 13s 4d for ilk tyme absence to
the comoune box except he send ane
lanfull reason that hes deteined him
& the Visitor to apoynt the officer to
pynd him for the sd soume.

Act for not
compearance

The sd day Gabriell Syeserf pothecar is
admittit freman and brother of craft
wt the rest of the brethren & he to
use hes anne calling who hes given
his oath to do his dewtie in defending
ther dewtie

freman
Syeserf

Quttermastores.
Mr Ror hamiltoune
Mr Robt Allasoune
Andro Mylle

dies 22 of September 1615
The sd day Andro mill be mearest
vots of his brethren is chosen Visitor

Visitor
Mill

for ys yeir to com who hes given his oath
for dew administration yrintill

Qrtermasters
Mr Rot hamiltonne
James dunkan
Gabriell Sysserfe
Jon Hall

The 20 of September 1617.
The sd day Andro myl is chosen
Visitor for ane yeir to com wha hes
given his oath for den administration
therintill

The 4 of Apryll 18
The 4k day Andro mill Visitor of the
airt of chirurgerie wt in the tonne of
glasgow acompained wt his masters &
haill brethren of that airt, finds James
harper ane qualified chirurgian to use
yt airt in all poynts and therfor
they have admitted him freman &
brother wt them & he to use the fredome
& libertie of his calling wt in the bound

of the fredome to us be his majestie as
frely as any of our selfs, wha hes
given his oath for dew administration
therintill, & hes payed 40 lib punds of
vpset & shall yirly intyme coming pay
10 s to the almous house of the craft of
glasgow, & be ther officer, provyding if the
sd James com & duell in glasgo yt he
shall mak him self burges of the toun
for the relieve of the craft theranent.

    sic subscribitur Craig clark
       James harper Chirurgian

    die 22 of September 1618.

Visitor hall

The qlk day son hall is chosen visitor
for ane yeir to com be unanimest votis
who hes given his oath for dew
administration therintill.

The sd day Isak fleming is admitit
officer for ane yeir to com.

    die 22 of Sept 1619

Visitor hall

The sd day the brethren of chirurge
being convenit they haue chosen Johne.

hall Visitor for ane yeir to com wha hes
given his oath

Qrtermasters
Mr Rot hamiltoune
Andro myll
Officer
James fleming.—

die Sept 22 1620.—

Visitor
hamiltoune

The sd day mr Rot hamiltoune is
admittit Visitor for ane yeir to com
+ hes given his oath

Qrmaster
Jon hall Andro myll
James dunkan
Officer
James fleming.—

die 22 Sept 1621.—

Visitor
hamiltoune

The glk day mr Rot hamiltoun is
continued Visitor for ane yeir to com

Msters of craft
Andro myll Jon hall
James duncan

Officer
James fleming.–

(II)

dio Sept 21. 1622.–

Mill Visitor

The glk day andro mill is admittit
Visitor for tho yeir to com

Qrmasters
Mr Rot hamiltoune
Johne hall
James dunkan
Officer
James fleming.–

dio 20 Septemb 1623.–

Visitor mill

The sd day andro mill is continued
deacon for ane yeir to com

Msts of craft
Mr Rot hamiltoun John hall
James dunkan

dio 20 of September 1623

Visitor Mill

The glk day andro myll is continued
Visitor for ane yeir to com

Mrs of craft

Mr Rot hamiltoune
Jon Hall
James duncan..

the deacon
ue pour to
to persons to
in courte...

The 9k day it is statute and ordaned
yt the deacon heue power to choise 2
or 3 of the optermists to sit wt him in
any publict court wt some frie of the
calling ether to admit fre men or do
any other thing relating to the calling..

The 23 of Sept 1624.

The sd day Johne hall put deacon
Clark
idwood
wt andro mull, James Read, James
fleming hes admittit James braidwood
yr clark for the yeir to com + hes maid
faith as use is..

The sd day In presence of the sd
e man
inday
deacon + brethren Mr Arch Linday is
admittit fre man wt the remanent
brethren who hes maid faith as use
is and hes given satisfaction for his
fyne..

man Rot
all
The sd day Rot hall con to the sd
deacon is admittit freman wt the rest

of the brethren & hes maid faith as use is
& hes satisfied for his fynes acording to order.

dic 29 of Sept 1626

Visitor
Mill

The sd day Andro mill be pluralitie of
votts is electit Visitor for the yeir to com
wha hes maid faith as use is

Mrs of craft

Mr Rot hamiltonn Jon hall

James duncan

Officer

Rot hall

Boxe masters

Mr Rot hamiltonne & Joh hall

(12)   22 of Sept 1627.

Visitor
Mill

The day andro mill is electit Visitor for
ye year to com be pluralitie of votts
who hes maid faith as use is.

Mrs of craft

Mr Rot hamiltonne Mr arch: lindsay

Jon hall

Boxe maste Mr Rot hamiltonne

Mr arch: lindsay.

36

Act for Convining

The 9th day the holl brethren being convined do all in on voce set doune ane act for compeirance which act is to stand to our successores in all tyme coming the tenor qrof is as fallowes That whair as it hes bine accustomet to compeir to courts when lawfully warned by the visitor we all in on voce ratifie & aprove the former act maid theranent & statutes & ordaines that who so ever brother does not compeir being in toune & lawfully warned be ye officer shall pay 13 s 4 d & the officer to pound for the sd soume. The sd day it is statute That giue any member speik scandelously of the present visitor upon tryall taken the facultie is to dischalge the sd member of being any chairge wit them and is to pay ane new upset & the present visitor before his admission to heue satisfactions.

26 of Sept 1637.

freman
Archibald

The sd day Rot Archibald is admittit
freman in the calling of chirurgerie
& in particular in the Incision of the
stone, cataract, hernia & all uthers
externall acts of chirurgerie & yt upon
his tryall qualification & practice had
therabout & hes given his oath de fidele
administ & that the sd rot shall
be ane obedient member to the brethren
& common will & hes payed the fynes
agreable to the chartor & leters raised
ther upon.—

dies primo novembr 1627..

freman
hamiltoune

The sd day Mr James hamiltoune son
to Mr Rot hamiltoune be examinatioun
is fund qualifi to proges the art of
chirurgerie & medicine be Andro Mylne
Visitor & brethren of the calling & therfor
hes admittit the sd Mr James freman
in the calling who hes maid faith
as use is & hes payed his fynes the
somme of 20 lib &c & no over the denner
to be given to the brethren wt hes

provisione that the sd Mr James mak
himself burges in the toune utheroys
his admission to be null..

Anno Novembris 1627..
The sd day Wm Swane is heir in buikit
prentise to serve Andro Mylne prnt visitor
as ane prentiso in chirurgerie for the
space of 7 yeires fra the dait hereof & hes
payd for his buiking 33 s 4 to the box..

The 9 of aprylle 1628..
The sd day Andro Mylne & remanent
brethren of the calling hes dimittit
Andro Mwir To exercise chirurgerie so
far as he has knowledge he had be the
said deacon & brethren hime grament
for the whyll he hes payed his fynes
agriable to the charter and letters
raisit ther upone..

The 20 sept 1628..
The 9th day the deacon & brethren of
ye calling being convenit in the new

Kirk for the trayll qualification of Alexr
dyes who being tryed the sd deacon +
brethren foirsd fand the sd Allexr only
able in practice to vent ge blood wt
ane horne alenerly for the qlk Alexr

obliges his aires raecatores to pay to
the sd deacon + brethren to the well of
the puir four dollores qhof the sex brethren
hes receivit two into ther box + obliges
him to pay to the sd puir ulther 2
dollores vpon whitsonday nixt to come
dykas the sd Alexr and him + his
foirsds to pay to the sd deacon + his
successores in office well of ye sd puirt
the somme of 40 S yeirly during all
the dayes of the sd Alexr his lyftyme
at two termes in the yeir beginning
the 1 termes payment at mertimes
nixt and sua furth termly during
his sd lyftyme du pritts qhof wryten
be James Braidwood notar our clark
+ subscribed be him at command of the
sd Alexr dyes day yeir + place foirsd
Befor thir witnes Wr heir Archib. Store

to ror: Arch: & william dvan servitor to
the sd Andro myle

   sic subscribitur Jacoubus
     Braidwood..

Visitor Mylne

The sd day Andro Mylne is electit Visitor
for the yeir to com be pluralitie of vots who
maid faith as use is

   Wrste of craft for the deacon
Mr Arch: Lindsay - Johne Hall -
    Wrste for the craft:
Mr Rot hamilltoune - Rot Hall -
    Bose masters
Rot Archibald Johne Hall

   die 8 october 1628:

Freeman Fleming

The 9th day Andro Mylne & brethren
of his calling being convenit for the
tryel & qualification of James fleming
who being tryet the sd deacon &
brethren fohed fund the sd James
qualifiet to be ane barbor & to use
simple woundis & obliges him to use
na farder & obliges him to use no farder
ws but the adyse of the most expert

(14)

brethren of the calling upon the qlk the
sd James hes payed to the well of
the puir the soume of ten pounds &
hes maid faith de fideli administratioune
as use is ...

officer fleming dykes — the sd James is admittit officer
for the yeir to com & hes maid faith.

      die 23 of September 1629 —

Visitor hall — The sd day Johne hall be pluralitie of
wottis is admittit Visitor for the yeir to
com who hes maid faith

    Mastis chosen be the deacon
    Andro Mylne. Rot: Archibald
    Rot hall crafts Mr James hamiltoune.
    Bose masters
    Andro Mylne Rot archibald.

discharge hulk of his intromissions — The sd day Andro mylne last deacon
hes maid compt and reckings of his
intromission the last yeir who hes maid
payment to the craft of ten pounds &
qlk is put in the bose and dischargis
the sd deacon of any farder for
ever ...

the sd day the deacon & Brethrin hes
ordanit 4 lib yeirly for ther clark & yt
for all tyme coming

21 Septembe 1630..
the qlk day in pntt of Johne hall
present deacon of the chirurgians & his
masters of craft Gilbert Marshell nottar
is admitt ther clark wha hes givin
his oathe de fideli administratione..

die 22 September 1630..
the qlk day in the black froir Kirk
Johne hall be pluralitie of voits is
continued Visitor for the yeir nyxt
fallowing wha hes givin his oath de
fideli administratione..

Visitors qrtermasters
Andro muil.. Rot hall
Crafts qrtermaster
Mr James hamiltoune
Mr Arch lindsay
Mr James Fleming
The qlk day in pntt of Johne hall present

Visitor and his masters of craft qua for
the most pairt was present Iohne
hamiltoune burges of this brughe
being fund qualifiet is admitit fre
man chirurgian & hes payed for
his admission as use is

Officer
Iohne hamiltoune

(15) The clark is payed for this pntt yeir

22 September 1631

the qlk day In presence of Iohne hall
dracon for the yeir preceiding Andro
mylne be pluralities of votts is Admitit
Visitor for the yeir fallowing

28 September 1632
Item Mr arch Lindsay James duncan
& Rot Archibald ther after comptis this
yeir is payed be Andro mylne deacon
& is anne be them to him
The qlk day Andro mylne be pluralitie
of votts is maid Visitor for the yeir
nixt fallowing and gaue his oath

4

conforme to ordor

    dracones   qrtermasters

    Johne hall   Johne hamiltoune

        for the craft

    Mr James hamiltoune And Muir

clark payed The qlk day the clark payed for the
yair last

            12 Julii 1633

Admission The qlk day in presence of Andro
ian freman mylne put deacon & masters of craft
who wer all put except Andro Muir
Villiam Suan is admitit barbor &
for curing of simple woundis who
geve his oath conforme to ordor &
payed for his admission 10 marks

        Officer
       Villiam Suan

      die 21 Septemb: 1633

The qlk day convenit in the black friar
Visitor kirk Andro mylne putt visitor of the
hamiltoune churugians and most-pairt of the
vocation who wer putt Mr James

hamiltoune professor of physick be
pluralitie of votts is maid Visitor of
the said vocation for the yeir next
fallowing wha geve his oath de fideli
administratioune.

             deacons qrmasteris

Andro mylne   Johne hall

         for the craft

    Johne hamiltoune

     Andro Muir

     Bose masters

     Jo hamiltoune

     Andro muir

       Officer

    Williame Suan

     die the 26 of September 1634
the 9fk day in the Blackfriar Kirk
Mr James hamiltoune be pluralitie
of votts is continued Visitor for the
yeir next fallowing wha geve his
oath de fideli administratioune

          deacons qrmasters

Andro mylne   Andro Muir

Visitor hamiltoune — marginal note

(16) — marginal note

46

Crafts qrtermasters
Jo Stall Rot Archibald.—
Boxe masters
Jo Stall Rot Archibald.—

die 7 of november 1634
The qlk day in presence of Mr James
Hamilltonne present Visitor & qrtermasters
wha for the most pairt wer present,
daniell Browne is admitt frermane
chirurgiano———————

freman
Browne

——————— and payed for
his admission 40 lib being ane stranger
and geve his oath conforme to order.—
Officer
daniell Browne
The visitor put in the boxe 40 S whlk
he gote from Alexr lyes for the year
1634.—
The qlk day the clark payed

die the 24 of Sept. 1635
The qlk day Be pluralitie of votts Rot
archibald is maid visitor for the

Visitor
Archibald

yeir neist fallowing wha geve his oath
conforme to ordor.—

Visitors grmasters
Mr James hamilltonne And Mylne

Crafts
Jo hall And Muir

Bose masters
Mr James hamilltonne Jo hall

James Reid officer for this yair to come
+ his grtercompts dischargit him this
neist yeir

die 23 of march 1636

The glk day du presence of Ro archib.
present visitor ane grtermasters Wm
didsdall servitor to Andro mylne
chirurgian is Buikit barbor + ane
chirurgian for curing of simple wounds
wt out fractures ruptures dislocations
or dyk + only to profes conforme to
his knouilage and gave his oathe
conforme to ordor + Mr James hamilton
obliges him to pay for his Buiking
tuentie marks at mertimas neist.—

taken from the end
of this minute Book

die 23 of March 1636

The glk day in presence of Rb archib:
present deacon James Bradwood is
bukit barbar viz to use only intyme
coming barbaryng, polling shewing +
making of bairds wt ak farder privilage
or poynts belonig to ther calling +
payed for his admission 40 ~~marks~~ + li
obliges him to pay in tyme coming
to the bose tiventie shilling money
at 2 tearmes whesonday + mertimes
this done with the denner or ten
merks this with his awone consent

Gilbert Marchell Notary

freeman
Braidwood
~i~er

Vigesimo nono junii 1636
The glk day convenit in the crafts
hospitall in presence of Rb archibald
jut visitor + qrtermasters who wer
present Ion Low son dawzull to
Mr Peter doie burges of ~this~ Burgh
doctor of chirurgerie for the low favor
+ respect they had to bir toward the
soued uingle Mr Peter and the

freeman
Loie

rather becaus he was the principall
procurer to this vocation of yr letters
of visitation under the prive seale they
heue admitit the Iohne freman who
hes given his oath conforme to ordor
yis for ye benefit of his children
                    Sic subscribitur Gulielmus
                    Marshell notarius..

(17) tie
Ratification
dow
                    Quarto Januarii 1652 yriss
Ion hall now visitor and haill brethren
being conveined in the craft hospitall
after mature deliberation (ye sd Ion doir
present) ratifies and, approves the former
act in all poynts notwithstanding the
declyning therof he payand after compta
intyme coming..
                    Sic Subscribitur Io Selkrit

                    die 22 September 1636..
The 9th day Convenit in the Blackfriar
Kirk Mr Archibald put visitor and
remanent of the vocation wha for the
maist pairt wer put for the electing

Visitor
Archibald

q ane visitor for the yeir nixt fallowing the sd kor arch: is continued visitor for the yeir nixt fallowing and gave his oath conforme to the ordor.—

Visitor qptermasters
Mr James hamiltoune
dor hall
Craftis qptermasters
dor low daniell Broune
Collector
daniell Broune
Boxe masters
dor lou daniell Broune
Officer
Vm Clidsdall

Ultimo Septembris 1637.

The qlk day convenit in the blackfrier kirk the hole Brethren for making chosse of ane visitor for the yeir nixt fallowing Mr James hamiltoune is maid visitor for the sd yeir who gave his oath conforme to the ordor.—

deacon qptermasters

Visitor hamiltoune

Jor Hall Ror archibald
Crafts
Andro Muir   daniell Browne
Officer
Wm Clidsdaill
Boxe masters
Jor hall   daniell browne
Collector
Andro Muir

The 9th day in presence of Mr James
hamiltonne putt Visitor and oftermasters
George Michelsonne is admitit freman
chirurgiane wha geve his oath conforme
to the ordor & payed for his admission
40 lib.

Penult Novemb: 1637.
Mr James hamiltonne present Visitor Johne
hall, daniell hall Wm Clidsdaill Andro
Muir ilk an of them payed upr
shilling for the oftercompts preceiding

(18)

die 23 of maii 1638 yeires
The 9th day conveinit in the Blackfreir

Kirk Mr James hamiltonne present
Visitor of the chirurgiano & apttermasters
who wer all present & Mes Thomsonne
Servitor to Mr Wr cosse doctor of phisick
is admitt be the said vocation to cur
dutyne cowing simple woundes & to use phlebotnne
ventosis Canters barborising & the sd James
acts himself to use no farder & in
caiso he transgeces in tyme coming
being tryed he obliges himself to pay
toties Quoties ten markes penalties (viz)
the on half to the provist balyies of the
brugh & the other half to the common
box of the vocation & payed for his
admission 20 lib & the Banckett.—
        Sic subscribitur James thomson

        die 30 September 1638.—
The 9th day convanit in the blackfries
kirk Mr James hamiltonne present
Visitor and remanent of the vocation
wha for the most pairt wer present
John hall be pluralitie of votts is
maid visitor for the yir next fallowing

and gawe his oatt conforme to the order

Visitors   qrtermasters

Mr James hamiltonne

Crafts

Andro   muir   daniell Browne

Officer

Groge   Micheleon

Box   masters

Mr James hamiltonne

daniell Browne

dischairg
hamiltonne   The qlk day Mr James hamiltonne for
the yeir preceiding maid compt of his
intromissione & chairge & dischairge
being laid is dischairgit

The 25 Sept 1639..

Visitor
haill   The qlk day Johne haw chirurgian is
continued visitor of the vocation for
ye yeir to come be pluralitie of votts
wha gave his oatt conforme to the
order

Visitors   qrtermasters

Mr James hamiltonne

Crafts

Andro Muir
daniell Browne
Boxe masters
Mr James hamiltoune
daniell Browne

die 28 of September 1639

Act contra
Braidwood
& utheris

The 9th day convenit in the crafts
hospitall Johne hall present Visitor &
his qrtermasters Richard allane deacone
conveiner James Braidwood Barbor is
fund in ane wrong for Railling upon
daniell Browne & the visitor and
qrtermasters therfor statute intyme coming
that gif the sd James or any other raile
upon the visitor or any of the brethren
shall pay to the box intyme coming
fine pund toties quoties & to the Balzies
40s unforgiven & he to remaine in
fast ward till it be payd.

(19)

die the 13 of decemb 1639.

The 9th day convenit in the crafts hospitall
Johne hall present Visitor & qrtermasters

the sd Johne hall maid compt & reckning
of his intromissione wt the crafts goods
for the preceiding yeir & anent his depursments
of the samyn & charge & discharge being
consent & considered the sd Johne hall
resta awand 40 s which he presently
payed & was put in the box & discharged
him for ever..
Item alexr dyrs hes payed his 40 s for
the yeir ———— 1639

                    die the 29 of Sept 1640

The qlk day Conveint in the crafts hospitall
Johne hall present Visitor & remanent of
the vocation who for the maist pert wer
present daniell Browne chirurgiane be
pluralitie of voots is electit & chosen Visitor
for ye yeir nixt fallowing wha geve his
oath conforme to ye ordor..

                    Sexto novemb: 1640.

The qlk day conveint in the crafts hospitall
daniell Browne present Visitor & remanent
of ye vocation wha for the most pairt

wer present the persons fallowing as electit
qrtermasters

Visitors qrtermasters.
Andro Muir Wm Archibald
for the craft
Mr James hamiltonne Jon hall

Officer
James Thomsonne

The gik day Jon hall Visitor for the
year preceiding maid compt of his
intromissioun & charge & discharge being
confered he is secoured of his intromissi-
for the sd year.

Boxe masters
Andro Munn Wm Clidsdall

die 23 of apryl 1641.
The gik day Convenit in the Bleckfrien
Kirk daniell browne present visitor
James Young sone lawfull to James
Young merchand burges of Edinburgh
is bukit prentiss wt George michelsonne
chirurg Burges of glasgow to remaine
wt him 5 yeires prentiss conforme to

the Indentor of the daite the 15 of Sept 1640 + payed for his Bouking fine punds to the Boxe + to the clark 33 s. 4.

(20)
Visitor
muir

die 24 September 1641

the qlk day the neaist pairt of the brethine being conuenit in the blackfrier Kirk Be pluralitie of uotts andro muir is electit Visitor for the yeir to come wha hes given his oath de fidele administratione as use is

Visitores qrtermasters
Wm Clidsdale daniell Broune

for the craft
Mr James hamiltoune
Jon hall

Boxe masters
Wm Clidsdall
daniell Broune

die 22 of decemb 1641

Selkrit Clark

The qlk day Johne Selkrit nottar is electit Clark for ane yeir to come wha is payed in hand + given his oath.

Hall prentise

The sd day Johne hall is Buikit prentise
wt Johne Hall lait deacon his guidsher
wha hes payed 40 s conforme to the former
act being on fremans sone to serve
5 yeires conforme to the Indentor—

Officer
James Fleming.—

Vigesimo novemb: 1641.—

The sk day daniell Browne maid compt
of his Intromission wt the craft guids
this yeir preceiding

die 10 of August 1642

obligement Wm muir

the sk day Andro muir visitor & brethren
of craft being convenit in the blackfrier
kirk ther was ane band grantit be him
& Jon boyd cationer conteaning fiftie markis
and 4 markis aniual rent at martimes
next whilk is ondew & les: & sk debt
being grantit be the sd Andro muir &
of his awne consent obligest him ather
to mak up ane new band for payment
yrof or then pay the sd sowmes & aniual

rent at the sd terme be thir pñts
subscrive wt his hand..

die the 23 of Sept: 1642..

The 9th day Mr James hamilton is electit
Visitor for the yeir to com who hes
givin his oatth as use is
  Qrtermasters for the Visitor.
   Andro Muir
   George Michelsonne
   for the craft
   daniell Browne
   Wm Clidsdall
    Officer
   Wm Calderwood..
   Box masters
   Andro Muir
   daniell Browne

(21)

The clark payed for this yeire fie
  24 of March 1643 yeiris

The quhilk day in presence of Mr James
hamiltoune present deikine James Braidwood
younger is buikit barbor & onlie to use
in tyme coming barbarising as polling

and scheuing and making of bairdes w^t
out farder priuiledge or poynts belonging
to the calling & payed for his admissioune
40 lib and obleges him to paye in all
tyme coming to the box tuente schillings
money at tua termes whitsondaye &
mertimes this with the denerer at his
admissioune or ten merks to the box
this with his awnie consent.

The 12 of Sept 1643.

the qlk day Convent in the new Kirk
Ioⁿ andersoune balyie & Wm Neilsoune deacon
conviner w^t the visitor & brethren George
michelsoune payed his gpter compts by gon
& is become aclit befor the sd persouns.
that he shall Krip good ordor & Krip
the crafts meetings in all tyme coming
under the paine of paying 3 lib toties
quoties unforgiven

die 22 of Sept 1643.

the qlk day the maist pairt of the craft
being convent in the blackfrier Kirk

Margin notes:
frie man
Braidwood
younger

Act
Gyanet
Mchelsoune

visitor
michelson

all w. on consent be pluralitie of voitts
hes chosine George Michelsounne Visitor for
the yeir to com & give his oath as use
is.

Qrtermasters Visitor
Mr Jam: hamiltonne daniel Broun
craft
Andro Min Wm Clidsdall
Officer
James Braidwood
Boxe masters
Mr Ja hamiltonne daniele Broune

Mr James hamiltonne maid his compt of
his Intromission w. the crafts guids chairgs
& dischairge confeeit & dischairgit

die 26 of appryll 1644
This 9ok day George Michelsounne maid ane
compt of his intromission befor Mr James
hamiltonne daniele Broune + Wm Clidsdaill
+ hes given the gift to the boxe w. the
new letters + hes given in of moneys to
the boxe 18 tib 3s chairge & dischairge being
consent he is exonerit

Compt
hamiltonne

discharg
michelson
intromission

die 24 of Sept: 1644.

The qlk day in the black frier Kirk of glasgou the sd George Michelsonne is continued Visitor for the yeir to com be pluralitie of vots who hes given his oath as use is..

die 23 of Ianuarii 1645.

The qlk day Mr Wr mains professor of medicine of his aune consent is admittit freman wt the calling conform to the patent wha hes givin his oath de fideli administratione as use is & his promised to be asisting to the visitor & brethren in all things belonging to the well of the calling & to bein burdrine wt the rest..

The qlk day Mr Iames diming doctor of phisick is admittit freman wt the calling conforme to the patent wha hes givin his oath de fideli administratione & hes promised to be asisting to the visitor & Brethrine in all thing belongeig to the well of the calling & to beire burdrine wt the rest..

(22)

die the 28 of julie 1645

The qlk day George michelsonne delivered
to Mr James hamiltonne the boxe &
wrytts conteined therin fyne & awarded
by reasone of his present infirmities &
gave 30 S for James dyrs dueties & payed
12 S for his anne qttercompts for the
yrir 1645 all put in the Boxe.

die the 29 of Sept 1645.

Visitor
Maine

The qlk day the holl members of craft
being convenit in the blackfrier kirk be
pluralities of vots hene electit Mr Rob.
Maine doctor of phisick Visitor for the
yrir to come

Qttermasters

Mr Ja hamiltonne daniell Browne
George Michelsonne

Collector

daniell Browne

Boxe maisters

Mr Ja hamiltonne daniell Browne

die 22 Sept 1646.

4

The 9th day the most pairt of the memb
bring convenit in the craftz hospitall
electit Mr Ja hamiltonne Visitor for the
yair to come wha hes given his oath
as use is

Visitores Quermasters

Mr James dining Andro Muir

Craftz

daniell Browne Wm Clidsdall

Boxe masters

daniell Browne

Vm Clidsdall

du 28 of Maij 1647..

The 9th day the Visitor & maist pairt
of the craft bring convenit in the
blackfrier Kirk of glasgou Johne hall
chirurgiane is admitit freman wt the
calling as professor of chirurgerie wha
hes payed his fyne & givin his oath
as use is ..

du 23 of Sept 1647..

the 9th day daniell Browne be pluralitie

Visitor
Bronne

of votts is electit deacon for the yeir to
com & hes givan his oath de fideli
administratione..

(23)   Qrtermasters for the deacon
                        Mr James hamiltonne
                        Wm Clidsdall
                        for the craft
                        Jon Hall
                        Officer
            Jon Roxbright for Jon Hall
                        Box masters
                        do Hall
                        Wm Clidsdall
Payed to Jon Selkrit clark 2 yeires fro
preceding..
daniell Bronne dischairgit of his
intromission wt the crafts grin..

                die 22 of Sept 1648..

Visitor
Hall

The 9th day Johne hall be pluralitie of
votts is electit Visitor for ye yeir to
come wha hes givan his oath de fideli
administratione as use is
                Qrtermasters for the deacon

daniele Browne Andro Muir
for the craft
Mr James hamiltonn
James Thomsonne
Boxe masters
James Thomsone
daniele Browne

die Novemb 14. 1648.

The qlk day Johne hall present visitor
+ brethrine of the calling being convenit
Mr Browne is Buiklit prentise to daniele
Browne for 5 yeires and hes payed
according to ordor.

Eodem die

Adam gray is admitit freman as ane
simple chirurgiane to the calling wha
hes given his oath as wse is + hes
payd for his admissiow 40 markis.

die the 12 of Maii 1649

The qlk day James dyre is admitit freman
to the craft in drawing of blood to ane
horne +/to do other things yt he hes

knoulage is who hes given his oath as
use is & obliges him to pay to the
craft 30 S yearly during his Lyfe..

The thrie of September 1649..

admittit on this 1654

The 9th daye du pns of Iohne hall deacone
and bretherine of the calling being convenit
in the craftes hospitall Archibald Bogill
barbour is buikit barber viz onlye to use
in tyme coming barbarising as polling
& shewing of beardes wt out farder privilage
or poynts belonging to that calling and
payd for his admissionne fourtye merks
and obeiss himself to paye yirlye in
all tyme coming to the craft box
twentie schillings at tua termes in the
yir whitsondaye and Mertimes this
witto the denner at his admissionne
or ten merks to the craft box this wt
his awine consent— sic subscribitur..

die 21 of Sept 1649..
The 9th day the most pairt of ye calling
being convenit be pluralitie of votts electit

(margin notes:)
sic
from the end
minute Book..

frieman
Bogill

Visitor
num..

Andro Unin visitor for the yrir to com
who hes givin his oath as use is
Qrtermaster for the Visitor
dor Hall   daniell Broune
for the craft
Mr James Hamilltoune
Adam Gray
Boxe masters
dor Hall
daniell Broune
Officer
Archibald Bogle

discharge
Halls

the 9th day dor hall Late deacon hes
maid his compt of his intromissio wt
the crafts guids & hes payed in to James
dyre Collector after specified seventrine
punds 18ᵈ & therfor the craft discharges
him of his intromissio.

Item the craft apoynts James dyre Collector
for the yrir to com

act for
the Clark

the 9th day the calling apoynts Johne
Selkrie ther clark to have yrirly intyme
coming 4 lib & is payed of all Bygons
preceiding this dait.

die the 13 of decemb: 1649 —

freman dockard

The q*lk* day Thomas dockard is admitit apothecarii + x to *xchirurgian* wse plebosomie w* putting in of potentiall canters *+ other piece of chirurgie* ~~dextously~~ wha hes given his oatte + admitit for y* effect + hes payed his fyne —

dischainge tyre

the *sd* day the erast dischainges James tyre of his intromission w* the erafts guids + ther is in the boxe 16 S sterling + 6 pence —

die the 28 of June 1650 —

freman frank

The q*lk* day James frank is admitit as ane ordinar chirurgian w* the calling who hes given his oatte as wse is + is content to obay the Visitor + to keip the qrtercourts —

die the 23 of sept 1650 —

Visitor Mur

The q*lk* day the holl eraft being convluit in the erafts hospitall be pluralitie of wotts Andro Mur is continued Visitor for the yeir to com wha hes given his oath de fideli administratione as wse is..

Qrtermasters for the Visitör

Mr Ja hamiltonne da Brown

for the craft

James Thomsonne

Jor Hall

Officer

Thomas Lockart

Boxe masters.

daniell Browne James Thomsonne

(25)   decimo septimo febrie 1653 yeirs

The 9th day Robert hamiltonne now servitör
to James frank chirurgiane is buikit
prenteis heirin for ye space of fyve
yeire fra his entrie yrto qlk was and
began ye sevintein of Nor 1652 yeirs
conforme to ye ordor preseryvil and set
downe of old guha hes payit to ye boxe
clark and officer conforme to ye set
maid grantet..

Eodem die

Gabriell conynghame is electit officer
during ye deikin and callings will..

Margin notes:

Prenteis
hamiltonne

Conynghame
officer

rode die

yᵉ clark payit of his fie preceeding
Michaelmes 1652.,

upon the 4 day of apryll 1653 yeires
It is statute and ordained that if
any member speak disdainfully of
the whiter or to the visitor after tryell
taken shall be discharged to heue ane
vott wt the facultie + be discharged
of his airt + the visitor to heue full
satisfaction

28 apryle 1654
The qlk day yᵉ visitor and brethreine
being conveind dn huchesounes hospitall
It is statute yᵗ if any brōᵧ sall slander
any aᵧ persoly or behind yᵗ bak
yᵗ they sall pay to ye ptie offendit
fourtie schillings toties quoties to ye boxe
and sicklyke to pay fourtie schillings
for ilk _

The qlk day being conveined as sd is
it is statute and ordained yᵗ at no

tym heir after any person qtsoever
bring a member of the facultie shall
Act for abusers of the deacon tak upon him to speak scandelously
of the visitor ather before his face or
behind his back for qtsoever cause or
occasion bot upon the contrar shall
dudivior to cary themselfs respectiuly
to him
+ giue him his due respect in
every thing relating to the calling
+ yt under the paine of 15 lib
unforgiven + this act to be put to
dew execution be the laid deacon the
present deacon complening to him
who is declared by thir pntts qtsver
he be to be competent judge et cet
therto –

2o The qlk day the clark payed q his
fiees by gou this dait..

die 19 September 1651
deacon The qlk day Jon hall be pluralitie
of uotts is electit deacon for the yeir
to come wha hes gioun his oatto as
use is

Qrtermasters for the deacon
Andro Muir
daniell Browne
for the calling
Mr James hamilltonne
Wm Clidsdale
Boxe masters
Adam gray
Thomas Lockard
Officer
James frank

Item the sd day andro muir mad
his compt of the crafts guids chaing
& discharge bring Confrrit they
hirby discharge hime of his intromisen
the last yrires. -

die 8 decemb: 1651 -

The 9th day the clark payed of his
by gon fies conforme to ye act.
The sd day the visitor & brethren of
yr calling bring convenit finding
that diverse persones wt in & wt out
the toune hes usurpit upon them

our liberties of our callings of chirurgerie
phiseck & others belonging to ther calling
and are w'out licence tryall &
reexamination contrair to the expresse
tennor of our gift for remeid therof
& for fortification of ther gift the sd
Visitor & bretheren hes hierby ordained
that ther be ane supplication maid
to the provist bailies & counsell of
this brugh to the effect they may
ether autthorize the old gift & hoic
privilages therof or thento give to the
calling such libertie & privilage as the
magistrats & counsell shall think
most expedient for affectuating hierof
it is therby allowit that Andro
daniell Browne, Tho: lockard & James
thomesones & maist pairt of them
w' the Visitor attend the sd magistrats

ultimo maii 1653 –
& the holl craft w' on consent
ane band of fiftie marks awand to
them be Mr tho mun as principall

Act for
Andro
muir and
Band
(27)

& Johne Kirkwood as caut for him
to andro muir our brother & that
in respect he lost so much of the
crafts guids at the incoming of the
English to this toune grof rested of
the sd principall sowme unpayed
twentie marks wt certaine bygon
anuel rents which was frely gifted be
the calling & farder three punds taken
out of the boxe also given to him
to help him to put the sd band to
execution..

upon the 20 day of September 1652
The 9th day in the crafts hospitall
the holl calling being convenit they
be pluralitie of wotts electit and chosin
sd Stall Visitor for the yeir to come
wha of new hes givin his oath de
fideli administratione as use is..

Visitor
Stale

Qrtermasters for the Visitor
Andro Muir
James Thomsoune
ffor the craft

James frank
daniell Browne

Irtio Octori 1653.

The qlk day anent ye electiounc of an
deikin for ye yeir to come upon ye
22 of September Last upon qlk day
daniell browne was electit deikin for
ye said yeir and being absent for
ye tyme to tak his chairge and
give his ayt This day in pñs of
ye craft he hes given his ayt de
use is ...

rodem die
Dterminis for ye deikin
Thomas Lokhart
James frank
Crafts
Do hall
Mr James hadonne
boxmris
Mr hall
Thomas Lokhart
Ordaines Do Selkrig to remaine clark for

one yeir to come

4 nor 1653

The ealing convenit in ye hospitale
Jon hall last deikin maid his copt
and is heirof dischairgit be ym of
his intromissionne in 29 tt h/S ye
comonne guids

sir Daniell brown ...

opt hall
29tt h/S..

Sxeto febric 1654

Andro Miller in pns of daniell broun
Visitor and members of ye calling
convenit in huchesonnes hospitale is
admitit and brukit barbor vz onlic
to use intyme conreing polling and
schaving of bairdis w out farder priviledge
or points belonging to the ealing and
payit for his admissionne fourtie pund
and obleiss him to pay yeirlie in
tyme comeing to ye boxe tuentie schilings
at witsonday & mertimes ye first gxter
at witsonday nixt and payis ten mks
for ye denner or yn ane dennar to ye

in tte end of
Book
Licence
miller

craft of his awin asent

ₚ I Selkrig clark.-

penultimo febrii 1654

Miller
ffïr

Andro Miller is of his awin consent
become ffïr for ane yeir to come to
serve ye calling quha hes gevin his
ayt as wse is.-

10 apryle 1654

The Visitor & brethrein conveint in huchesone
hospitall be pluralitie of votis they
ordaint ye deikin to send for new
dres on ye deceit ye last dres being
lost and according to his debursement
he is to be repayit qn ye dres sall
returne.-

(28)

5 maii 1654

delyverit bak ye dd and dres according
to ye act for said sikis dres ar
delyverit to ye visitor.-

5 maii 1654

frieman
Chrichtoun

The qlk day Mr Lou chrichtoune professor
of medicine of his awin consent is
admitit frieman wt ye caling conforme
to ye patent quha hes gevin his aithe
de fideli administrane as use is and
hes promrist to assist ye visitor and
brethrene in all things belonging to
ye weill of ye ~~weill of ye~~ and to bein
burdein wt ye rest of ye caling in
all things belonging ylto..

12 maii 1654

frieman
hareis

The qlk day Robert hareis is admitit
be pluralitie of vottis of ye haill caling
frieman simple barbor chirurgiane onlie
to medill wt simple woundis allenarlie
and on na termes to medill wt
phisick tumors, hulsors, dislocanes,
fractors nor nothing yt is composic
qll he be farder qualified, quha hes
gevin his ayt as use is and payit
his fynes conforme to actis
sg Robert Arris

Eodem die 12 maii 1654

James dougall gairdner in obedience
of ye chairge of horning gevin to him
and declairit he wey had doone
nor wocit chirurgianrie or phisick and
oblist him not to wse any in all
tyme comeing under ye paines contein-
in ye dres ressept for his awin wse...

&c. I Hovsgate...

Eodem die

John holl in Kilbarchane is heirby
dicentiat by ye Visitor and brethrein
to wse & exerce sik poittes of ye
airtis and caling of chirurgianrie
and medicine as qof he hes knowledge
experience and practyze and according
to ye quhaster and elder of testimonis
quha hes gevin hes ayt to ye will
of ye caling and oblrisst to meddle
wt na farder nor qof he hes knawledge
nor na operatione wt in ye brut of
Glasgow, and hes payit his fynes
and als obleiss him to pay yeirlie
to ye caling twentie schillings at

hallowmes, yᵉ first yeir at hallowmes
next.—

Sᵍ I Stoll.—

(29)   Eodem die

Nathan Grey is admittit freeman
simple chirurgiane wᵗ yᵉ ealing onlie
to exerceice and cuir simple woondis
and in pᵃrticular in euting of yᵉ
gravell and stone wᵗ yᵉ haill cuir
of yᵉ gravell and stone and is
restrictit fra curing of humors, fractors
dislocatiunes and all apostit wounds
till his farder knawledge and efter
his knawledge to be admittit and
approvin and allowit to exerceice
accordinglie quha hes gevin his
aÿt as use is and payit his fynes
conforme to yᵉ actis and is to keip
courtis and pay his quttercomptis.—

26 maii 1654.

The 9ᵗ day daniell browne pᵗ Visitor
wᵗ his querteris and remanent of
yᵉ facultie of chirurgianes and

82

Licence
Grahame

phisicianes of ye brut of Glasgow and
boundis belonging yto being convenit
in ane publict court anent ye
examinatioune and qualificatioune of
Mr Ard Grahame apothecar quha
being examinat be ye said facultie
as licentiate to profes farmacie and
medicine wt in ye boundis (except ye
brut of Glasgow) as is content wt in
ye lres of gift and obliss him at
na tyme heirefter to use nor exerce
any point of chirurgianrie wt out
ye consent of ye visitor or ane or
mae of ye saids qrtermris and yis
his act of licence to practize as is
alon said to be alwayes wtout prejud
of ye toune of Glasgow yr libertiea
in relatioune to ye burges fyne and
qr he is burges we obliss us and
our successors in office to mak him
altogither frie wt ye ealing as we ar
our selfis gratis in quhat he is bund
now to profes and hes payit his fyne
and hes givin his ayt de fideli

administrane as use is --

Sr I Selkrig clk --

26 Maii 1654

The qlk day daniell browne pnt visitor
gptenrs and brethrene of ye caling
apprit befor ym Dr mathies in cokhue
quha being rexamined on his airts and
is fund to have litill skill of ye said
airts except allendirle to cuir simple
woundes and smithing of brokin banes
gf the fleshe is nd cut so upon his
compeirance we have grein him that
tolleraunce for ye saids cuiris Sf ye cume
nd in any eplaints again him and hes
grein satisfactioune for his fynes and
obleiss him in tyme coming to pay
yirlie to ye caling twintio shillings
at michaelmes and ye first yeir payt
to be at ye nixt michaelmes 1654 and
yis licence nd to be extendit nor
to   Wm ye brut
of glasgow and hes grein his agt as
use is --   Sr I Selkrig

penultimo maii 1654

freeman
Wallace

the 9th day williame wallace for ye
pnt residenter in paislay professor of
medicine of his awin consent is
admitit freeman wt ye caling conform
to ye patent quha hes gevin his ayt
de fideli administratione as use is
and hes promisit to assist ye Visitor
and bretherin in all thingis belonging

(30)

he is to pay 30 ß
be yair tethe caling
for the use of
the poore

to ye weill of ye caling and to beir
burdrine wt ye rest of ye said caling
in all thingis ptenning yairto.

ß J Selkrig

penultimo maii 1654

the 9th day daniell Browne present
Visitor qtermaisters + hole facultie
being conveined in the craftis hospitall
considering yt the dying upon us
conteined unto our charter that we
tak notice of the poore gratis hes
apoynted + be thir presents apoynts
Johne hall + ħis archib Grahame to
present to ye common sessioun our

desire in relation to the poore in
wryt the tennor qrof is as fallowes.
Unto the reverend moderator remanent
ministers elders & deacons of the
session of glasgow Humbly sheweth
I daniell Browne present visitor of
the chirurgians of yis brugh for my
self & in name of the haill members
of yr sd calling for the reet vnder
wryten That we being met in our
ordinar way of convention and taking
to consideration how yt by the lords
wyse dispensation our number wch in
ther fri yeires is much increesed
& yt ther is dayly a number of poore
sick people Increesing destitute of all
worldly help crying for christian
charitie & supplie & especially at your
hands whose it is in the first place
by providence to act your pairts &
wt all pondering our duties & considering
qt may best contribute for the well
of these poore sick people shall from
tyme to tyme hereafter happen to be

wᵗ in this citie do mak offer of our
service to your upon behalf of the
poore Humbly entreating yᵗ sin ther
is some respect amongst us of physik
chirurgeri & pharmacie our number
being greatly increassed & we mor
fitted for yᵗ dentie we oght to your
    for the poor then formarlie That ye
may accept of our service & inact
our offer wᵗ ane ordinance That it may
be ordered yᵗ any knowno deceassed
poore so represented to the session or
sessions or comitie for the poore or the
ministers of the later gf they duell
by ane elder or deacon shall be
by the sd minister be recommendit
to the visitor of the calling for the
tyme who is to nominat such of
our number as may contribute ther
best skills for the well of the poore
diseased wᵗ out any payment or
reward for ther panis rexpt the
payment of such medicaments as
shall be displaysd & boght from the

apothecairie which will be at ane rate
not considerable & such other ordores
apoynted by you as shale be thought
(31) fitting du relation to this undertaking
of oures & of we crave ane answir
may be givin to Mr Arch Grahame
& son hall two of our number who
is apoynted to present thir putto to
you & to returne ane answir to us
And we the said facultie obliges us
and our successores to stand be were
particular of the sd obligatioun presented
to the sd session be thir foir namied
persons under the paine of fortie
pund & to obey the Visitor in every
imployment he puts upon us in
relation to the diligent attendents of
the sds poore sick or hurt peopee
under the paines of other fortie punds
& the sd act to have the force
of any decreit gt ennroer it being
by the unanimous consent of the haill
callieg & subscrived by us all at
day yeir & place foirsd before

witness - sic subscribitur daniell broun -
Arch Grahame - Jo Crighton - Ja during
James ffrancke - J Hamiltonne - Adame
gray - J Hall - Robert Morris - Andro
muir - Tho Lockhart -

Second June 1654 -
The 9th day daniell broune and
bretherine of yr ealing being conveinit
in ane court James Sclr Mchand
is licentiat and tolleral to cur
simple woundis and to mak and
compose pillounes according to his
skill practize and experience quha
hes gevin his ayt de fideli administra[tione]
as use is and hes payit his fynes
as use is according to yr ealing
yr actis and ordinances -

Eodem die -
The 9th day yr facultie being conveinit
anent yr examinacone and qualificacon
of Jo Patersonne in paisley quha
being examined barberchirurgid is fund
qualified to cur simple woundis practis

(marginal notes)
2
Licence
Sclr

3
freman
Patersonne

yt yr is no flesh cutt whairis phlebotomie
applicatine of brutois potentiale contenis
and is restraitit hu all tyme coming
fra using of phisick and pharmacee
and also him to beir burding wt ye
rest of ye ealing and hes payit his
fynes and gevin his ayt de fideli
administratno as use is—

Second June 1654

The qlk day Johne dies wrivar is by ye
Visitor and brethrein dicentiat and
tollerat to draw bloode wt ane horne
and sik things as pertinis yairto
allundirlie quha hes gevin his ayt and
payit his fynes as use is, and is
to pay twelf schillings yeirlie to ye
boxe qlk he harby oblissis him to
pay.—

Last Julie 1654 yeir

the qlk day The facultie hes consentit
That the Visitor cause putto William
fleyming in hamiltonne. Thomas.

Wair in auld machane and Robert
forguesonne in air to the horne
because of yr disobedience as the
secrutiones beirs.—

&c I Selkrig.—

14 September 1654

The qlk day in ye craftis hospitall
being conveind danieta browne visitor
and brethrein of ye facultie anent
ye reeximinatiun of Johne miller
in Kilmarnok concerning his skill
and knawledge of ye airtis of ye
calling The visitor and bretherine
doeth hereby licentiat ye said Johne
miller to sell drogis, Let boode give
ane cleister apply ane conter and to
compone medicaments, be advyse of
professors of phisik except it in ye
brut of glaspow and obliese him to
pay ye dutie to ye calling tuelff schilling
and in ye meintyme hes payit for
his prit warrand as use is and givin
his ayt de fideli administracone conforme

freman
miller

To use pharmaceu
and give simple
potiounes
I Selkrig.—

to yⁱ ordor..

g⁻ d⁻ Miller – Selkrig ck..

Licence
Sod

14 September 1654

The qlk day in yⁱ craftis hospitall beig
convrinit Daniell browne Visitor and
brethrein of yⁱ facultie they doe heirby
dicentiat Iohne Sod gairdner in deir
to draw bloode, to put in   making
of treit and curing of simple woundis
(except wⁱin yⁱ brut of Glasgow) and is
heirby obleist to yⁱ eating twelf schillingis
yeirlie and hes payit for yⁱ warrand
according to yⁱ ordor..

26 of September 1654

The qlk day yⁱ haill brey (except doctor
doung & doctor chrichtoun) beig convrinit
in yⁱ craftis hospitall be pluralitie of
voris all in ane voyce electit d⁻ Hall
Visitor for yⁱ yeir to come quha hes
gevin his ay⁻ de fideli administra⁻no
as use is..

Visitor
Hall

                Eodem die

(33)

qtermrs for yr visitor
daniell browne
Thomas Lokhart
for yr Facultie.-
Mr James hamiltoune
James Thomsoune
boxemrs
daniell browne
Mr Ard grahame
officer
Robert hairies

Glasgow yr 13 of octor 1654 yeirs
The alk day yr visitor and Remanent
brethrine of facultie being convrinit
in ane publict court anent yr
examina'ne and qualifica'me of
Robert forgushill pharmaciane, burges
of air quha being examined be yr
said facultie to licentiet an all
tyme coming to practize pharmacie
and medicine w'in yr boundis
contrinit in yr lres of gift grantit
be yr deceist King James to yr facultie

of ye sd vocærie for ye tyme and yair
successors in office Except win ye citie of glasgow
and ye said Robert is herby obleist at
na tyme heirafter to exerce any of ye
saids airtis win ye said brut of
glasgow and yis his act of dicentia'mie
to practize as is above win to be
alwayrs but prejudice of ye liberties
of ye said brut of glasgow in rela'ne
to ye burgesschip of ye said Robert and
qn he is burges ye said faicultie and yair
successors in office are herby obleist
to mak him altogither free wt ye
vocærine becaus he hes now payit his
fynes and gevin his ayt de fideli ad
ministra'ne as use is and is herby
obleist to pay yirlie to ye said vocærine
and ye successors yintill threttie
schillings scotis money ye first yeiro
payt beginand at mdtimes 1655.
sic subscribitur. JRrgashill
J Selkrig eP.

Eodem die et anno

The visitor and remanent brethrein being
convrinit as said is anent the
rexaminatne and qualificatne of
Thomas Chisholme, chirurgiane, burges
of air Duha being examinat be ye
said facultie ar fund qualified and
is licentiat to practize and profes
chirurgie in all tyme coming win
ye boundis of yair jurisdictioune about
spet (except win ye citie of glasgow)
and ye said Thomas is hereby obleist
not to exerce ye said airt of chirurgie
win ye said brut of glasgow and ye
pnt det to be but prejudice of ye
liberties of ye said brut and citie of
glasgow in relatne to ye said Thomas
his burgesschip and gn he is burges
ye said facultie obleiss ym and yr
successors in offic to mak him free win ye examne
anent ye said airt becaus he hes not
payit his fynes and grein his ayt de
fideli administratne as use is and
is hereby obleiss to pay to ye said
examne yeirlie thrittie schillings usual

money at urtimes begи and yᵉ first yᵉᵃʳᵉ
at urtimes 1655.
sic subscribitur   Tho: chisholme
           J Selkrig clk..

tertio Novᵣ 1654

The qlk day being conveinit in the
craftis hospitall yᵉ visitor and facultie
anent daniell browne said Visitor

payᵗ browne

his compts of his Intromissiounne wᵗ
yᵉ caling yᵉ gnids + sommes yᵉ last
yeir qrin he was visitor after dew
examinaᵗiounne and consideraᵗiounne yᵉof
charge and discharge being confeilit
yᵉ caling all in ane voyce dischaᵣges
himpᵗ yᵉ said daniell of his yeirly
Intromissiounne wᵗ yᵉ caling yᵉ gnids
and sommes..

          Sⁱᶜ J Selkrig clk.

Eodem die

Thesᵣ browne

yᵉ visitor and facultie electit yᵉ said
daniell browne Thesʳ to yᵉ vocaᵗiunne
for yᵉ yeir to come to him they
have delyverit In readie money anᵈ

hundretho fiftie four pund sixtein
schillings aucht pennyes And he hes
ressavit ane bond of Gabriell thomsoune
in Langsyde + his cane of ane
hundretho punds prinll somme
being arent Item ane band of
thr hairies etrining twentie merk and
bring arent Item ane band of
Jor Mathies etrining ten merk and
ane band be Nathan grefis etrining
twentie merk prinll somme and
arent wt yr gift del and dres —

(35)

decimo sexto nov 1654

The 9th day being convenit in the
New Kirk steiplle of glasgow yr visitor
doctor Jor chrichtoune daniell broune
thomas dokhart Nathan grey and
thr hairies anent yr examinatioune
of John Kid burges of air anent
his Knowledge of chirurgianrie guha
being reexamined is Licentiat to eur
Simple woundis allendirlie and obleiss
him self not to medill wt

Licence
Kid

tumoures, ulceris, disclariounes, fractures
nor any thing y^t is composed and
y^t undir ye paine of ten pund toties
quoties all his farder qualificatiouns,
and efter his qualificatiouns to be
admitit and obleiss him no^t to
practize w^t in ye brut of glasgow, untö
sik tyme he be burges of ye s^d brut
and lykwayes obleiss him to pay
y^{rlie} to ye facultie saxteen schilling^s
ilk money at ye terme of witsonday
ye first y^ers pay^t to be at witsonday
nixt and swa furth y^rafter y^rlie
during his lyftyme and he the mein
tyme hes pay^t his fynes and givin
his ayt^t de fideli administratioune
as use is.—

die subscribitur   Johne Hird
                    Selkrig clt.

Eodem die.

Convenit as is above writtin anent
ye reexaminatioune of archibald boyle
concerning his knawledge of chirurgie
quha being reexamined be ye faculties

is fund qualified to practize simple
chirurgie yt is to say to cur simple
woundis in yr flesh and obleiss
him at na tyme hereafter to
medill wt fractors, ulcers, tumors
dislocacounes nor any thing yt is
eposit and yt under yr pains of
ten pund toties quoties qll his
farder qualificacoune and efter qualificacounes
to be admittit quha hes payit his
fynes and hes grown his dyt as
use is.—

die subscribitur Archibald Boyle
            I Selkrig clr

                20 Nov 1654.—

The qlk day yr visitor & brethrein
conveind in yr craftis hospitall for
yr tyme be pluralitie of votis it is
ordaint yt James Dies inchand
sall onlie his quarter complett
yirlie ~~all yr rest of yr vocacoune~~
fourtein schillings yirlie as sd is
in tyme coming during his dyttyme

(36)

Dies

die
168

to yᵉ clk he herby obleiss him and hes payit bygane epts..

sic subscribitur   James die..

feb 8. 1655..

Convinit I tho craftis hospitale the most prt of the facultie & all in on voice hes statute & ordaint that the holl grer comphs be payʳd upon the day that yᵉ visitor is electit & whosoever trangreses shall not hene ane vor in the election..

The day it is ordaint that daniell broune give to Wᵐ Selkrig 2 lib for his desceised father service & so our new clark begins at Candelmes 1655..

The sd day it is ordaint to guir dʳ Rosbrugh officer 1 lib 4S for half yris servie..

The sd day the present visitor is to chairg all the people that professes phisick or chirurgerie wᵗ in the toune of aire & he to be allowed for his chairges..

The sd day we have maid choise of
Mr Rbt Govane to be our clark bot
is not present

The sd day it is apoynted that
daniel Broune be apoynted if the
aduyse and consent of hath: Gregs
Mr arch Gihame & James thomsonne
Adam gray to visit the execntionne
of those persones that ar chargit
wt horning & cause dennve them
& they ar to be allowed ther
charges.

decimo nono Februarie 1655.

The Visitour and facultie having met
in the crafles hospitall Mr Rbt
Govane being sent for cam & acceptit
the place as being clerk and gave
his aithe de fideli administracune
And it is enactit That in all tymes
coming during his exerceing the place
as clerk That he shall have ten merkes
yeirlie of fie attonn the usuall dewis
payable by the friemen entering and

others casualities.

The sd day by ane unanimous consent
William Soutter is admittit and receweit to
be on of ther number So whom they
herby grant libertie to exerceis his airt
of cuting of ~~the stone~~ people of the
gravell and preparing of the patientes
in regeine therto w't out the citie of
glasgow Swa far as they have libertie
by ther gift ay and qll he satisfie
the toune for his burgesship and
after puting to the pint visitour of
his burgess ticket after he is admittit
They herby declair his libertie to be
extendit w't out any exceptioune And
ordaines him to pay Twentie merkes
for his fyne to daniell browne
thesaurer and other quarterlie comptis
as the use is in all tyme cowing
who being put gave his oathe of
fidelities.

Septimo Martij 1655.

The 9th day Johne Hall Visitour Tho

102

James Hamilltonne, Wr ard Grahame,
daniell browne, John dow Adam
brays, Wm Clydsdaill Thos Starues and
ard bogle members of the sd faculte
being convinent in the craftes hospitall
Compririt before them James Tobias
chirurgiane in Air sone to son
Tobias chirurgiane ther And having
putit to them ane petitioun anent
his earnest desyre to be admittit
ane of ther number And that his
said old aged father who was
not able to travell might be
licentiat to exerce his sd airt of
chirurgianrie during his lyftyme
they both being such as ar bothe
to be refracter to good ordour of the
sd facultie after reexaminatioun and
sufficient tryall taken of the sd
James they all in on voyce do
licentiat him to exerce his sd airt
Wt in the toune of air allangerlie other
places convine to ther trust conforme
to ther gift & power authorising them

Tobias
licentiat

d.c

for that effect except w'in the citie
of glasgow & suburbes belonging therto
the sd James alwayes yearlie at the
terme of Lambmes paying in to
the boxe threttie shillings scotes for
the use of the poor begginand the
first terme at Lambmas nixt And
if he failyie that two yeares com to
go ther unpayit Then and in that
cause The sd facultie heirby declaris
this his admission and tollerance
of exerceing the sd airt To becom
null voyd & ineffectuall in all tyme
thereafter who being put hes givin
his oathe as use is And hes
payit to daniell broune Collectour
for the use of the poor fourtie pennies
money dykas they heirby declair
ther pryces to extend to his sd father
during his lyftyme upon ane
testificat to be reportit to the present
visitour under the put or last
magistrates of air & these ther of
ther brethering burgesses of the sd

brughe or ar authorized to exerce the
sd airt ther handis of his qualificatioune
age & inabilitie to travell & which
being done the sd Johne Tobias
is to give ane act extend it to him
for the effect afo'rsd And upon
which termes ther putis ar grantit
and no otherwayes And is subt be
the sd James

Sic subscribitur   James Tobias
                    R Govrane clt

Vigesimo Secundo Maii 1655.
The 9th day James Caruthers sone to
the deceist James Caruthers of
holmendis is bookit prentise heirin
to Thomas Lockhart apothecaire for
the space of foure yeiris conform to the
Indentour produceit past betwixts
the sd Thomas on the ane ptie
The sd James and Mr Johne Lockhart
of prentis as burdener for him of
the dait the second day of october
1654 last bypast for the entire

Prentise
Caruthers

pras of the sd dait of the forsd
Indrulour conforme to the accustomed
ordour To the end That he may
have the benefit of the accessary
present redounding to priviliscis
of the lyk Rynd Quho being put
gave his oathe as use is and payit
his ordinar dewis usit & wont.—

payit to the thr
—2—18—0—

25 Maii 1655.

Glasgow
merchandis

The gfk day the put visitour and
most pte of the faultie being
convenit in the craftis hospitall
They ordainit all exercing to
ceass against the merchand of
glasgow till farder ordour.—
dykris dohne McClae scholmaster being
present and declairing being spoken
to That he would not medle heirafter wt any poynt of chirurgianrie
or prescribe any physick Therfor
the faultie all in on voice did
discharge the sd dohne to medle
in any of the sds arts on any

McClae

tyme heirafter w't ȝifpearime that they
will proceid against him w't all rigour
of the law..

21 Junii 1655..

The qlk day the prit visitour + most
pte of the facultie bring convenit
in the new Kirk sessioune hous
They all in on voice did ordaine
That Thomas Weir in Auld machaue
be prosecut be all legall wayes +
that the visitour give to some
agent or other ane rex dollar to
wait upon the calling of the suspensione
raisit be him against them..
Item the sd day ordaines the
lies of capoun agt whom they ar
raisit to be put to all executione
and the lies to be copied That
alse many copies be drawne up
as ther is personnes contenit in
the sds lies + that messingeris be
imployit for yt end..

deb:
Weir

lies of
capoitue

18 Septbr 1655

The pnt visitour and most pte of the facultie being conviniit in the Craftse hospitall Compeirit Quintein

Muir Muir in Paislay who being apprehendit by lres of captne for using & exerceing the airt of chirurgainrie & others wt in the compas of ther gift And being inquyred anent his carriage theranent Confpit his guilt befor the charge givin him but not sine and declairit his resolucune to

discharge abstein in tym coming And therfor of his owne consent is heirby content of his owne accord to deceist & ceise in all tyme coming from exerceing of the sd airt or using or pscribing to any patient of summrven any medicamentis And that under the paine of 40 lib toties quoties he sall be found to trahsgres And therfor in the caice of his abstinence the heirby fris him of all lres & exercecunes therof used

against him upon the pay.t maid
to the collectour of fystie right
schillings for defraying the charges
impendit — Sub.r befor Mr Rd govenour
& Rd Symisonne his Servitour ..

     Dure
      R. govrane witnes
      Rd Symisonne witnes ..

    21 of Sep.ber 1655
The qlk day the pnt visitour Johne
Hall w.t the wholl facultie except
James Scott and James frank being
conveenit in the craftes hospitall
of the sd citie anent ther electionne
of ane new visitour for ane yeir
to com By pluralitie of votes The
sd facultie electit nominat choise of
and continued the said Johne hall
visitour of the said facultie for ane
yeir to com who being pnt acceptit
of the sd office and gave his oathe
de fideli administratione as the use
is ..

Lykas the sd Visitour did nominat
for himself Thomas Lockhart and
James Thomsone to be quarter masters
of the sd facultie for ane year to
cum.—

As also the sd facultie did nominat
+ by pluralitie of votes elect Mr
Johne Crichtoune and James
hamilltoune to be quarter masteris
for them for ane year to com,
which quarter Mrs being all put
(except the sd James Thompsonne)
acceptit of ther receive offices and
gave ther oathes as use is.—

Item the sd facultie did nominat
+ appoynt Johne Low + Mathow grey
to be boxe masters for ane year to
com and dellyvered to ilk ane of
them ane kye of the sd boxe.—

Item by pluralitie of votes Mr Ro-
Bovrane is continued clerk for a
year to com + daniell broune is
ordered to pay him fyve merkis for
his half yearis service bygaine, who

qtr masters

boxe
mrs

Clerk

accepit & gave his oathe as use is —
Item they appoyntit Robt Harris officer
for ane year to com who
accepit

22 Septr 1655 —

The qlk day being conveinit in the
new Kirk sessionne hous The Visitour,
Mr Johne Crichtonne, Thomas Lockhart,
Johne Low, Nathan grey Wm Clydsdaile,
Robt Baxter & Ard bogle Mr Ja Hamiltonne
& daniell browne Compeirit Allane
Kirkwood at the grein and being
wtin the shyrredome of Renfrew
and being examined anent his
qualificatne in using chirurgianrie
in mending of woundis and broken
bones They did licentiat him to
continue in acting the lyff and
curing all simple woundis wtin
the boundis conteint in ther gift
except wtin the toune of glasgow
and subscrivis thereof He paying to
the collectour fourtie pounds for his

(margin left: Harris officer)

(margin left: Kirkwood licensed)

bygane fyne in not obeying the charge
givin to him and putting the facultie
to the charges of recentinge cap[tio]ne
against him And for his licentia[tio]ne
heirafter during his lyftyme And
30 S payin[g] yearlie XXX s to the boxe
of the s[ai]d facultie begining the
first termes pay[t] therof at Michaelmas
next And if he failzie in pay[t] [th]of
yearlie dewa that twa yearis runne
in the thrid unpayit Then and in
that caice this his licentia[tio]ne is
heirby declairt nulle and sall becum
insffectuall in all tyme coming
And upon the q[uhi]lk condi[tio]nes thir
pntis ar granted and no otherwayes.
band for The s[ai]d day the s[ai]d Allan gave
40 lib band for 40 lib q[uhi]lk is delyvered to
the collectour.

Octavo Octobris 1655

The q[uhi]lk day being conveine in the
sessioune hous of the new Kirk,
the pnt visitour, N[o]r D[oc]tor Crichtoune,

and James hamiltoune & Ard grahame
Thomas Lockhart, James thomsonne
daniell browne, adam grays, nathan
greg Wm Clydisdaill Rot harris and
Ard boyle The sd daniell gave in
his compt of intromissionne wt
the faculties guids as being ther
collectour the former year.
Qlk by charge & discharge is as fallowethe
Charge
Imprimis the sd daniell charges
himself wt of somever was fund
by compt the former year being
the third of Nober last restand
in his hand pade   —154 —16 —8
Item receaved from Gabriell
Thomsone that he wasdue
be band   100 — 0 — 0
Item for ane year and ane
halfis Dirint   9 — 0 — 0
Item from nathan greg Johne
Boyd & Rot harris eache of
them being dew be band lide 40 — 0 — 0
Item from Johne Mathie for

(40)

Collectours
Compt

his fyne   6 — 13 — 4

Item from James Tobias for his fyne   40 — 0 — 0

Item for James Caruthers booking
     prenteis to Tho Lockhart   2 — 18 — 0

Item from 21 persones of quarter
     comptes being the number of
     those w in the toune yo ar
     burgesis and friemen as they
     ar in use to pay..   13 — 4 — 0

Item from Wm Soutter for his fyne   13 — 6 — 8

Item from Allan Kirkwood for his fyne   40 — 0 — 0

Item of quarter comptes from
     nyne persones licentiat w
     out brucht   9 — 10 — 0

          Suma — 429 — 8 — 8.

          discharge

Imprimis the sd daniell comptes
     discharges himself by payt
     of the soumes fallowing &
     others under & retrowritten
     To wit first by order from
     the facultie to Wm Russell
     messinger.   2 — 15 — 0

Item by ordour from the visitour
to Mr Rovaine messinger for
charging severall personnes   6 — 12 — 0
Item to James Watsonne bedle
for attending the faculties at
severall tymes   0 — 18 — 0
Item to Mr Rud officer for his fie   1 — 0 — 0
Item to Sor danield for charging
severall personnes   10 — 13 — 4
Item to Johne Rosebrighe officer
for his service   1 — 4 — 0
Item to Wm Selkirge for his deceast
fathers fie   4 — 0 — 0
Item for the registra'ture of the
lres of hotning denuncing of
the personnes to the horne,
raising of captionne any lex
doubling of of conforme to
ane compt producit   12 — 14 — 0
Item to Johne Muir collectour
to the crazies hospitalls   3 — 6 — 8
Item to Johne Jamiesonne drumer   0 — 12 — 0
Item to the clerk for his fie
half year past   3 — 6 — 8

Item he discharges himself by Wm
Souter his indt payt of his fyne   13 — 6 — 8
Item be Allan Kirkwood his bandy   40 — 0 — 0
Item be a band of Ard Andersones
and his cautioneris of   266 — 13 — 4
Item by indt payt of James frank
his after compt for the sd year   0 — 12 — 0
Item by indt payt of the nyne
outtound prisoners ther quarter
comptes and of   9 — 10 — 0
Item as indt receaved from James
dies of his quarter compt 48
and of Androe Millares 8s inde   0 — 13 — 0
Item grein to the visitours that
he gave to the Mr Weir to
agent   busines   3 — 0 — 0
                Suma 380 — 15 — 8
Swa restes dew be the compter
the soume of   48 — 13 — 0.

Alk compt aforsd being calculat it
was fund as is above written That
the compt of charge com to four
hundreths twentie nyne poundes

eight schillingis and eight pennies monye
By which then rested dew by the
compter the forsd ffourtie eight pounder
threttin schillingis which the sd
daniels did wᵗ the forsd twa bandis
of Ard Andersone & Allan Kirkwoods
exhibit & produce before the sd facultie
And thereafter he and Thomas Lockhart
bring removed to the effect on of them
might be collectour for a year to com
be pluralitie of votis the sd daniell
was continued collectour for a year
to com who accepit therof and gave
his oathe as use is to whom the forsd
twa bandis and fourtie eight pounder
threttin schillingis was redelyvered wᵗ
which at his nixt putting of his compt
he is to be chargeit ᵗʰᵉ and for the forsd
accompt they did approve in the
haill articles as is aforsd –
The sd day James Thomsone gave
his oathe as a gⁿ master for a
year to com –

decimo septimo Martii 1656.

The sd day being convenit in the
craftes hospitall Johne Hall, visitour
doctour Chrichtoune Mr Ard grahame
Thoms Soutter, Thomas Lockhart, daniell
Browne, James Thomsone Rot harris,
Ard bogle, Adam gray, John Low &
Wm Clydisdaill They did appoynt the
lies to executioun
visitour, doctor Chrichtouns Mr Ard
grahame, daniell browne & Thomas
Lockhart To speak the Magistrates
anent the executione of ther lres
of captioune Speciallie agt Catherine
Robiesone and Elspethe Murray.

The sd day daniell browne collectour
collectour
20 lib
acknawledgit his recept of Twentie
pounde fra the ladie   who
was incarcerat by lres of captioune
for her bygaine transgressiounes, whom
they in caice of her insisting to
transgress heirafter ordaint to be
reincarcerat againe.

Item the sd daniell grantit his
recept from James frank of 24s Scots

of bygaine quarter comptes.
Item the sd day ordains the collectour
to give Gabriell Conyinghame officer
thrie poundes for his extraordinar paines.
The sd day Walter Nielsone deacon
convriner having representit to the
facultie the meaines of ther fyve
merkes ꝑ yearlie they pay in to
the sd deacon conveners hous for
the use of the poor of the hospitall

They all in on voice ordered the
augmentarune of other fyve merkes
and so yearlie to pay in to the
collectour of the craftis hospitall
Ten merkes Beginand for the first
year at Mair day Noel to com
and so to continue Upon condicune
The deacen convriner & deacones
augment of the facultie on of thes
number Jarder to be of ther number
& on his conncell wt the two they
have That so heirafter the facultie
may have thris of ther number

wt the two they have on the

deacen conviners hous And that the
draconis joyne to intreat the magistratis
concurrence in recceutiounes of ther
landable actis estableshed in ther
favouris.-

4to August 1656
Conveint in the craftis hospitall
the prit visitour wt Mr James
hamiltoune, daniell broune, Jor
dow, Nathan greg, Wm Clydisdaill
Rot harris, Adam gray + Ard bogle
who all in on voice did condiscend
and aggrie that ane seal of caus
or letter of deaconrie be purchest
from the toun councell in favouris
of the facultie, but prejudice of the
old gift grantit to them be the
deceast K James and this to be
allenerlie in favouris of chirurgianes
and barbouris.-

the sd day they ordaint the
collectour to give to Catherine Spang
daughter to the deceast Mr Spang

chirurgiane four poundes
supplie..

       Octavo Augusti 1
Conveint in the new h
hall put visitour wt Wr
hamiltoune, And grahan
dow, daniell broune, tho
James thomsone and ?
Anent the tryzall of d

chirurgiane who hes b
these ten yearis or the
in cutting of the stone
sight of severall creditab
did licentiat him al
source the cutting of th
in the boundis contai
gift. And therfor hes

bose ffourtie merkes wt
in hand and the res
ticket and is to pay y

his quarter comptis thre
beginand the first yea
Whitsunday muet and

in payt therof yearlie Swa that two
yeares rune in the thrid unpayit
That in yt caice this his licentia'une
is heirby declarit hull and shall
broom inoffectuall in all tyme
coming who gave his oathe as
use is.

22 Septr 1656.

Convent in the hospitall the prnt
Visitour wt the wholl facultie except
Mr James hamiltonne, James frank
James Scot & Wm Soutter Anent the
electionne of ane new visitour for
ane year to com By pluralitie of
votes they did elect & make choise
of James Thomsone chirurgiane as
Visitour for ane year to com who
being prnt acceptit and gave his
oathe as use is.

The sd day ane new lre of deaconrie
was put up in the boxe.

(42) dykas the wholl persones prnt being
sractrin in number sightit ther bygaines

quarter compte And it w

by unanimous consent

q^r compte burgess inhabitentis w

facultie pays alyk in

convning & nan to rece

year So that what we

upon James dies & An

is not to be exactit

Item the 2d day the

did nominat for hims

and daniell browne to

masteris of the 2d fa

a year to com

And the facultie & plur

Mr did elect Thomas Lock

Nathan greg to be of

for them during th

spaces

Item they did nom

Ard: grahame & Nor

browns masteris for a year t

delyverit to eiche of

his of the box

Clerk Item they continued

Govrane clerk for a year to com.—
Item they did by pluralitie of
votes liberat and frie Mr Ard: grahame
of his being officer this year it being
his turne & ordaint Gabriell
Cunyinghame to supplie upon the
faculties expense.—

7 Nover 1656.—

the 9th day being convint the
prnt: visitour wt the wholl facultie
except doctour Crichtoune, James
frank, Wm Soutter, Thomas Lockhart,
and James Scot & Alexr Joiphray
deacon of the   men & Robt:
Carruthers deacon of the tailyouris
in the crafts hospitall for heiring
of daniell browne collectour his
compt 2th accordinglie was done
and was as followethe by charge
and discharge.—

            Charge
Imprimis the sd daniele charges
    himselff wt of soume was resterd

at the last yeares compt   48 — 13 — 0

Item w^t merkes that is

dew be Wm Soutter   13 — 6 — 8

Item w^t a band of allane

Kirkwoodis of   40 — 0 — 0

Item w^t a band of Ard

Andersones of   266 — 13 — 0

Item w^t James frank his

g^{ta} comptis these two

yeairis past   1 — 4 — 0

Item w^t the g^{ta} comptis of the

whole facultie of

being 19 in number payis

price   18 — 11 — 8

Item w^t a yearis @rent of

Ard Andersones band to wit

fra Martimmes 1654 to

Martimmas 1655   16 — 0 — 0

Item of fyne recrouerit fra

the ladie dimrod   20 — 0 — 0

Item of fyne frou dver Nichal   26 — 13 — 4

Item of g^{ta} comptis receauit

fra Joⁿ how, Joⁿ Millar

and Joⁿ Tod   4 — 8 — 0

Summa 448 _ 6 _ 8

discharge

Imprimis the compter discharges
himself as having the bandis
fallowing debursing of the cowmes
afterspecit To wit w^t Ard:
Andersoun his band of   266 _ 13 _ 4

Item a band of Johne Millie lent
at Candrelmas 1656 of   66 _ 13 _ 4

Item a ticket of Jvis M^c willie of   6 _ 13 _ 4

Item to the collectour of the
craftes hospitall   5 _ 0 _ 0

Item to the clerk for his fie   6 _ 13 _ 4

Item by not pay^t of Wm Souttars
fyne of   13 _ 6 _ 8

Item givin to Catherine Spang
upon warrand   4 _ 0 _ 0

Item for a plaistoring ag^t Wair
in auld machane & for
raising   9 _ 0 _ 0

Item to the drumer and James
Watsoune   1 _ 16 _ 0

Item to the deacon convriner officer   1 _ 0 _ 0

Item to Sr dounald miss for service 13—0—0

Item to Gabriell Conyngham officer 3—0—0

Item for the new Kall of Arms 12—17—8

Item to the Jaylour of the tolbuithe

    for booking of the lade dinnrod 0—12—0

Item spent at the receipt of allan

    Kirkwoodis fyne 0—12—0

Item to Gab- Conyngham

    officer this day 1—10—0

Item Wr Broun for charging Jvr

    Mc neill 0—12—0

    Suma 412—19—8..

Swa restes deu be the compter the sowme of

    35—17—0..

Qlk compt aforsd being red was allowit

and approvine and ordanit to be bookit

and the twa bandis & note aforsd

was put in the box and they

(+3)   ordanit the sd daniell to pay in

to Ard boyle whom be pluralitie of

votes they electit collectour for a year

i vii   to cow ye acceptit and gaw his oathe

Box   the forsd sowme of thrittie sex poundis

sex schillingis. Qrupon they woouer him

of his Intromissioune.

gter mr · Item the visitour did nominat Mr
And Grahame as a gter mr for
a year to com who gave his oathe
as use is as being addit in
place of dr Hall.

It is to be remembred that Wm
Non payte · Wallace, dr Pattersoune he sargonshill
Thomas Chisholme, dr Reid, Jam
Tobeas have not payit ther
comptis, this upon 1656 & an
awand the former year also 1655
and allan Kirkwood for michaelm
1656 as they ar sett doune in
first pt of this book.

Glasgow 28 day of Januare 1657.
the sd day compeirit James
dowgall gardiner and is becom
actit of his owne confessioune That
he shall abstein in all tyme
hirafter from useing & exerceing
any pairt of the airt of chirurgain
or prescribing of any medicamints

or physick to any persoune of
similar ather w^t in this citie
or w^t out wherby he may fall
under the censur of the chirurgiane

dowgall

of the s^d burghs And y^t under
the pain of Twentie poundes so
often as he shall transgres Having
payit fyve poundes Scotis for his
bygane transgressioune In witnes
q^r of this p^ntis ar subscribit day
yeir & place fors^d Befor thir
witnessis Mr R^t gowrane writter
clerk to the s^ds chirurgeans and
writter heiro and R^t symisone
his servener..

    die sub^tis James Dowgall
      "   MR gowrane witnes
      "   Robert symisone witnes

      23 f^r 1657.-
Conuenit the visitour, d^or Hall
doctour Crichtonne, Thomas Lockhart
daniell Broune, James Lies, d^or
dow, Ard boyd R^t harlee, W^m

Clydisdaill, Iames braidwood, nathan
greg & Androw Millar.

The 9th day Iohne Logane in
gorballis having acknowledged that
he had exerceised the airt of
chirurgainrie to some persones &
of his owne consent is content
and herby oblidgit That he sall
not exerce the sd calling any
manner of way more or less
directlie or undirectlie in all
tyme coming except of he can do
to himself or any sd in his owne
familie under the paine of fourtie
poundis in caice he sall transgres
and do in the contrair.

Item the said day they did licentiat
Robt muir in gorbalis to exerce
the airt of barbourizing ther ptz
paying yearlie to the box 16 s
beginning at michaelmes nixt.

Item Iohne diddell is admitit
barbour and to exerce the sd airt
wt in this citie and the boundis

comitt to the charge of the facultie
paying yearlie his quarter comptis
Beginand at michaelmas nixt
who hes to the collectour ten pd
for his admissione.

Item James Mowat Servitour to
doctour Rolage is admitted to
exerce the art of pharmacie to
applye dochlitchis and cawteris
And if he proceed any farder
he is heirby actit to pay fourtie
peris Sua oft as he sall transgres
paying his yearlie qtr comptis
biginning at michaelmas nixt &
who hes payit to the collectour
Ten poundis money.

Item the 2d day John Crichtoune
sone to hir dr Crichtoune is
bookit prentis to his said fatter
for seavine yearis conforme to the
Indentour betwixt them qlk entres wt
the first of maii 1652 & hes payit to
the box 30s.

Mowat
is tit

Jhon
Crichtoune
30 s

19 Maii 1657.

The sd day compeirit in p̄ns of
the visitour and masteris of craft
Elspethe Murray widow And being
incarcerat w't lr̄es of cap̄nes for
usurping & taking upon her to
prescribe and give phisick & use
the airt of chirurgaine And now
liberat upon mair favour is becom
actit of her owne consent and
dr̄ bell merchand is ca̅ner for
her That shoe sall not medle
directlie nor indirectlie in all
tyme coming to exerce phisick
or use the forsd airt to any
persoune of quumever except to
those of her owne familie under
the pain of fourtie p̄ds so oft
as shoe sall transgres to be
payit the sd facultie of chirurgianes
of this brughe and shoe is actit
to releiff him be this act su̅r
before Gabriell Conynghame & Jo̅
Jamisone

Octavo Junii 1657

Convaint the ptt visitour Johne
Hall, doctour Crichtoune, Mr Ard
grahame, Thomas Lockhart, Mr Jon
Hamiltoune, Nathan greg, Ard
bogle, Rot haries, Wm Clydisdaill
And Adam Craige Concerning ane
letter direct to them be the chirurg
& apothecaris of Edgr anent the
letteris of patent grantit be the
protectour for erecting ane colleg
of physitianis ther They did all
in on voice comissionat and
Impower Johne Hall & Mr Ard
grahame to goe to Edgr to
advocat & oppose the same befor
the counsall of Stait To whom they
grein ther gift & del Simondis &
lres of horning Allero they ar to
returne back againe And ordaine
the collectour to advance them

visitoune
Hall &
...hame

(44)

monye for that effect~

         duodecimo Junii 1657~

the forsds personns having met
and dor Hall & Mr Ard Grahams
having mad ther report and
presentet the double of petitionne
Report given in be them to the counsall
of Steat together wt the double
of aur comissionns grantet be
them to Wm brodie & Mr Wm
dightbodie to agrue in ther
absens the facultie did approve
therof & render them thanks
and ordered each on of ther
number to think upon the
phisitiones patint and upon
objectiones ther against And did
again commissionat them upon
the first occasions to repair to Edr
for the effect aforsaid~

         Sexto Augusti 1657~

the sd day being convuint the

Visitour, baillie Hall, doctour Crichtoune
Mr James Hamiltoune Ard Grahame
Thomas Lockhart, Dor Lowes, Nathan
greg, Adam gray, Mr Clydisdaill
Ard boyle, James dies, Rot Staries.
They did all in on voice condisced
and appoynt that the sex personis
fallowing To wit Dor Hall, doctour
Crichtoune Mr James Hamiltoune
Ard grahame Thomas Lockhart, Rot
Staries & Ard boyle Act & doe yt
is necessar & Incumbent in reference
to all transactiones for the good of
the faeultie Whereunto they obliged
themselves to stand but contra=
dictionne —
Lykas they ordaine that ther be
ane visitatne the 17 of this instant
of all the pharmaciaus chopes
of thess wt in this bruglt that ar
fremen and memberis of the faeultie
And for yt effect doe nominat
the visitour, doctour Crichtoune
Mr Ard grahame & Tho Lockhart. —

opis

As also they did ordaine Mr James
Hamiltonne, Ard grahame & Johne
Lowis wt the first conveniencee to
goe to doctour Rotray and crave
a sight of his letteris of graduatioun
and if he refuis that they may
have a sight therof To report.

28 August 1657.
Convrint Johne Hall, baillie James
Thomsone visitour, doctour Crichtonne
Mr James Hamiltonne & Ard grahame
Thomas Lockhart, daniell browne
Johne Lowis, Rot harieis Wr Clydisdall
Ard boyle, and James dies.
the qlk day Compeirit befor them
Elspith Murray spous to Johne
wallace, wright and Johne Rollo
merchand as cawer for her being
lawlie warnit To whom ther was
ann act subt wt ther handis of
the dait the 19 day of Maii last
bypast oppinlie read Brи and the
sd Elspith who was them

widow to becom actit of ther
owne consent and the sd Iohne
Killo as ca°ner for her That shoe
sould not medle directlie nor
indirectlie in all tym coming to
give or administrat phisick or
use the airt of chirurgie to any
persouns quhunever except to those
of her owne familie under the
pains of fourtie poundis scotes
monye swa oft as shoe should
transgres To be payit to the sd
facultie And the sd Elspethe being
interrogat whither or not since
the dait of the sd Act shoe
had given any phisick to any
persounes Speciallie to on Iames
Watsoune shoe oppinlie confest the
sam in swa far as he having
had as shoe calld it The
gentilmannis seiknes Shoe gave
him first Ialup & then ointment
of olibey galtanne & quiksilver
all mixt together and quarter of

Act

Murray

vnce of everie on of them, and
that scho gave his child som
quoliquislida. Wherupon the sd
faculties all in on voice did
dicerne and vnlaw the sd
Elspithe and the sd Johne Rollo
her caven in the forsd sowme
of fourtie poundis And that
becaus of her owne confessioune
And of the forsd Act subt be
them glk scho had broken To
be imployt as the magistratis
and the faculties should judge
expedient Intreating the magistratis
of this brut to Interpon ther
authoritie to the puting of this
ther decreit to executioune wt in
termis of law.

the sd day Anent the complaint
givin in befor them be James
Andersone relict of the deceast
James Rodger merchand of this
brughe against Margaret Cranfield
spous to david Sorrell merchand

(45)

mentiouns that q[uhi]lk upon the sext
day of this instant monethe the
sd Jannet her deceast husband
being heavilie diseased wt ane
mortall diseas q[uhi]lk of he departit
this lyf And hear tell that the
sd Marg[are]t had gevin out herself
as ane most expert phisician
he caused her goe for her who
cam to visit him And after sho
had griped his pulsis sho told
him that his diseas was cureable
and promeist to cuir him therof
wt in fyftein dayes thereafter
saying that sho would sell her
lyf for his if he would bestowe
upon himself And he being thus
persuadit be her did in end agrie
wt her for thrie poundes ten
schilling sterling monyes for the q[uhi]lk
sowme sho promeist to cuir him
perfectlie wt in the space forsd
And q[uhi]lk sowme sho receavit in
hand according to her owne desyre

And trw it is shw sent him some
Sowley in our eair w other two
things Ulkrs ar almost reelant to the
for to be saim Ulkrs medicamentis
the prrorwar supposed to be
mor hurtfull nor helpfull to
him in swa far as he depairtit
this lyf upon the ellivinthe day
of this instant and being present
wtin thrie or four momentis of
tyme before his departour shw
told that ther was no dratho
working wt him Wherthrow of all
law equitie and reasoun the sd
Margt nor onlie aught to be
delairit incapable of the forsd
sciencie and art of medicine and
chirurgainrie and punished for the
forsd wrong But also aught + sould
be drecernit to giv bak the monys
forsd receavit byfor fra the complener
and to receave bak the medicamentis
which shw sent doune And albeit
it be of veritie that the petiwar

has oft requyit the defender to gev
her back her monyis and to receave
back her pretendit medicamentis
alse muche therof as is restant qlk
is almost the qhole Nevertheles
shoe refusit to doe the samyne
w'out shoe be compellit Craveand
therfor the sd bailie, visitors &
remanent members of the facultie
to determein therin according to
justice And anent the exta'nne
grein to her Compeired the sd
Marg't & her sd husband and
after hearing of the sd complaint
lead to her shoe denyit the whole
expressiones conteint in the narrativ
aforsd but acknawledgit the recept
of the forsd monyis And that shoe
did giv to the defunct the particular
medicamentis conteint in a papper
grein in be her So wit Two pyntis
of   two pyntis of claret wyne
two leaves of sugar three once of
syrup of   three onces of

garnfield

madinhair wt sum syrup of gilleflowrs
and declarit he died of ane
hydropocie be reasone of his legis
war all swalit downward, had
ane harch coche and ane drought
and tirgd in his belles and being
Interrogat who was put at the
bargaine making shoe declarit on
Mr anna Crawfurd daughter to
the deceast laird of Carssmuir
whom shoe was content should
be receavit sole witnese in the
wholl particularis and that if
shoe upon oathe should declair
shoe spek the wordis lybelled shoe
was content to succumbe and
undergo the censur of the faculte
and for the prit would pay back
all the forsd thrie pund ten
schillings sterling to the perswar.
And being demandit if shoe had
any warrand to exerce medicine
or testimonialle from any in
authoritie to pas throughe the

142

natione wherby her honestie & willd
cariage might be knawne Shoe
denyit the having therof Alk
being considered The sd facultie
all in on voices did unlaw,
unveiat & dreeme the sd Marg.t
and her sd husband for his
entries to pay to Ard bogle ther
collectour fourtie pound srves for
her bygane transgressione for the
use of the poor to be disposed
upon by the baillie & facultie
for her usurping to exerce the sd
calling wt in ther boundis wt out
any testimonialls And to act
themselves That shoe salle not
prescribe or gro any phisick to any
patient of summver wt in his citie
or the boundis comitit to the
faculties trust & that shoe salle
not practise the airts of chirurgianie
or pharmacie in any tym cong
under the pains of ffourtie pounds
sres monye for ilk transgressionne

(left margin, upper:) grausield 40 tbt

(left margin, lower:) sic
And yt because
her confessionne
and of the sd anna
Crawfurd hir
depositione upon
oathe that lybelled
was of truulth shoe
deny willing gto

Swa oft as comitit And that in
respect also of her contumacie to
appear befor gᵐ they war eitit
befor them. The sd day in obedience
to the forsd act The forsd david
Sorrell & Margt granfield spouss
becom actit of ther owne consent
That They sall not medle directlie
nor indirectlie in any tym coming
to gev phisick or use the forsd
airtes to any personne of enuiron-
ed in this toune or any pairt
wt in the rest ptes of this natione
comitit to the trust of the medicians
and chirurgians of glasgow under
the paine of 40 lib scotts monye
to be payit to them for the use
of the poor Swa oft as they sall
transgress Be this act subr befor
Rot allans writter Wm Reid, Rot
hodge & gabriell Connynghame officers
sic subr Wm govane no pub
at comand of the sds personnes

rill
haugit

(46)

Quarto Sep^{bris} 1657.

Convveint the visitour, doctour Crichtoune
daniell broune Mr Ard grahame
Johne dow, Rot harris, James dies
Adam gray & ard boyle.

The sd day they having taken to
ther consideracne the petitione givin
in to them be Marg granfield
spous to david Sorrell Inglishman
makand mentune That yf by
invitatioune by the decease James
Rodger shoe way imployit to visit
him upon his dealth bed and did
prescribe to him some medicamentis
upon her receipt from him of
thrie pound Ten schilling's sterling
2Ck shoe had redelyvered back
to his relict And he being departit
this lyf And compleaint mad
againes the petitioner by his sd
relict The sd petioner did ingennouslie
canves what was trueth therinto
And being considered by the
facultie They war perswaded to sentence

her in the soume of ffourtie poundis
Scotis as our fyne for her transgressioun
in usurping to medle to prescribe
physick wt in the boundis comitit
to ther trust And seeing the treuthe
is shoe was altogether ignorant of
her being censurable Therfor shoe
humblie craved the facultie would
pitie her conditioune being our
stranger and being most willing
to submit herself to them And
all judicatouris of the land So
refund to her her sd fyne since
shoe had inactit herself to desist
from using the forsd airt wt in
ther bounds They did all in on
voice ordaine And boyse ther collectour
to delyver the forsd ffourtie poundis
of fyne to doctour Crichtoune &
Mr Ard grahame to be disposed upon
be them as they shall think expedient.

Octavo Septbris 1657.
Convint the visitour, doctour Crichtoune

146

Mr James Hamiltoune, Ard grahams,
Thomas lockhart, Johne low, Wm
Clydisdaill, Ard bogle, Adam grays
James & Johne dirs, James braidwood
Mr harris & Johne Riddell.

The 2d day the visitour did shaw
that upon Saturday last the
magistrates & councell did send for
him & desyred he might convocat
the facultie and demand of them
whither they would adher to ther
old gift or joyne wt the privil colleg
of phisitianes. They did all in
on voice adher to ther old gift.

Thomas lockhart as quarter master
protestit against the act mead the
former day in giving up the fourtie
pound of fyne to Mr Johne Brichtoune
and Ard grahame and that it be
not disposed upon but for the weill
of the facultie.

    decimo octavo Septr 1657.
Convent in the hospitall the wholl

protestacon Lockhart

14

Visitor
Compsone | facultie receipt Mr Souttar, Ja frank
Thomas dockhart and nathan greg
anent the collection of our new
visitour for our year to com
Be pluralitie of votes they did
continue James Thomsone visitour
for our year to com 2° acceptil
and gave his oathe as use is —

Item the sd day the visitour
9th novr | did nominat for himself Mr
James Hamiltoune + Ro Maries to
be quarter masters for the facultie
for a year to com. And the facultie
be pluralitie of votes did elect
Thomas Lockhart + Mr Clydisdaill
to be quarter masters for them
during the sd space of all receipt
Thomas dockhart accepto + gave
ther oathes as use is —

Item they did nominat Johne
box mrs | dow + Adam grays box masters
for a year to com + delyvred
to eache of them ane Kye
of the box —

clerk.
Item they continued Mr Ro: gouvane
clerk for ane year to com & gave
his oathe as use is.—

Soutter
Item they ordaint Wm Soutters fyne
to be scoirit out of the book &
remitit to him.—

decimo sexto octobris 1657.

The qlk day being convint in the
craftes hospitale the visitour, Jon
hall baillie, Wm Ja: hamiltoune, Ard
grahame, daniell broune, Thomas
lockhart, Jon low, Adam gray, Ro:
harris, Wm Clydisdaill, James dies
James braidwood Wr George Clerk
of the skinnars and michaell
watsoune deacon of the wobsters
appoyntit for hearing the accomptis
of Ard boyle ther collectour qlk
accordinglie was done, read &
allowit and ordaint to be
bookit and is as fallowithe
by charge & discharge.—

Charge

Imprimis the sd Ard boyle
compter chargis himselff w^t
the sowme he gott from
daniell browne last collectour.. 36—6—8

Item w^t the prinll sowme dew
be Ard Andersone   266—13—4

Item the @ rent therof fra
Martinmas 1655 to Martinmas 1656   16—0—0

Item w^t the prinll sowme dew
be Jon Neill   66—13—4

Item the @ rent therof fra Candlmas
1656 to Candelmas 1657   4—0—0

Item that he receavd from Jon
M^cneill that he was dew be hise   6—13—4

Item for his ofr comptis this year   1—10—0

Item from Jon Liddell and James
Mowat ther upsetts   20—0—0

Item from Elspeth Murray of fynes   4—12—0

Item from James dougall of fynes   5—0—0

Item from Mistress Sorrell of fyne   40—0—0

Item from Elspeth Murray of fyne   40—0—0

Item from dot Creichtoune of
booking monys   1—10—0

(47)

Item from Ro Muir in gorbalis
of qter comptis   0 — 16 — 0
Item the qter comptis of all
the facultie pint bring 19   11 — 8 — 0
          Suma — 521 — 2 — 8 —

                    discharge
Imprimis the compter discharges
   himself wt the having of the
   bandis fallowing in the box
   and deburssing of the soroms
   after spent So wit wt the band
   of Ard Andersone of   266 — 13 — 4
Item ane band of Johne Neilis
   2CR is mead   100 — 0 — 0
Item to the collectour of the
   hospitall deburst   6 — 13 — 4
Item to mr Reid for his fie   1 — 0 — 0
Item to Ro fymisone for parchmine
   and writing   3 — 8 — 0
Item to the bidle of the new kirk
   for his painis at the faculteis
   mittings   1 — 10 — 0
Item to mr gair for the sextrael of ane act 2 — 18 — 0

Item for charges imprendit upon
    lres agt Mr hew Montgomrie   7 — 10 — 0
Item of charges imprendit be ther
    comissioners two severall tym
    at Edgr & to advocalis & agents . 117 — 14 — 0
Item to the post-for carieing of lres   0 — 12 — 0
Item to Jo bryssonns for writieng   0 — 12 — 0
Item to James lockhart for his
    charges in attending upon the
    councell of Stait & the chirurgians
    of Edgr   12 — 0 — 0
Item for half ane years rent of
    50 merks bandrol for the
    faculties accompt   1 — 0 — 0
Item to the officers for apprehending
    Mr Sorrell & to the meng filld the Iaill   0 — 2 — 4
Item to the clerk for his fie   6 — 13 — 4
Item to Wm brades ther agint this man 12 — 16 — 0
Item Mr Sorrells fyne qlk was remitt
    as the act Bears   40 — 0 — 0
Item by nor payit of Elspethe
    Murrayis fyne of   40 — 0 — 0
         Suma — 622 — 8 — 4 ..
         Sua charge & discharge bieng

calculat ther restes dew br
the facultie to the compter the
somme of   101 _ 5 _ 8

Cole

Item br pluralitie of votes they continued
the sd Ard boyle collectour for ane
year to com: qo bring pnt acceptil +
gave his oathe as use is _

Wallace

The sd day in answer to the
supplica'ne givin in br Sr Wallaces
husband to Elspethe murray The
facultie w consent of Sr hall baillie
ordaint the collectour to accept of
Ten pound in satisfactione of the
whole fyne of 40 lib The baillie
having remittt his half totallie
to the poor And did frithe Johne
Rollo of his ca'ne in tymecoming _
Item they ordaint the collectour to
geve Gabriell Comynghame ther officer
three pound for his bygain service
Item to Catherine Spang supplicant
three poundes _

c_7^h

Item they appoyntit Johne diddell
officer for a year to com qo acceptil +

gave his oathe as use is —

Item Thomas Lockhart gave his oathe
as a q[uarte]r master for a year to com —

(48) Item it is to be remembred that
W[ill]m Wallace, Johne Patersonne, Ro[bert]
Jarqushill, Thomas Chisholme, Johne
Reid, James Tobias ar awand ther
q[uarte]r comptis the years 1655, 56 + 1657
Allan Kirkwood the year 1656 + 1657
and James frank this year 1657
as they ar sett doune in the
first page of this book + Jo[h]n Low +
Jo[h]n Millar —

17 of October 1657 —
The sd day comperit Johne Wallace
wright + Elspethe Murray afoir =
men[tioned] and now his spous And is
becom actit of ther owne consent
for freithing Johne Rollo merchand
who was formerlie ca[utio]ner for her
That the sd Elspethe sall not
medle directlie nor indirectlie in
any tym coming to gave or

prescribe physick or use the airt of
chirurgianrie to any persounr of-
unnoun except to those of ther
oune familie and that under the
paine of ffourtie pounds so oft
as shot salle transgres to be
payit to the collectour of the
chirurgians of this burghe bring
qualifiet as accordis of the latter
before them be this Act subr befor
Ard boyle & Mr Tho govrane
            see subtt   Jor Wallace
            -          Tho govrane witnes
            -          Ard boylle witness
The sd day Johne Nride band givin
out of the boxe to Ard boyle
collectour.-

            Undecimo febrii 1658.
The 9th day being convint Johne
hall baillie, tho visitour, doctour
Crichtoun, Mr Jor Hamiltoune, Ard
grahame, Tho lockhart, daniell
broune, Jon dow, nathan greg, adam

gray Wm Clydisdaill, Wr harris, And
boyle Compeire tho Robesone knitoun
to the laird of Cauldwell being
under cap'oune for usurping the
airt of chirurgienre vsin ther
bounds specialle of making their
clothes of Keit & mending broken
bones And they having remitit &
forgivin him for all his bygaine
escapes upon assurance not to
transgres in tyme coming he is therfor
becom actit of his owne consent
never to medle therin directlie nor
indirectlie heirafter and if under
the paine of fourtie pds for the
first transgressione And for eache
oy therafter so oft ashe sall transgres
sub at glasgow the   day befor
Wr Rot gorrane & Rot symsoune his
kinitour.
      sic sub   tho Robertsone
                    Elk gorrane witnes.

            19 Junii 1655.

the sd day in the crafts hospitale
being convent The visitour dor hall
doctour chrichtoune, daniell broune
thomas lockhart, dames frank, nathan
greg dames morsat & wr Clydisdaill
Mr David Speirs putit a pappen
desyring he might upon tryall &
admitit a brother of the faculti
for professioune of pharmacie wt
that pte of chirurgie as drawing
of blood bend applica'ne of cauteris
bend putit his indentour wt
Johne foullie apothecar in Edgr
and bine discharge therof wt his
burges and gild brothers ticket
Qr upon they prescribit to the sd
Mr David to mak these compositiones
fallowing To wit Consectio Hamech,
Pilulæ Cochie majores, Emplestrum
de musilaginbus dimenentium
Mier and Trochei albi rasis And
that at the sight of thomas lockhar
and mr And grahame in the sd
thomas his chamber — And for

blood drawing and applica'nes of
cauteris They ordered that first byfor
he be admitit therto He practice the
same befor two chirurgians of the
facultie and upon a sufficient
report They declarit they would
admit him to the exerceis therof
And prescribit to him to have
his compositi'nes readie ag' the
25 instant Qlk they ordered to be
the day of ther meiting. --

22 Junii 1658. --

Convenit the Visitour, do' halls
doctour Crichtoune Mr James hamiltoune
and Ard grahame, James hamt
Adam grays, Johne Lowe Rd Harvie
and Ard Boyle,
The said day Andro Ralstoune
by petitione having desyred to be
admitit w'in the facultie and
licentiat to exerceis chirurgie Suche
as mending of fractours, dislocaines
and amputa'nes They unanimouslie

orderd that befor he be receavit he
acquaint the visitour when any
patient did imploye him to use
any pairt of chirurgianrie who
could tak two of his number
w.t himself to see his applicane
And in the main tyme that he
nather prescribe physick nor use
pharmacie nor transgres this
ordour under the pains of Ten
poundis toties quoties Q.to into the
s.d Andros acquiescit.

"Prentice
Sprull

(29)

The s.d day Alex.r Sprull sone
to M.r Andros Sprull is bookit
prentice w.t James frank for the
space of Sevine yeairs conforme to
the Indentour past betwixt them
dautit the first day of februarie
1655 His entrie being the s.d day
And whose tyme the facultie
frielie did quat.

25 Junii 1658
The s.d day in the crafts hospitll

being convein the haill forsds personus
in the last sederunt and daniell
browne Thomas Lockhart Nathan
grey & James Mowat the sd Thomas
Lockhart declairit he did so Mr
david Sherp wright the simples &
mixe the same ordourlie wherefter
he mad these compositiones aforsd
pescribit to be mad be him And
they being exshibit & produceit upon
the table byfor the facultie And
inspectioune & tryall yof taken be
oathe of them They all unanimouslie
approvid therof as being yria
perfyttlie dispensrd And having
appoyntit The sd Thomas in ther
pns & hearing to exeaminn him
upon som termes of his airt &
calling qruuto he mad perfyt answr.
They did admit & receaw the
sd Mr david to ther fallowship
as ane pharmaciane Kmiting his
exerceis of any pairt of chirurgie
conteint in the act of the dait

Sherps
admissioune

the 19 instant till his tryall Ʒof
+ report be mad who payit by ordour
to the collectour Turntie Menkes of
tyme..

The sd day they ordaint the collectour
to gev to Catherins Spang supplicant
fourtie schillingis Scotts monys..

Vigesimo Septeno 1658..

Convint in the hospitall the whole
faculteis except doctour Crichtoune
James frank + Wm Clydisdaill anent
the electioune of a new Visitour
who be pluralitie of votes mad
choice of Thomas Lockhart for a
year to cum who being put accepted
and gave his oathe as use is..
Item the sd day the visitour did
nominat for himself James
Thomsoune + Nathan greg and the
faculteis Mr James hamiltoune +
Ard boyle to be quarter masters for
a year who accepted and gave ther
oathes as use is..

Officer   As also James Mowat officer for a year.

21 Sep^br 1658.

Conveint the fors^d sederunt except
Mr Barns Ja^n & Jo^n Lies & Androw
Dies   Miller q^o ordered the pay^t of James
Mudie messenger for his panes
taken in his office & ordered the
die   renewing of the dies of horning &
poinding cap^ouns in the new
Protectours name.

Clerk   They continued ther clerk for a year
to com and ordaint him to have
yearlie heirafter of seill right pound
scots.

Box m^rs   Item they appointit M^r david Sherp
and James Mowat box masters
for a year & gave each of them
a Kye of the box.

Item they ordered Mr Ard grahame
and david Sherp to speak all those
censurable w^t in the toune betwixt
and the nixt meiting and to
report.

Harris
Collector

Item they mad choice of Rot Harris
to be collectour for a year to com
+ gave his oathe and appoynat Ard
boyle to gev in his compt the
Niset writing..

Nono No^{bris} 1658..

The 9th day being conviint the
visitour doctour Cuchtoune, d^r
hall m^{rs} James hamiltoune + Ard
boyle James Thomsone, d^r dow
Nathan greg Rot Harris, Adam grays
m^r david sherp, James Mowat + Ard
boyle anent the auditing of the
sd Ard boyle his compt of
Intromissiohns which being read
was approvin and ordered to be
bookit and is as follows by charg
and discharge..

Charge

Imprimis he charges himself
wt ane band grantit to the
facultie be Ard Andersone +
his ca°new of   266 — 13 — 4

Item to the Rent thereof fra
    Martinmas 1656 to Martinmas 1657   16 — 0 — 0
Item ane band of Jor Neills of   100 — 0 — 0
Item the Rent thereof fra Candelmas
    1657 to Martinmas thereafter   4 — 10 — 0
Item fra Elizt Murrays or fyne   10 — 0 — 0
Item from Jor hous in Kilbarchan
    for two years quarter complis
    to wit fra Michaelmas 1656 to
    Michaelmas last   2 — 0 — 0
Item from Mr david Sharp at his
    admissioune   13 — 16 — 8
Item fra Allane Kirkwood two
    years qr complis preceding
    Michaelmas last   3 — 0 — 0
Item from dor Mc Neill for his qr
    compt fra Michaelmas 1657
    to Michaelmas last   1 — 10 — 0
Item from Ror Muir in Beyrnd   0 — 16 — 0
Item from James frank his qr complis 1657   0 — 12 — 0
Item from yr faeultie at the
    eleetione ther qr complis being
(50)   the usuall tyme they pay
    yearlie being twentie in number

Mr da Sharp not entering no
payt till the next years   12 — 0 — 0
Item from Mr Wm Wallace of after
comptis who payrs yearlie
40 s yearlie his admissione
to Michaelmas last is   4 — 0 — 0
Item from Dr Patersoune the lyk   4 — 0 — 0
Item from Dr Miller in Kilmarnock
for the year 1657 & 1658   1 — 4 — 0
Item from Mr Farqouhill in Air
36 s yearlie & is since his admissione
being four years preceiding
Michaelmas last   6 — 0 — 0
Item from Thomas Chisholme ther the lyk   6 — 0 — 0
Item Dr Reid in Air who payis
yearlie 16 s and is since his
admissioune to Michaelmas last
being four years   3 — 4 — 0
Item from Dr Mathie in Cockhill
yearlie 20 s and is since his
admissioune to Michaelmas last
being four years   5 — 0 — 0
Dr Tod in Aran yearlie 12 s and
is since his admissioune

to Michaelmas last being four
yearis   2 — 8 — 0
     Suma ____ 462 — 4 — 0 __
Say four hundreth thriescoir
twa pounds four schillings
  monye __

discharge

Imprimis the compter discharges
himself w' the having of the
band of Ard Andersoune law
in the box of   266 — 13 — 4
Item by reteining of pay' in his
oune hand of the sowme of
ane hundreth and ane
pounds fyve schillings right
pennies due to him be the
facultie at his last compt
suting inde   101 — 5 — 8
Item disburst to Gabriell Conyngham
  officer   3 — 0 — 0
Item to Catherine Spang supplicant
  by two severall warrandis   5 — 0 — 0
Item to ane poor man upon his

James durhames disyr   1 — 4 — 0

Item to Mr Wm Weir for calling

of auld machowse suplica'ns   2 — 18 — 0

Item to the post for carriage of lres 0 — 4 — 0

Item to the deacon conveinrrs

officer his years fiall   1 — 0 — 0

2 Item to James Watsonnr bedll

of the caighe Kirk   0 — 12 — 0

Item to the deacon conveiners haw 6 — 13 — 4

Item to the clerk for his fiall 6 — 13 — 4

Item to James Mudie wres' for

his paines in executing the captnes 6 — 0 — 0

Item for renewing of the generall

lres of horning & the cap'ns

and to the post   8 — 4 — 0

Item by not payt of Mr Jon

Crichtoune, daniell browne

James frank & Wm Clydisdaill

ther 9ter comptis this year 1658 2 — 8 — 0

Item by not payt of Mr Wm Wallace

his 9ter comptis conteint in the

charge   4 — 0 — 0

Item of Johne Patersonnes 4 — 0 — 0

Item of Jo Millares   1 — 4 — 0

Item of Rot Jarqushillis	6—0—0
Item of Tho Chisholmes	6—0—0
Item of Jo Kidis	3—4—0
Item of Jon Mathew	5—0—0
Item of Jon Jodie	2—8—0

Suma —— 443—11—8—

Say four hundreth fourtie thrie pound
ellevine schillings & eight pennies—
Swa charge and discharge being calculat
ther restis dew be the compter to
the facultie the soume of eightein
pdes twelf schillings & eight pennis.
Qlk is presentlie delyvered be him
to Rot Karris pnt collectour—

Symie
prentis to The sd day Alexr Symie ~~of Renfrew~~
is ~~bookit~~ sone lawll to the deceast
Johne Symie baillie of Renfrew is
bookit prentis wt Thomas Lockhart
pnt visitour for the space of ffyve
yeiris furthe & fra his entrie yrto
Qlk was be vertew of the Indentour
past betwixt them at the dait
therof Qlk is the twentie twa of julii
last by past And hathe payit to

the collectour fyve poundes scotes mony.

Vigesimo Januarii 1659.

Convint the Visitour, doctour Crichtoun,
Jo. hall, Mr. James hamiltoun, Ard
grahame, david Sherp & daniell broune
Nathan preg, Ard bogle, Wm Clydisdaill
Ro. haries & James thomsone Anint
ane supplicaoune putit to them
be Mr. Thomas younger residenter
in Argowane Mentiouning his being
chargit wt lres of horning to desist
from exerceing the airtis of cherurgianie
and pharmacie or prescribing or
giving of phisick to any patientis
wt in any of the schyres of the
west ptes of this natioune And his
woll desyre to be Acntiat to exercee
chirurgie allenerie upon such satisfaone
as the sd faculteis should judge expedient
and his qualificaone should deserve.
Who being reexamined be them was
found qualified to exercee the sd airt
wt out the towne of Glasgow & suburbis

(51)

Younger
40 lib

therof and is in the wholl west
pairt of this natioun contrair in
ther patent Excepting alwayes from
this present licentia*ne* to him to medle
w[i]t[h] dissectiones Imbalmingis, amputa*ornes*
Repairingis and other compo[i]s[i]d woundis
untill he war farder tryed & fund
qualifi[e]d thereunto — And did ordour
him in the future to buy his drugs
from such of the facultie as he
should find to have the same as
occasiounis offred, And putte to
pay to the collectour for the box
fourtie merkes and yeirlie hereafter
threttie schellingis Beginnig the first
yeiris pay[t] at Michaelmes nixt.
The sd day also upon petitione givin
in befor them be Johne forster in
Auchinclerk men*ti*ned his being
chargit to desist to exerce the art
of chirurgie at ther instance And
his desyr to be executiat upon his
qualificatio*ne* and tryall They
having reexaminned him in what

Licentiaone
frasser
40 lib

he resolvit to profes & essence did
licentiat the sd Johne to cur green
woundis & brokin bone wher ther
is no wound and to oppin and
varie as necessitie shall require
allenerlie And did ordour him to
pay to witt the boundis of the terri-
ples of this natioun conteit to ther
trust and exprest in ther patent
but not w^t in the citie of glasgow
or suburbis therof And did ordour
him to pay to the boxe for this his
licentiaone & bygaine transgressions
fourtie pound and yearlie heirafter
30 S beginning at Michaelmas nixt
and that he buy his drogis from
friemen of the facultie as he hathe
to doe therwithe & occasioune offeris.—

22 Januarii 1659

Licentiaone
Robiesone
16 lib

The sd day the visitour & facultie
did licentiat Thomas Robiesone To
mak ther clothes and green salve
for curing simple woundis w^t in

the boundis committ to ther charge
but not wt in the toune & suburbis
of glasgow And not to transgres
under the penaltie of ffourtie pds
toties quoties who hath payit pntlie
to the box sesetein pds And is
yearlie at Michaelmas to pay twentie
schillingis begunnand at Michaelmas
nixt And gave his oathe of fidelitie
as use is ..

This
10th
The sd day also They did licentiat
Johne Weir in Cambusnethen To mak
grein salve And being incapable to use
any pairt of chirurgie or pscribing of
phisick & specialie to medle wt
quicksilver They did therfor discharge
him in all tymis coming from the
exerceis therof except of the use of the
sd salve wt in the schyre but not
wt in the toune & suburbis under the
paine of 40 tlb toties quoties as he
shall happen to transgres And for
his pnt transgressione to pay in to
the box Ten pds ..

Item having reexamined Johne Rising
in dumbartaine whom they fand
not qualifiet as he profest by his
papper did therfor for his incouragment
suspend the charge of horning givin
to him and ordered him to studie
farder for the space of half ane
year and he to appear befor them
for a reexaminacne betwixt and
lambmas nixt.-

17 Septr 1659.

The sd day they did licentiat Wm
flemyng gardiner in hamiltoune
after reexaminacnis to mak ane
grein salve + to distill planting +
rose water allenerlie but not to
medle any farder And yet not
in the shyre but not the toune +
suburbis of glasgow under the
paine of 40 lib so of as he sall
transgres to be payit be them to
ther collectour for ther comoune
boxe and for the put to pay Ten

pds & yearlie 20 S heirafter beginand
at Michaellmas niset who gave his
oathe of fidelitie as use is.

22 febru 1659

The sd day being conveint the visitour
and the most part of the whole
facultie of chirurgians of this brughe
upon ane petitioune givin in befor
them be Mr Alexr Dunlop in
hamiltoune Which being read &
having excaminied him according
to his bill they did find him
qualifiet to use some small poyntis
of chirurgie kill drogis and to give
phisiekes to patientis according to
ane approven doctours recept as ane
pharmaciens And to act the pti
of phlebotomie And therfor did
licentiat him to exceree the samyne
w in the boundis comitit to ther
trust But not w in the citie of
glasgow and suburbs therof under
the paine of ffourtie pds so oft as

Licentiatoune
Dunlop

(52)

he sall transgres to be payit be him
to ther collectour for the use of ther
poor And for qlk he hathe payit to
the collectour pntlie tuentie poundes
And is to pay yearlie at Michaelmas
to ther box thrittie schillings beginand
the first yeare payt at Michaelmas
next and hathe givin his oathe
as use is

20 lib

Recto Maii 1659

diceimo
gilbert
Kennedie

The qlk day being convent the
visitour and far most parte of
the whole facultie of Chirurgianes
of the sd burghe in ther ordinar
place of meiting Anent the reexaminacone
and tryeall of the qualificacone of
gilbert Kennedie chirurgiane in
Mayboill last prentice to david
Kennedie chirurgiane burges of Edr
To exerce the sd airt of chirurgie
With the boundis & shyres comittet
to ther trust according to the desyre
of ane petitionne givin in befor them

to that effect And having reexamined
him and fund him qualifeit They
did all in one voices dicentiat the
sd gilbert to exerce the sd airt of
chirurgianrie wt in the forsd boundis
But not wt in the toune of glasgow
and suburbis therof under the pain
of fourtie poundes mony to be
payit be him to ther collectour for

on the margin
the use of ther poor — So of as he sall
transgres — Provydit alwayes betuixt
and this day twelf monethes That
he exhibat and produce befor them
ane sight of his indentour and
ane discharge therof otherwayis thir
prttis to be null — Who is to pay

26 — 13 — 4
to the collectour fourtie merkes qrof
the on half prttie and the other
halfe at the productioune of the sd
discharge And is to pay to the boxe
yearlie 30 S at Michaelmas Begimand
the first yearis payt at Michaelmas nixt
hathe geven his oathe as use is —

Vigesimo Augusti 1659.

Conveint in the hospitall the visitour
Johne Hall Mr James hamiltonne &
Ard grahame. Ja Thomsone, Nathan
Gregg Mr da Sherp, Johne low and
Mr Clydisdaill Quho upon representa'ne
of Adame Gray ane of ther number
His waiknes of meanes did ordour
and appoynt fourtie pounds Scots
money to be givin to him be ther
collectour out of the readiest of ther
meanes belonging to the facultie.
And yet for to help to putt ane of
his childrine to a calling And for
ther secceuritie to tak his band
and ane assigna'ne to ane
band the sd Adam hes of 100 lib
of Wm basteiris in Rutherglen and
yt it bear rent fra the dait
and during the not payment W
provissionne that when the ane
hundrethe ponndis is gottin to
restor the rest that sall be moir
to Adam then 40 lib & d rent

w{t} all expensis that shall happen
to be expendit upon obtaining
therof being first allowit and
defaulkit.—

decimo septimo Sep{bris} 1659.
Convein in the hospitall Thomas
Lockhart p{n}t Visitour w{t} Johne
hall, Johne Low, James Thomsone
Ro{t} harris, nathan greg, Johne Lies
Ard bogle, Adam grayr, Johne
Liddell, M{r} david Sherp & James
Mowat membris of ther faculties
Anent the electioune of ane new
Visitour of ther calling for ane
yeir to com Who all in on voice
did continue the s{d} Thomas
Lockhart visitour for a yeir to
com who being p{n}t acceptit and
gave his oathe of fidelities as use is.
Item the s{d} day the visitour did
nominat for himself quarter=
masters Ja Thomsone & nathan
greg And the faculties by pluralities

Lockhart
Visitor

q{r} m{rs}

did elect James Mowat + And boyle
who being put acceptit + gave y
oathes. And Wr da Sherp + James
Mowat bose masters.
Item the sd Wr da Sherp to be officer
for a year.

bose m[r]

Office[r]

Sexto octobris 1659
Convenit the put visitours Johne
hall, James Thomsone, Nathano
greg, Wr Harvie Wr da Sherp, James
Mowat, Adam graye, Johne dies,
And boyle, Johne Liddell.
The 9th day they continued thir
clerk for a year to com g° gave his oathe
Item they acceptit of Johne haill
cordonar to serve for a year in sted
of Wr da Sherp as officer g° gave
his oathes.

Cl[er]

(53)
1660

Vigesimo octavo Septembris 1660
Convenit in the hospitall of the sd
brughe be lawll authorities and be
vertue of ane warrand from ye

Magistrats & Counsell under ye subscription
of . . . . . . yair ye deput daitit ye
27 of September instant James frank
present Visitor of ye Chyrurgians wt
severall oyrs of ye members of ye sd
facultie Anent the choyseing of ane
new Visitor for the yeir to come
And after yt Gabriell Conyngham ye
officer hood givin his aith he haid

warned the haill members — receept
ye secluded members — They proceedded
to ye sd election and be pluralitie
of votes They elected of new againe
ye said James frank to continow
Visitor for ye sd yeir to come, quho
gaive his aith as use is —

The sd Visitor appoynts doctor Croghton
and daniell browne his quarter masters.
The sd Visitor & members maik choyse
of Mr James hamilton & Williann Clidsdaill
quarter masters for ye yeir insuring —

The Visitor & members elected Hector
Stewart no in glasgow ye clerk to ye
sd calling for ye yeir to come who gaive

his aith for faithfull discharge of his
ductie yrin as use is And the clerk
is appoynted to haiv ye benefit and
priviledges of any former clerk ..

They electit Gabriell Conyngham yr
officer to the sd facultie for ye yeir
to come ..

              first of Nov 1660 yeirs ..
Convint in ye steapl hous of ye new
kirk of glasgow James frank present
Visitor of ye chirurgians of glasgow
wt severall quartermasters & uyrs of
ye members of ye sd facultie They
did admit & receave Androw Elphingston
son laull to James Elphingston soutyn
portioner of woodsyd to yr fellowship
as ane pharmaceau And yt in regitura
the sd Androw gaive in to the sd
writting contine in ye sd place upon
the 20 day of octor last ane huble
supplicaoun subr be him for ye effect
And Breans that the sd Androw
gaive in ane subscrivd papper also

Elphingston
his admissione
giueman

continuing the particulars of pharmacie
y[t] he desired peaceable to haue
fur libertie as a bro[yt] of exercise
viz the distellation of simple and
compound waters, decoctions comoine
and pectorall, all syrops except
purgatives, mel mercurials, mel
rosatum, Robs or sapa, as barbaris
cheris &c, dochoch as farin et respectum
et dochoe de pulmone vulpis consernis
and tablets no wayes purgative, the
powders as romatieum Rosatum et
diamoschidubris, conform to y[r] prescription
of y[r] doctor, pills, as pilule de aloe
lota, et cothice minoris et pilule
russii, pilule stomathice, pilule de
succino, et imperiales Troches as
trochii albi, Rosis, et crochisci birhisci
albi, rolule pectorale trochisci gallie
muscat et crochisci dearadon, oyle
as oyle of Roses, of camobyle of hipperion
of water lillies and of walflours, onguents
ongurentum album, ongurentum egyptiacum
ongurentum amodiaceum, basilicon may[s]

(54)

et minus unguentum, de u
unguentum rosatum, de u
rubrii, unguentum pectoral
pantalinum, Emplastroum
or fours of oyntruents, bal
onitions, Salcp, Lykas th
Elphingston did not only b
of Mr James hamilton an
bretherin appoynted for y
ye sd Mr Solms his cha
and persyttie as it becam
simples mixe and compou
ordorlie of ane pairt of yr
his paper and produced
ym to ye visitor + his b
ye table suficientlie mad
satisfactions Bot right for
doctor Crichton + Mr ard
yr severall demands + ge
pharmacie Quher for the
and brethere admitted hi
felloroschip as a broy² to
dispensing + compounding
particulars, only for this ty

such tyme he attin to mor skill. Quho
payed of Compositions tuentie merks
give his aith of fidelitie and produced
his burges tickel.--

ffourt of decr 1660.

daniell   Convent In ye new Kirk steipl hous
broune
Collector the Visitor wt severale of his masters
of craft & vyrs of his bretherin Who
haive appoynted daniell broun ther
thesaurer & collector till ye next ellection.
The sd day delivered to daniell broun
daniell has ye thesaurer the band grantit be
Ard andersonnes
band   ard anderston & his cairs to ye
calling of 400 merks to waive in ye
Drent owing yrof & to bring to ye
court ye last dischargo.

Elphingstoun The sd ffacultie appoynts Androw
officer   Elphingston officer for a yeir.

Prentis   The sd day William Semple of dalmonk
Semple   is bookkt prentis to Iames franck
present visitor to ye calling quho is
to serve dise yeirs efter ye dait of his
indentur gfk is ye 25 maii 1659 yeirs

184

And hes payrd of fyn fyve pund q[d]
is givin to gabriell coningham for his
1659 & 1660 yeirs service—

The sd day the twentie merks of fyn
payex be Androw Elphingston is gibin
to the sd daniell ther thesaurer to be
furthcomand to yr calling—

The sd day duncan mackindo gaive
in a supplicatne to haive libertie to
exercise the calling of barbouris and
In respect he was a lopur wt yr
King severall tymes as he allegs dyka
they dicentie him till candmas nixt
provyding that if he mack not himselff
burges & frieman betwixe & yn that
he of his own consent descharge himself
of yr sd calling & from yr burt & to
pay 40 lib of penaltie attor—

In sua   duncan mcdoo—

The lyk don wt James Wilson his
libertie is grantit also to candmas
under yr lyck penaltie of 40 lib—

5 ffebrie 1661.

Convint in ye steipl hous James frank visitor livo of craft & vyrs members of ye calling the sd duncan mackind be convint to yis court accordinglie compeirand in obedience to ye warning & this Act, they ordain him to leek in his lissins and fries him of ye 40 lib becaus he is not burges and poetre.

(55) The sd day ordaines James Wilson to leek in his lassins becaus he is not burges nor frie wt ye calling And ordaine him frie of ye 40 lib of fyne.

Act anent ye delivering to daniell brown of Edward Robisons band. The sd day Edward Robison prinl & Nicol Roton cautr yr band of ane hundreche punds bearing dait ye nyntein febrii 1659 then is givin to daniell brown to ract in two yeirs @ rent yrof yt is due to at candlmes last & to report his diligence ye next writting.

Act anent delivering to daniell gilbert kennedies band. The sd day givin to daniell gilbert kennedies band of twentie merks.

no cravein of ye sume & to rent ye of
ye band is daittit ye 16 maii 1659 yeirs.

14 febrii 1661.
Convnit in ye new Kirk stipl hous
Sa frank Visitor, daniell broune,
James thomsone Wr Ja: hamilton &
Ard graham, Androw Elphingstone
Johne liddell, Son dies. Wr david
Seharp declared that he woold not
keip court wt ye Visitor & chirurgiens
anent ye auditting of Rob hareis compt
except yt ye haill brethrin wer presen
and yron took instruts & imediatlie
left ye court and vpon ye glk carriadg
of ye sd Wr david Seharps James
frank Visitor asked instruts and
protested for remeid of law agt him.
Vnto glk the Visitor declared ther wer
a prll of ye number secludded from
ye court and notwithstanding Wr david
said he woold have him to be ye
befoir he would acknowledge ye court.
Item daniell broune hes Ard anderstow

his band of ffour hundreth marks to
wawr in ye bygain @ rent yeof + to
report his diligence ye next court yter
witsonnday 1661 yeirs instant gff is
markd befor vpon ye 4 deer 1660 —

9 Maii 1661 —

Act ordouring
daniell to persew
flor hareis + oyrs Convint in the new Kirk steiple
hous James ffrank prt visitor
daniell broune collector + severall
quarter mrs + brethren of ye calling
of ye chirurgians of glasgow And
appoyntd the sd daniell broune to
Call + persew befoire ye magistrats
of glasgow as condie grof flor hareis
last collector to giv due accompt of
his two yeirs intromissions to wit 1658
and 1659 wt ye sd callings yr poores
moneys in his hand And also to
persche all oyrs out of ye toune
for ye quarter compts that ar yet
due be ym + be compteris wt his
intromissions to ye calling —
sic snbr   James ffrank —

sic sub.   J Hamilltoune
"   Andro Elphinstoune
"   James dies
"   J Stewart

(56) Convint in the visitor Ja franks hous
ye 9 Julii 1661 the sd visitor himself
Mr James hamilton daniell broune
and James dies members of ye
calling ye rest of ye calling being
warned to ye meitting

Act for   Quho understanding yt daniell broune
daniell broune   is going to Edgr appoyntit him to go
for our bus.   to Wid bradie to receve yer deed
on yer gift & give him satisfaction
and cause new lres of horing yr on
and to satisfie daniell broune for
his painis

follows a minuta completly obliterated.

5 Septr 1661

Jeieman   Convint in the clipt hous of ye
Muir   new Kirk of glasgow yis fyst Septr 1661
James ffrank pnt visitor of   ye

Chirurgians wt two of ther quarter mrs
and severall of the brethren of calling
Anent ye admissioun of and receving
of Mr Jor Muir son lawll to umqle
Androw Muir chirurgian in ye sd
brughs Confirin to his having sealled
Patent or datters of graduaсne
produceit be him & red over befor
ye sd Court Quho hes fund him
kfter reeaminaсn qualifiet And yrfor
admiits & receivs him a frieman
of ye sd calling conform to his sd
gift who hes givin his aith & payed
his fyne & oyrs dues as use is
Cforni to a frimeans sone lyek as
he is to produce his bruges ticket
befoir he gt rextract heirof.

1661

friman frank

Couveint in ye new staple hous of
ye new Kirk of glasgow ye eightline
day of September James ffrank Visitor
wt severall of his quarter mrs & bretherin
of ye calling of ye chirurgians

Anent ye electing of James ffranck
younger chyrurgian burges of ye sd
brughe ane frieman chyrurgian wt
ym in ye sd calling who hes
givin his aith as use is ~~payed~~ gevin
satisfaction of fyne & is to produce
his burges ticket ye nixt meitting —
And efter reeaminaon was fund qualef
quherfor they admittit him frieman
as sd is gk burges ticket produceit &
schew & gevis the dollors of fyn to
do ma mssr for his service bf the
Visitors ordor —

su

frieman
Wilsone
to be barbor only

The said day admits James Wilsone
barbour upon supplicaon admitted
frieman wt ye sd calling to dress
barbourise & trim alluverli & to do
no further who hes givin his aith
and hes payed his fyne & is to pay
his quarter comptt as use is efter
Michaelmes approching —

(57) Convent in ye new steiple hous of ye
new Kirk of glasgow ye 20 day of

191

September 1661 yeirs James ffranck present
Visitor of ye chirurgians of glasgow wt
his quarter masters & bretherine.

The callings dernate lres brought hom & put in ye box — The sd day daniell bronne hes
broght hom from Edr the calling
ye drecreit from Wnd braddes &
raisd new lres of horning yron
            charles ye second his nam
glke boith of yu are put in ye box
for ye use of ye calling.

James Wilson band — The sd day put in ye box ane band
granted be James Wilson of threl
pound Scots.

ffranck Visitor — The sd day The haill bretherine
by pluralitie of votes hes continourd
James ffranck Visitor for ane yeire
to come who hes givin his aith
as use is.

quarter mrs bronn & Muir — The Visitor chuses daniell bronne &
Mr Jon Muir his quarter mrs who
gaive aithes as use is for a yeir
to com.

quarter mrs thomson & Elphingston — The Visitor & calling chuses James
thomson & Androw Elphingston quarter mrs

for a yeir to com who hes given recept
James thomson ye aithes as use is
for a yeir to com...

Muir & Elphingston bose muro

The visitor & quartermro wt ye bretherin
of calling chuseo Mr Jo Muir and
Androw Elphingston bose muro unto
yu ther is a key givintill ane of
yu for a yeir to com...

Jon Muir muaro to ye facultie to yu givinyu their housing

Convint in ye new Kirk stiple hous
ye 11 octor 1661 the visitor his quartermro
and severall of the members of court
who elected Jon Weir muast ye mroso
and servand for yis insewing yeir
to sret yu unto yu they gave
ther lres of horng wt a comissiow
to waue strangero quarter compt. &
give discharge accordinglie & he to be
comptable to ye facultie of his recept
who gave his aith to be ye faithfull
servand & mroso & referred his payt
to ye visitor & his quarter masters...

sic eub   J Weir

James thomson sworn quarter mro

The sd day James thomson gave

his for yis yeir, as quarter mr in
ye calling.—

gilbert Kennedies band givin to Jon Wm to warrant.. Item givin to Jon Wm gilbert Kennedie
chirurgian in may boill his band to
ye facultie of Paisltie merks deattit
ye 6 maii 1659 to crave in ye sd
soum breauss he is going now to
ye west.—

Gabriell Cunyngham ordered to git 10 S.. Ordered yt daniell browne give to
Gabriell cunyngham fourtie eight schilling
for his service ye yeir 1661 to buy ane
pair of new schoon.—

(55) Conveint ye visitor qrmrs of facultie
and oyrs membris yrof in ye new
Kirk stiple hous ye 22 Octo: 1661.—
Compeirrd Adam Patersoune in
paisley who desired to be admitted
as a brof of ye joind facultie to
wilt to ye curig of simple wounds
~~simple~~ ~~fracture~~ opining of vaines applying
of doch leeches & contars who being
fund qualyied & able to perform ye
sam efter escamination, Are payed

instantlie of fyue twentie pund Scots
of fyne & is to pay twentie schillings
Scots be yeir And is not to exerceise
his calling wt in ye brughe nor
suburbs & hes givin his aithe as
use is And if tuo yeirs run in
ye thrid unpayed then his admission
to be null befor ye sd Visitor &
facultie hes received him freman
wt pow to ye exerceise of ye sds poynts
as witnes his subscon

se subr   A Paterson

d Stewart Clk

I confes my self payed of a yeirs
siluer of ye calling yis 22 of Octor
1661 be danell broun being right
pund Scots

se subr   d Stewart

2 Novr 1661

Couvent in ye new Kirk stiple hous
Mr James hamiltoun deput Visitor
electit be James frank put Visitor of
ye calling of Chirurgians & mediciners

in glasgow Conform to ye sd James frank
his comission ye last of octor last &
quarter now & byis members of ye
facultie— And Comperied befoir ye
sd facultie Robert hamiltoun in toune
of Camislang who desired to be
admitted to ye curing of simple
wounds & brokin simple fractures qr
the fleshe & skin is not broken Who
after examinaon was admitted and
priviledged be ye sd facultie to do
ye sam wt in ye bounds of ye
gift except wt in ye toune of glasgow
and is restricted from doing or meereing
any furder in Chirurgianrie and
medicin nor as sd is And hes payed
instantlie of fyne twentie merks
begining his band at ye sd mritting
ye ordor to ye Colrector— to ye Colrector
& givin his aith as use is, and is
to pay of quarter compt yeirlie thrittie
schillings Scots— sic sub Robert hamiltoun
sic subr   I Stewart Clk.

15 Nov 1661.

(59)

Convenit in the new kirk stiple hous
the Visitor mr of craft & severall
of ye calling Anent ye admitting
of Jon Sproule med in pasley
to be frieman wt yn to ye selling
of drogs & macking of receipts according
to phisicians ordour Quho efter
examination (was) fund him qualified
and admitted him frieman to yt
effect he no wayes to do any thing yrin
wt in ye brughe of glasgow & suburbs
yrof who hes payed of fyne twentie
merks & is to pay yeirlie twentie
schilling And hes givin his aith of
fidelitie as use is & lyckwyes sall
have priviledge to apply doch leiches
and apply couters.

frieman
Sproule

glasgow ye 11 febrii 1662.

The qlk day convenit the Visitor mrs
of facultie & oyr members of ye
calling They ordains & Commissionat
danieel broune (he intending otherwhes

broune
commissionat.

197

for Edgr) to caus denunce certaine
persons contravinners of ye gift &
lres yron for ye practice of phisick
and chirurgianrie who ar nayr
warranted nor skilled & he to have
his charges allowed & to bring hom
lres of Caption agaunst ym..

sic subr   d Stewart Clr..

ordains to ye   The sd day ordains hector Stewart.
clerk.   ye clerk to try if Ard Andersons.
wyf be infeft in his tenerd & gif
~~debi~~ ~~yeire sho nevre yron & gif~~
~~is past yeire for~~ infeftments is yron
And ye visitor & facultie is clear
provydding scho be not infeft yron.
or if scho be infeft yrin provydding
scho removes judiciallie so teck Thr
darroch & don young yr right to Ard
Andersons band & discharge ym..

13 febrij 1662.-
The sd day Ard Andersons wyf gaive
hir aith & cartifies Thr dorroch & don
young infeftment of Ard Andersons ho..

198

Order for discharging dorroch & young & taking ye oblist of and Andersons hous

Dykes the visitor da frank hes dischargd
for himself & in name of ye facultie
Rot dorroch & don Young of ye cawtin
for Ard to ye facultie dimispotts yto
the sds Rot dorroch & don Young haivg
assignt & dispont ye right to Ard
Andersons hous & ye facultie, glke
band of Ard Andersons   ye band
of securities fra Ard Anderson wt ye
imprisinent of Ards hous & ye sds
Rot dorroch & don Young ye right
to ye facultie are all delivered to
daniele broune..

(60)   28 Maii 1662..

The glk day convint in ye new
Kirk steiple hous the visitour wt
severalls of his quarter masters &
members of ye facultie Unto qm
was presented a subd supplicaon
be James Watt burges of ye brughe
desiring he might be admitted for
ye priviledge wt ym in ye bounds
to ye drawing of blind applying coulers

James
Watt

dochleithes to ye rincrod venis giving
of a clrister + macking of green treit
for curing of simpl woundis Weh Iames
Wat (efter he was reeaminrod be ye
visitour + mr ard grahame + fund
qualyied to do ye same) was admitted
frie wt ym to do ye same + to doe
no furder under paine of tb for
ilk faulyie who gave his aith +
payed twratie pund of fyne + is to
pay his quarter eoumpts conforme to
ye use of ye hous.
the sd day Ion Ewing in Paisley
presented to ye Visitor + facultie his
wlt supplicaon desiring they would
licentiat him to sell drogs + mack
up reeips according to ane doctors
direction geh he is to receave frae
ye doctors only in Sedo languadge
becaus he has no uyr languadge
So geh privilsdge the Visitor and
facultie admitted him haiving efter
reeamina on fund him qualyied for
ye effect who gave his aith ae use is

payed of fyn twentie marks & is to
pay 20 s yeirlie of quarter compt
and he is nayr to maell recipies
nor sell droge in glasgow & he is
to pay 20 lib Scots for ilk tym he
does any thing mor nor he is
licentiat to doe ..

Conyngham   The sd day ordaines daniell broun
to give to Gabriell Conyngham ye
faculties officer fourtie eight schilling
Scots qr wt to buy a pair of schoone
for his yeirs service 1662 yeirs ..

Clerk Stewart   The qlk day hr of calling & hail
continued   members of ye facultie convenit
Ordonred Hector Stewart ye Clerk to
remove to ye dore quhen they all
in one voyce being called in — continued
to be ye clerk till michaelmas niext
And tuek his aith for faithfull
discharge of his duetie And ordored
daniell broun presentlie to pay him
his pension of eight pund + tuck
his receipt yer of in ye buk qlk they
could allow ..

off ye gch aught punds Scots & grant
ye receipt from ye sd danuell browne
discharging him & ye faculties yro..

     sic subr   J. Stewart..

         16 Jun 1662

Convent in ye new Kirk steiple hous
James ffranl present Visitor with
severall of his quarter masters - and
membres of ye faculties - Anent ye
admitting & heiring of danuell browne
ye present colcetor his Compt of his
intromission wt ye moneys Blgnand
his intromission ye 4 day of decr
1660 yeirs untill yis instant 16 day
of Jun 1662 yeirs -

        ffollowes his charge
        of his intromission
Imprimis fra Andrew Elphingston.
  quhen he was receed fra man 013 — 06 — 08
fra Allan Kirkwood for his
  quarter compts fra candlmas
1658 to candlmas 1661   003 — 00 — 00
frae Edward Robson for two yeirs

annuell to wit frae candlmas
1660 to candlmas 1662 of 100 lib
priall somme . . 012 — 00 — 00
fra don how in Kilbarchan of
quarter compts conform to his
discharge as his booking bеirs 002 — 00 — 00
fra don Miller in Kilmarnock
conform to his discharge of
quarter compt at 12 Sh anu 001 — 04 — 00
frae don Tod in dran from his
booking of quarter compts as
ye boock beirs 003 — 12 — 00
frae don ffoster in news wark
cform to his booking of quarter
compts cform to his discharge 001 — 10 — 00
frae doctor walace in paisley
sise yeirs quarter compts frae
his booking 009 — 00 — 00
frae don Patson in paisley for
fyve yeirs quarter compts to
wit from his booking 005 — 00 — 00
frae Rot dorrock for Ard Anderson
two yeirs annuell of 400 mks 032 — 00 — 00
frae Wm don Muir qn he was maid frie 011 — 12 — 00

frae Robert muir in gorballs of
   quarter compts frae Octor 1659
   to Octor 1661..   001 _ 12 _ 00

frae mr Alexr dunlop in hamilton
   of quarter compts frae Sepr 1659
   to 1661   003 _ 00 _ 00

frae Adam Paterson qn he was maid frie 020 _ 00 _ 00

frae Jon Mathie in Cockhill of
   qtr compts   003 _ 00 _ 00

frae Rot hamilton qn he was maid
   frie I receivd a band of 20 mks
   qrof I am now payed   000 _ 00 _ 00

frae Jon Spreule in paisley qn
   he was maid frie   013 _ 06 _ 08

frae Jon ffoster in new wark of
   qtr compts   001 _ 10 _ 00

ffrae Jon Young for ye annuel of
   ye sd 400 mrks due be
   Ard Anderson

frae James Watt qn he was admitted
   frieman   020 _ 00 _ 00

frae Jon Ewing in Paisley for his opeel 013 _ 06 _ 08
      Sume of his intromission
        is 190 lib.

Say ye compt of his
intromissions is ane hundreth
four score ten pund..

follows his discharge of his
intromissions

Imprimis to ye deacon conueners
officer for ye yeire 1661 for a
yeirs fie   001—00—00

To Katharin Spang supplicant
eform to ye visitor & bretherine order 008—00—00

(62) To Mr Rowauld enrost to go to ye
west countrie to bring in quarter
compts being imployd be ye
Visitor & bretherin according to ye order 012—00—00

To his son who went wt him &
wrot ye discharges   000—12—00

To James Clerk schoolmr for capping
our gift geh lyes in ye boxe..   001—04—00

To david Robieson collector to ye
crafts hospitall eform to his
discharge for ye yeire 1661..   006—13—04

Giuen to a distrest minister mr
androw aitton who was going
to Irland be ye deacon conuener

and visitors order tuo rex dollors   005—16—00

disbursed qn Rot Harris was appre
hended don Ker being bailyie
The visitor James frank & his
brether complining on him becaus
he woould not maek his colrator
compt.   003—00—00

So tuo officers yt apprehended him   000—06—00

Item disbursed qn he did maek
his compts bfoir bailyie Ker &
ye deacon conviner, ye visitor &
severall of our brether being
present.   003—00—00

Givin to Wud braidie advocat for
getting our dreraxte geh don hall
and Thomas Lockhart left in his
hand qn we wer at law gainse
ye Colledge of phisicians they
not having payed him say
disbursed yn tuo dollors.   005—16—00

Item givin to a writter to yt siqnet
to raise new bres of horning in
King Charles ye secunds name
on our gift.   006—13—04

Item to Wnd braidie to get ye bds
past going throw ye lords for ye
effect & agreeing ye sd busines   006 _ 13 _ 04
Item to his man   000 _ 12 _ 00
Item to ye Compter for his owine
    paines in attending Wnd braidie
    and James borthick for seeking
    out of our deernt geh was left
    be don hall & Thomas dockhart
    tue yeirs in ye Chirurgians hous
    of Edg, & yt be ye spaice of ten
    dayes or yrby conform to ye comission 012 _ 00 _ 00
Item to don Wir for charging Thomas
    dockhart Mr david Scharp
    James Mowat don lamb Elder &
    younger Andro gibson Kendrie
    Craig Adam Ritchie George
    boyl Alexr mackinnie George
    dumb and to sell salton pison
    or as nick   003 _ 12 _ 00
Item to don Wir for charging of
    James fairie smyth in Ingland
    coho hes givin band to abstein
    from our calling   000 _ 06 _ 00

It for charging Ro: hamilton to enter
wt: us—   000_06_00

It to Gabriell conyngham officer
at ye visitors ordour & his brotherin
gt with to buy a pair of schoes
for his yeirs services 1661   002_08_00

It to don weir for charging don
broun to deciss from our calling   000_06_00

(63) It to don patson, allan anderson
and Gab Conyngham for putting
don broun out of ye toune at
magistrats ordour   000_06_00

It for putting of ye sd don broun
in ye tolbuith to two officers—   000_06_00

Item to strector stewart his yeirs
fie 1661   008_00_00

It to katarin spang supplicant
conform to ane warrand   010_00_00

It to da guididie for charging of
don Robson to deciss   000_06_00

It to Ro: saunders for printing ane
hundreth charges on ye visitors
ordour on out horning   003_12_00

It be ye deacon conviners officer for

his yeiro fie 1662   001_00_00

It to a poor gentleman going to
Irleand at ye visitors ordor who
was once deacon convinier in
Idbrughe...   002_18_00

It to don Weir qu he went to ye
wist to charge unfirman +
to lyft ye bygain quarter compts
ye conform to ye visitor and
bretherins ordom   003_00_00

It to william Cruckschanke be ordor
frae ye visitor, who was going to
Irland being heavilie diseased
of ye trimbling fraons   002_08_00

Item to James Watson Kirk officer
for his attending us at ye steple hous 000_18_00

It to a distrest broy of calling who
came out of Edgr going to Irland
at ye visitors ordom...   002_18_00

Item to david Robson colretor to ye
deacon convinirs hous for yeyeir 1662   006_13_00

So a messr for drumming thrittie
dace persons at ye croce of Edgr
conform to our free abbey price inte 010_16_00

for ye receqution yrof   000 _ 12 _ 00

for regratting ye hanning + recequtions

    yrof   002 _ 18 _ 00

Item for caption on ye eds tres geh

    contins two scheits of papper 002 _ 18 _ 00

for my own paines to get ym don

    according to ye faculties comission

    and attending else dres _   006 _ 00 _ 00

To Rot Miller post for bringing hom

    of our caption + recequ'n yeon

    conform to ye visitors ordor   000 _ 06 _ 00

To a pour distrest gentloowman

    who was hidropick + haid

    thrie chrildreon wt her named

    anna hoorn _   002 _ 08 _ 00

To Walter graham mrset for charing

    Androw Ralston gardiner   000 _ 06 _ 00

To Walter graham for charging of

    Lamrs Watt who gave phisick   000 _ 06 _ 00

Item disbursed qn Lamrs Watt + don

    Ewing was recd freman   001 _ 16 _ 00

Item given to Gabriell Conyngham

    officer to buy a pair of schoon 002 _ 08 _ 00

(64) To Lamrs Watson who keeps ye

new kirk dor for his attending 000_06_00
to hretor Stewart Clerk for his fiell
 to Michaelmas 1662   008_00_00
             Suma of yr comptars
             discharge is 160 lib gs 4d
Say ane hundreth thriescor pund
9 s 4d
Charge & discharge being compaird
the compter rests to give in 29 lib
10 S 8 d Say turntie nyn pund
ten schilling eight pennies
QlK compt the sd visitor quarter mastrs
and members of court haiving heard red
over & considered on yr same ffinds
yr samyn just & ressonable & yrfor
hes ordaint yr samyn to be bikit and
allowes yr samyn haill foirsds compts
of charge & discharge & continowes yit
the sd danell colleclor To ye calling
to Michaelmas nixt And he to be
comptable of his furder intromission
till yr sd term of Michaelmas nixt
dyekas in testimonie of ye approba on
of yr sd accompt the finll above

brocked compt is allowed & subscrivit
be ye visitor Seimes frank, doctor Jon
Crightoune Androw Elphingston, Mr
Seimes hamilton & me ye sd Rector
Stewart ye clerk & is put in ye boxe..
sic sub   H Stewart Clk.

Glasgow ye tent day of Septr 1662.
Conveind the Visitor wt severall of his
quarter mrs & Sverrall of ye humbers
of ye calling And Compeired Androw
broune chirurgian in hamilton who
desired to be admitted & receaved a
frieman of ye sd calling of chirurgianrie
who in respect of his knowne
qualifications sufficient to yt effect
and in respect of his payeing of his
fyne of Swentie schilling sterling of
fyn to the use of the poore of ye
calling is licentiat to ye excerceisrie
of ye sd calling of chirurgianrie wt
in ye bounds of ye gift who hes
givin his aithe ad use is and is
not to excerceise ye sd calling wt in

Glasgow or suburbs and is to pay
yuirli 30 s.

dic sup^a   H Stewart

Vigesimo secundo die mensis
Sep^{bris} 1662 –

The qlk day James Frank Visitour
w^t ane considerable pairt of his
bretherine being conuenit Anent the
electioune of on of ther number to
be Visitour of ther calling for a
year to com Qⁿ be pluralitie of
votes maid chois of James Thomsone
to be Visitour for a year to com –

decimo quarto Nov^{bris} 1662
The qlk day the sd James Thomsone
in pns of the far most pairt of
the bretherin of the calling being
togither Conuenit in New Kirk Steple
hous gave his oath as visitour to
Inchargemas viset de fideli administratione –

Item the sd day they maid chois

of Mr Rot gowrane to be ther clerk for
a year to com who gave his oathe
as use is.

Item the 2d day the sd visitour did
nominat James frank + Wm Clydisdaill
And ye sd calling mad chois of
Mr david Sherp + And bogill to be
quarter masters for a year to com
Do gave ye oathes as use is.

(65) Item they mad chois of James dirs
and Johne liddell as box mr for
a year to com Do being put gav ther
oathes also as use is.

Item they mad chois of Gabriell
Conynghame to be ther officer for a
year to com qo also gave his oathe
as use is.

Quinto febii 1663.

The 9lk day in pns of James Thomsone
visitour and a grit many of his
bretherin of the facultie being together
convaint Hughe hunter youngest laull
son to Rot Hunter of Hunterstonne

Hunter
printeis
5 lib

is bookit printeis wt Mr david Sherpe
apothecar for the space of fravine
years whose entrie [1600] to was at
lambmas last fyft nyn years
Conforme to the ties of Indentour past
betwixt them of the dait the tent
day of September last by past 1662
& hes payit to the collectour ffyve
pounds scotts monye.

Prenais
gray

The sd day also Adam gray sone
to Adam gray maltman is bookit
printeis wt Ard boyle for the space
of fravine years whose entrie was
at ye dait of the Indentour past
betwixt them being of the mynt of
September 1659 years Quhess booking
monye is forgivin him be the
calling as being the sone of a
member of the facultie.

Mc neill
printeis

The sd day Ever Mc neill sone
to umqll duncan bane Mc neill sone
tym in drunma muckloche is bookit
printeis wt Ever Mc neill chirurgian
for fravine years whose entrie was

at beltane 1656 Conforme to the ties of
budrutour past betwixet the sd Evin
the elder and donchlan Mc Nrill in
Andreushr as burdriner for the sd
preutris of the dait the sesot of Mai
1660 2ᵒ hes payit to the Collectour ffyftie
two schilling Scotes moнуε...

                    decimo septimo februarii 1663
Convient the Visitour Johne hall Mr
Ard grahame + david Seterp, Ard bogle
Androe Elphingstoune. Evar Mc Nrill
dames + ɛᵒ dies. daniell broune +
don diddell.
The sd day the sd daniell gave in
to the put collectour eighteen pound
ten schilling and eight pennies Scotes
moнуε as that was fund on his
hand of the faculties moнуε intromittit
wt be him as finding to be ther
collectour the tyme som differнеis
was amongst them as his compt
did bear QlK they could not ordour
to book in regard of the informaliti

coll
charge

therof And of his imprudeing of severall
sowmes which they could not approve
of And wt the gen sowme the pnt
collectour is to be chargit wt at his
compt sentvig.

Item he pducit a band of Mr Wm
Wilkeis of ane hundreth poundos Scots
daitit 17 fer 1662; a ticket of Rd hamiltoune
of twentie markes daitit the 2 of Nor
1661; a band of Gilbert Kennedies of
twentie markis daitit 6 Maii 1659 which
war delyverit to Ard bogle pnt collectr.

decimo Octavo Septbrio 1663.
Conveine in the hospitall the whole
faultie during publie in towne Anent
the electionne of ane of number
to be visitour for a year to come
who be pluralitie of votes woid choos
of James feank elder who being
pnt gave his oathe de fideli
administratione.

Visitor
feank

The sd day the sd visitour did
nominat Thomas lockhart & James

9ber 1663

Thomsone to be qarter masters. the sd
calling did nominat Mr david sharp
and Ard bogle.

box mris   Item they did appoynt Andro
Elphingstoune & Iames dies box mr
of rec the Ries of q.

Clerk   Item they continued ther clerk.

lies of horning   The lies of horning ar taken out of
the box & givin to the visitour.

Vigesimo nono decbris
1663.

Convient in the new Kirk striples the
visitour wr Ior Hall, Mr Ard grahame
Thomas lockhart, Iames Thomsoune
daniele broune, William Clydisdaill
(66)   Andro Elphingstoune, Archibald Bosill
and Ior liddell Anent the auditing
of the sd Archibald his compt
of intromissioune wr the faculties
maines which being read was
approvine and ordered to be
bookit and he excoenered And is
as fallowethe be way of charge

218

and discharge.

Charge

Imprimis he charges himselffe
w^t ane band grantit be Ard
Andersone and his cau^{o}ner
to the facultie of   266—13—4

Item w^t the @rent therof from
Candlemas 1662 to Lambmas 1663   24—0—0

Item w^t ane band grantit be
Mr Wm Wilkie + his cau^{o}ner of   100—0—0

Item the @rent therof from
Candlemas 1662 to Lambmas last   9—0—0

Item w^t Allane Kirkwood his quarter
comptis from Michaelmas 1660
to Michaelmas 1663 at 30^s
per annum inde   4—10—0

Item Johne Stow his quarter
comptis the sd twa yeares   2—0—0

Item w^t Ro^t Muire his g^ter
comptis twa last yeares at
16^s per annum inde   1—12—0

Item w^t doctor Wallace his q^ter
comptis fra Michaelmas 1660
to Michaelmas 1663 at 30^s

per annum inde   4 — 10 — 0

Item doctor Crightorne his gtter
    comptes for the yearrs 1658
    1659, 1660, 1661, 1662, 1663   3 — 12 — 0

Item Mr Ard grahame his gtter
    comptes for 1659 & fine   3 — 0 — 0

Item from Iames ffrank his gtter
    comptes the eds yearro   3 — 0 — 0

Item Nathan gregs his gtter
    comptes for the year 1660 & fine   2 — 8 — 0

Item Iames Mount his gtter
    comptes the eds 4 yearro   2 — 8 — 0

Item do dow the lyft   2 — 8 — 0

Item daniell browne his gtter
    comptes for 1658 & fine   3 — 12 — 0

Item do diddells for the last 4 years   2 — 8 — 0

Item Andros Miller for the eds
    4 years   2 — 8 — 0

Item wt Iames Wilsone his fyne of   12 — 0 — 0

Item his gtter compts for 1662 & 63   1 — 4 — 0

Item Mr Ion Muir his gtter
    comptes for the 1660, 62 & 1663 yearro   1 — 16 — 0

Item do Mathie his gtter compts for
    1657 & since at 20s be year inde   6 — 0 — 0

Item from daniel broune that he
had intromettit w⁰ of the
calliegrs monyis   18—10—8

Item Mᵐ Clydsdaill hisqᵗᵉʳ compts
for the year 1658 & since   3—12—0

Item for booking Eon Mᶜ Nrill
his prentieo   2—12—0

Item Lames Thomsone his qᵗᵉʳ
compts for last 4 years   2—8—0

Item lor Hate, Iho lockhart, Mᶜ david
Sharp, lon dieo Eon Mᶜ Nrill &
the compter himself thereqᵗᵉʳ
comptis the sds 4 years ilk
ane of them being 48 S inde   16—16—0

Item Audros Rephirgetoune his
qᵗᵉʳ compts for 1661 & since   1—16—0

Item Lames Braidwood his qᵗᵉʳ
compti for 4 years   2—8—0

Item Lames Wat for 1663   0—12—0

Item dor lod his qᵗᵉʳ compto from
Michaelmas 60 to 1663 at 12 S
per annum inde   1—16—0

Item ane ticket of Gilbert
Kennedieo of   13—6—8

Item his q^{ter} comptis fra Michaelmas
1659 to Michaelmas 1663 at 30s
per annum   6—0—0

Item ane ticket of R^d hamiltonne   13—6—8

Item the @rent therof   1—4—0

(67) Item his q^{ter} compts for the year 1663   0—12—0

Item d^r foster his q^{ter} compts for
the last 4 yearis   6—0—0

Item tho Robertsone his q^{ter} compts
for the sds 4 yearis 20s per annum   4—0—0

Item M^r alexr Dunlop his q^{ter}
compts for 2 yearis at 30s
per ann   3—0—0

Item d^r Miller his q^{ter} compts for
the year 1659 & since   3—0—0

Item d^r Orvine in Paislay his
q^{ter} compts for 62 & 1663   3—0—0

Item fra Adam Patersoune y^r from
Michaelmas 1662 to Michaelmas 63   1—0—0

Item fra Ja frank y^r his q^{ter}
comptis for 1662 & 63   1—4—0

Item d^r Patersoure in Paislay his
q^{ter} compts from Michaelmas 62
to Michaelmas 1663. 20s per ann   3—0—0

Item fra Jo: Sproull ther for 62 & 63   2 _ 0 _ 0

Item for booking Mr david Sharp
  his prenteis   5 _ 0 _ 0

Item fra Mr Jho younger for 3 yeares
  30s per ann inde   4 _ 10 _ 0

Item fra Ro: Harvies that restit
  in his hand at the fitting
  of his compt as collrctour
  the year 59   33 _ 13 _ 8

      Suma   611 _ 9 _ 0 _

  Say sex hundrethe & elleavine
  poundes nyne schillings
  scots monye _

     fallowis his discharge of
      Intromissioune the forsd year _

Imprimis the compter discharges
  himself is the having of the
  boundes fallowing now put in
  the boxe is pay & debuorsmts
  of the soumes under writtin
  And first is And Anders oun his
  bound of   266 _ 13 _ 4

Item is the nd payt of the rcut therof
  fra Candelmas 1662 to Lambmas 1663   24 _ 0 _ 0

Item is mr william Wilkie his bandg 100 — 0 — 0

Item is the a rent y of the forsd spaie 9 — 0 — 0

Item is the rest pay^t of Allexr

    Kirkwoods q^ter comptes 4 — 0 — 0

Item of doctor Wallace his q^ter

    comptes conforme to the charge 4 — 10 — 0

Item of Mr Jon Aughtounns conform

    q to — 3 — 12 — 0

Item of Mr Ard grahames 3 — 0 — 0

Item of James franckes but allowit

    and payit for ane leasing 2 — 8 — 0

Item of Nathane gregg 2 — 8 — 0

Item of R8 Maries 2 — 8 — 0

Item of James Moisets the forsd 4 years 2 — 8 — 0

Item be Jon Jous the lyk 2 — 8 — 0

Item daniel Browns his q^ter compts

    for the year 1663 0 — 12 — 0

Item be Jon Riddall the lyk 0 — 12 — 0

Item be Andro Millar the lyk 0 — 12 — 0

Item James Wilsone his fyne 12 — 0 — 0

Item his q^ter compts the year 62 r 63 1 — 4 — 0

Item Mr Jon Moors 61. 62. 63 1 — 16 — 0

Item is Gilbert Tinrdies his

    ticket of 13 — 6 — 8

Item his gr̄ compt fra 1659 to 63
   inclusive   6 — 0 — 0
Item Don fosters gr̄ compts the sds
   years   6 — 0 — 0
Item Johne Mathieo since Michaelmes
   1657 being sex years   6 — 0 — 0
Item Johne Sodes gr̄ compts fra
   Michaelmas 1660 to 1663   1 — 16 — 0

(68) Item Thomas Robiesons gr̄ compt
   for 4 years   4 — 0 — 0
Item Wm fflemyngss for 4 years   4 — 0 — 0
Item Mr Alexr dunlopes for twa
   years   3 — 0 — 0
Item Don Millers for fyve years   3 — 0 — 0
Item Don Youngers for 2 years   3 — 0 — 0
Item James franck ys for 62 & 63 1 — 4 — 0
Item restand in Ro. Harris his
   hand at his compt fitting   33 — 3 — 8
Item Don Patersons gr̄ comptē
   3 years   3 — 0 — 0
Item givne to the bedell Andro
   Thomsone   0 — 12 — 0
Item to the deacon conviners
   officer   1 — 0 — 0

Item for his paynes in warning
the facultie   1—4—0

Item to Gabriel Cuninghame
at 2 severall tymes for his
schoov & siall   5—8—0

Item to Androe Somsone   0—6—0

Item to the Clerk for his siall   8—0—0

Item to the deacon conviners hous 6—13—4

Item to the drumer   0—12—0

        Summa   554—17—0

Say fyve hundrethe fyftie four
poundes seavintein schillings Scotis
mony—

Swa charge and discharge being calculat
The compter restis dew to the facultie
The soume of fyftie sex poundes twelfe
schillings mony forsd—

Collector

Item be pluralitie of votis they continow
the forsd Ard bogle collectour for a yeir
who gave his oathe as use is—

Item they ordaint the collectour to gro
to Androe Muir his relict supplicant
for her pnt supplie Sevntie markes
mony—

duodecimo Januarie 1664..

Convenit the Visitor Johne hall, daniell
broune, Ja Thomsone, Tho lockhart
Mr david Scherp, James dies, Ard bogle
and Ever McNeill..

The sd day Johne Hall & daniell broun
mad report that they had seine
Hughe Montgomerie weght the samples
and ordowrlie dispens the same Dr upon
the faeultie upon reeamina'ne did
admit him to be a pharmatieiane
wt libertie to oppine a veine applye
doch leitches and cauters at the sight
of the visitour of Jon hall and James
Thomsone or any ane of them &
upon report to be mad if ordowrlie
done they permit him to practice
But not to medle any farder in the
exereeis of chirurgie And that under
the paine of twentie pds tories
quotis in caice of his transgressione
And ordaint him to pay to the collector
Twelffe poundes Scotts mony..

Vgesimo sexto Septembris 1664..

Convenit in the new Kirk stieple James
franck put Visitour, wt Jon Hall
Thomas Lockhart, Mr david Sherp, James
Thomsone, Andro Elphingstonne, Ard
Bogle, James & Jon Lies, Wm Clydisdaile
James Beardwood, Andro Miller &
Jon diddell Anent the electionne
of one of ther number to be
Visitour for a year to com or the
nixt elections who be pluralitie of
votes mad chois of the forsd James
Thomsone who gave his oathe as
use is.-

Item the sd Visitour did nominat James
franck & Wm Clydisdaile to be quartermasters and the sd calling did elect
and nominat Thomas Lockhart &
daniell browne for a year to com
who gave ther oathes.-

Item continued Andro Elphingstonne
& James Lies boxe masters for a year
to com.-

As also ther clerk during ther pleasure

yf gave his oathe as use is :—

Wilsone Item having convenit James Wilsone
byfor them as he who exerceis his
calling as a barbour and yt hathe
nather payit his fyne nor yet compeirs
They therfor all in on voice ordaint
(69) that he should tak in and not
putt out hinging basings towards
the street byfor his dwelling hous
or chamber And that ay and
whill he pay his fyne & all
bygaine yet compeirs, And the Visitour
to seik the Magistrates authoritie
for putting of this to execution :—

Officer Item they continued Gabriell Conynghame
ther officer yt gave his oathe And
ordaint the collector to gve him
four poundes ten scots monys for his
bygaine years service and his constant
faill be year heirafter To be onlie
thrie poundes :—

Quinto decembris 1664 :—
Convenit in the New Kirk steiple hous

the visitouris wt Johne Hall, James frank
Mr Ard grahame + david Sherpe Andw
Elphingstoune, Ard bogle, Mr Clydisdaill
James dies, Ivar McNeill, Jon diddell +
James Wilsone. Anent the auditing of
the sd Ard bogle collectours his compt
of intromissiounis wt the callings meaing
QlK being read was approuine and
ordered to be bookit + he reconered
And is as fallowethe be way of
charge + discharge

Charge

Imprimis he charges himself
wt ane band grantit be Ard
Andersone + his cautiners of   266 _13_ 4
Item wt the @rent yof fra candelmas
1662 to Lambmas 1664   40 _00_ 0
Item ane band grantit be Mr Wm
Wilkie + his cautioneris of   100 _00_ 0
Item the @rent yof fra Candelmas
1662 to Lambmas 1664   15 _00_ 0
Item wt Allane Kirkwood his gth
compter from Michaelmas 1662 to
Michaelmas 1664   05 _00_ 0

Item for how his qter comptes from
Michaelmas 1663 to Michaelmas
1664 20 S and wt 32 S of Rot Muires
at brigend being 16 S per annum
fra Michaelmas 1662 to Michaelmas
1664 Itt 6 ttb of qter comptes fra
doctor Wallaces fra Michaelmas
1660 to Michaelmas 1664 Itt 20 S
as ane years qter compt of
Lon Sprewls wt 3 ttb for two
years qter comptes from Lon
Ewine Itt 4 ttb for four years
qter comptes preceiding Michael
mas fra Lon Patersone wt 5
ttb being 20 S per annum of
qter comptes fra Thomas Robiesn
from Michaelmas 1659 to Michael
mas last. Item wt the lyk fra
Mr flemyng. Item wt 4 ttb 10 S
being 30 S per annum fra Mr
Alexr dunlops for the years
1662, 1663 & 1664. Item wt 24 S for
the two last years qter comptes
fra Andros browne wt 30 S for

this first years qter comptes fra
Rot hamilltoune is 8 lib being
20S per annum yearlie the
years 1657, 58, 59, 60, 61, 62, 63 & 1664
from Lon Mather - 48S for the
4 last qter compts fra Lon Lod
Withe 3 lib 12S at 12S per annum
fra Lon Mather 7 lib 10S at 30S
per ann fra Lon foster the years
1659, 60, 61, 62, 63 & 1664, 30S for this
years qter compts fra Wm
Thomas Younger - 4 lib 4S for 8
years qter comptes fra Wm Lon
Chrichtoune - 3 lib from Rot Fareis
for his qter compts 1660, 61, 62, 63
& 64 - 12S from Lon Siddell for
his qter compts for 1663 - 36S of
qter compts fra Wm Ard graham
1662, 63 & 64 - 3 lib from Nathan
grey for his qter comptes 60, 61, 62
63 & 64 - 3 lib for the lyk fyve
years fra James Mowat - 1 lib
4S for the twa last years qter
comptes fra daniell Brown

36S for thrie last years q^{ter} compts
fra James Wilsone – 12S for this
put year fra James Wat – 12S
fra Norie McneIlle for the lyk
12S fra Hugh Montgomerie for
the lyk, 36S for the thrie last
years fra James frank y^{or}
and 36S for the lyk fra Wr
don Wmr   Incle   81 – 16 – 0

Item w^t ane ticket grantit to Gilbert
Kennedie in Mayboill of   13 – 06 – 8

Item w^t the sd Gilbert his q^{tter} compts
fra Michaelmas 1669 to Michael.
mas 1664   07 – 10 – 0

Item w^t Hughie Montgomerie his fyne of   13 – 06 – 0

Item w^t James Wilsone his band of   12 – 00 – 0

Item y^t remanit in Wo Hareis
last collectour his compts   33 – 13 – 8

Item y^t was left in the compter
his own hands at his last
compt suting   56 – 12 – 0

Item y^t he receavit at the last
electiouns fra 14 of the calling
of q^{tter} comptes   08 – 08 – 0

Summa 652_16_4

Say sex hundreths fyftie twa
poundes sextein schilling four
pennies Scots monyes.—

fallowes his Discharge of
intromissioun the forsd year..

Imprimis the compter discharges
himselfe wt the having of the
bandis fallowing how pittie in
the box + daniell browns
his hand + debursments of the
sowmes underwritten + non
paymentis aftersped + first wt
Ard Andersons band in daniell
his hand of   266_13_4

Item wt the rent yof restand
awand forme to the charge 40_00_0

Item wt ho Wilkie his band of 100_00_0

Item wt the rent yof restand
awand forme to the charge 15_00_0

Item wt the non payit of the yfts
compter aftersped To wit of
50 S awand be Allane Kirkwood
of 16 S awand be Ro. Innes

(70)

of 6 lib be doctor Wallace - of 30S
be son Ewine - of 4 lib be son
Patersone - 5 lib be Thomas
Robiesone, 5 lib be Mr Flemyng
4 lib ten schilling - be Mr
Alexr dunlope, 24S be Andros
browne, 30S be Mr hamiltonne
8 lib be son Matthie. 48S be
son Tod - 4 lib 10 S be son Miller
7 lib 10S be son foster - 4 lib
4S be doctor Crichtonne 3lib
be Nathanie greg, 3 lib be James
Mowat, 12S be Mr Ard grahame
36S be James Wilsone, 12S be
James Wait, 36S be James frank
yor + 36S be Mr son Muir
12S be Rorie McNeill   inde   70 - 8 - 0
Item dew be Gilbert Kinnedie   13 - 06 - 8
Item dew be liun of after comptes 7 - 10 - 0
Item be Hughe Montgomerie for
his fyne 20 merkes + 12S of
after comptes inde   13 - 18 - 8
Item dew be James Wilsone
for his fyne   10 - 0 - 0

Item restand awand be Rt Stauis
  of his former compt—33 lib 3S
  8 & three pounds of qtr compt 036—6—8
Item givine to sd Corbet supplicant
  be warrand   13—6—8
Item payit to the dracon
  conveiners hous   6—13—4
Item to his Officer   1—4—0
Item to our Clerk & his servant 8—12—0
Item givine to Johne douglas   1—10—0
Item to our Officer   4—0—0
Item to the Kirk Officer   1—4—0
Item to the drumer & two
  Officers for service done   0—13—0
  Summa of the discharge is 610—13—4.
  Say sex hundreth and ten
  poundes threttein schillings
  and four pennies monye.
So charge and discharge being compared
the compter restis dew to the calling
the sowme of fourtie twa pound and
three schillines monye.
  sic sub   Wm gowanis clr
The sd day they continued the sd

Collector
Boyle

Ard Boyle be pluralitie of votis to be
collectour for ane year to come & gave
his oathe of fidelitie as use is.
Item they taking to ther consideratioune
Landis belonging
to the facultie
the renewing of the securitie of four
hundrethe merkes dew to them be
Ard Andersoune & his cautioneres As
being done be daniell Broune at his
own hand unwarrantablie in passing
from the cautioneres And taking to ane
impytrment of his landes qlk standes
affeltit wt mor nor they ar worthe
As most prejudiciall intending to the
los of the monye. They all in on voice
did nominat Johne Scott, Mr Ard
grahame, Wm Clidisdaill & Ard Boyle
to remonstrat the same to the toune
counsall and to craive redres And for
ane band of Mr Wm Wilkies qlk
unwarrantablie he also did tak in
ther names they did appoynt the sds
Johne Scott & Mr Ard grahame to speak
to Mr Andersoune theranent And as
they ar answerit to report.

decimo dec^rio 1664

Act anent the Craftes Hospitall The sd day being convenit in the new Kirk stripl hous the visitour & Johne Hall, daniell browne, James frank, Androw Elphingstonne, Wm Clidisdaill, James & Johne dies, Ard boyle, Rorie M^c neill, James Braidwood & Johne liddell And that be ordour of the deaeone conveiner & numbers of the trades hous Anent ther consent giving of the casting downe of the craftes hospitall & rebuilding yof after ane mor large & comlie forme They did all aggrie and consent in on voice to the casting downe & rebuilding of the sd hospitall According as ane selectit number of the craftismen of the citie w^t the deacone conveiner sould aggrie upon and that for ther pte conforme to ther quantities of stock in box they ar most willing to contribut yto Which altho small in ~~number~~ proportioune Being yf industrie of ther numbers brought to ane litle

quantitie & chenged in its securitie by
the sd daniell Browne w'out consent of
the calling And put by him to the
hazard of the los of all w'out the
deacon conveiner And the members of
his writing ther endeavour for ane redres
which they humblie respect for from
ther members as will wisheres to the
supplie of the poor.--

17 August 1665.--
The sd day being conveinit the visitours
Wm Hall, Wr And grahame Wr david
thorpe, James franck, Andro Elphingstome
Johne dow, Ard Boyle, Johne Liddell,
James dies, Andro Miller, + James
Braidwood in the laighe Kirk steeple
They upon ane representacoun made to
them be the sd visitour That Walter
Wilsone deacon conveiner had desyred
him to conveine ther calling And to
signifie to them That his matie &
estates had imposed ane greater taxatioun
of monys upon the countrie nor formerlie

239

And that the magistrates of this brughe
had ordered him to desyre the callinges
to mett To the effect they might know
how the samyne should be payed whither
by a comoun stent or augmentacoune
of the excyse of malt who all in on
voice agreed that fyve schillinges scots
monye mor of augmentacoune sould
be laid on upon ilk mask of malt
nor is pntlie exactit And yt allennarlie
during the space of fyve yeares That the
pnt imposit teseacoune salt indure.

Vigesimo Secundo Sepbris 1665.
The sd day being conveind in the craftes
hospitall the haill calling except dauid
Browne Ion dow Iven McneiL & Mr Ard
grahame Anent the electioune of ane
of ther number to be visitour for a
year to come or the niest electioune
who be pluralitie of votes made choice
of Mr Clidisdaile who gave his oathe
as use is.

them the sd visitour did nominat

James frank & James Thomsone to be
quartirmasters and the sds calling did
Elret & nominat Mr david Sharpe &
Ard Bogle for a year to come qo gave
ther oattes..

boxe mrs
Item they doe nominat James Braidwood
and Johne liddell boxmr.–

Nono febrii 1665..

prentecie
Tod + Clerk..
The sd day in presence of the Visitoris
and most pte of the sd calling Johne
Tod in deanis is bookit prentiss wt
Thomas lockhart
As also Jon Clerke sone to Jon Clerke
this + the former
act would have bein
booked befor.– maissoune is booked prentiss wt Jon
Hall..

Seseto Martii 1665.–
The sd day being conveint tho visitoris
Jon Hall, Wm Ard Gray, Andros Elphingstoune
James Lies, Evin Mc.uill, Wm Clidsdaill
James Braidwood, Ard Bogle, James
Wilsone, Wr david Sharpe, Jon liddell
Quintene Mc.adom in Watrihead qo

M:adam Garvane upon supplicacune is to be
dischargit of the charge of horning givne
to him and is upon examinacune
licentiat to oppen a vaine or cur
a broken arme & leg or the lyk &
mend a simple wound & the lyk
small curis and to applye ane
couler or any thing of that nature
by order fra a doctor of phisick & is
to pay the collector fourtie merks in
satisfaccune of all bygains fynis or
any qk comptis to become during his
lyftyme.—

band   The sd day Quanteine Kinnedies band
Kinnedie of twentie merks is given to And: Bogle
to be put to execucune.—

Vigesimo tertio octobris 1665.—
The sd day convenit in the blew kirk
Sriphous the Visitour dr Hall, James
frank, daniell browne, Mr David Sharpe
James Thomsone, Johne Lowe, Androw
Elphingstoune, And Bogle, James Braidwood
dr liddell, dr Lies & James Wilsone.—

anent the auditing of the said Ard Boyle
Collectour his compts of intromissiounes
w'the callings inranis gfk bing read
was approven & ordered to be bookit
and he recorned and is as fallowsithe
be way of charge & discharge

Charge

Imprimis he charges himself w'
a band of Ard Andersoure &
his cautioners of   266. 13. 4

Item w'the @rent therof fra Cand:
1662 to Lambmas 1665   056. 00. 0

Item ho Wm Wilkies band and his
cautioners of   100. 00. 0

Item the @rent therof fra Cand 1662
to Lamb: 1665   021. 00. 0

Item w'Allane Kirkwood his gen'
compte fra Michaelmas 1662 to
Michaelmas 1665   003. 10. 0

Item w'dow his gen' compte fra
Mich: 1663 to Mich 1665 – 40s, be
Ro'r Unui 32s, be doctour Wallace
7 lib 10s, be Lamer Tobias for four

years 5 lib, be Adam patersonne
40s, be Jor patersonne 5 lib,
be Jor Spruill 40s, be Jor Ewing
3 lib, be Thomas patersone in
Cauldwell fra Mich 1659 to
Mich 1665 6 lib, be Wr Alexr
dunlope fra Mich 1661 to Mich
last 6 lib, be Andro Browne
fra Mich 1662 to Mich last 30s
be Wr Hamilltonn in Pambuslay
fra Mich 1663 to Mich last 3 lib
be Jor Mathie in Corsgates 9 lib
don Lod in deans fra Mich
1660 to 1665, 3 lib, be Jor Miller
fra Cand 1663 to Mich last,
33s, be Jor foster in Auchinleck
fra 1658 to 1665 bring exavine year
10 lib 10s, be Wr Tho younger
fra Mich 1663 to Mich last
3 lib. Inde   73 . 01 . 0

Item our band grantit be Gilbert
    Kinnedie of   13 . 06 . 8
Item tho sd Gilbert his gth compts
    fra Mich 1659 to Mich 1665   09 . 00 . 0

Item James Wilsoun his band of   10 .. 00 .. 0

Item y[t] remainit in Rot haries
last collectour his compt   33 .. 03 .. 8

Item Rot haries of qrt[r] compters fra
Mich: 1661 to Mich: 1665. 3 lb 12S, be
James Wilsoun fra Mich 1661 to 64
1 lb 16S, be James Watt fra 1664 to
1665. 1 lb. 4S. be Hughe Montgomrie
for 1664 & 65. 1 lb. 4S. be James frank
y[e] for 1662. 63. 64 & 65. 2 lb 8S, be Wm
d[o] Muir for 1662. 63. 64 & 65. 2 lb 8S;
be James Mowat for 1660. 61. 62. 63. 64.
& 65. 3 lb 12S; be Wm and grahame
daniell broun & Edw. M[c]neill
for 1665. 36S inde   18 .. 00 .. 0

Item that the collector ret at the
election[e] of qrt[r] compters fra the
members of the calling   8 .. 08 .. 0

Item for Tho Lockhart his prenticebooking 3 .. 06 .. 8

Item fra Quantein M[c]adam of fyne 26 .. 13 .. 4

Item for d[o] clerk his booking   02 .. 00 .. 0

Item y[t] was restand in the
compters hand   42 .. 03 .. 0

Item y[t] the compter gott from

Mr and grahame son McneiLL
for 1664 quarter comptes   01 .. 4 .. 0
Item 18 Nighe montgomerie his ffyne 13 .. 6 .. 8
              Summa — 700 – 16 – 4 –
          Say sevine hundreche poundes
      Sextein schillings + four pennies.
              fallowes his discharge of
              intromissioun the forsd year

Discharge

Imprimis the compter dischargse
himself wt the having of the
bands fallowing, disbursmentes
of the sowmes vnderwritten
+ nonpayt after spent and
first wt ard andersones band
whilk is in the boxe of   266 .. 13 .. 4
Item the @ rent yrof fra Land
60 to Land 65   56 .. 00 .. 0
Item Mr Wm Wilkies band of   100 .. 00 .. 0
Item the @ rent therof fra
   Candlemas 1662 to Lambmas 1665 21 .. 00 .. 0
Item do stores quarter comptes fra
   Mich: 63 to Mich: 65, 2 tt , b

doctor Wallace fra 60 to 65, 7 ℔
10 S, be James Tobias for 1662,
63, 64 & 65, 6 ℔, be adam patersone
for 65, 1 ℔, be dor patersone fra
Mich 60 to 65, 5 ℔, be Jon
Sprull fra 64 to 65, 1 ℔; be
Johne Swine fra Whyt 63 to 65
3 ℔; be Tho Rot Sone fra Mich
59 to 65, 8 ℔ be wr alexr
dunlop fra 1661 to 65, 6 ℔; be
andro browne conforme to
the charge 36 S, be Rot hamilltoune
3 ℔, be dor Mathie 9 ℔, Dor
fralin 10 ℔ be wr Tho yor 3 ℔
be Gilbert Kinnedie twenties
merkes Item of his gratr
compts 9 ℔, be Hughe Montgomry
13 ℔ 6 S. 8 d; be James Wilsone
of his fyne 5 ℔ Item the sd
James his gratr compts 35 S,
be James Watts 24 S, be Hughe
Montgomrie of gratr compts 24 S
be Ja frank yor of gratr compts
48 S, be wr Jon munn 48 S. James

Mowat 3 tts 12s inde	117 .. 11 .. 4
Item be Rt Marco restand of his compt setting	33 . 03 . 8
Item of after comptes	03 .. 12 .. 0
Item for Dr clerks booking	02 .. 00 .. 0
Item be hir and grahame, daniell browne, Ever mcneill of after comptes	01 .. 16 . 0
Item disbursit be the compter to the deacon convimers hous	06 .. 13 .. 4
Item to the clerk & his errvand	08 . 12 .. 0
Item to the deacon convenurs office	01 .. 04 .. 0
Item to thos that went to burialrs by the deacons order	06 . 08 .. 0
Item to the messgr for charging dor Gardiner	00 .. 06 .. 0
Item to a notar for an Instrut takeing agt daniell browne & wrytting of a bill to the grall	00 .. 15 .. 4
Item to ther officer for his fialle & shoes	06 .. 08 .. 0
Item to the Kirk officer	00 .. 08 .. 0
Item to a poor woman by the deacons order	00 .. 12 .. 0

(73)

Suma _ 631 _ 13 _ 0 _

Say one hundreth threttie ane
pounds and thretteine schillings
Sextir mony_.

So charge + discharge being compared
the compter restis dew to the calling
the soume of thrie scoir nyne pounds
thrie schillings and four pennies mony_
forsd _.

　　　　　sic sub　　　Alr gouvans

Kinnedie The sd day they ordainit Gilbert
band Kinnedies band of twentie merkis
to be put to executione w'out any
dylaeacoune _

Boyle Item they ordainit Ard boyle q was
collector continued collectour be pluralitie q
votis for ane year to com to signifie
by a letter to Mr Maries that his letter
direct to them was read publicklie
in ther audiences and that they
Maries ordred him to show him that y
he cam not w'in aught dayrs therafter
+ payit all bygaine compts that then
falzieng they ordainit his band to be

put to execution.

Item they appoyntit Johne Hall and
James frank to speik to Johne Robiesone
anent his exerceising the airt of
chirurgie and of relaitis to ther
calling And that he alter desist
or enter & to returne his answer
agt the next meiting.

Item they continued the collectour &
clerk as formerlie.

The sd day Johne Gardiner obleidged
himself not to appeyr or make any
plaister without licence of the facultie
and of his own consent was content
if he did in the contrair his shop
sould be closed up and that any
drogs therin not fund sufficient by
suche sworne men as they sall
appoynt sould be confiscat and that
he sould not cuir any wounds with
out ther licence.

Nono Januarii 1666

Conviene the Visitour wt Johne Hall, mr

david Scharpe, daniell Browne, James
Thomsone, Mr and grahame, Johne dow
doog Mr neill, James Braidwood, Ro
diddell and James Wilsone -

The sd day Johne Logane du Torballes
being desyrous to be licentiat to cur
ane simple wound they after discoursing
wt him & tryall of him anent his
qualificatune did pas by any bygaine
transgressioune comitti by him and
discharge him to meddle in ther
calling untill he ware reexamined &
fund qualified upon what he sould
put to them in ane papper under
his handis -

Twentie erset of Junii 1666 -
Convenit James Thomsone last visitour
in absence of the prnt visitour wt
Johne Hall, Mr david sharp, daniell
Browne & James Braidwood Byor qm
the sd daniell did exhibit ane
regrat band in the townes bookes
of the prnult of Junii 1661 grantit to

the facultie be ard: Andersone cordoner
as princl. Rot Brook + Johne young as
cautioneres for him for 400 merkes
princl: bearing @rent & penaltie. Item
a band of the dait the crostme day
of Junii 1659 grantit be the sd ard
wt consent of his spous in favoures
of his sds cautioneris wherin for ther
releiff of the forsd band Brarand
obleismnt to infeft them in his land
in trongait. Item ther erasing fallowing
theropone daitit the 18 Jarii 1662. Item
a disposicone of the sd band & band
grantit be the sds cautioneris in
favoures of James frank visitour for
the tyme daitit the 14 of febrii the
sd year wt the sd callings erasing
fallowing theropone daitit the 8 of
Julii theroyter. Whilkes wrytes they
appoynt to be put in ther boxe after
the clerk hes done ther wt in pascitit
for the mailles of the forsd land.—

vigesimo primo Septembris 1666.—

the sd day being conveniet in the
regalitie court Hall Wm Clydisdaill
fuit Visitour Wm Johne Hall, daniell
browne, Androw Elphingstoune, Johne
Low, Ard bogle, Iames Braidwood,
John dies & Johne Liddell anent the
elseeine of ane of ther number to be
Visitour for a year to come or the
next elseeune who be pluralitie of
votes maide choice of the sd Ard
Bogle who gave his oathe as
use is:—

Item the sd Visitour did nominat
the sd daniell Browne, Iames
Thomsone & Wm Clidisdaill to be
quartermasters And the sd calling
be pluralitie of votes Mr david
Sharpe, Androw Elphingstoune qo gave
ther oathes as use is:—

Item they did nominat Iames
Braidwood & Jon Liddell boxe masters:—

Item be pluralitie of votes they did
nominat Mr david Sharpe collectour
for a year to come & gave his oathe

(marginal notes)
Bogle Visitour

(74) quartermrs.—

boxe mrs

Collectour Sharpe

as usr is.

Clerk & officer   Item they continued ther clerk and
officer as formerlie.

Vigesimo sexto Octobris 1666.
The sd day conveint in the new
kirk sessionhous the visitors, Johne
Hall, James Thomsone, Mr ard grahame
Mr david Sharpe, Johne Low, daniell
browne, Johne dies, James Beaidwood
ivor mcneill + Johne liddell anent
the auditing of the auditing of the
sd and Bogle his compt of Intromissions
wth the callingis meanis of the being
read wer approvine + orderit to be
bookit and he escourned And is
as followis by way of charge +
discharge.

Charge
Imprimis he charges himselff
wth a band of Ard Andersons
+ his cautioneris for qlk they
have inststrument du ard

Andersones band   266 – 13 – 4

Item w^t the @rent y^{of} fra
 Cand: 1662 to Lamb 1666 072 – 0 – 0

Item w^t ane band of lui^r w^m
 Wilkies of   100 – 0 – 0

Item w^t the @rents y^{of} fra
 Camds 1662 to Lamb 1666 027 – 0 – 0

Item w^t the quarter comptes
vnderwittne To wit d^r Stows
fra Mich 1663 to Mich 1666, 3 lib
allane Kirkwoods for 1666 1 lib
10 S, Ro^t Mure fra Mich 1665
to 1666, 16 S. doctor Wallace fra
Mich 1660 to 1666, 9 libs, James
Tobias In Air for 1662, 63, 64,
65 & 1666 7 lib 10 S Adam Patersons
1664, 65, 66 2 lib, d^r Sprewll
1665 & 1666 2 lib, d^r Patersone
for 1660, 61, 62, 63, 64, 65 & 1666 6 lib,
Jo^r Ewine In Paisleays, 64, 65
& 66 4 lib 10 S, Thomas Robiesons
In Cauldwell for 60, 61, 62, 63, 64,
65 & 1666, 7 lib, lui^r alex^r dunlop
for 62, 63, 64, 65 & 1666, 7 lib 10 S, And^w

Browne 63, 64, 65 & 1666. 2 lib. 8S. Johne
Mathie du Cockhill for ten
years 10 lib doline foster du
auchinleck 12 lib. Johne miller
for 1666. 12 S. Mr Thomas younger
for 1664, 65 & 1666. 4 lib 10 S. Hughe
Montgomerie for his fyne 13 lib
6S 8d. Item his quarter comptes
1664, 65 & 1666. 1 lib 16S. James
Wilsone restand of his fyne
5 lib. for his quarter comptes
fra 1661 to 1664. 1 lib 16S. Mr Maries
for 1660. 61, 62, 63, 64, 65 & 1666 4 lib 4 S.
James Watt for 1665 & 1666 24 S.
James frank yor for 1662, 63, 64
65 & 1666 3 lib. Mr Johne Muir
for the same fyve years 3 lib
James Mowat for 60, 61, 62, 63, 64, 65
& 1666. 4 lib 4S. Mr ard Grahame
& daniell Browne for 1665 & 1666
48 S. Ivor McNeill for 1665. 12 S.
James Wilson for 1666. 12S. Item
at the collectioune yr compter
receavit 6 lib. 12S. James dies for

1666, 12S. James frank elder for
1666, 12S. mde   129 – 4 – 8
Item Mr Harris is dew of old compt 33 – 3 – 8
Item the compter had restoird
   in his hand at the last
   compt futting   69 – 3 – 4
Item a band grantit be Gilbert
   Kinnidie in maybole for   13 – 6 – 8
Item the @rent therof   04 – 13 – 4
Item the sd Gilbert his quarter
   comptes fra Mich 1659 to 1666   10 – 10 – 0
      Sumes – 725 – 15 – 0
     Say havine hundrithe, twentie
   fyve pound, fyftine schillinges.
      ffollowis his discharge of
       intromissiouns the forsd year.

       discharge

Imprimis he discharges himself
   w^t andro Andersoun + his
   cautioneris band of   266 – 13 – 4
Item the @rent theroff fra Cand
   1662 to Camb 1666   072 – 0 – 0
Item Mr Wm Wilkies band of   100 – 0 – 0

Item the Orent therof fra Cand
1662 to Lamb 1666   027 – 0 – 0
Item w' the quarter comptrs
undrawin So wil be Allan
Kirkwood for 1666, 1 lib 10 s
doctor Wallace fra Mich 1660
to 66, 9 lib. James Sobias 1662,
63, 64, 65 & 66, 7 lib 20 s, Adam
Patersone 1666, 1 lib Sr Patresone
fra 60 to 66, 6 lib, Johne Spreull
for 66 2 lib, Johne Cuming fra
Whytel 1663 to 1666, 4 lib 10 s Thomas
Robiesone fra 1659 to 66 7 lib, Mr
Alexr dunlop fra 1662 to 1666
7 lib 10 s, Andros Browne fra 1662
to 1666 2 lib 8 s Johne Mathie In
Cockhill 10 lib, Sr foster Inn
anchinleck 12 lib, Johne miller
for 1666, 12 s, Mr Thomas younger
for 64, 65 & 66, 4 lib 10 s Gilbert
Kinnedie fra 5? to 66 10 lib 10 s
Hughe Montgomrie his fyn
13 lib 6 s 8 d Item his after comptrs
for 1664, 65 & 66. 36 s, James Wilsone

fyne 5 lib. his quarter compt. fra
1661 to 1664 & 1666 48S restand of
Rob. Maries old compt. 15 lib. 3S. 8d.
Item his quarter compts for 60,
61, 62, 63, 64, 65 & 66 4 lib 4S, James
Watt for 1665 & 66 1 lib 4S, James
frank yor for 62, 63, 64, 65 & 66 3 lib
Mr John Muir the lyft 3 lib
James Mowat for 60 & sine 4 lib
4S. Mr Ard grahame for 65 & 66
24S. daniell Browne the lyft
24S, Jon Mcwill for 1665, 12S
James frank older for 66, 12S
James Lees for 66, 12S, Item to
the deacon conviners hous
6 lib. 13S 4d Inde   149 — 3 — 8
Item to Mr Rob. Govrane for his
   fiall   8 — 0 — 0
Item to his man   0 — 18 — 0
Item to the Keiper of the door
   at the electiouns   0 — 06 — 0
Item to Gabriell Cunyghame   3 — 00 — 0
Item for summonding & dit agt
   Rob. Maries   4 — 01 — 0

Item to Johne donald for charging
a man in Grinock   1 – 4 – 0
Item in recovering pay.t of Gilbert
kinnidies band   0 – 12 – 0
Item upon band w. @rent of the
faculter to Ard Gray   66 – 13 – 4
Item to the deacon convriners
officer   1 – 4 – 0
        Summa – 700 – 15 – 4 ..
        Isay sevine hundreth poundes
        fyfteine shillings four peneis
        mony ..
So charge and discharge bing compared
The compter rests dew to the calling
the sowms of twentie four pound
nynteine shillings eight penneis QlK
sowme was delyvrt at the table b.
the compter to Mr david Sharpe fin:
collector w. thritto sex shillings. of
quarter compters that war dew to Mr
Ard grahame & dvor mc.urill Together
w. the pnce pt ag. Ro. Stancis w. his
ticket + letter – Item the forsd Ard grays
his band of ane hundreth mirkis

was put in the box.—

Bogle printer

The sd day Wm Bogle sone to Wm Bogle messgr was bookit prentiss wt the forsd and bogle visitour for the space of thrie years & ane for meit & fie conforme to the Indentour past betwixt the sd and Bogle & the sd Wm Bogle elder his burdener for his sd sone of the date of thir presents And for his verie booking monyis to the sd calling They all du on voce did frielie forgive & quyt the samyne to the sd Wm Bogle elder for his undertaking to doe them all service he can wt in burgh du giving of charges of horning or any other service.—

Logans admissioune

The sd day Johne Logane chirurgiane du gorballis vpon suplicacoune and reexaminaoune of qt therin he did professe was licentiat by the sd calling to make use of greintreit he was fund du use to make to any cut or byle or simple wound As also to applye ane corter provydit he

dos it by advyse of on approven by
the faculties for yt end or licentiat
bi them And paying putties to ther
box Twentie merkes & twelf shilling
scots yrarlie of quarter comptes during
his lyftyme to ther collectour Or so
long as they sall tollerat him to
dos anything relaiting to ther calling
Beginning the first years payt Dof at
michaelmas niset to come 1667.–

Quarto debris 1666.–

The 9k day being convened the prit
Visitor is Dr Hall, daniell Browne
James Thomsoun, Wm Clidisdaill, Jor dow
James Watt, Jor liddell, Wr david Sharp
James Braidwood, John Pantone chirurgiene
Mr hamiltoune gave in ane petitioune
under his hand befor them Mentioning
his being chargit is lres of horning
at the faculties instance To desist
from the using & practising of the
airts of phisick & chirurgie is in
the bounders comitit to ther trust.–

And that in obedience therto he
acknowledgd That near thes ffteine
years bygaine since he came from
france as he had occasione he
proffest to cur all sort of wounds
Impostumes, Vlcers, fracters, disloca°ns
flebotomies, applica°ns of couters and
in use to giv phisick to woundit
persons q(n) necessitie requyres And
therfor desyred they might be pleasd
to admit him to sserce the same
is in the foursds bounders being
fund qualified after sexamina°un.
Wherbpon they did sexamine the
sd Johne vpon Chirurgie and having
fund him qualified expert therin
according to his ansirs made to
ther questions They did all in on
voyce fund him qualified to be admitit
approvine & licentiat to sscerce the
sd art of chirurgie is in the west pts
of this Kingdome comitit to ther
trust and ordaind him to pay to
ther collectour for his admissione for

the use of the poor Servitie pound Sedrs
and zearlie during his lyftyme To pay
for his quarter comptrs 30S sers for the
use afors Begimand the first years payt
at Michaelmas next to come —

Decimo Nono Martii 1667 —

The glk day being conveinit in the new
Kirk steeple hous of Glasgow; And
Bogle Visitour wt Johne Hall, daniell
Browne, Mr david Sharpe, Androw Elphingstoun
Johne Low, Johne diddell and James
Braidwood Compeirit Johne Rrid in
Briryairdes befor them being challengd
for taking upon him wt out ther liecence
To exerce the airt of chirurgie wt in
the bounds comitit to ther charge by
ther gift grantit be his Matie In useing
of orall applicaions To sundrie kynds
of wounds, cutes & Sores Who absolutlie
denyrd the same and he being ane
old man and the sd calling not
desyrous to trouble him provydit he
doe not midle wt ther calling to the

264

futur He therfor of his own accord
did bnact himselff and be thir
prentes Inactes himself neuer to midle
or soeerce any ptt of chirurgie by
making of any applicatiounes to
any woundes, cutes or sores unles
he be authorised be the sd calling
at any tyme heirafter Under the
payne of fourtie pound to be payit
be him swa oft as they sould prove
any transgressiounes and yt for the
use of ther poor And for the pnt payit
to the collectour for charges dispendit
58S feirs moneyes —

Secundo Apprilis 1667 —

Rot dunlope   The sd day being conveind In the
pays 20tb fyn foirsd steiple hous the pnt Visitor wt
+20S grantie John Hall, daniell browne, James
Thomsone, Mr david Sharpe, John
Wilsone, James Braidwood & James dirs
and that at the desyre of Rot dunlope
In Domine desyring he might be
admittit to soeerce the airt of chirurgie

wᵗ in ther boundes as bevig willing to
be reeamined vpon his qualificaⁿs
and abilitie to reeeveг the same And
bevig at lenthe reeamined by them
they be pluralitie of vots fand the
sd Kⁿ qualified at pnt to reeeвее the
sd aint for euring of disloeⁿns fraetons
woundes, applicaⁿs of eoveleᴿ, and if
to the futur he attevur to farder
knawledge therin vpon his supplicaⁿs
and reeaminaⁿs they eoneludit yᵗ he
sould be admitit to praetis as he sould
be fund qualifit And ordaint him
to pay twentie pound for his admissions
putten (geh he payit to the eolleetor) and
to be frie heirafter reecept yrarlie during
his lyftymr to pay of gπteᴿ eompteᴿ for
the her of thr poor 20ˢ Beginnand the
first yrars payt at michaelmas next
who gave his oathe as usr is.—

Ultimo Maii 1667.—

The sd day bevig conveint du the erafts
hospitall the visitors, Johne Hall, daniell

Browne, Mr david Sharpe, James Thomsone
Andro Elphingstonne, Iohne dow, Ion Mcnille
James Braidwood & Iohne dies Compirired
Philipe Bowie sone to Mr Iohne Bowie
ane of the ordinar ministers of the
sd brughe Who desyred to be admittit
friman wt the sd calling Who appoyntit
him befor he sould be admittit To mak
and compone the particulars fallowing
as his say & tryell vz diascordium
coratium sentalium pilula rudii
diapalma, Who receptit of the sd tryell
and undertook To make & compone the
samen brevisel & the last day of Junii
nixt to come and then to enter himself
frie mane wt them And the sd calling
ordainit the forsds daniell Browne &
Andro Elphingstonne to be his say
masteres—

As also the sd day david flemyng
Mr Villelane was admittit frimane wt
the sd calling for drawing of blood &
curing of a simple grein wound
allenarlie of his own consent being

(7)
flemyng
admitit frie

only yᵗ which he after he was examined
could doe. And in order yᵗo gave his
oathe and payed to the collector Twentie
mrk for his fyne.

dreimo tertio Augusti 1667.

The qlk day Ard Bogill prᵗ visitour of
the facultie of chirurgians wᵗin the
sd brughe Wᵐ Loᵘ Stall, daniell Browne,
Mʳ david Sharpe, James Thomsone, Johne
dove, Mᵗ Loᵘ Muir, Androe Elphingstoune,
Wᵐ Clidisdaill, Ivor Mcnrill, James diev
& James Braidwood being conveinit in
the new Kirk belhous of the samyne
brughe anent the entrie and admitting
freimans wᵗ the sd calling of Adam
Gray laitt servitour to the sd visitour
who being reexamined and his sd
master dielairing he haid dewlie
servit him all the years conteinit in
his indentour They did all in on
voyce find the sd Adam qualefied
to practise simple chirurgie or to
cur simple wounds in the flesh

Gray
freimans

discharging him to medle w^t fracturs
olcers, tumors, dislocac^{ns} nor any
thing y^t is exposd and y^t under the
payne of ten pounds totirs quoties q^ß
his jardin qualificac^{ne} and after
qualificac^{ne} to be admitt As also
they fand him qualified as ane
comonne barbour for dressing and
polling of heads & bairds and in making
of periweeks Who gaw his oathe of
fidelitie as use is And payd to the
collectour fyve pound sextein shilling
for his fyne And is to pay his ordinar
quarter comptes as the rest of the
calling —

Robersone
friemans
The sd day John Robersone enrd
after examinac^{un} is fund qualified
to practis apotheccarie And of consent
he is to be exempt from ever bearing
place or office wⁱⁿ the sd facultie
as visitour, quartermaster or box master
Except y^t he is obleist to give his
best counsell & advyse to the visitor
qⁿ called for concerning the sd

vocation and paying his quarter compts
as the rest of the calling Whose fyne
is refeired to himselfe to pay to the
collectour and hes gevin his oathe
as use is.—

Continua^on As also The 2d day They continued
Bowie Philip Bowie his giving in of his fayes
In respect he pretendit the samyne was
not readie as yet.—
As also they approve of Johne drume
and his calo^uris band.—

Anno nono Septembris 166[?].—

flemyng The 9th day being conveinit In the
friemane new Kirk bell^ous And Boyle visitour,
Johne Hall, W david Sharpe, W Ard
Grahame, Androw Elphingstoune, daniell
Browne, Ro^t Robisone, do. liddell, James
Braidwood, Ro^rt mc^nrill, Johne dow,
James Watt and adam Gray, Johne
flemyng is admitit friemane as a
comone barbour for polling & dressing
of headis & bairdis q^o gaws his oathe
as use is and to pay four dollars to

270

to the collectour and 12S yearlie of
quarter compts.—

The sd day anent the petitioun futil
be Wm Currie in the parochine of douglas
go futil a testificat under the ministeres
hand craiving licence to practis the
use of hearbes for externall applica-on
onlie who being examined upon his
sd knowledge finds him able to practis
hearbes in externall applica-ons allenarlie
and obleisis him in all tyme coming
not to exerceis medicine, chirurgie, nor
pharmacie under the paynes of Twentie
pounds toties quoties except he appear
befor the sd calling & he finds farder
qualified upon reexaminaene at whilk
tyme he is to be farder admitted to the
practis of ther airtes who gave his oaths
as use is And is to pay for his pnt
admissioun fourtie merkes scotts whereof
the on halff pntlie And is to give band
for the rest and to pay twentie shillings
scotts yearlie of quarter compts.—

Vigesimo quarto Septembris 1667

Bogle
Visitour
The 9th day Archibald Bogle, Visitour, John
Hall, James Thomsone, James Braidwood
John dow, James Watt, Wr and grahams
Androe Elphingstoune, Wr John Muir, Rot
Mcneill, John diddell, Wm Clidisdaill, Wr
david Sharp, John Robisone, Androe
Miller, John flemyng & Wr dow & adam
Gray being conveind In the laigh kirk
betuous anent the electioune & making
choyse of ane of their number to be visitour
for the year to come Who be pluralitie
of votes continued the sd Ard Bogle
for a year to come Who being first
acceptit of and gave his oathe as
use is ..

quarterms
Item the sd visitour did nominat Wr
Ard Grahams & James Thomsone to
be quartermasters and the sd calling
electit Wr david Sharp and Androe
Elphingstoune go gave ther oathe as
use is ..

box ms
Item they continued John diddell and
James Braidwood to be box masters for

a year to come. 24th September 1667

The sd day Complaint is givin in
by the sds Ard: Bogle & Wm Currie
makand mentione that of Wm Clidisdaill
vpon the 19 day of the sd monethe in
presence of the haill brethereine Vpon
reading of the sd Wm Currie his supplicatioun
anent his admissione to exerce such
ples of chirurgie or apothecarie as he
could be fund qualified unto Trew it is
the sd Wm did in ane most unavill
manner w out any offence givin
upraid the sd visitour by uttering ane
number of vyll expressions as perticularlie
yt he was ane meir fool & ane asse
not worthie to carrie office in his place
and did call the sd Wm Currie ane
Warlock & Runnagaile going fra door
to door As the sd complaint mor
fullie comportis Whilk being read in
presence of the sd Wm Clidisdaill confest
the article agt Wm Currie and denyed
the article alleadgit spoken be him
agt the visitour wherfor the faculttie

(78)

Complaint
agt
Clidisdaill

admittit the samyne to the visitour's
probaoun who for proving therof produceit
famous witnesse viz Mr Ard grahame +
david Sharpe apothecaries + gabriell
Cunnynghame officer sworne + admittit
who proved the forsd article spoken
be the sd Wm agt the visitour And
therfor the sd faculty all in on
voyce did fyne the sd Wm Cludisdaill
in twentie markis money for the use
of ther poor And yt the sd Wm sould
never carie office nor have a vott in
the sd calling in all tyme coming
except the visitour put ane to command
the faculty see his good behaviour to
the futur.

Decimo quinto Octobris 1667.

admissioun
Wiviine The 9th day The visitour, John Hall
James Thomsone, daniell Browne, Mr
david Sharpe, John Robisone, Ror
McNrill + Adam Gray being conveinit
in the belhous anent a supplicaoun
givine in be John Wiviine in dumbartane

desyring therby to be admitit friemans
wt them to recover the curing of a grin
wound, the opning of vynns at a
doctors direc°uns, the using of coulters
and applying lochleitches be advyse
forsd Who being reexamined at tenths
be the sd faculter was fund onlie
qualifird to recereis the curing of a
simple grine wound, the opning of
vyns be the advyse of a physiciane
The using of coulters & applying of
lochleitches by advyse forsd discharging
him for midling wt any poyntis of
chirungie & mediecine recept othr
particulares aforsd and yt under the
payne of fourtie pounds. And yt he
sall nor middle wt no thing of his
calling wt in the toune of Glasgow gif
he be first admitit burges therof under
the lyk pernalties du obediences gr of
he gave his oathe as use is and
payit to the collector fysteine pound
for his fyne and twenter shilling
yearlie for his quarter complt

25 of Nov 1667.—

The q[uhi]lk day the visitour, Johne Hall,
Mr and Grahame, Mr david Sherp, Johne
Robisone, James Thomsone, Androe
Elphingstoune, James Beaidwood and
Adame Grays Being conveniet in
the bilhous anent what course
should be takin with ane advocatioune
produceit ag[ains]t them in the caus
persuit be facultie befor the comissar
of Glasgow ag[ains]t the thrie sons of
umq[uhi]le Mr Aro Blair for ane hundreth
pounds with the @renles therof q[uhi]lk is
dew to the sd calling be Mr Wm
Wilkie as prin[cipa]le and the sd of Mr
Aro as can[tion?]ner for him conforme to
ther band Who all in ane voyce
ordaint the double of the advocatioune
putti to be sent eas to James
Galbraithe wryt with tua rise dollours
to procuir ane remett if possible And
what farder charges the said James
shall happin to be thereanent They
ordaine the sd Mr dawid ther collectour

To satisfie the samyne.

The sd day also the sd facultie convenit
as said is havein spoken amongs
themselvs anent the four hundreth
merkis deu to the sd calling be
Ard Andersoun and what course
should be takken theranent to recuir
the calling therin Who all in ane
voyce condiscendit and ordaint The
Visitour, Johne Hall, Johne Robesoun
and the quartermaisters To mit w[t]
Johne Binnie in ordour to exte with
him theranent And in caices they
can aggrie with the said Johne
and git good securitie fra him for
the forsaid prinll sowme of four
hundreth merkis They ordaint the
forsds psones to quat the haill
bygane @ rentis therof restand awand
preceiding Martimmas exsetr ceaving
granis.

The sd day they ordaint Mr david
Sharpe thr collectour to give to Johne
Grahame wryter tua rex dollars.

At anent Binnie

for his paynes done in the sd caus agt
the airs of the sd deceast Mr Hughe Blair
and of other charges he hatte debursit
theraunt and to Ro fynnisone ane
rose dollar –

19 december 1667 –

The glk day The visitour, Johne Hall
James Thomsone, Johne dow, Evin
M'nill, James Braidwood, Mr
david Sharp, Johne Robisone, Androx
Elphingstoune + Adam Graye Being
convrinit die the forsd Bilhous anent
the report making be the sd Johne
hall, Johne Robisone + the sds quarter
mr of they had done wt the said
Johne Binnie concerning the foun
hundrethe marks dew be Ard
Andirsone who reportit to the sd
faculti convrinit That they had
aggriet to take ane band of foun
hundrethe markes fra the sd Johne
Binnie + Margt Knose his spous clining
ane assigna'ur for ther fordir ecuritie

of the mailers & duties of the sd
And his lands ay & gfl the calling
sould be payd of the forsd 400 merks
Bearing @ rent fra Martinmas last &
yt they had qual all bypast @ rents
of And Andersons band preceiding the
forsd terms of Martinmas In favors
of the sd John Binnie And yt they
wer to procuir ane assigna°tne &
dispositione of the right granted be
And Andersone fra the sd faculte
In favors of the sd Jo Binnie gfk
report bring deva made be the sd
John Hall, Jo Robisone & quartermrs
Conforme to the former appoyntment
The said faculte convenit as sd is
all in on voyce was weele satisfiet
& pleased w the sd agrieement And
did ordeine & appoynt the sd And
Boyle visitour to subscryba the right
to be drawne vp on the sd And
his band for himself and In name
and behalff of the haill calling In
favors of the sd Jon Binnie and

appoyntit the sd Mr david Sharpe to
receave in fra the sd Do binnie &
his sd spous the forsd band conteining
ane assigna'ur as sd is to the
mailtrs & dewtirs –

The sd day also Wm Kelso lawll brother
to Ro Kelso of hallrig is bookit printtis
wt Do Hall for fyve years as printtis +
twa years for meat & fie fra his entrie
thertoo qlk was at Whytsonday 1667
conform to ane indentour past betwixt
them theranent dailit the 12 & 29 of
appryll 1667 who gave his oathe and
payit to the sd Mr david collector
forsd 5 lib. –

As also The sd day they ordainit the
sd collectour to give to Do donnald
merss'r 6 lib monye for giving of nyne
charges of horning at the callings
Instance conform to ane resceno'ur
theranent to be given in be the sd
Do to the sd collector –

As lykwayes they made choyce of
Ro fynnieson to be their clerk till the

niet ordinar election of being put
acceptit of.—

13 of Marche 1668.

The 9th day the Visitour Johne Hall
Johne Robisone, Andro Elphingstoune,
Johne dow, Jamis Thomsone, Jamis
Braidwood, W Ard Grahame, W
david Sherp and Adame Grays Being
Convrint in the bilhous W Mathow
Miller conr call to unngll Sor
Miller apothecarr in Killmarnock
Anent ane supplicacur givin in be
him befor them desyring therby to
be admitted freeman w ym So wccres
the airt of pharmacie the opining of
veins by the advyce of physitians
the applicacur of coulters and
ventosis the curing of simple wounds
and the imbalming of corpis Who
being rcamined at lenth was
fund quallified to wcercise the foirsd
airt of pharmacie the opning of veins
by advyss aforis: the applicacur of

coulters and vrutoris the curing of
simple wounds And imbalming of
corpes And in caice it shall happin
at any tyme heirafter the sd Matthew
to attaine the more knowledge +
skill of his sd calling Being fund
quallified be the sd facultie That he
shall be admitted yrto accordingly
gratis discharging him to medle nor
any poynt of his sd calling win
the toun of glasgow Whill first he
be admittit burges yrof under the
payne of fourty pund Scots or as
he shall happin to transgress the
samine du obedience qrof He gave
his oathe as use is And payes to
the Collr fourty punds for his fyne
And to pay yearly for the use of
the poor twenty schilling or
after compts.—

    Admission Matthow Miller

(80)

       12t May 1668.—
The qlk day the visitour Jn Hall

Admission
Thomas
Harper

Mr david Scharpr, John Robinson, Androis
Elphinstoun, Dr Liddill, Evar Mcneill
Jas Braidwood, Wr ard Grahame &
Mathow Miller being conveen in
the billhous Anent ane supplicaoun
givin in befor ym be Thomas
Harper in Kilmarnock desyring
yrby to be admittit freiman wt
ym ffor curing of simple wounds
bloodletting, fractures wt out loss of
substance who being reexamined
Accordingly bi the sd faculty
 qrupon was admitted to practise
the curing of simple wounds the
opning of veinis at the command
of physicians and to cure fractors
qr yr is nor loss of substance And
to repone the dislocations allenrly
And in caice it shall happin him
to transgress the limits he is
admittd to in manner above
writn He is heirby obleist to pay
toties quoties ewa oft as it shall
happin him to transgress the

...amine the soume of twenty pounds
Scots to the sd calling for the use
of ther poor dischairging him hard
from medling wt any of the foirsd
airts wt in the foirsd brugh of
Glasgow Whill first he be admitted
burges grof Under the lyk pennalty
In obedience grof has givine his
paithe as use is and payed to
the colle Twenty pundle for his
freedom fyne and is obleissd to pay-
graciis to the sd calling for the
use of yr poor twelve schilling
monye of gfter comptd And in
caice he attaine to farder knowledge
in the foirsds airtes being fund
qualified to the sd facultie at
any tyme heiraftr he is to be
admitted be yu yrto accordinglig
gratis..

8d Junii 1665.-
The gfk day the visitour Johne Hall
Jnr david Scharpe, Jno Robinson

284

Act anent
Blair

Jo: diddell, Jas Braidwood, Adam
Gray being mett & conveined in the
billhous Anent ane overtour made
be Jo: Blair sone lawll to umqll
Mr Androw Blair of the money dew
be Mr Wm Wilkie as princll And the
sd umqll Mr Androw Blair as cautionr
wheirby the sd Jo: Blair offred to the
sd faculti the princll soume being
ane hundreithe punds upon conditiones
allwayes they wold quyt the bygaine
annuelrents grof And prinally overist
yrfor And to assigne him to the
sd band Whilk overtour the sd
faculty having takine to yr
consideratioun To eschus all farder
pleas and the waisting of the
poors money All in ane voyes
did condescend to take in the
forsd hundreithe punds And to
quyt the bygaine annuelrents and
prinaltye And to assigne the forsd
band In favoors of the sd John
Blair And ordained the visitor &

coll to subscryve the samine which
soume of ane hundreth pund was
instantlie payed in to the david
schairper coll —

Tertio Augusti 1668 —

Admissione
Lockhart The 9th day the visitour, Johne Hall
mr david scharpe & ard grahame
Jon Robisone James Thomsone, Androe
Elphingstoune, James dire, Jo Liddell
James Braidwood, Rovr mc uille, Jo
flemyng, James wat & Adam gray
being conveinit in the craftis
hospitall wt George Lockhart sone
laull to the deceast Thomas Lockhart
appothecarie burges of the sd brughe
anent the supplicatione givin in
be him desyring therby to be
admittit friman wt the sd calling
who being examined be them upon
trall poynts of phermaeie was
fund qualified to practise the forsd
airt of phermaeie as lykways gn
he hes the occasione to cur simpll

wounds, phlebotomie, apply cultters
use ventosis & silomis he taking
alongst w him some of the
bretherine and they accordinglie
making report is to be admitted
therto and if he attrine to mor
knowledge of chirurgie upon
examinaoun is to be admitted
(81) yeto — who has given his oathe as
use is and payit to the collect
for his fyne twelf pound
Scots —

              18 of September 1668 years —
Visitour   Tho 9th day the visitour, dohne
Grahame   Hall, who and Grahame, who david
Scharpe, dohne Robisone, Androw
Elphingstoune, George Lockhart, dohne
dow, dames Thomsone, dames
Braidwood, dohne diddill, dohne
fflyming Adame Grays, Androw
Miller and dames Wilsone Being
convienit in the billions of the
leigte Kirk steiple of the all bright

of Glasgow Anent the making choise
of ane of ther number to be
visitour for the year insewing who
be pluralitie of votis they made
choise of the said Mr And Grahame
to be visitour for the year to com
who being put accepted of and gave
his oathe as use is

gr maisters Item the said day the forsaid visitour
did nominat and appoynt for him
Mr david Shirp and And Bogill to be
quartermaisters And the said facultie
electit and made choise of James
Thomsone and Androw Elphingstone
who being put accepted of and gave
ther oathes as use is

Box maister The said day also they made choise
of James Braidwood and Adame
Gray to be box maisters who being
put accepted and gave ther oathes
as use is

**Symmisone
Clerk** As also they made choise the sd
day of Mr Symmisone to be ther clerk
for the year to com who accepted

and gave his oathe as use is.—

Officer Item they continowed the sd day ther officer for the year to com.—

9 of No. 1668 yeares.—

Collectour Elphingstoune The 9th day the visitour, Jo Hall Jo Robirsone, Mr david Sherp. And bogill, James Thomsone, Androw Elphingstoune, George Lockhart, daniell Browne, Evir M'urile, James Braidwood Johne Liddell, James Watt, James Wilsone, Adame Graye and Johne Flemyng Being convenit in the bellhous Anent the making choise of ane of ther number to be ther collectour till the next ordinarie tyme of collectioning who be pluralitie of votes made choise of the sd Androw Elphingstoune to be ther collectour Till the ordinar tyme forsaid who being put accepted of and gave his oathe as use is.—

Stowstoune fynnd As also the said day they fynnd Ro Stowstoune in 20 lib for using of

pharmacie, chirurgie & for learning
of others to make drogis sirupes &
others this halfe year bygane since
his mistris was mariee And
dischargit him from using the lyk
in all tyme coming & the sd fyne
not to be exacted till it be
thought fit.

9 of November 1668 yearis.

The said day the facultie within
writt sett doun the forsaid day on
the other syd ordanit Mr Charles
Mowat in ordour to his desyre to be
admittet friman wt them To mak
and compone the particulars following
for his say To wit trochisci bechici
albi looch formun et expertum
electuariunn lince totum pilula
factoda mayoris emplostomum diapalma
And to have the samyne reade
betwixt and the first day of Januarie
nixt 1669. And appoyntit Mr david
Sherp and John Robersone to be

lay maisters for that effek,—

4 of december 1668 yearis..

The qlk day convenit in the laiche kirk
the visitour, Johne Hall, And Baillie
Johne Robirsone, Mr david Sherp, Androw
Elphingstoune, Johne dow, James
Braidwood, Adame Gray, James Thomsone,
George Lockhart, Jon Mcneill, James
Wilsone and Wm Clydisdaill anent the
auditing of the said Mr david Sherp
his compt of intromissioune with
the callingis meanies And that
fra the twentie ane day of September
1666 being the tyme of his admissioune
to the forsaid fourt day of december
1668 Whilk compt being read was
approven And ordourit to be bookit
and the sd Mr david recourit Which
is as follows be way of charge +
discharge..

Charge
Imprimis the compter charges

himselfe is the sowme of   lib _ 8 _ d
twentie four pounds nyntein
schilling right pennies scotis
monye receavit be him fra
and Boyill last collectour that
was resting in his hands
of the callings remaines to
ballance his compt of intromission
inde ..   024 _ 19 _ 8

Item is ane band of and Andrason
to the said faculter of 400
merkes priull inde   266 _ 13 _ 4

Item is the @rent therof since
Candelmas 1662 to Mart 1667
being fyve years and thrie
quarteris extending to   092 _ 00 _ 00

Item and band to Mr William
Wilkies as priull and ungle
Mr Hew Blair as cawner to
the calling of   100 _ 00 _ 00

Item is the @rent therof fra
Candelmas 1662 to Whit 68   037 _ 00 _ 00

Item with ane band of Mr and
grayer of priull   066 _ 13 _ 4

Item with the a rent therof fra
marts 1665 to marts 68   012 – 00 – 00

(82) Item with ane precept obtaint
at the faculteis instence agt
Rot Harris wherof restand   020 – 03 – 00
       fridome fynes

Item fra Johne dogans 13-6-8 fra
Johne Reid of expenss 2-18-0 fra
david fleming 13-6-8 fra Ion
Robersone 12-0-0 Item fra Wm
Currie 26-13-4 fra Wm Kelso for
his booking 5-0-0 fra thomas
Harper 20-0-0 fra dor Panton
20-0-0 fra Robert Dunlop 20-0-0
fra Adame Grays 5-16-0, fra
Johne flening 11-12-0 fra dor
Irivine 15-0-0 fra Matthow Millar
40-0-0 fra George lockhart
12-0-0

      Extending the fresde fynes to   217 – 12 – 8
Quarter comptes of firmant
others at 12S by year

Item fra Jo Hall for 66)768 – 1 – 4 – 0
Mr And Grahame for 1665-66-67-68

2-8-0. James Thomsone 1667r1668
1-4-0 James dies for 66-67. 68
1-16-0 Ard bogill 67.68. 1-4-0
Andrew Millar 67 r68. 1-4-0
Mr david Sherp 67. 68-1-4-0
James Wilsone 1661.62-63-64-65
66-67-68. 4-4-0 Ja Watt 65-66.67
r68. 2-8-0. James frank Elder
66.67.68. 1-16-0. Mr Jo Muir 62
to 1668. 4-4-0 Andrew browne
1663 to 1668. 3-12-0 John Robinsone
for 1668. 0-12-0 George Lockhart
for 1668. 0-12-0 Thomas Harper
for halfe ane year 0-6-0. Rot
Harris fra 1659 to 1668. 5-8-0
damuel browne for 1665-66-67.68
2-8-0. Wm Clydisdaill 67r68
1-4-0 Wo dies for 66) r68. 1-4-0
James Braidwood 67r68. 1-4-0
John diddell 67r68. 1-4-0 Andrew
Elphingstoune 67r68-1-4-0 Jon
Mcnill 67r68 1-4-0 James
frank younger fra 1662 to 1668
4-4-0. James Morsat fra 60 to68

5_8_0. Hew Muntgomerie fra
64 to 1668_3_0_0. Iohne Logane
67.68_1_4_0. Adame Grayz for
68_0_12_0. Iohne flemyng 1668
0_12_0_

    Suma of the forsds qter
    Comptes extendis to   058_10_0
    Strangeris quarter comptis
Allane Kirkwood 66.67.68_4_10_0
Iames Lobias 1661 to 68. 10_10_0 Iohne
Patersone fra 61 to 68_8_0_0. Iohne
Ewing fra Wit 63 to Mart 68_5_10_0
Mr alxer dunlop fra 1661 to 68
10_10_0. Iohne foster fra 1658_15_0_0
Gilbert Kennidie fra 1659 to 1668
13_10_0. Iohne tantan 67.68
3_0_0 Wm Currie for 68_1_0_0.
Mathow Millar for halfe ane
0_10_0 doctor Wallace from
60. to 68_12_0_0 Adame Paterson
66.67.68 3_0_0 Iohne Sprewll
66.67.68 3_0_0 Thomas Robisone
fra 1659 to 1668 9_0_0 Iohne
Mathie fra 1656 to 1668_12_0_0

Mr Thomas younger fra 64 to 68
7-10-0. Ro Neur in Gorballs
1667 r68. 1-12-0 Ro dunlop ane
year and ane halfe 1-10-0
do uriving 68 .1-0-0
  Suma of the Strangers
   quarter comptts is   122-12-00
Item the compter chargrs himselfe
 w 13-6-8 that was dew be
 Steis Montgomrie for his
 fredome fyn dues   013-06-08
Item fra James Wilsons for his
 fredome fyn   005-00-00
Item w four pounds mony for
 ane years @rent of 100 lib dew
 be ungle Iohne drunie + his
 cautioners to the sd faculti
 fra Mart 1667 to Mart 1668 dues 004-00-00
Item with other four pounds mony
 as for halfe ane years @rent
 of 200 markis dew to the calling
 be Mr Gilmour and his cauners
 fra Wit 68 to Mart 68 dues 004-00-00
  Suma of the wholl charge

is – 931 – 11 – 08 –
say nyne hundrethe threttie
ane pound elleavine schilling
eight penneis –

discharge –

Imprimis the compter reconris
himselfe w^t thrie pds givin to
Gabriell Conynghame officer for
his fiall   03 – 0 – 0

Item to him for erraving in of
Sr Matheis aftr compts   00 – 12 – 0

Item to Rot Adame the deacon
conviners officer for 1667   01 – 04 – 0

Item to the said Rot Adame
to the deacon conviners
hospitiall for the year exactlie
cravine   06 – 13 – 04

Item to Thomes Wilsone messr
for erravine charges of horning 03 – 12 – 00

Item to Sr Ban messr at the
visitours command   00 – 12 – 00

Item to the kirk officer at
command forsaid   00 – 06 – 00

Item to daniell Browns wyff
that Catherin Spang wes
dew her   05 – 00 – 00

Item to the Kirk officer 6S To the
drumer 12S and to Gabriell
Cunyngham to buy ane pair
shoone 48S inde   03 – 06 – 00

Item to Mr Ro Gowrane for his
siall fra 66 to 67   08 – 00 – 00

Item to Jo Greir & Ro Adame at
comand of the visitour   00 – 06 – 00

Item to Johne Hutchison the
deacon convriners officer   01 – 04 – 00

Item to Jo Grahame twa full
dollars and to Ro ffynnison
ane sixe dollour of pror six
for the faculties caus agt the
caus of unngle Mr Aru Blair
as caruner for Mr Wm Wilkie   08 – 14 – 00

Item the sd caus being advocat
from the comissar befor the
lords the compter gave to the
said Johne grahame to and
reist for ane remitt therin

at the faculteis dreyer 020–06–00

Item for ane lybell summonds
calling in the said caus
befor the said comissar for
actes of court for sentence
monye + drink monye to
the comissar clerkes man
and to Johne Grahames man 003–18–8

(83) Item to Johne donnald messer
for giving of severall charges
of horning in the contra
at the faculteis instance. 006–00–00

Item given to dr Grahame for
writting the faculteis disposition
of and Andersones band to
Johne Binnie 004–07–00

Item to his man of drink mony. 000–18–00

Item for ane instrument taking
in Mr haires hand when
Johne Binnies wyff gave her
oathe that shoe was not
compelit to the subscrybing
of the right grantit be Binnie
to the faculteis and for the

extract of the ratificatioun   001—13—04

Item to the erosis hospitall for
   the year 1668   006—13—04

Item to the Kirk officer 12s + to
   the drummer 12s incle   001—04—00

Item to Gabriell Conyngham for
   his fiall 1668   003—00—00

Item for tua horse hyres to the
   ladie nwsarkis buriall   003—14—00

Item to the Kirk officer   000—06—00

Item the compter recovers himself
   with ane band grantit be
   Johne Binnie + his wyff in
   favours of the facultie   266—13—04

Item wt ane years rent of the
   cuinyie to Wil fra Mart 1667
   to the terme of Mart 1668   016—00—00

Item with ane band gunsgt
   Johne drunkis of   066—13—04

Item with ane years rent
   thereof fra Mart 67 to Mart 1668   004—00—00

Item with ane band of Wr Gilmour
   and his cautioners of   133—06—08

Item with halfe ane years rent

therof fra Wit 68 to Mart 1668   004_00_00

Item with ane band of Ard:

graye's & his cautnr of   066_03_04

Item with ane years @rent

therof fra Mart 1667 to Mart 68   004_00_00

Item he reconers himselffe of

20 lb 3s restand be Robert Haras

of his precept at the callings

instance agt him inde   020_03_00

Item the compter reconers himselff

of the sowmne of 92_0_0 that

was gevin downe of the

bypast @rentes of Ard Anderson

band be the forsaid facultie

to Johne Binnie at the

granting of his forsaid band

above writt to them conforme

to ane particular act in this

booth dailit the 19 of december

1667 inde   92_00_00

Item he reconers himselffe of the

sowmne of 37_10_0 that was also

gevin downe be the said facultie

to Johne Blair of the bypast

@rentis that was dew of Mr
Mr Wilkie's band and umqll
Mr Hew Blair as eacenrs the
tyme the said faeultie aggreit
wt the sd Johne for the prinll
sowmr conform to ane other
aet in the sd book dait the
8 of Junii 1668 inde   37 _ 10 _ 00

    Non payrentes of gth comptes
    of priemrn + others at 12S
    a year ..

James Watt for 65 66 _ 1 _ 4 _ 0 Wm
Clydisdaill for 68 _ 0 _ 12 _ 0 James
Wilsone for 61 _ 62 _ 63 _ 64 + 66 _ 3 _ 0 _ 0
Ja frank elder 66 _ 67 _ 68 _ 1 _ 16 _ 0
Mr Johne Muir for 65 _ 66 _ 67 _ 68
2 _ 8 _ 0 Androw Browne for 63 _ 64
65 _ 66 _ 67 _ 68 _ 3 _ 12 _ 0 Rot Stairis
for 60 _ 61 _ 62 _ 63 _ 64 _ 65 _ 66 _ 4 _ 4 _ 0 _
Johne Aeo for 68 _ 0 _ 12 _ 0 James
frankll younger for 62 _ 63 _ 64 _
65 _ 66 _ 67 _ 68 _ 4 _ 4 _ 0 James Mowat
for 60 _ 61 _ 62 _ 63 _ 64 _ 65 _ 66 _ 67 _ 68 _ 5 _ 8 _ 0
Hew Muntgomrie 64 _ 65 _ 66 _ 67 _ 68

3-0-0. Thomas Harper for halfe
a year - 0-6-0

Non payments of strangers
after compters.

Adame Kirkwood for 1668 - 1-10-0
doctour Wallace 66-67-68. 12-0-0
Johne Patersone from 66 to 1668
8-0-0 Johne Ewing from Wit
1667 to Mart 1668 - 1-10-0. Mr Alexr
dunlop from 1661 to 1668. 10-10-0
Johne Wallace from 1656 to 1668
12-0-0 Gilbert Kennedie from
1659 to 1668. 13-10-0 Rot dunlop
one year and ane halfe.
1-10-0 Johne Ewing 1668-1-0-0
Jamie Lobias from 1661 to 1668
10-10-0 Adame Patersone for
67 and 68. 2-0-0 Johne Spreull
for 66.67.68. 3-0-0 Thomas Robisone
from 1659 to 1668. 9-0-0 Johne
forster from 1662 to 1668. 9-0-0
Mr Thomas Younger 1667 and
1668. 3-0-0 Johne Pantane 1667
and 1668. 3-0-0 Wm Currie for

1668 – 1–0–0 And Matthow Millar

for halfe ane year 0–10–0.

    Suma of the forsaidis

      9ᵗ compter is   102 – 10 – 00

Non paymentis of fridome

fynne

Item be Hew Montgomrie   013 – 06 – 08

Item be Wm Currie   026 – 13 – 04

Item be Thomas Harper   020 – 00 – 00

Item be James Wilsone   005 – 00 – 00

Item restand be Johne Nivine

of his fyne   003 – 08 – 00

    Suma of the discharge is 877 – 09 – 4.

      Say eight hundreth

      seaventie seavine pound

      nyne schilling four pennies

      monye. –

This charge and discharge being

compaired the compter restis dew to

the forsaid facultie to ballance the

forsaid charge the sowme of fyftie

four pound twa schilling four pennies

monye QuilK sowme the said compter

hathe instantlie dlyvrid at the

table to Androw Elphingstoune junt
collectour With ane band of Johne
Binnies of 400 merkis Ane band of
umqll Johne dennies and his
cauconers of 100 merkis Ane band of
And Grayes of 100 merkis Ane band
of Wm Gilmours and his cauconers of
200 merkis Rob Staviers precept wt his
band And ane tickat of Johne Usingis
of 3-08-0 And recovers and simple
discharges the sd Wr david his airs
and executors of his forsaid intromissiounis
be thir putis for now and ever...

The said day also the forsaid facultie
all in ane voyse ordained James
franck elder and Andw Mountgomrie
to be frie of ther haill bypast quarter
comptis and in tyme coming during
ther residence in the Kingdome of
Irland As also Gilbert Kennidie his
bypast quarter comptis in respect he
is departed this lyfe.—

Item the said day they fialie quatt
Wm Clydisdaill of his twentie merkis of

fyne upon conditioun allwayes he behave
himselfe towardis the said facultie as
becometh in all tyme heirafter.—

Wilsone As also the forsaid day the quatt
James Wilsone of his bypast quarter
comptis provyding he pay his fridome
fyne and quarter comptis in tyme
coming.—

Prentis The forsaid day Johne Robinsone sone
Robinsone lauch to umqll Wm Robinsone merd in
Glasgow is bookit prentis wt Mr
david Sherp for the space of fyve
yeare as prentis and twa yeares for
meitt and fie conforme to ane Indentour
past betwixt them theranent who
halter givne his oathe as use is And
payit to Androw Elphingstoune collectour
for his booking twa pounds money.—

first of Januaris 1669 yeares.—

Admissioune The 9th day the visitour Johne Hall
Wm Charles James Thomsone, Johne Robinsone, Mr
Mousat david Sherp, daniell Browne, Wm
Clydisdaill, George Lockhart, Ard bogill

Adam Grayr, James Watt, James
Braidwood and Androw Elphingstoune
Being convenit in the erastes hospitale
with Mr Charles Mowat who produceit
befor the said faculties his say appoyntit
to him to mak and compone conforme
to aur former Act sett doune particularlie
in his book upon the nynt day of
november 1668 yeirs Together with ane
supplicacioune Wherby he the sd Mr
Charles desyrit to be admittit fraeman
with them to practis the airt of
phormacie Qlk say the said faculties
approveit to be sufficient And after
reexaminatioune of the said Mr
Charles upon the forsaid airt of
phormacie was fund qualifiet be them
to practis the samyne And therfor the
forsaid faculties all in aue voyce Admittit
the said Mr Charles Mowat fraeman
with them to practis the forsaid
airt of phormacie allanerlie And who
is heirby onlie astrictit therto And
haithe payit to the collectour for his

fredome fyne thrittie pounds scotts mo[ney]
And gave his oathe as use is — The sd
Mr Charles bring heirby obleist for his
yearlie quarter compters conforme to the
rest of the rest of the faculties —

Act anent
admissions
of friemen The forsaid first day of Januarie and
year of god w^t in Aprile The said facultie
haveing taken to ther serious considirat[ion]
the great hurt and prejudice the poor
of ther said vocationne hathe thir
manie years bygaine sustinit And
daylie does sustein throughe strang[ers]
coming in and receiveing within
this brughe And ar admittet friemen
by the said facultie for litle or
nothing fyne at all By ther making
of monye with the said calling
Notwithstanding they ar rather
friemens sones, sones in law hor
arveit ther printriship within the
said brughe of Glasgow And that
the patent and gift grantit in
favours of the calling Ar therby
altogither slightit The skaithe and

damage wherof dothe mightilie
redound to the poor of the forsaid
vocatiouns. Therfor and to the effect
that good ordour may be keipit in
all tymes coming And that the
said gift and patent be not slightit
But dewlie observit heirafter And
the weill and behuife of ther said
poor advertit to At the admissiouns
of strangers firmen wt them Whose
intent is to leive wt in the forsaid
brughe of glasgow the forsaid faculties
within writt all in one voyse nemo
contra dicente Heirby inactit
statut and ordeint And by thir
prntis inactis statutis & ordainis
That qtsumevir persones that sall
happen in all tymes heirafter to
enter friemane with the said faculteis
Ather as a phormacianes or chirurgianes
or bothe that is to leive wt in the
said brughe Sall pay at his admissioune
to the collectour of the sd calling
for the use of ther poor ane hundreth

merkis scottis mony QlR sall be the
least soume of thir that sall be
statit and proposit be the said faculties
befoir the said admissioune And which
of the forsdis thir soumis swa to
be statit in manner as said is
that sall by vottis be cariad that
the samyne soume sall be first-
payit befor the admissioune be bookit
for the use aforsd - and ilk barbour
bring ane stranger befor his admissioune
sall pay fourtie pounds mony at
least of fyne sie sub R Tymnisoune -
Proovyding alwayes dykas it is hierby
represlie proovydit that this prnt-
act be nowayes roetendit to frimmens
childrein whither they serve prentis
ather within or wout this brughe
And to prsisis that serve ther
prentishipes within this brughe
with frimen As lykwayes that it
be not roetendit to those that learne
in the contrie But that the sd calling
sall have ther frie libertie as to

these vij formmers sones, prentisis
and those that leaves in the contrie
that is to be admittit as in former
tymes. And for performance and
observing of the haill heads and
annow of this ther pnt act and
ordinance they all in on voyes in
manner above mentional ordaint me
undersubscryband clerk to the said
calling to subt the samyne for them
and in ther names.

Sic subt   R Symisone Clk.

          At Glasgow the erect day of
          Appryll Jawi threscour and
          nyne yeares.

The whilk day Wm and graham present
visitour of the chirurgianes of the
forsd brughe of glasgow, John Stall
James Thomsone, Wm david Sherp and
Charles Morsat, Androw Elphingstoune
Daniell browne, Archibald Bogill
James Kerr, George Lockhart, James
Braidwood, John diddell, Adam Gray

Twelf of the brethrein of the said
facultie Being convrint in the bell
house of the laigh kirk steiple of
the said brugh of glasgow Anent ane
bill of complaint givin in befor them
be Margrat Millar relict of umqle
John Risk quariour in glasgow Against
william Clydsdaill on of the brethrein
of the sd vocaciun of Chirurgians And
Catherine Muir his spous Makand
Mentioun That wherabout Twentie dayes
since or yby The said umqle John
Risk having ane pain in his breist
went himself to the said williame
and his said spous And acquainted
them yrwith Who upon the morrow
yrafter the said defenders came to the sd
defunct and agrict with him for
ane certaine sowme of mony wherof
the equall half was delyvred in
hand to them be the defunct At
which tyme the said Wm Clydsdaill
faithfulie promisit to cur sufficientlie
the said defunct of his said pains

And in ordour yrto the said defunct at the leist his said spouse gave to the defunct in twa Cockell shells ane porne of Antimonie which they declared to him was ane porne of phisick wherof pairt is yet reclent in the said shells And that the saidis defunders ane or ather of them ordourd the defunct to make use of the samyne for purging upward and downward And that according yrto the said defunct made use yrof upon the marrow yeafter being a sabouth day And after that the defunct hade takin and made use of the samyne according to the defunders directions That it did no wayes in the leist work with the said defunct untill munday at night at which tyme That it wroght the defunct to death And the ptinan having sent for doctor Hamiltoune upon the foirsaid day Being the tyme of the height of the

defunct his working And the said
doctour having come and sighted
the said defunct alitill befor his
drath did declair expresslie that
the said vncle William Kirk the
pursuars husband hade gotten wrong
yeby And thrugh which the pursuar
is left in ane pitifull conditioun
with twa poor children And nothing
wherwith to mentaine them nor
the pursuar herselfe Crvand yefor
for the lords saik that the foirsaid
facultie would take the premiss to
ther serious considerations And not
only to punish and fyne the said
defender and his said spous for giving
of the samyne But also to recomend
the saids defenders and the caices
and conditioun of the said matter
to the civill magistrat to cognosce
yeupon to the effect that they may
be deemed to mentaine the pursuar
and her said poor children in tyme
coming According to Justice as the said

complent in itselfe at lenth proports
Qlk bill of Complent bring at lenth
redd to the saidis defenderis bring
personalie present and warned for
that effect They denyed the samyne
simpliciter And the said William
declaired in puts of the foirsaid facultie
at the said tyme that he never gave
phisick in his lyftyme to the said
persewaris husband Except about ane
quarter of ane yeare since the said
defunct having meaned himself to
the defender William Clydesdaill that
he hade ane paine in his back And
the said William in puts of the
foirsaid facultie and persewar declaired
and confest that he did give to
the said defunct in ordour to the
curing and mending of the said
paine some oyles and some pills —
Which confessione and declaratione
bring at lenth considered be the said
facultie And they being therewith weill
and wyslie advysed Be this ther decreit

and sentence ffyns and decerns the
said William Clydsdaill defender to
content and pay To Androw Elphingstoune
ther collectour the sowme of ffourtie
punds Scots mony to be applyit for
the use of ther poor Or otherwayes as
the said facultie should think fit &
convenient And that becaus of the
said defender his confessioun of the
giving of the foirsaids pride The
samyn being altogither contrar to
his act of admissioun wherin he is
nowayes licentat to practise the
samyn And yrfor the said facultie
ffyne and decerne the said defender
In manner as said is And ordaine
ther said collectour to present this
ther decreit to the magistrate of the
foirsaid brugh and to crave ther
assistance and concurrence therin—

13 of Maii 1669 years.
The glk day being convenit in the
billious the visitour Johne Stark, hw

david Sharp, Jo: Robinsone, damiell
Browne, And Bogill, George Lockhart
Mr Charles Mowat, Androw Elphingstoune
Adame Graye and James Brandwood
ansrt the supplicaoune givin in
befor them be Petter Boill wriwar
in Wallacishewghe Creavand therby
to be admittet frirmane is them
to oppine veinis, place culteris
applye lochleitchis, making of
grintrett, giving of cleisterus, and
ane potioune of phisick for the
gut And therby crewit to be
reeaminird theropon Who being
reeaminird conforme be the forsd
faeultie They all in ane voyes
fand him onlie qualifit to mak
grintrett and applyeing of
lochleitchis allanerlie And discharge
him heirby in all tyme coming
from using any pts of chirurgie
medeein or pharmacie Except he
be fund qualifit heirafter be the
said faeultie after reeaminatioune

to practise the samyne And in caice
it sall happin him to transgres
any pairt of this pnt act The
said Petter or the tennour heir of
of his owne conssent binders & oblissis
him to content and pay to the
said calling toties quoties for ilk
tyme it sall happin him to brick
any pts of this pnt act the sowme
of fourtie pounds Scotts monye and
to pay yeirlie to the collectour of
the forsaid calling for the use of
ther poor the sowme of twentie
schilling And in the meantyme
tyme he hatthe payit to the pnt
collectour twelfe pounds monye
for his present admissioune And
gave his oathe as use is And
that he sall not mak use of
nothing wherinto he is licentiat
wt in the toune of glasgow ghe
he be first admittit burges under
the lyk penaltie and to pay
yeirlie

24 of Maii the forsaid
monethe and year 1669. —

The 9th day the dracons, Johne
Hall, Mr david Sharp, Mr Charles
mowat, James Thomsone, And
Bogill, daniell Browne, Androw
Alphingstoune, Johne flemyng, Ja:
braidwood and Adame Crage Bring
conveined in the laigh kirk Anent
the supplicatione givin in befor
them be Gilbert Nicolsone induellar
in Straven wherby the said
Gilbert craved to be admittit
firman wt the sd faculte to
sell drogs in his chop, to mak
purintrie to cur simple wounds
in the flesh To oppine vaines
To use ischoirs in legs & airmes
by incitioune To applye lockbritches
To give vomitouris of graciola And
craved to be examinrid therupon
to the effct he might be admittit
accordinglie who being at lenthe

examined be the said facultie They
all in on voyce onlie admittis
the said Gilbrt to sell drogs
in his chop but not to compose
non But be the advyce of our
assistance or apothecar and to
cur simple wounds witho the said
grin tritt discharging him heirby
not to middle with blood letting
applying of lochleitches & making
of ischous without the speciall
advyce of thois who is knawin to
be expert and skilfull in their
airtis As also from giving of
vomittouris of graciola directlie or
indirectlie without the speciall
advyce of our phisitians in all
tymis coming And in cace it
sall happin the sd Gilbrt to
transgris any ptt or poynt of
this pnt act he be the tennour
heirof of his own consent binds
and obleisis him to content &
pay to the said calling totiens

quoties for ilk tyme it sall happen
him to breck any pte of this
pnt act the soume of twentie
pounds Scotts money to the
collectour of the sd calling to
be applyed for the use of the
poor of the samyne And to
pay yearlie to the collectour of
the sd tred for the use of
the sd poor twentie schilling
And that he sall not weeve
any pte of the forsds airtes
whereunto he is admitted wtin
the toune of Glasgow while first
he be admitted burges therof under
the lyk penalties above written
And in ordour therto hathe givin
his oathe as use is and payit to
the collectour twentie pounds pnlie
and one band for other twentie
pounds payable upon Whitsonday
nixt 1670 for his admission

29 Julii 1669

The 9th day the visitour, Jon Hall, Mr dewid Sharpe & Charles Mowsat, deniell broune, Dr Robirsoune, Ard bogle, James Thomsoune, Androe Elphingstoune, Adam Gray, George Lockhart, Dr Liddell, Androe Miller, James Braidwood, Johne flemyng & James Wilsone, being convenit in hutchisones hospitall anent the desyre of Ro Houstoune desyring the said faculter to prescrybe a dyr to him to the effect he may enter firmaine in the said calling Who in ordor to his desyre the sd faculter appoynted the sd Ro to epose the particulars underwrin viz extractum redii de recordum diapalma, diaphanicon torchisci de myrchir ung: diapompholigos and to have the samyn reader beliveisd & the first of Sept meet and appoynted

to be his examrs for yr effect.

As also the sd day The sd
facultie considering the desyre of
Dr Clark ordained him to make
himself first burges.

Last of August 1669

The 9th day the visitour, Dr Hall
Mr Charles Mowat, Archibald Bogill
daniels browne, William Clidisdaill
Ivor McNeill, Andros Elphingstoune
Ja breidwood, Dr Robisone + Adam
Gray being convint in hutchisones
hospitall wt the forsd Rd Houstoune
who gave in his forsd cry wt ane
supplicacne desyring therof he might
be admitted frimane wt them
accordinglie and the sd facultie
having taken inspecone of the
forsd eposicns exponed be the sd
Rd in maner as sd is and
Examined him accordinglie ypone
the sd facultie fand him treulie
qualifeid to practice the airt of
formaine allenarlie and admittit

(87)

him yto and heirby dischargit the
sd nor from useing of any other
airt nor yt he is admitit to in
manner as sd is being the desyr
of his supplicacon givine in by
him yaurnt And in caice it sall
happene him this his sd admissione
to transgres he is heirby oblist to
pay to the sd calling the sowme
of twentie pounds Scots tolies
quoties it sall happen him to
transgres for the use of the poor
yof And in order yto produceit his
buyers tickit and payit to the
collectorie ane hundrethe markes
monye for his friedome fyne And
gave his oathe de fideli administratione
as use is.—

Anent the Clerk As also they have appoyntit Ro:
fyuirsone ther clerk to wryt: east to
a wryter to the signet anent the
componing of this qo hathe gottine
a charge of horning at the callings
instance to enter friemane wt them

in order to the payees at the signet
to get the samyne als easie as can
be and the said Mr to report
to them.—

24 of September 1669 yearis.—

The alk day the visitour, Iohn Hall
Mr Charles Morsat, Iohn Robertsoun
Iames Thomsoun Androw Elphingstoun
Iames Bradwood, Androw Millar
Archibald Bogill Robert Housetoun
Roor M'neill, Iohn fflemming, Mr
dawid Sharpe, Adam Gray, Iohn
diddell and Iames M'at Being
convenit in the crafters hospitall
anent the making schois of ane
of ther number to be ther visitour
for the year to come who be
pluralitie of vottis made schoise
of the forsaid Archibald Bogill to
be ther visitour untill the next
ordinar tyme of erectioun who
being present acceptit of and
gave his oath as use is.—

qr maisters

As also the sd day they made choise
of ther quarter maisters as fallowes To
wit the said visitors made choise of
Mr Ard grahame and david sherp
for his maisters and the sd calling
made choise of James Thomsone and
Androw Elphingstoune for ther qr maisters
who being put accepat of & gave ther
oathis as use is—

Act anent
officuris in
tyme coming

Item the foirsaid day is in wrytin
the said faculter all in one vote
hath statut and ordainit And
be ther puts statute and ordaines
that cohatsoumever persowne or
persoumes that sall be admittit
frimane with the said faculter in
all tyme coming that sall happine
or resolves after his admissioune
to reeird withine this brugh aither
to pay to the said calling ther
punds sets mony for ther opern
fir by and attour ther fridoume
fyne Or then to save officer
themselves to the said faculter

326

for ane years space.

Box Mr

The said day the said calling made
sehois of Mr Charles Mowat and
Adame Gray to be box masters
for ane year to come who being
present acceptit of and gives their
oath as use is.

Clark
Jymmisoun

Item the said day the said calling
continoured Robert Jymmisoun wryter
to be their clerk for ane year to
come who being present acceptit
of and gives his oath as use is.

Conyngham
officer

The said day also they continoured
Gabriell Cunyngham to be their
officer for ane year to come And
ordained the collector to give to
him fourtie eight shilling To buy
ane pair of shoone.

15 Nor 1669

Visitours
Iunibus

The sd day the visitours, Dr Hall,
John Robisoun, Mr Ard Grahame,
Androe Elphingstoune, George Lockhart
Dor McneilL, James Braidwood

Adam Gray, James Thomsone, Johne
Liddell & Mr david Sharpe all in
on voyce consentit to lend out
their hundreth merks of ther
poor monye to Johne Turnbull yor
and to take Mr Inglis right of
the sd Johne Turnbull lands for
securitie therof and appoyntit &
ordaind the visitour & collectour to
borrow ane hundreth merks upon
band To make out four hundreth
(88) merks to the sd Johne Turnbull
and ordaint the sd collectour
to make his compt readie betwixt
and the 22 day of the sd month
or no for that effect

22 Nor 1669

The qlk day The visitour, Johne
Hall, Mr Ard Grahame, James
Thomsone, Johne Robisone, danuell
browne, Wm Clidisdaill, Groy doekhart,
Nr houstoune, Mr Charles Mowat
Nr liddell & James braidwood being

convened in hutchesons hospitall
wt the forsd Androe Elphingstoune
collectour Anent the making of
his compt of the sd faculties
maines sine hallowmas 1668 to
hallowmas 1669 who in order therto
made just compt reckoning &
payt of his haill intromissions
the sd year And that by charge
and discharge in manner
underwritt —

Charge —

Imprimis The compter charges
himselfe wt the soumm of
54 lib 2s 4d receavit be him
fra wr david Sharpe last
collector glk was restand in
his hands of his intromission
the former year inde   054 — 2 — 4
Item wt a band of Johne Binnes
of 400 merks wt two years
@rent gof fra mart 1667 to
mart 1669 inde   298 — 13 — 4

Item a band of umqll Johne
drumes & his cautr is the
@rent therof fra Mart 1667
to Mart 1669 of ane hundreth
marks prinll inde   074—13—4

It Wm Gilmours band & his caus
of 200 mrks is @rent fra
Whyt: 1668 to Mart 1669 inde 145—06—8

It a band of Ard Graye & his
caus of 100 mrks is the @rent
therof fra Mart 1667 to Mart
1669 inde   074—13—4

It is a precept of Ro Haries
cluning   020—03—0

          freedoms fynes

It fra Wm Currie of fyne 26 lib
3s 4d It fra Wm Livine as the
remainder of his fyne 3 lib
8s It fra Mr Charles Morsal
for his freedome fyne 30—0—0
It fra Gilbert Wilsone for his
fyne 40—0—0. It James Wilsone
remainder of his fyne 5—0—0
It James Harpers fyne 20—0—0

Jr Peter Bogilles fyne 12-0-0

Item Rb houscomess fynn

66-13-4

And fra hr david Sharpe for

booking his prentis   2-0-0

Friremens quartercompts

fra Johne hall for 1669. 12S hr

And Grahame 1669 12S hr Charles

Mowat 1669. 12S Wm Cleddisdaill

1668 +1669. 1 lib 4S, James Watt

1665. 66 r 69 1 lib 16S, James Wilson

1661. 62. 63. 64. 66 + 1669. 3 lib 12S -

James Mowat for ten years

6 lib Thomas Harper for a

year + a halfe 18S Androe

Miller 1669 12S daniell Browne

1669. 12S, Ivor McneiIl 1669. 12S

Johne Logane 69. 12S Adam

Gray 69. 12S And Bogill 1669

12S hr david Sharpe 69. 12S

Jo Robison 69. 12S. James

Thomsone. 69. 12S Jo Dro 68 +

69. 1 lib 4S. Rob Harris for 59 to the

foord 22 hr 1669. 6 lib - James

frank y{e} for eight yeares 4 lib 16 S
Androe broune for seavine
yeares 4 lib 4 S. James Sirs for
69. 12 S George Lockheart 69. 12 S
James braidwood 69. 12 S Johne
diddill 69. 12 S + Jo fleming
for 1669. 12 S.

    Strangers quarter compt
Jra Allane Kirkwood for 1668 +
1669 3 lib. James Tobias for eight
years 12 lib. Jo Patersone for
nyne yeares 9 lib Jo livine twa
year + a half 2 lib 10 S ho
alsoe dunlope eight yeares 12 lib
Johne mathie for 13 years 13 lib
Johne Tambane for 67. 68. 69
4 lib 10 S. W{m} Currie 68+69 2 lib
mathow Miller a year +
half 1 lib 10 S. Jo hos 67. 68+69
3 lib doctor Wallace 9 year
13 lib. Adam Patersone 67. 68. 69
3 lib. Jo Sprull 66. 67. 68+69 4 lib
Thomas Robertsone for ten years
10 lib. Jo foster 7 year 10 lib 10 S

Mr Thomas yo for 67. 68. & 69. 4 lib. 10S
Ro dunlope tisa years & a
halfe 2 lib. 10S, Johne huine
68 & 69 2 lib & fra Ro huie in
Gorbald for 1669. 16S.

    Summa of the haill
    Charge is — 1027 – 02 – 08

discharge

Imp: to Ro ffynniesone for his
fiall fra Mich: 1667 to Mich:
1669 being tisa yearrs   16 – 0 – 0
It to Adam Wilsone 18S to Pat
Muirhead 12S to Kirk Birdale
6S inde   01 – 16 – 0
It to the dracon cvriurs hous
6 lib. 13S. 4d & to his officer
24S   07 – 17 – 4
It for four hors hyrs to
Walkingshaus buriall   03 – 06 – 0
It for thrie hors hyrs to Montrois
buriall   06 – 16 – 0
It for four horses to my Lord
Elphingstouns buriall   10 – 13 – 4

It for tua horsa to Rot Donnaldsone
   buriall   02 — 00 — 0

(84) It to supplie Gilbert Currie his
   jaylor fie   01 — 10 — 0

It to Johne Wru messt for chargs
   of horning givn be him at
   the faculties dreyre   08 — 14 — 0

It to dor Jannirsone 12S and to
   the Biddell 6S   00 — 18 — 0

It to Gabriell Cunynghame to buy
   a pair of shoes   02 — 08 — 0

It to Rot ffynnirsoun for regra'ne
   of Sr Binnies band + for horning
   Jupon 5 lib 4S for post of cap'ne
   2S   05 — 06 — 0

Item Johne Binnies band of four
   hundreth merks is the @ceut
   therof pra Candelmas 1669 to
   Mart 1669   278 — 13 — 4

It Sr Dunnes + his cau'n band of   066 — 13 — 4

It Wm Gilmour +his cau'n band of 133 — 06 — 8

Restand by Rot Harvie of
   the preysl +expense in
   eland   020 — 03 — 0

Nonpay^ts of tounsmen +
others q^lt compts at 12 S
p annum.–

Imprimis Robert Maries for ten
years 6 tlb Wm Cliddisdaill 1669
12S Jo^r dures 1668 r1669 24S, James
Watt 1665 r1669 24S, James Wilson
1661.62.63.64.66r69 3 tlb 12S James
frank yor eight yeares 4 tlb 16S
James Mowsat ten yeares 6 tlb
Andro Broun sevin years
4 tlb 4S J^r Thomas Karpen a
year + a half 18S daniell
Browne 1669 12S + J^r flemyng
for 1669. 12S.

    Strangers nonpay^ts
Imp: allane Kirkwood 1668 r1669
3 tlb. doctor Wallace nyn yeares
13 tlb 10S. James Tobias eight
year 12 tlb Jo^r Paterson nyn
year 9 tlb Jo Spruell 1666.67.68r69
4 tlb Jo^r Ewine fra Whyt 1667
2 tlb 10S. Jho Robertson ten year
10 tlb W^r Alex^r dunlope eight

years 12 lib. D° foster craving
years 10 lib 10S. D° Mathew
thritteine year 13 lib W° Tho
yo[r] 1669 1 lib 10S D° Pantaine
67. 68. 69 4 lib 10S R° dunlops
tua year & a half 2 lib 10 S
W[m] Cunie 68 & 69 2 lib John
liveine 68 & 69 2 lib Mathow
Miller a year & a half
1 lib 10S.

 freedome fynes unpayit.
Imp: restand of James Wilsons
fyne 5 lib It of D° liveins 3 lib
8S It of Tho Harpers 8 lib of
Gilbert Nelsons 20 lib R°
Houstonne fyne 66 – 13 – 4
 Summa of the haill
 discharge is   802 – 06 – 4
Restis in the compters hands to
ballance the charge the which
I haive consignd to be given
to my successor   224 – 16 – 4
 which doth ballance the
 charge & contra   1027 – 02 – 8

336

John
Turnbull

As also the sd day they all in on
voice ordained the Visitour and
collector To barrow ane hundreth
markis And to grant band yeror-
and to putt thrie hundreth markis
of the callings Qlk is remaining in
the collectors hand yt to To mak up
four hundreth markis And to lend
furth the samyne to John Turnbull
upon securitie of his land Conform
to ane former act sett downe in this
booth datid the fyftene day of No
1669 years.

As lykwayes the foirsaid twentie twa
day of November is in wrytten Ohry
all in on voice continowed the forsed
Androw Elphingstoune to be ther collector
till the nixt ordinar tyme of electiouns
Who being present acceptit of & gaue
his oath as use is And ordained that
John brown being now dreist hes nott
to be qualt.

7 febru 1670

Act anent
Binnis

The 9th day the visitors Mr david
Sherp, Mr Archibald Grahame, Mr
Charles Donald, John Robisone, Androw
Elphingston, John liddell, John fleming
and James Braidwood Being conveined
in the craft hospitall To sie what
sall be done Anent the ending
rast So call John Binnis suspensioun
raised be him against the faculteis
four hundreth merks band draw be
him to them Who all in on voice
condescendit To send rast to call
the soumyne and mony yt with for
that yffet With the first occasioun
Except the sd John Binnis give
ane new band of corroboracioun To
pay the foinsd soumne at Whytsonday
nixt and to be obleist be the band
of corroboratioun To pas fra all
benefit of the foinsd suspensioun
And not to mak use yrof in
all tyme yrafter Wpon qch conditioun
they ordainred to accept of the
foinsd band of corroboracioun

Jacksone — The said day also thay continowrd Thomas Jacksone's band till the first of March nixtocome.—

15 March 1670.—

Jacksone — The qlk day the visitors John Neill Mr And Grahams Mr Charles Mouitt John Robison, daniell browne, Androw Elphingstone, Evar McNeill, John fflenning, Adam Gray, and John Liddell All in on voice ordaind furth with that Jacksons band be puit to all drw execution lres of horning and caption to be raisrd yeupon

(90)

Houstoune — Item they ordaind that if Robert Houstoune give not satisfacion of his fsedome fyne That the dracone convining and the rest of the dracons to be acquainted yerwith That some course may be taken anent the payt of the samyne.—

Clark — Item the sd day they appoynted the visitors To sprak with John

339

Clark anent his admissione.

Hunter Item they ordained Mr david Sharp
to wryt to hew hunter in ordour
and to the effect he may mak
himself friman with the sd
faculty.

13 of Mait 1670.

The qlk day the Visitors, John Hall
Mr david Sharp Mr Archibald
Grahame, Mr Charles Moüat,
John Robisone, daniell broune,
Williame Clydidsdaill, Adame
Grays, Androw Elphingstone, James
Thomsoune, John diddell & James
Baidwood Bring conveined in
New Hunter Hutchisons hospitall with the
admissioun foiresd New Hunter Who presented
ane suplicaune to the foiresd
faculty desyring yeby that he
may be admitted friman w them
Who being examined Was fund
qualified to practise the art of
phormacie And if it sall be fund

hereafter that the said Steu seele
be able to practise the airt of
chirurgie at any time hereafter
he is to be admitted yeto provyding
he have the approbation of one
phisieiane of his abilitie to practise
tho samyne Without any farder
fyne Nor twentie pundes which
he hath presentlie payed for his
admissione to the collector And to
pay his quarter comptes yearlie
Conforme to the rest of the frimen
of the sd faculltie And hath giorn
his oath as use is ―

Will Weir   They also all in on voice ordained
all papers relaiting to the faculltie
that ar in John Weirs hands to
be taken up from him What paines
he hath ben at that he be
satisfied yrfor except the taking
of Thomas Jacksone wt captione
in respect he apprehendit him wt
out ane warrant from the
Visitour ―

Jacksone   As lykwayes the sd facultie all in
on voice condescendit to take ane
band fra the said Thomas Jacksone
of fourtie pund as barrowd mony
in favors of the said calling And
to pay in præsentie to thrie
scoring pund six shilling eight
pennies of expensis they have
beine at And to give in band to
the calling not to practise any
thing of his calling ws in the brugh
of Glasgow or liberties yrof in all
tyme coming Upon which conditions
they ordained the sd Thomas to be
sett at libertie.—

Kennedie   The sd day the sd facultie ordained
twa rex dollars to be takine fra
George Kennedie for charges & expensis
they have bein at and the sd George
to be quatt heirafter in regard of
his old age.—

19 Sep° 1670.—
The gß day the Visitor Johne Hall

Visitor
Elphingstoune

James Thomsoune, Johne Robersoune
Andro Miller, Andro Elphingstoune
James Braidwood, James Hall, James
Wilsone, Johne flemyng Adam Gray
Wr david Sharpe, Wr Charles Mowat
daniell Broun + Wr diddell being
convenit in the Crafts hospitall
aurnt the electioun and making
choyse of ane of ther number to
be ther visitor for a year to come
who be pluralitie of votes made
choyce of the sd Andro Elphingstoune
to be ther visitor for the year to
come who being put accepted of
and gave his oath as use is.—

11 October 1670.
The glk day the visitors Johne Hall
Ard Bogill, daniell Broune, Wr
Charles Mowat, Wr Robersoune, George
dochhart, Wr flemyng Wr Houstoune
Adam Gray, James Thomsoune, James
Braidwood, Wr david Sharpe + James
Wilsone being convenit in the

(91) crafts hospitall anent the making choyce of ther masters for the year to come viz the sd visitor made choyce of the forsd Ard Bogill and James Thomsone for his tua And the calling be pluralitie of voices made choyser of the forsds Mr david Sharpe and Mr Charles Mowat for ther tives who being all plie accepted of and gave ther oathes as use is—

Boxmrs
The sd day also they made choyce of the forsdrs Adam Gray & John firmyng to be boxmrs for the year insuing who being plie accepted of and gave ther oathes as use is—

Act anent Binnie
The sd day they allowat the intaking of Tua hundrethe marks fra John Binnie be the said Ard Bogill and the said Androw Elphingstoune in plie payt of ffour hundrethe mark dew be him to the facultie by band—

Collectr Mowat
As also the said day they made choyce of the sd Mr Charles Mowat

to be ther collector till the niext
ordinar tyme of electioune who
gave his oathe as use is –

Act anent Houstoune Lykwayes the sd day they ordeand
the sd Rot Houstoune ather to pay
in his friedome fyne or then to give
in band gyfor putter glk if he refuis
that the samyne be representit to
the deaconvrimers & deacons to the
effect they may present the samyne
to the provest baillies & counsall

Act anent Wair As lykwayes they ordeand the forsd
Androw Elphinstoune & Ard Bog to
conveine Dr Wair niesser befor any
ane of the baillies of this brught
in order to the delyvering up of all
the papers he has belonging to the
sd faculter.–

Bands in the bose Item ther is in the bose Johne Binnies
band wt the band of corrobora.ne
of four hundreth marks wherof
twa payit in manner befor
mentioned. Item Wm Gilmour & his
caut.rs band of twa hundreth marks

St Johns drmur & his cautioun band of
ane hundreth merks, Johne Turnbulls
band & securities of his band for
four hundreth merks Mr Curries
band in a blank persons favors for
the behooff of the calling conteining
ten merks wt a precept of Robert
Harrisis. —

Clerk Item they conteinued Ro ffynnasoun
to be ther clerk till the next ordinar
tyme of electioun Who being put
accepit of and gave his oathe
as use is. —

officer As also conteinued Gabriell Cunynghame
to be ther officer for the year to come
who being put accepit of and gave
his oathe as use is. —

24 of November 1670
The qlk day Androw Elphingstoune Visitor
John Hall, Mr Archibald Grahame
James Thomsoun, Archibald Boyell, Mr
Charles Morrice, Mr david Sharp, John
Robisoun, Evan McNeiII, Ro houstoune

Adam Gray, Johne fleming and
Jo diddell Being conveined in the
craftis hospitall wt the sd visitour
Being last collector anent the
making of his compt of intromissions
wt the callings meanes as collector
yrto since hallowmes 1669   to
hallowmes 1670 And that of charge
and discharge in manner under
wrytten —

Charge

(92) Item the charger compters
himselffe witht the soume of
Twa hundrethe & thirtie four
pundis sixtein shilling ffoure
pennies quhilk was restand in
his handis to ballance his
accompt as collector the year
preceiding inde   234 – 16 – 0

Item with ane band of John
Binnies of ffour hundreth markis
with annuel therof fra Candlemes
1669 To lambmas 1670 And the

@rent of Two houndreth
mrkes that then rested
unpayit therof from the
said terme of Lambmas
1670 so Martinmas the said
year inde   292—13—4

Item Williame Gilmour & his
cau'nars band of Two
hundreth mrkes with the
@rent therof fra Martinmas
1669 to Martinmas 1670 inde 141—06—8

Item umqle John dennis and
his cau'nars band of Ane
hundreth mrk with @rent
fra Martinmas 1669 to
Martinmas 1670 inde   70—13—4

Item Robert Mairess precept
obtent be the calling conteining 20—03—0

ffridome fynes
Item he charges himself with
5 lib restand be James Wilsone
of his fyne Item be Cuthbert
Wilsone of his fyne 20 lib be
Ares Hunter of his fyne 20 lib

Item fra Ia: Crawford in
Cumnock and Georg Kinnindie
in air for raising of lris
of horning and captions agt
thim each of them tua
rix dollours is 11 lib. 12S
Thomas Harper of his fyn
8 lib Ro: Howstoune fyn of
66 lib. 13S iiii d:.

Quarter comptes
John Hall for 1670. 12S Wo: Ard:
grahame 1670 12S Androw
Elphingstoune 1670. 12S Wo:
Charles Mowat 1670. 12S William
Clydsdaill for 1669 12S James
Watt for 1665. 66 and 1670 1lib 16S..
James Wilsone 1661. 62. 63. 64. 66.
69 and 1670 4 lib. 4S James
Mowat Wraving years 6 lib
12S Thomas Harper tua year
and ane half 1 lib 10S Androw
Millar 1670. 12S daniell Broune
ffor se 1669 and 1670 1 lib 4S.
James Braidwood 1670. 12S

Johne Logane 1670 12S Adam
Gray 1670. 12S Archibald Bogill.
1670. 12S Mr david Sharp 1670
12S John Robieone 1670 12 S.
Iames Thomsone 1670 12S John
Aris for 1668. 69 and 1670 1lib 16S.
Robert Harris ffor elravine years
6lib 12S. Iames ffranck ye
nyne years 5lib 8S. Androw
Broune eight years 4lib 16S
Iames Aris for 1670 12S George
Lockhart for 1670 12S John
Liddell 1670. 12S Evan McnrilL
1670 12S Mr ffleming for 1669
and 1670 1lib 4S Robert Houstoune
for 1670. 12S.

Straingers quarter comptr
Allane Kirkwood 68 69 and 1670
3lib Iames Tobias for nyne years
at 30S per year 13lib 10S. John
Patersone for ten years 10lib
John Ewing three years and
ane half at 20S per year 3lib
10S Mr Alexander dunlop nyne

years at 30S per year 13.10S John
Mather ffourteine years at 20S
per year 14 ℔ John Pantoun
for 67. 68. 69 and 1670 at 30S per
year 6 ℔ Mathow Millar
tua year and ane half at
20S per year 2 ℔ 10S John
Stors for 1670 1 ℔ doctor Wallace
tru years at 30S per year
15 ℔ Adam Patersone for
1670 1 ℔ John Sproull for 66. 67
68. 69 and 1670 at 20S per year
5 ℔ Thomas Robertsone ane
year 2 ℔ John foster eight
years at 30S per year 12 ℔
Mr Thomas Younger for 69
and 1670 3 ℔ William Currie
for 69 and 1670 3 ℔ Mr Mun-
in Corbells for 1670 16S

  Summa of the haill charge
  extendis to   1137_05_04

   ffollowes the
   discharge

Item the compter recovers himself
wt the counts underwritten givne
to the persons after respret So
witt John Weir missd ffor his
bypast service 8 lib 14S And to the
post 4S So Gabriell Cunynghame
12S So Robert Andersone the
dracone conveiners office 1lb 4S.
So Alext Pilegrew for new lres
of horning at the callings
instance and caption yeon
And for his owne painis taken
ye in 30 lib So Patrick Bryce
collector to the deacone conveing
house Sex markis And to the
said Gabriell Cunyngham 12S.
Rt ffynnisone ffor his fiall
fra Michaelmes 69 to Michaelms
70 8 lib ffor the expenses for
the registratione of Jacksons
band dres of horning and
captione raised yeupon 7 lib
6S 8d ffor expenss of insiftmen
of John Turnbulls house 5 lib

(93)

Itt to ane poor man att the
visitours command 1 lib 4s Item
for thir hors hyres to Collaine
Campbells buriall 2 lib 14s.

ffridome fynes nott payit.

Item ouvand be James Wilsone
of his fyne 5 lib Item be Gilbert
Wilsone of his fyne 20 lib Item
be Thomas Harper of his fyne
8 lib Item be Robert Houstoune
of his fyne conforme to his
band 66 lib 13s 4d.

Item the compter secures himself
with ane band of Johne
Turnbulls containing   266 – 13 – 4

Item ane band of John Binnies
wherof ordir extand to the
calling   133 – 06 – 8

Item is mugle John drumries
band of   066 – 13 – 4

Item Williame Gilmours band of   133 – 06 – 8

Item is ane years rent of the
said Mr Rumble his band from
Martimas 1669 to Martimas 1670   016 – 00 – 0

Item with Robert Hairies precept
contening   020 – 03 – 0
Item to the sd Ro fyrmisour
that was dew to him be
the calling or band   069 – 13 – 4
            Non payment of quarter
            comptis of firmrie + others
Mr Archibald Grahame for the
year 1670 12S James Wilsone for
61. 62. 63. 64. 66 and 69 3 lib 12S
Thomas Harper for tua years
and ane half 2 lib 10S John
dogans for 70 12S Robert Hairies
for Elravine years 6 lib 12S –
Androw Browne for eight years
4 lib 16S James Watt for 65. 66.
1 lib 4S James Mowat for Elravine
years 6 lib 12S daniell Browne
for 69 and 1670 1 lib 4S John
dui for 68. 69 and 1670 1 lib 16S –
James frank yor for nyne
years 5 lib 8S Edan McneilL for
1670 12S.
            Non payments of quarter

compte of Strangers

Allane Kirkwood for 68. 69 and 1670
3 lib. James Tobiae for nyne
year 13 lib 10S John Patersone
for ten years 10 lib John
Ewing ffor ane year and ane
half 1 lib 10S. Mr Alexander
dunlop for nyne year 13 lib 10S.
John Mathie for fourtine
years 14 lib John Pantone
for 67. 68. 69 and 1670 6 lib Mathew
Myllar ffor tua year and
ane half 2 lib 10S John How
for 1670 1 lib doctor Wallace for
ten years 15 lib Adame
Patersone for 1670 1 lib John
Sproull ffor 66. 67. 68. 69 and 1670
5 lib Thomas Robertsone for
eleavine years 2 lib John foster
ffor eight years 12 lib Mr
Thomas younger for 69
and 1670 3 lib Williame
Currie for 68. 69 and 1670
3 lib Robert Muir in

Corbells 16s.

Summa of the haill
discharge extendis to Ane
thousand twentie nyne
poundis ane schillingis
monye Scay   1029 – 1 – 0

Swa charge and discharge
being compaired ther restes
in the compters handis to
ballances the forsaid charge
fourscoir aughtein pound four
S four prunris Scay   0098 – 04 – 4

Ilk the compter hes instantlie
delyvrd to Mr Charles Monod
present collector for the use
of the poor.

And therfor the sd faculten all in one
voice recours guytclames & simpliciter
now and for ever discharges the said
Androw Elphingstoune his airis and
exerors of his foirsd intromissioun
with the callings merins sins the
said terme of Hallowmes 1669 to Hallowmes
last bypast 1670 And of all actiouns

persewit and instance competent to
the sd calling against the said
Androw ye anent for ever And ordained
their clerk undersubscryband to
subscryve their pnts for them in favours
of the sd complen.

sic sub   R fynnisone Clk.

3 of Januarie 1671.

The qlk day the visitors John Hall, Mr
Charles Maxat, Mr Archibald Grahame,
daniell Browne Archibald Bogle, Robert
Houstoune and Adam Groye Being
convined in the crafts hospitall anent
their adhering or not adhering to the
Articles drawen up be the calling to
be presented to the phisitians who
ar desyring to be incorporat wt the
faculte To stand as ane aggriement
Betuixt the sd calling and them
who by pluralitie of votis condiscendit
That the foirsds articls alredda drawen
up upon half ane shirt of paper undr
their clerks hand should be observed

and keiped as ane aggriment as sd
is And nothing to be altered therof
As also they ordained the visitour
John Hall Mr Ard Grahame, John
Robisone and Archibald Bogill to
writt is the forsaids phisitianes
To the effect that they may present
the forsaids articlles to them And
that they should not condescend to
no mor And to heir what the sdrs
phisitians had to say theranent
And to report back againe to the
sd facultie their dilligence y2 of

douglas As lykwayes the sd day they
ordained the collector to give to
Williame douglas mess. for his service
done to the calling in the west
countrie their xxe dollours

2 of ffebruarii 1671

The 9th day the visitour, John Hall
Mr david Sharpe, Mr Archibald Grahame
John Robisone, Archibald Bogle, Robrt
Houstoune and Mr Charles Monac Burg

convent as sd is w James Loudoune
gairdiner in air who was charged
w horning at the facultie instance
for alledgit useing of thir calling And
the said calling have reeaminet him
upon his skill yeament And after
the said facultie reeaminet him
They fand him not able to reeerce
any pairt or poynt of thir calling
And thirfor in respect of ane band
givn in to the facultie that he
shall no dirrectlie nor indirectlie
hirafter dureing his lyftyme middle
w any pairt or poynt of medicine
pharmacie or chirurgie under the
paine totar quoties mentiond in
the sd band upon which conditions
the said facultie All in one voce
reeonens and simpliciter discharges
the said James Loudone of the forsd
charge of horning givn to him as
said is With his or horning raised
therupon And all that has followed
may or eann follow therupon the

samyne upon the conditionis aforesaid
be this prits for ever And in testimonie
of the said facultie ordained the
undersubscryband clerk to the said
calling subscrybe thir prits for them
and in thir names to the sd James
for his reconveratione in thir
premiss.—

7 of februarii 1671:—

The 9th day the visitour John Hall
Mr Archibald Grahame, Mr Charles
Morsat, Mr david Sharp Archibald
Bogle, John Robinsone, James Thomsone,
James Aris, James Braidwood, Andrew
Millar, Adam Grey, John fleming
John Liddell, Robert Houstoune and
Evar McnvilL Being convint in
hutchisons hospitall Anent the
writing of the forsdrs phisilians
To witt doctor John Colleuhoune, doctor
Mathow Birsbane and doctor Thomas
Hamiltone Anent thir dreyrs in
ordour to thir incorporatne wt the

facultie the said facultie in ordour
to ther dryers did condescend that
tua of ther number should meit
w^t the sds phisitians in ordour to
the settling and agreing w^t them
And the sdrs phisitians declairing
that it was ther intentiones to know
the mynd of the sd facultie whither
they had any right to the kings
patent as phisitians w^t in the brugh
of glasgow or not And the sd facultie
having putt the samyne to ane
vots It was votted be the sd Visitour
Mr Charles Brouat, Mr david Sharp
Ro Houstoun, John Robisoun and
Archibald Bogill that the sdrs
phisitians had any right yrto And
the rest of the sd facultie declaired
themselves non liquet And yr after
being condescendit be the sd facultie
Whither to admitt or not admitt of
the saids phisitians accordinglie By
pluralitie of vottes it was caried
That the forsaidrs phisitians should

be admitted upon fryday nixt
Being the tent of this instant month
of februarii.—

21 of Aprill 1671.—

The qlk day being convint the
deacon and severall of his brithrine
of the calling comprised Thomas
Brunnill in Blackwood in obedience
of our band granted be him to the
sds facultie Being takin w^t caption
for using and usurping some pairtis of
Chirurgie under our penaltie for his
sd appeirance befor the facultie betuixt
and the first of Maii nixt to come
In ordour to his reeaminacun of the
forisdrs pairtis of chirurgie And being
reeamined be thim yeanent Was funde
altogether ignorant of the knowledge yof
And in respect yeof the sd Thomas
Brunnill of his own consent Hath
granted our obleismint in favours of
the sd calling of the dait hinof
oblidging him in all tyme hireafter not

362

to middle or use any poynt of chirurge
medicine or pharmacie under the
paine of fourtie poundes toties quoties
Qlk band the calling ordainit to be
putt in the box for preservacone And
yrfor in regaird of tho foirsd
obleismentt grantit to the sd facultie
thay all in on voice ordainnes ane
discharge to be grantit to the sd Thomas
of his foirsd band for his appeiranc
And of the foirsd lres of captione With
all that has may or cane fallow
yrupon. To be sub. be Robert ffinnisone
thir clerk for the sd Thomas his
reconoracone yrof who payd to the
collector three hundrs for defraying
of charges.

25 of Aprile 1671.

The qlk day bring convenit the
deacone and severall of his brethrine
of the calling Comprired John Loudone
gairdiner in Auchinerris wt in the
parochine of st cullochis who heaving

being takin ws exceptioun at the
callings instance ffor using and
usurping some pairtes of chirurgie
did give band for his appeirance
befor the sd faculties of chirurgians
wtin the sd brugh in ordour to
his examinacoun And being examined
be the sd faculties upon the sds pairtes
of chirurgie ffor qlk he was chalengd
was be the sd calling found altogither
ignorant of the samyne And in
respect therof the sd John Loudoune
of his owne consent hath granted
ane oblaisment in favours of the
sd calling of the dait heirof Oblidgeing
him in all tyme heirafter to meddle
or use any poynt of chirurgie, medicine
or pharmacie under the paine of
fourtie pundis totis quoties Qlk
band the calling ordainit to be putt
in the box for preservacoun And yefor
in regaird of the forsaid oblaisment
grantit to the sd faculties they all
in one voyce ordaines and discharge

to be granted to the sd John of his
foirsd band ffor his apperirance And
of the foirsd lres of captions with
all that hes may or canr fallow
yrupon To be sub br Robert symisone
thir clerk ffor the said John his
recornorae ur yrof who payit to the
collector thrie pundrs ffor defraying
of charges —
Therafter the calling queitt the forsd
thrie pounds —

21 of Junii 1671 —

Act anent
donald The 9th day the deacons John Hall
Archibald Boggils, Mr david Sharp
and Adam Gray being convrint
Consentit To lend ane hundreth
mirks of the poors meanes To John
donald mrsr as prinll and Mr
John Cruickre and Archibald dennrston
indwellars in glasgow as cautnrs
for him upon thir band And
ordanrs Mr Charles Mowat thir
collector To delyvr the samyn

accordinglie.—

7 of September 1671.

The 9th day the visitour John Hall
Archibald Bogill, James Thomsoune
John ffleming, John Liddell, Andrew
Millar, James Watt, Adame Gray
James Braidwood, Mr david Sharp, George
dockhart & Mr Charles Mowat being
convenit in the croytis hospitall wt
John Hall barbour sometyme indweller
in Edr now residenter wt in the sd
brugh of glasgow who gave in his
supplicacne to the sd facultie dreyring
grbyt to be admitted as ane of ther
number to excercise the office of
ane barbour which dreyre the sd
facultie thought most reasonable and
grfor and in respect of his burges
and gild brother ticket rexhibitit
befor them did all in on voice
admitt the said John Hall frieman
wt them to practise the office of ane
barbour allanarlie And ordainit him

(46)

366

To pay fourtie pundrs scotis money
to ther collretoun ffor his fridome fyne
Qlk he did instantlie pay in
accordinglie And gave his oath as
use is—

Ordour for
giving back
20 lib to Johne
Halls
Thirafter the said facultie hraving
takin to ther considraoun the
respect, kyndnes, favour & courtacie
the sd John Halls had showen to
the said calling and guid dids done
be him to them They all in one
voice Ordaint ther colleetor to give
back Twentie pundrs as the equall
halff of the sd fridome fyne Qlk
was done accordinglie—

donnalds
100 m̃ allowit
The sd day also the sd facultie all
in one voice did allow and approve
of the outlending of the hundreth
markis to John donald and his
caͣutions—

Aet anent
Howstoune
and Gilmour
As lykwayes the said day they ordain
the colleetor to speak to Robert Houstoune
to provyd his hundreth markis againis
Martinmes next And to continow

the insyking of ung^ll Williame
Gilmours monry dew by him and
his ca°nus to the sd calling be
band wntile the sd trme of
Martinmas nrset to come –

=2 September 1671 –

Visitor
Bogill

The 9th day The Visitor John Hall
Mr david Sharp, Mr Charles Michat
James Thomsoune, Archibald Bogill
Georg Lockhart, Adam Gray, James
Watt, Robert Houstoune, Evn M°nill
Jo ffleming, John Lus, James Braidwood
Jo Hall yo Bing convenit in the
Crafts Hospitale anent thir making
choyse of ane of thir number to
be thir visitor or deacon for the
insuing yrir who by pluralitie of
votrs elected Archibald Bogill to be
visitor who being prsent gave his
oathe de fideli administratioune
he had accepted   the
sd office

368

13 October 1671

The 9th day the visitor, John Hall
James Thomsoune, Robert Houstoune
John Fleming, John Liddell, Mr
Charles Miñal, George Lockhart, Adam
Gray, James Fredwood, dow Hall
yor, Mr David Sharp and Mr and
Grahame having conveined have
elyted William Stirling is Robert
Ffinnersoune then late clerk they
be pluralitie of votes have admitted
the sd Wm Stirling to be their clerk
ad vitam et ad culpam who
being put accepted and gave his
oath as use is. —

As lykewise the visitor did nominate
for the insuing year for glen mastes
who gave their oathes as use is
as follows

for visitor
Andrew Elphingstoune
James Thomsoune
for the calling
Adam Gray

George Lockhart
Rose masters
Robert Houstoun
John fflemming.–
Robert Smellie officer for
the Houstoun admitted and
sworne.–

The facultie ordaines Mr Charles
Muat their collector to give in
his collector accompts upon the
27 or last dail of Octor instant
or first or second dayes of
november next to come.–

Printie Young to George Lockhart

The said day John Young cow-
laur to John Young wallethincar
Ingleston is bookrd prentise to
George Lockhart in his calling of
chirurgry and pharmacy for seven
yers space croy two yers for mril
and six ffrae his entrie glR is the
twentie aught day of September 1671
bring the dail of the ducdenter
past betwiset them thereanent who
hes made faith and hes payit to

Mr Charles Mowat present collector
ffyve punds Scots.—

(97)

Penult day of October 1671.—
The 9th day the Visitor, John Hall
Mr Archibald Grahame, Mr david
Sharp, Mr Charles Mowat, Robert
Houstoun, ever McNeill, Andrew
Elphingstoun, Adam Gray, George
Lockhart, James Thomsone, Jo⁰
ffleming, John Liddell, James Watt
John Hall barbour Being conveened
in Hutchisonnes hospitall Compeired
Andrew Ralstoun garner who presentit
to the sd faculta ane supplica°n
desyring therby That he might be
examined of his practise of
Chirurgerie and efter tryall might
be admitted freeman with them—
Who being examined wer found
qualifud for making grein treit
of herbis and uther Ingredientis
yrof And to cure grein woundis
wher ther is no loss of substance

Admission
Andrew
Ralstoun

and to cure simple fractures and
dislocations And did admitt him
thirto allanerly And hereby discharges
the said Androw from using any
farder prts of chirurgerie untill
his farder tryall Who hes produceit
his burges and gild brother ticket
and payed to the collector twelve
punds Scots for his present admissioune
and gave his oathe de fideli
administratione as use is.—

<del>Act anent</del>
<del>Jonet stood.</del> The sd day compeirit also Jonet stood
Being citd befor the faculty upon
a complaint givin in aganist her
for giving phisick to Barbara Hart
servitor to James Muir merchand
the tyme of hir service q of shoe dard
Who being reexamined thereupon did
in presence of the sd faculty confess
that shoe had givin to the sd
Barbara the night befor shoe dard
certain vinice tryacle As als that
shoe gave her that day shoe dard
some jalap. Wherupon the Joined

faculta having sent for the sd
James Muin his master for ther
jardin clring in the sd master
ats being by them reeximined therupon
dreclard that frae the tyme that
the sd Jonet stood gave his servant
that phisick tho frae then furth
vomited until shoe reepyred. Alths
being takin by the foirsd faculta
to ther serious consideraoun they
recommendd her to the magistrats
for her condigne punishment and
for procuring of ane act upon her
oblissing her never to give or
preserve any phisick to any prsons
gtewin at anytime hirrsf shoe
being neither burges or gild brother or
having right therto by her husband
nor having entres nor priviledg wt
in the burgh of glasgow.

Continuaoun
of the
collector

the sd day the foirsd faculta all
in on voyce did continow Wr Chanes
Murat to be ther collector untile
the nixt ordinar tyme of ther

election who being put accepted and
gave his aith as use is.—
The sd day Robert Houstoun hes
payed in to the boxe ffourtie pounds
Scots in satisfactioune of his friedome
fyne And tho faculter have in
testimony they will exact no mor
from him yrof, givin up to him his
band qlk he had grantit to them.—

The last day of October 1671.—
The qlk day ther being conveined in
the visitors hous The Visitor, James
Thomsoun, Mr david Sharp, Mr Ard
Grahame, Mr Charles Unnat, Andrew
Elphingstoun, Georg Lockhart, Rot
Houstoun, Wer Mc̄neill, Adam Gray
Andrew Ralstoun, John ffleming. John
Liddell. They have lent to the sd
Mr Ard Grahme at his desyre
Twentie pundis Scots ffor qlk he hes
givin band payeable at Whitsounday
1672 with a Annes Rent and is
put in the boxe.—

The sd day Mr Charles Michal being
conveined w the foirsd faculty as
collector for making compt with
the faculties mrmrs of his intromission
thrwith sine the 24 November 1670
to the 12 of Nor 1671 and yt of charg
and discharg in maner underwrit
glk wrs red and approven and
ordred to be booked

Charg

Imprimis the Compter charges
himself with the somme of
of 98 lb 4S 4d receivid be him
fra Andrew Elphingstoune
last collector glk wrs resting
in his hand the former
yrir of his intromissioun   lb . S . d
inds.   98 - 4 - 4

Item with the somme of 200
mrnk resting of Jo Binnies
bond for 400 mrnk w the
Ornt yrof fra Lammess
1670 to Martimes 1671 inde 143 - 16 - 8

It a band of umqll John denny
and his executors for 100
merks princll wt @rent fra
Mertimes 1670 to Mertimas b)inds 070 – 13 – 4

It a band grantit be Williame
Gilmour and his ex'rs for
200 mrks pll witt @rent fra
Mert 1670 to Mert 1671 inde 141 – 06 – 8

It do Turnbulls band for 400
mrks pll wt @rent fra Mert
1669 to Mert 1671 inde 298 – 13 – 4

(98) It Robert Henris precept conteining
the soume of 20 lib Scay 020 – 03 – 0

ffirdoune fynes

Item the compter charges himself
witt 5 lib resting be James
Wilson of his fyne It witt
20 lib resting be Gilbert Wilson
of his fyne It witt 8 lib resting
be Thomas Harper It witt
66 lib 13 s 4d of Robert Howstoun
his fyne It witt 20 lib of
John Scale his fyne It witt
6 lib 13 s 4d resting of Wm Curra

his fyne. It with 6 lib 13 S. 4 d
of Groy Lockhart his prentis
entric –

      Quarter comptes –

Archibald Bogill for 1671 . 12 S
John Hall for 1671. 12 S . Mr
And Grahine for 1670. 1671 . 24 S
Mr david Sharp for 1671 . 12 S
Andrew Elphingstoun 1671. 12 S
Mr Charles Murat for 1671. 12 S
John Robisoun 1671. 12 S. James
Watt for 1665 : 1666 and 1671 36 S
James Wilsoun for 1661. 62. 63. 64
1665. 69 and 1671. 4 lib. 4 S James
Murat for 12 yeirs 7 lib 4 S
Thomas Harper 3 yeirs and
a half 2 lib 2 S. Andrew Milne
for 1671. 12 S daniel Broun 1669
1670 and 71. 36 S. John Logane
1670 & 1671. 24 S. Adam Gray
1671. 12 S. James Thomsoun 1671
12 S. John Ders for 4 yeirs 2 lib 8 S
Robert Henris 12 yeirs 7 lib 4 S
James ffrank 10 yeirs 6 lib.

Andrew Brown 9 yeirs 5lb 8S
James derr 1670 and 71. 24S
Geog Lockhart 1671. 12S. John
diddell 1671. 12S doir m^c urill
1670 and 71. 24S Robert Houstoun
1671. 12S James Braidwood 1671
12S John flenning 1671. 12S –
    Strangers quarter compt..
Allan Kirkwood 4 yeirs at 20S
pr yeir 4 ttb. James Tobias
10 yeirs at 30 ttb per yein
15 ttb. John Patersoun 2 yeir
at 20S per yeir 2 ttb. John
ewing 2 yeirs and a half
at 20S per yeir 2 ttb 10S. Mr
Alexr dunlope 10 yeirs at 30S
pr yeir 15 ttb. Jo^n mathie 15
yein at 20S pr yein 15 ttb John
Paulan 5 yeirs at 30S pr yein
7 ttb 10S Mathew muller 3 yeirs
and a half at 20S pr yeir
3 ttb 10S John Aois 2 yeirs 2 ttb
doctor Wallace 11 yeirs at 30S
pr yein 16 ttb 10S. Adam Paterson

two yeirs 2 ℔ John Spreul
6 yeirs 6 ℔ Thomas Robisoun
12 yeirs at 20 S pr yeir 12 ℔
John foster 9 yeirs at 30 S pr
yeir 13 ℔ 10 S. Mr Thomas Young
3 yeirs at 30 S pr yeir 4 ℔ 10 S
William Currie 4 yeirs at 20 S
pr yeir 4 ℔ Robert Muir two
yeirs 1 ℔ 12 S. Hew Hunter two
yeirs 2 ℔

    Summe of the wholl charg
    extends to   1092 _ 12 _ 00

    ffollowes the discharg
Item the Compter recours and
discharges himself with the
soumes of mony underwrin
givin to the persons efter
mentionat viz.t To Gabriel
Cunnynghame 2 ℔ 16 S And
to the clerks man 13 S. It.
to the deacon conviners officer
24 S. It. to John Weir messer
11 ℔ 12 S It. to wm douglas messer

8 lib 14S It to John donald 2 lib
10S It to the deacon conviner
house 6 lib 13S 4d It to thee oficer
12S It for regraters of Wm
Gilmour's band 20S It for
having ye upon 2 lib 18S It
to georg Pollok at the faculties
direction 6S It to another
poor man 12S It to the
present preciter to be given
to the drummer 24S It to
the town's officer for bringing
a woman befor the Bailie
2S

freedome fynes unpayit
Item awand be James Wilsone
of his fyne 8 lib It & Gilbert
Wilsone 10 lib It be Robert
Houstoun of his fyne conform
to his band 66 lib 13S 4d It
be Thomas Harper of his
fyne 8 lib
Item the compter discharges
himself with ane band of

John Binnie grof only resting
to the calling 200 merks of
princi somme and @rent
since downbruns 1670 to Mert
1671 dude in haill   143 _ 6 _ 8

It wt umqll John drunnes band
of 100 mk prll and a yers
@rent at Mert 1671 mdr   070 _ 13 _ 4

It w William Gilmours band
of 200 mks and a yrs @rent
grof at Mertimes 1671 mdr   141 _ 6 _ 8

It w Turnbulls band of 400 mery
with two yeirs @rent at
Mert 1671 mdr   298 _ 13 _ 4

It w the remainder of Ro
 Anes precept   020 _ 03 _ 0

    Non payments of yeirs compts
    of townsmen and uthirs

Mr Aird Grahme 1670 & 1671. 24 S.
James Watts 1665 and 1666. 24 S
James Wilson 1661. 62. 63. 64. 66
69. 71. 4 lib. 4 S. James Umal 12
yeirs 7 lib 4 S. Thomas Harper
3 yeirs and a half 2 lib 2 S.

Daniel Broun 3 yeirs 36 S. Son
Logan 1671. 12 S. Son legs two
yeirs glk wer forgivin 24 S.
Robert Henris 12 yeirs 7 lib 4 S.
James ffrank younger. On
yeirs 6 lib. Andrew Broun
nyn yeirs 5 lib 8 S. James Lees
1671. 12 S. John Liddell 1671. 12 S
Non payments of opter-
compts of Strangers at 20 S
per yeir. followeth.—

(99) Allan Kirkwood 1668 69 70 and
1671 inde 4 lib. John Patersoune
11 yeirs inde 11 lib. John Ewing
two yeirs and a half 2 lib
10 S. Mathew Miller 1671 20 S.
Hew Huntar 1671. 20 S. John
Mathie 15 yeirs 15 lib. John
How 1671. 20 S. Adam Patersone
1670 + 1671 2 lib. Thomas Robisoune
12 yeirs 12 lib. Wm Currie 4 yeirs
4 lib. Rot Muir in Gorball
for 1671 he payes 16 S.—

ffollowes the non payts

of grter comple at 30S
a yrir.—

James Lobien 10 yrins 15 tt— Inr
alexr dunlope 10 yeirs 15tt
John Pantan 6 yrirs 7tt 10S
doctor wallace 11 yrirs 16li8 10S
John ffoster 5 yrirs 7 tt 10S..
Inr Thomas Younger 3 yrirs
4 tt 10S—

Item the compter recouers
himself wt Sr donalds band
to the Calling dailie in
dunie 1671 bring @rent for
While last contraning the
Soume of   066 – 13 – 4

It wt the Soume of thritta
pund nyn shilling debursit
be him at the visitors
direction to James paires
to make up to him 500
mks lent by the calling
conforme to his band   030 – 09 – 0

It to a poor man at the
visitor direction 4S And to

To ffinnieson late clerk to
the calling for his fiall
from hallowmes 1670 to hallowmes
1671   008 _ 04 _ 0

   Suma of the haills dischay
   extends to Ane Thousand
   thriescoir nyne punds
   savintein shilling four penns 1069 _ 17 . 4
Swa Charg and Discharg brug
compaint ther rests in the
compters hand to ballance
the foirsd Charg the somme
of twentie two punds fourtein
   shilling aught penners Scots 0022 _ 14 _ 8
And thairfor the sd faculter
Allan on voyce recovvrs quyt-
claims and for now and evir empire
discharge ther sd Mr Charles Innnat
his airrs and ssers of his foirsd
intromissiouns wt the callings menns
fra the foirsd twentie fourth day
of Novr 1670 to the twelve day of Nov
last bypast And of all other prsent
and instanes compitent to thim

therfor be this pñts for ever And
ordaines the ther clerk undersubscryband
to subscryve this pñts for them in
favours of the sd compter and his
foirsds..

sic sub:. H Stirling clk.

The fourtein day of december 1671 yiers..
The 9th day Being conveined in the
hous of Ard Rogills present visitor
the sd Archibald, John Hall late
baillie Mr Archbald Grahme Mr david
Sharp, Andrew Elphingstoune Mr Houstoun
Andrew Ralstoun, Adam Gray John ferrie
Jo hall barbour and James Watt
Compeirit Mr Robert Naper broye
to the Laird of Killmakill befor
them Who being interrogat by the
sd visitr, If according to his former
desyres he wold enter friesman
wt them who answered that he
intendit not to enter tradsman
albeit he had in order yeto givin
his band to the deacon conveiners

hous for his gild brothers fyne Bot
altogether refusit to enter with the
sd facultie only he declared he
was content & offered to give bond
to the sd visitor ffor himself and
in name of the sd facultie not
to make any compositiounes nor
ansuer any phisicians receit nor
to use any pairt of Chirurgia or
pharmacie at any tyme to come
under the paine of ane hundreth
punds scots penaltie totius quoties
And yt sine his setting up he
had not usit anything relating to
aither of thes airts - qrupon he offered
to give his solemn oath at subscrybing
of the sd bond qlk being done he
respected yt might satisfie them
Qlk premiss being takem by the
sd faculty to ther serious consideratio
they declarit to him ther consent
to his desyre upon his granting
ane performance of his offer And
for yt effect ordred the bond of yt

matter and tenner foirsd to be
drawin agains thir next meitting
The sd day Compirit also Iohn
Hall son to the sd Iohn Hall
late Baillie who gave in his
supplica'ns to the sd faculty
dosyring therby to be admittit upon
tryals to the exercise of Chirurgry
and pharmacie Qlk desyr they
thought reasonable and for y' effect
ordained Mr And Grahm, Mr david
Sharp, Andrew Elphingstoun and
Mr houstoun or any two of them
to be his key masters and to see
the compositions underwritten made
up in order to his tryall in pharmacie
viz Elect. diaphionicon, empl diapalma
Gratum, santalinum Crochisi albi
Rasis pilulæ cochiæ minoris and
ordains the foirsds compositions to
be publictie producit before the sd
faculty upon the twentie aur or
twentie fyft dayes of this instant
as they sall have best occasioun

Act anent
Mr Hall younger
for his trys

(100)

to meet And ordaines y{t} the sd Ioh
Hall be publictlie reexamined by
them the sd day upon the prts of
Chirurgerie befor his admission And
y{t} upon his tryall and reexaminacn
foirsd they wold grant his dreyre
as they found him qualifeid —

25 dec{r} 1671 —
At the keads hospitall —
The 9{th} day convened the pnt visitor
John Hall late baillie, Wr and
brahins, Wr Charles Muat. Andrew
Elphingston — Iorr Mcneill Rt houstoun
Adam Gray, Andrew Ralstoun, Io{r}
ffleming, Io{r} liddell, Iorr hall barbour
James Watt and James Braidwood
And having perusil the last
erdrumt Cohrrin Wr Rt napn had
offred to the visitor and faculte ane
band therby oblrissing him not to
make at any tyme w{t} in ther
bounds Compositions nor to ansuir
any phisitians receits nor to use

or exerce any prt of Chirurgery or
pharmacie under the paine of
ane hundreth punds scots toties
quoties And to give his solemn oath
that he had not since his setting
up used any of thes airts for
the tyme past; Who being callit by
the bhallie offen to the sd facultie
at ye direction Compeired not to
have performed what he had at
the last meeting promised to
doe and is perticularly abov writn
Therfor the sd Visitor and thes
of the facultie present remine
contradicente Ordained that the
Visitor and the sd Baillie Hall
sould goe to the sd Mr Rd hapen
and require him to subscryve
ane bond of the tennor forsd
ofh the facultie had caused make
And to compeir before the faculty
to depone as sd is And upon his
refusall to make thir applicaōne
to the magistrats or to use all

legall wayes for compelling him
thirto And y^t it sould be doon
by them in order thereunto They
dreland ye approba'ne therof And
hirby obleiss them to stand and
abyd y^{at} And ordainrs them
to report ther diligne at the
nrset meeting.

Act of admission — Lykeas the sd day compeirit also
John Hall youngest — John Hall eldest laull sone to
the sd John Hall late Bailler in
obedisne to our former act of the
calling in ther last sdrminut And
producit upon the table in presene
of the sd faculty the reseve composg
ordered to be made be him as his
say byor his say masters Who being
prsent declared they did sie the
sd John Hall wreigh the simples
and mixe the same orderlie And
efter inspection takin by the haill
faculty pnt yrof They did allow
and approve of each of the sd
compositiones made be him as

wsell dispensit and as yf they had
been doon be on of a longer practise
And having reexamined him in
ther presence upon the termes of
the arts both of Chirurgrry and
pharmacie quinto he made pirfyt
answers They all in on voyce
declared That they found him
able and sufficiently qualified both
for the practise of chirurgrie and
pharmacie and all prts relating
thrito And yftir production of his
burges and gild brother tiekit did
admitt and receive him as Chirurg.
and pharmacian who payit for
his admissioun To the collector
ffyve punds sextein shilling scots
money And gave his aith as
use is: —

    The Twentie aught day of
    februarii 1672 yeirs. —
The gfth day being convrined in the
hous of Archibald Bogill pnt visitor

the said Archibald, John Hallers
eldest and youngest Andrew Elphingstoun
Robert Houstoun, Evin M'nrill
Adam Gray, Jo[hn] ffleming, James
Thomsone and John Liddell, Comperand

Act of admission
William Sempill
of dalmoot

befor them William Sempill of dalmoot
in obedience to our band grantit
be him So them ffor his apperance
befor them And tutiring w[i]t[h] them
q[ui]lk was redelyvered to him, who
is admitted to practise Chirurgery
and y[a]t becaus he were found
qualifeid efter reexaminacone upon
some poynts of Chirurgery And
had servit as prentisse to James
frank somtyme visitor of the s[ai]d
calling As an Act y[ai]rupon daitit
the 4 of d[ecembe]r 1660 sein by the s[ai]d visitor
and members joisd of the s[ai]d
faculty at lenth beiras With this
express provisioun That he sall not
practise any part of chirurgerie
w[i]t[h]in the brigh of glasgow or
territorie y[air]of untill sic tyme as

he be admitted burges or gild
broye of the sd brugh under
the paine of aur hundreth punds
Scots money totiss quotiss he sall
be found to transgresse And is
ordainned to giv in bond for
twintie punds scots for his admission
pyrable at whilsonday nixt and
to pay yirly for the use of the
poor twelve shillings Scots who gave
his oath as use is._

(101)

                    The aught day of March
                    1672 yeeres._
The glk day conveined in the
sd And Bogill, visitor his house
The sd And Bogill, son Hallan
eldest & youngest, Andrew Elphingstoun
Mr Charles Maat, George dockhart
James Watt, son Hall barbour,
Adam gray, Mr Houstoun, son
fleming & son diddell Compeired
befor them James Weir put servitor
to doctor John Colquhoun professor

Act of admissons
James Weir

of medicine who gave in his supplicacone
to the faculty desyring therby to
be admittit upon tryall to the
exercise of Chirurgerie having
learned the same (as he declared)
from his father yet living. Qlk
desyre being found reasonable
he wes examined by the foirsd
facultie upon the poynts of Chirurgrie
And being found qualifiet were
admitted by them to practise
Chirurgry and wes ordained to
pay to the collector for his admission
twentie marks And to pay yeirly
for the use of the poor twelve
shilling scots who (having producit
his burges ticket in pñc of the
foirsd visitor the sds Ioh Mälles
eldest + youngest, Wr And Grahme
Ion diddell + divers uyrs) gave
his aith as use is.—

The aughtein day of Junii 1672.
The qlk day Convened in the

Visitors Chamber. The Visitor John
Hall late bailie, John Hall his sone
grorg lockhart, Adam gray, James
Weir, John ffleming and James Bredcom
who callit for William dowglas messr
who had the trust of the lres
of horning ffor charging through
the countrie And of ther lres of
captioun And ordained him to
delyver up the samin to the visitor
or clerk betwixet and the twentie
day of this instant And ordains
the lres to be givin to Jo donald
messr to charg such who sale
be givin to him in a list by the
visitor And the sd John donald
to returne the lres and execucours
back to the visitor And ordains
Jon Sod to be writtin to so come
and ruin againes the fair of
glasgow.

Glasgow Twentie nynth of August 1672.
The sd day conveined in And

Anent Wm dowglas
messr & Jo donald
admission to be
yt messr

Bogill Visitor his Chamber the sd Ard
dolm Halkes eldest and yr and
youngest. Mr Charles Miriat, Iames
Thomsone, grorg lockhart, Adam
gray, Robert Houstoun, dr Ileming
dr Liddell all members of the
faculty Befor gou ther wes a
blank in originis
supplicaone givin be   Gavan
in Grinok for the pnt a prisoner
Act anent Gavan
in anrr to his
supplicaone.
in the tolbuith of glasgow at the
sd faculty ther instane ffor
transgressing ye acts and bring
ane infirmane in exerceing ealls
pits of ther airts of Chirurgry or
pharmacie within ther boundrs;
grby the said   Gavan dreyred
to be sett at libertye The gth
supplicaone being considered by
the sd faculty Thry condescended
to the supplicants dreyer upon
this conditiouns he sould befor
he wes sett at libertye find them
sufficient caoune not to exerce
any pits of the airts of Chirurgry

or pharmacie is in their boundars
of this Charter untill he wer
guytted w^t the sd faculties and made
friemen under the paine of ane hundy
punds Scots toties quoties he sould be
found to contraveen the same And
y^t he sould pay to don donald mrs
for apprehending of him sex punds
scots in satisfaction for his paines
And this their answer they ordaine
their clerk to return subt w^t his
hand at their direction.—

Anent charging The sd day the faculty ordained
Robisone don donald mrss to charg w^t horning
Robison soulder for intruding
himself on ther priviledges betwixt &
the nixt meeting.—

(102)
first day of sept^r 1672.—
The 9th day Conveened the visitor,
don Halls eldest and youngest, Mr
Charles Munat, Mr ard Grahme, Roi
M^{c}neill, R^t Rowstoun, James Thomsoun
Adam Gray don diddell; Andrew

Miller, James Braidwood _

Admissioun
John Lod _

Compeired personallie John Lod apothecarie
in Kilmarnock in obedience to ane
charg of horning given to him at
the faculties instance ffor practising
pharmacie not being entred w[t]
them as frieman And desyred to
be reexamined in order to his
admissioun w[t] them as ane of
ther number who being tryed
and reexamined by the s[d] facultie
put wes found sufficientlie qualified
for using & practising of pharmacie
allanarlie Qurunto they admitted
him with this express provisioun
That he sall not use or practise
the same within the brugh of glasgow
or territorie yrof untill he be
burges and gild brother of the s[d]
brugh under the paine of ane
hundreth punds scots toties quoties
he sall be found to transgress
Who made faith as use is And
payed in to M[r] Charles Muat

ther colledtor Swentie four punds scotz
for his friedome fyne and is to pay
yirly for the use of the poor Swentie
shilling scots.—

Admission
Mr alexr Porter

And Lyklyke the sd day Compririt·
also Mr Alexr Porter apothreacur in
brith in obedience to ane uther charg
of horning givin to him for plactiong
pharmacie not being entird wt the
sd faculties Who upon his desyre
to be reexammed upon his qualificaons
and upon the faculters finding him
sufficiently qualifird yttir tryale for
practising pharmacie allowwrly was
by them admittd thirto Also not·
practising the sam wtin the tenitorie
or brugh of glasgow untill he be burges
and gild brother yrof under the forsd
fyn botirs quotirs he sald contraverme
the sam who made faith as use
is And payed in to Mr Charlrs
Muirat Colledtor Swentie four punds
scots for his friedome fyne And
is to pay yirly for the use of

the poor Twentie shilling Sess
mony.–

Glasgow the Twentie Sept: 1672.–
The 9th day convened in the Crafts
hospitall The put visitor Jon Hall
late Baillie, Jon Hall his cour.
Mr david Sharpe, Mr Charles Innat
James Thomsone, Mr Ard Grahme
Andrew Elphingstoune, geoy lockhart
Ths Houstoun, Jon Liddell, James
Birdwood, Adam Gray, Evar Mc neill
Andrew Miller, Andrew Ralstoun
Jon fleming, Jon Hall barbour &
James Weir members of the facultie
Anent the electioune of ane of
ther number to be visitor of ther
calling for ane yeir to come Who
be pluralitie of votts did continow
Archibald Bogill To be ther visitor
for the yeir ensuing Who being put
accepted and gave his aith of
fidelitie as use is.–
And siclyke the foirsd day The visitor

400

Clerk confirmit

and members of faculty put Ratifyed
and approved of the clerks former
admission wt the act yeupon the
preceiding yeir ad vidam or culpam.

Officer

And ordaines Jon Hall barbour to
be officer for the nixt yeir & Rot
Smellie to serve in his place
conforme to use and wont.—

Glasgow the 14 of Nov 1672 yeirs.—
The qlk day conveened in Hutchisouns
hospitall And Bogill put visitor, Jon
Hall late Baillie, Mr david Sharp
and Charles Muat, Georg lockhart
John Hall youngest Adam Gray
Mr And Grahme, Jon Hall barbour
Jon diddell, James thomsoune, Androw
Elphingstoune, Evin Mc neill, Rot
houstoun, James Braidwood, James
Weir and Jon fleming.—

(103)

Anent ther nominaoun of a collector
quter masters, box masters + the
particulars esd mentionat they be
pluralitie of votts make choyce of

Ralstoun Collector | Andrew Ralstoun to be collector for
the yeir ensuing untill the ordinary
tymes of ther election —

Qter mrs | And sielyke the sd visitor did
nominat and appoynt for him
Mr david Sharp and James Thomsoune
to be qter mrsts for the sd yeir
ensuing And the sd faculty did
by pluralitie of vots nominat and
elect Andrew Elphingstoune, Robert
Houstoun and Adam Gray who
being put accepted and made
faith as use is —

Box mr | And sielyke the sd day did
nominat and elect the sd Adam
Gray and Jon diddels to be box
mr who being put accepted and
gave ye aithes as use is —

Act anent
paying to the
minr 3 lib | It the sd day It is ordained that
Mr douglas mrsst sall have for
his painis in executing ye lrs of
horning against severall prsons
conforme to the recenrs givin
in be him Thrie punds scots And

the collector to pay it—

Act ann.t a discharg to Don Donald for exe[cutin] acc.nt of his exe.—

It ordaines a discharg to be granted and sub.t in favors of Don Donald mess.t for exe ffunds sects as a yeirs and a half accompts of the soume he is indew to the facultie ffor his bygain painer and service to them.—

act ann.t changing the officer yeirlie and every intrant paying to the box.—

And sieliyke the sd day the foursds members of facultie taking to their consideracoune the loss and damadg they sustein through ane former act gibg every intrant wer ordaint to serve as officer successivlie red ye admissione within this brugh So y.t in some yeirs then will be brurades admitted and yearly moe addit. It is after deu consideracoune had yr.of for the use and behove of the poor statut and ordaint that all who have been admittit as members yr.of since the admissioune of Don Hall barbour And who sall be hreafter admittit ffrimen w.t

Act ordains every intrant to pay at his admission to the collector in lieu of the officers fiall a dollar.

the sd calling sall pay to the
Collector ane rise dollor at ye sd
admission for the officers fialls and
ordains thes alredy admittit who
have not servil by thimselvos or
some oyr as officers to pay the
same to the collector, and declares
that the calling will hireed satisfy
ther officers thimselves Conforme quento
ye was instantly payit to Andrew
Ralston Collector be Son Hall youngest
ane sone to Baillie Hall ane rise
dollor. It Son Halls Barbour payit
to Tho Smallie ye officer his rise dollor
for his fialls this yeir ensuing.

The Ratificon of the Kings Gift procurit by Baillie Hall delyverit or put in the box.

It the sd day John Hall laic
Baillie producit ane Ratificacour of
the Kings gift in favors of Chirurgians
pharmacians and Barbours of this
brugh, qlk he had of his own proper
moyen & meines procurit in ther
favors Qlk being red over in the
hiring of the sd faculty thay
approvid therof as being a deid

doon be him in als y{r} favors and
for y{r} advantadg And declarit
after the sam wes delyverit and
put in the box that since the
procuring yrof wes expensive to
him and his repayment from
the faculty wold waken ther
stock and ther poors envines He
wes content to lye out of his
money and to supersoeid the
craving yrof uncill sic tyme as
therby yr sould be als much
money gott in as sould defray
the expense of the sam—Extending
to fyve hundreth marks money
glk they ordain the collector to pay
at the sd day The sd visitor &
faculty put taking to ther
consideraon the conveniencie y{t}
some phisitians residing wt in ther
bounds yr concurrane be had ffor
the right and legall exercise of the
power of visitaon and uyr duties and
priviledgis conteined in ther gift-

written subsequently

Act in favor of the Visitor and Brutin Hall ffor treating wt doctor Colquhoun & Hamilton for yr concurrence wt the faculty

(105) grantit by King James the sixt of
blessed memorie So the now dwelling
Mr Peter dow and Robert Hamiltoune
and ther successors And Ratificaoun
yrof in favors of the sd faculty
By this pnt partial they ordained
the pnt visitor wt John Hall late
Baillie to treat wt doctor John
Colquhoun and doctor Thomas Hamiltoune
thereanent And to draw wt them
for concurring wt the sd faculty
anent the regulaoun of medicine
wt in ther bounds and sitting
wt them upon honnrable termes
And ordaines them to report ther
diligence thereanent at ther nixt
meeting ‒

And sicklyke The sd faculty taking
to ther consideraoun the frequent
grivances and complaints givin
by ther collector yeirly of the
unnecessar paines they ar yeirly
at in making ther comptes by
inserting the names of severall persons

now decesit yrin and the gptrn
compts drw by thrm 2rof ther
is no hope to get any thing
recovrrd of thr rapresintans 2os
namrs and gptrn compts yrirly are
a prt of thr charg and most
again dischargs thrmselfs yr with
as non paymrnts Thry have thrrfor
thought fitt that ane sseatt compt
of all such prsons be takin and
kriprd out of the Collectors charg
for eviting of trouble and painrs
hrinaftir And for yt spret have
nominatrd and appoyntrd the
prt visitor John Hall late Baillie
Mr david Sharp Mr Charles Mnat
Robert Housetoun Adam Gray and
Andrew Ralstoune thr prt collector
to revise thr compt pittly givin
in be the sd Mr Charles Mnat
thr late collector And to transcryb
thr sam keeping furth yrof the
namrs of all such who are
decrissit And to booke thr samin

in this book conforme and that
the late collector compt be given in
perusil and recommend & therof
booked.—

Glasgow 19 Nov 1672.—
Conveined in the visitor his chamber
The Visitor, Baillie Jon Hall, Mr
Charles Muat, Robert Houstoune,
Adam Gray and divers uthirs
members of the faculty.—
Comperied Andrew Ralstoune in
obedience to our former act and
accepted in and upon him the
office of being collector for the yeir
insuing whar made faith as
use is.—
The sd day Mr Charles Muat the
last collector having given his comp
& intromissioune with the faculties
meinis since the 12 Nov 1671 and yt
by charg and discharg in maner
underwrin wes red and approvin
by the sd faculties and ordered

to be booked and he dischargit
grof as followes viz.-

Charg frae 13 octor 71 to
14 Nor 72.-

ffridome fynes.

Imprimis the compter charges
himself with 5 lib resting
of James Wilsone his fyne.
It with 8 lib resting of Thomas
Couper his fyne It with 10 lib
resting of Gilbert Wilsone his
fyne It with 12 lib resting of
Andrew Ralstoune his fyne
It with 5 lib 16S of Jon Neill
youngest his fyne. It with 24
lib of Jon Lod his fyne. It
with 24 lib of Mr Alexr Porter
his fyne Soa is   88-16-0

It the compter charges himself
with the soume of 500 merk
in Wace brooks hand gfh
is the (rent grof is   353-06-8

It with a band of 200 merk

dew be Jon Binnie wt two
yeirs @rent at Mart 1672 is 147 — 6 — 8
It With anoyr band drew be
him & his ca'riers for 100
merk wt two yeirs @rent at
Mart 1672   74 — 13 — 4
It with Jon donald his band
of 100 mirks wt the @rent
yrof frm whitsondy 1671 to
Mertimas 1672 extendis to   72 — 13 — 4

(106) It with William Gilmour his
band for 200 merk with a
yeirs @rent at Mertimas
1671 is   141 — 6 — 8
with 3 lib 18 S of expenses inde 145 — 4 — 8
It of Ror Houstoun his fyne
of   40 — 0 — 0
It with 22 lib 14 S 8 d as the ballans
of the last compt in the
collectors hands   22 — 8 — 8
It wt Ror Harris precept of 20 lib
3 S of expense of play inde 20 — 3 — 0
Soa of bonds 885 — 02 — 4.
Quarter compts at 12 S pr yeir.

It the compter charges himself
with 12S drw yeirly the yeirs
1670 1671 1672 inde. 36S drw be
Wr and Grahme. It with 12S
drw be Ion Hall late Bailley
for 1672 It with 12S drw be And
Bogill the yeir 1672 It with 12S
drw be Andrew Elphingstoune
the yeir 1672 It with 12S drw
the yeir 1672 be Wr david Sharp
the yeir 1672 — It with 12S drw
be Ion Robisone the yeir 1672
It with 12S drw be Wr Charles
hunat the sd yeir 1672 — It be
Ion dras for 1672 12S It be Iames
Thomson for 1672 12S It be
Rot Henris 13 yeirs inde lib
16S — It be Iames ffrank 11
yeirs inde 6 lib 12S It be
Andrew Broune 10 yeirs 6 lib
Iames Watt 1665-66 and 72
1 lib 16S It Iames Wilsone
1661. 62. 63. 64. 65. 69. 71. 72 inde
4 lib 16S It be Ion Hall barber

12S for 1672. It be James Gero 1670
71.72. 36S It be James Umat
13 yrs indr 7 tib 16S. It be
georg dockhart 12S for 1672 it
be Thomas Harper four yrs
and a half indr 2 tib 14S.
It be Jon diddree 1671 r 72 indr
24S It be Andrew Miller for
1672 It 12S be Roir McNeill for
1672. It be daniel Brown 1669
70.71.72 indr 2 tib 8S It 12S
drw be Rob Houstoun for
1672. It be Jon dogeur 71 r 72 indr
24S It 12S drw be Adam
Gray for 1672. It 12S drw be
Jon fleming for 1672. It 12S drw
be James Braidwood for 1672.

    Suva is   55 _ 10 _ 0

Strangers gitir comptes at 16S
and 20S pr anny.
It the compter charges himself
with 20S yrirly drw be Allan
Kirkwood 1668.69.70.71 r 72 indr
5 tib It with 3 yrs drw be

Adam Jackson indr 3 ttб dt
wt 20S bг Jon Sprull for 1672.
dt wt 12 yrs drw bг Jon Patsone
12 ttб dt bг Jon Ewing 3 yrs
and a half indr 3 ttб 10S —
dt with Math Miller 71 г 72
indr 40S dt bг Jas Hunter
1671 г 72 indr 2 ttб bг Jon Mathie
16 yrs indr 16 ttб dt bг Jon
Stow for 1671 г 72 2 ttб dt bг Jh:
Robisone 13 ttб indr 13 ttб dt bг
Wm Currie 5 yrs is 5 ttб dt bг
Rd Munn in Gorballs 16S yrs
71 г 72 indr 1 ttб 12S —

    Lisa is   66 — 2 — 0

Quarter compts at 30S pr annum
dt with 30S yrrly drw bг James
Tobias for 11 yrs space indr
16 ttб 10S dt bг Alexr dunlope
11 yrs indr 16 ttб 10S dt bг
Jon Rankine one yr indr 9
ttб dt bг doctor Wallace 12 yrs
18 ttб dt bг Jon foster 6 yrs
qoJ 5 are prieceding 1666 г now

1672 inde 9 tt It be Mr Tho.
younger 4 yeirs is 6tt.

    Swa is   75 — 0 — 0

It the compter charges himself
wr Wm Simpill of Dunook his
band of 20 tt and half a yeirs
@rent at Mert 1672 is   21 — 4 — 0

    Swa of the haill charg
    extends to — 1191 — 14 — 4 —

Imprimis the compter reconers
himself with the sowmes of
money underwrin givin
out by order of the prsons
aftermentionat viz lent to
Mr Ard Brahine by band
20S. It givin to the deacon
convriners his offien 24S. It
givin to a poor man yt
had his hous brunt 30S.
It givin to two poor men
by order 24S. It givin to the
deacon convriners hous
6 tt. 13S. 4D. It givin to a poor

(107)

chapman James him 12S. It
givin to a poor woman 12S. It
to anoy poor man 12S. It to
bury Adam Gray his son 3lb
It givin to bury Wm Currie 5lb
12S. It to the trads officer 12S.
It to him for shose 3lb. It to the
clerk for his fialb 8lb. It to the
hospitalb poor 6S. It to the drumer
12S It to Roin Meurill for a
poor man 30S. It to Patrick Bryce
for the trads prt of the street
120 lb.

  Sua is   174 — 19 — 4

ffiredome fyres unpayit.
It with 5lb remaining of James
Wilsone his fyra It with 10 lb
resting of Gilbert Wilsone his fyra
It with 8lb resting of Thomas
Harpers.

  Sua is   23 — 0 — 0

   Bands

It with Walter Brodfes band of 500
mrke is   333 — 6 — 8

It with Ion Bunias band of 200 mks is   133 — 6 — 8

It with Ion donald his band of
100 mks with a yeir and a
half @ rent at hent. 72 is   072 — 13 — 4

It with Ion dunia his band of 100 mks 066 — 13 — 4

It with Tho Herris precept is   020 — 3 — 0

    Siva is — 626 — 03 — 0 —

    Non payments of qtrie compt
    at 12S pr anny —

It 12S yeirly dew be Mr And Grahm
1670 & 1671 inde 24S dt 12S dew
be Ion dars for 1672 It be Tho
Herris for 13 yeirs inde 7 lib 16S
dt be James ffrank 11 yeirs 6 lib
12S. dt be Andrew Brown 10
yeirs is 6 lib. It be James Watt
for 1665. 66 & 72 is 36S. dt be James
Wilson for 1661. 62. 63. 64 66. 69. 71 &
72 inde 4 lib 16S. dt be Thomas
Harper 4 yeirs and a half is
2 lib 14S. dt be Ion diddell 671
12S It 4 yeirs be daniel brown
2 lib 8S. dt be Ion dgans 24S —

    Siva is   45 — 6 — 0

Non payments at 20S p annu
Item the compter recovers himself
with 5 yeirs drew be Allan
Kirkwood indr 5 lib It be
Adam Pateour 3 yeirs indr
3 lib. It be Jon Irving 3 yeirs &
a half indr 3 lib 10S. It be
Mathew Miller 1671 72 indr
2 lib It be Arch Hunter for 1671
and 72 indr 2 lib It be Jon
Mathie 16 yeirs indr 16 lib It be
Jon Stow for 1671 72 indr 2 lib
It be Jh Robison 13 yeirs indr
13 lib. It be Jon Sprule for
1672 indr 20S. It be Wm Cunie
5 yeirs indr 5 lib It be Jon
Pateour 12 yeirs indr 12 lib.—

Sua is   64 – 10 – 0

Non payments at 30S p annum
Item tho compter recovers himself
with 11 yeirs drew be James
Tobias indr 16 lib It wt 11 yeir
drew be Ro Alexr dunlope
indr 16 lib It with 6 yeir drew

be Son Panton indr 9 lib. It
with 12 yeirs draw br doctor
Wallace indr 18 lib It with
6 yeir br Son foster indr 9 lib
It with Mr Thomas yor for
1672 indr 30S.

Suva is   70 — 10 — 0

It the compter excouers himself
with a band for 200 mk draw
to the calling br Mr Boils
indr 133 lib 6S 8d. It wt a band
grantit br Mr Sempill of
damook for 20 lib and a
trimer @ rent at Mart 1672
indr 21 lib 4S. It givin to the
miset collecter Andrew Ralston
for ballancing the compt
of charg 32 lib 13S. 4d.

Suva of discharg is — 1191 — 2 — 4.

And yrfor the sd faculter in on voice
excouers and simpr discharges the sd
Mr Charles Iruat his airs and sccers
of his sds intromissionires with the
Callings minurs for the forsed 30 yr

octor 1671 to the 14 nor 1672 and ordeines
me then clerk under subscryband to
subscrybe ther pnts in ther names in
favors of the compter and his
foirseds.—

sic subr   W Stirling Clk.—

(108)

The sd day John Bryce sone to James
Bryce mrest is bookit prentice W Robert
Houstoun for fyve yeirs space and twa
yeirs yeift for meit and fie as they
can aggrie furth and fra his entrie
qlk wes begane at the dait of the
indentor viz 21 Sept 1672 who made
faith as use is. And in place of the
fourtie shilling qlk sould have bein
payed in to the collector and is quat
to him for his fathers undertaking
to eng the prisons following at the
faculties instance viz Allan Kirkwood
Jon Patsoun, Jon Ewing, Th Robisoune,
James Tobias, Mr Alexr dunlope for
the bygain yptrecompts and the sd
James Bryce is to report to the faculties
ane prsonall recentr̄ (if possible) agt

them betwixt and the   day of
Misel to come.

At the sd day the Collector Andrew
Ralstoun is to compt for a croe
dollor for his officers fiall as the
rest have payit who have not servit.
The sd day the Collector wes ordered
to pay to thir clerks servants 12S.
It to a poor man 6S. It to James
Grayes relief 40d qlk are ordained
to be deducit off the soume given
in to him by the last collector.

Eik to Gilbert Wilsoun forme admission
The foirsd day the facultie taking
to thir considera*ne* ane supplica*ne*
given in be Gilbert Wilsoun in Straven
qrby he craves to be admittit to
let blood and apply caulers beyond
qt he is formerly admittit to. They
finding it reasonable and the sd
Gilbert qualifeit qrfor dois hereby
admitts him thereunto and no farder
to qt is in his former admissioune
in urgent necessity and als to administrat clisters in
caises of necessitie in absence of

Gairner absolvit
for bygain transgressions
upon payt of 6 tt to
the Collector

phisitians) & to pay 20S yir only.
The sd day John Gairner mire in
Glasgow Being convened befor the
sd faculten for transgressing yr acts
in practising yr airts of Chirurgery
and pharmacie w out being licentiat
and being desyrous that the faculten
wold frie him for bygain transgressions
upon his faithfull undertaking to
observe the sam in all tyme coming
they wer pleasit to grant this
desyre upon payment to their collector
of thrie punds Scots for the masser
expenss the faculten wer at in
raising bivs and executing yrof..
against him Qlk he accordingly
payed in to the collector and upon
payt grof the faculty ordaines the
clerk to grant him a discharg
of his bygain transgressions and
of all diligence yt follosit agst
him upon the sds bivs with the
express provisioun that he observe
their acts for the future under the

yein continuid —

minut the charg givin collector.

The foirsd day the last collectors charg and discharg being considered and reexamined And the faculty put finding that the grivances givin in be thir collector to be very just in regaird that all prisons who wer debtors in all yeirs grtin compts are now dreussit And yt ye is no hopes of any gitting any pit grof brought in or gott off the representars of the sd defunct prisons Aur conform to aur act of the last facultie drawin over aur charg and altered nothing yrin Bot only Reiped out the names of thes who are dreuist for roitteg of troubll and pains to ther put collector & his successors in making ther yeirly compts and ordains the clark to book the sam and bring booklit salls be sub. by the put visitor and Jon Hall late Baillie two of thes number of R is to be

(109)

the p'nt charg with q't sale be hirinf
addit or payit in to the collector
and is to continow untill the
faeultie sale think convenient to
alter the sam by kriping out q'rof
the names of such who sale
hirinf happin to dreris ffollowers
the charg for 1673.—

Imprimis givin in be the last
collector off ballane of his
accompt 32 lib. 15S. 4d. It payit
be Ion Hall youngest, Iame
Vir, Ion Hall barbour each
of them a one dollor for
officeris fiale geh it the
p'nt collector his one dollor
for geh he is to compt-
rertends to 11 lib. 12S. It ye is
in the boxe a bond grantit
be Walt Book for 333 lib. 6S
8d with a yeirs @rent at
martimas 1673.
It a bond be Ion Binnie for 133 — 6 — 8

wt a yeirs @rent at Mart 1673.

It a bond be Jon dennie for 066 _ 13 _ 4

wt a yeirs @rent at Mart 1673.

It a bond be Jon donald nasso for 066 _ 13 _ 4

wt a yeirs @rent at Mart 1673

It a bond be Mr Boill mr for 133 _ 06 _ 8

wt a yeirs @rent at Mart 1673

It a bond be Mr Sempill of damoth 020 _ 00 _ 0

wt 3 termes @ rent at Mart 1673

It is tho Harper his bond of 008 _ 00 _ 0

It is a precept gft Rd Andros 020 _ 03 _ 0

Charg ffollowes the fredome

fynes --

Imprimis be Gilbert Neilsone

10 lib It be James Wilsone

6 lib

ffollowes the comptis wt in brugh

Imprimis be Ard Bogill for 1673 12s

It be Jon Hall late Baillie

12s. It be Mr david Sharp

12s. It be Mr Charles Minat 12s

It be Mr Ard Grahme 12s. It

be Andrew Elphingstonne 12s

It be Jon Robisone 12s. It

be James Thomsoun 12S. It be
Jon Liddell 12S. dt be Andrew
Miller 12S. It be Rot Houstoun
12S dt be Adam Gray 12S. It
be Win McNeill 12S. dt be
daniel Brown 12S. It be Jon
Hall youngest 12S. dt be Andrew
Ralston 12S. It be James Weir
12S. dt be Jon Fleming 12S.
It be James Birdwood 12S.
It be Jon Hall barbour It be
georg Lockhart 12S Ther abov=
un for the year 1673. It be
Jon Ers for 1672 & 73 24S. It be
James Will for 72 & 73. 24S.
It be James Ers for 70. 71. 72 &
73. 2 tib 8S. It be James Frank
for 12 years indr 7 tib 4S. It
be Rot Arriris for 14 years indr
8 tib 8S. It James Wilsoun for
9 years indr 5 tib 8S

ffollowre getrecoup w'out brigh.
Item be Andrew Broun 12S yrely
for 11 years space indr 6 tib 12S.

It br Allan Kirkwood yeirly
30S for 6 yeirs space indr 9tt
It br Jon Sproull 20S yeirly
72 & 73 indr 2 tt It br Jon
Patsone yeirly 20S for 13 yeirs
at Michaelmes 1673 indr 13tt
It br Jon Ewing 20S yeirly for
5 yeirs space indr 5 tt It
br Mathew Miller 20S yeirly
for 3 yeirs space indr 3 tt
It br Jon Hall 20S for 3 yeirs
indr 3 tt It br Thomas
Robissone 20S yeirly for 14 yeirs
space at Michaelmes 1673 indr
14 tt It br John Muir in
Corballs for 1673 16S It br Jon
dogan yr 12S for 3 yeirs space
indr 1tt 16S It br Jon Sobiae
at 20S the yeir for 12 yeirs indr
12 tt It br hir Alexr dunlop
at 30S pr yeir for 12 yeirs indr
18 tt It br Jon Paulon for
30S a yeir for 7 yeirs indr
10 tt 10S It br Jon foster 30S

(110)

426

yeirly 1672 + 73 inde 3 lib It- bi
Mr the younger 30s yeirly 72 +
73 inde 3 lib It- bi Mr Kimpill
of dannok 12s for 1673 It- bi
Son Sod 20s for 73. It- bi Mr
Abxer Porter 20s for 1673 - It-
Gilbert Wilsone 20s yeirly for
4 yeirs inde 4 lib It the
collector is to compt for
6 lib red fris of fyne fra
don Gainer.-

31 Nov 1672.-

In the Visitor his house Convened the
Visitor, don Halls late Baillie Mr david
Sharp, Mr Charles Kincat, Mr Ard
Grahame, James Thomsone, Andrew
Elphingstone, don Halls youngest, Evir
Mcnill, Georg Lockhart, Adam Gray
don fleming.-

Compd in presen of the sd faculty
James Kar som tyme residenter in
Hamilltoune in obedience to our
citacone givin to him ffor his appeirance

befor them ffor his exerceing the airts
of Chirurgery & pharmacei nor being
licentiat who desyrit to be admittit
fr<u>e</u>man with them and in order
yrto So be examined upon his
skill and practise both in Chirurgery
and pharmacei who being examined
yeupon was found groslie ignorant by
the sd faculty as to both the sds
airts And yrfor thay hirby discharg
him in all tyme coming So exerceise
any of the sds airts or to give
any potous or phisik And to give
bond for yt effect under the pain
of ffyve hundrith marks toties quoties
quoties And to pay in to their collector
the ffunds for their charges & expenss
in raising of this & executing yrof
against him.—

Glasgow 16 dec. 1672.—
Conveened in the Visitor his Chamber
The Visitor, Jon Hall late Baillie, hw
Ard Grahme, James Thomsone, Wm

428

david Sharp Mr Charles Mureat, Andrew
Ralstoun, Jon Hall youngest, Ro=
Houstoun, Adam Gray, James Win
Andrew Elphingstoun + Evir McneilL.—

Bailie Hall +
And Bayllis Report
to the facultie of
their diligence.—

Anent the sd Visitor and Baillie Hall
reporting to the facultie ane accompt
of ther diligence and the lenth they
came in order to ane aggriement
wt doctors Jon Colquhoun + Thomas
Hamiltoun anent ther joyning wt
the facultie By giving ye adyce
and concurrane with them Conforme
to the Lres of gift grantit to the
facultie By King James ther 2sect of
blessed memorie By virtue of ane
act in ther former ordinance, Who
dreclaret they had spok wt them
and propost overtures Bot had not
fullie endit and befor they could
fullie accomodat that again they
found some necessitie for ane act
of the sd facultie in ther favours,
impowering them for yt effect Or if
the facultie sould rather think fitt

(III) that the sds doctors or aither of them might be desyrd to be put at their nixt meiting of they and the facultie might speik coram and the aggreement yeby the mor unanimous. The facultie put thought it fitt efter dew considration had of the premiss to meet and comuin with the sds doctors and yt doctor Colquhoune might be desyred to be put at their nixt meeting qlk wes appoynted the nixt day in the efternoon And that the invitacn qlk wes ordred to be drawin in a paper apairt might be red over in the hiring of the sd faculty to the effect the same might either be approvin or not. Qlk being divers tymes red was una voce approvin and ordred to be bookit wt qt farder could pas in order to the agreement & subr by the visitor & qlk Qrof the tenor followes.

Wer the visitor of the Chirurgians

Double of the
invita'ne to the
phisitians.

and pharmaticians of the brugh of
Glasgow and brethrein of the sds
callings Taking to considra'ne The
lre of gyt grantit to Mr Peter dow
and Mr Ro: Hamiltoune and their
successors Be King James of blessed
memory Be vertue grof we & or
predecessors wer then incorporat and
constitut and established into ane
societie and corpora'ne and having
procurit ane Ratifica'ne of the sd
gift in our favours By this present
parliament We find by expres words
of the sds lres of gift and Ratifica'ne
grof that the concurrence of some
phiisicians reiding w' in the bounds
sprit thairintill is injoyned and
necessarie (if it can be had) for the
richt and legall exerceise of the
power of visita'ne and uther duties
and priviledges conteined in the
sd gift And may justlie impute to
the defect grof the girt prejudice
the Countrie did and yet does sustein

By the multitud of ignorant and
arrogant pretendars to medicine and
Chirurgry who not only practise
Chirurgery in all poynts qrof thry
have no skill nor licene Bot also
take upon them in all internall
diseases to prescrybe and administer
phisick contrair to the tennor of the
sd gift and in contempt of the
authoritie grantit to the sd visitor &
his brethren to inhibit and suppress
the same Wee being therfor willing
to use all indevor and meanes
to discharg faithfullie the trust
committit to us as being now constitut
in ane incorporaone according to
his Maties gracious intentiounes for
the good and advantadg of his
subjects yrin concernit And to
obviat all objections or exceptions can
be made by any against the sovereign
of the power of visitaone according to
the sd lre of gift and Ratificaone qrof
Doe for the tyme to come resolve to

procuir (if it can be had) the concurrence
and assistance of some phisicians one
or more within our bounds according
to the sd gift And for yt effect being
sufficiently preswaded of the ability
and goodwill of doctor don Colquhoun
Doz by thir presents earnestly obtest
and desyr him To take upon him
and exerceise the office of visitor
conjunct with the pnt visitor of the
Chirurgians and pharmacians as
fully frielie and honourlie in all
poynts as Mr Robert Hamilton did
or might have doon with Mr Peter
dow according to the first intention
and at the procuring of the sd gift
And for yt end ordaines two of
our number (untill the next meeting)
viz the pnt visitor and don Hall
late Baillie To invit and represent
this our desyar To the sd doctor
And to satisfie him in any scruples
he may have yearnt And to
condiscend to all overtures he sall

(112)

make to yt purpose qch are nor-
destructive to the sd incorporacōn or
to the Ratificacōn of the sd gift in
our favours And in particular So
reject the joyning in of all uther
phisicians wt in the precincts of our
jurisdictioun or yit wt in the toun du
the sd union and power of visitacōn
Sine trts of graduacōn or sojurning wt
in the bounds gives no richt to
phisitians to claime any interrse
in the sd gift Bot phisicians of
Glasgow who are called & acknowledged
as such by the pnt faculty in gos
favours the gift is now ratifird in
this current parliat With qch
reservacōn imediatlie abovwrin all
things els he sall demand for the
securing his honor and reputacōn
from aspersions or for easing of his
binding in the sd charg sall be
accordit unto by the sds comrs
and approvin by the haill incorporacōn
With this provision allwayes that

this put invita͞ons and all y͠t hes
followit or can follow yrupon sall
no wayes for the future prejudg us
of our s͞d gift and ratifica͞on yr of
in our favours.

Glasgow 17 d͠rer 1672.

Convined in Hutchesounes hospitall
The Visitor, Jon Hall late Baillie, James
Thomsone, Andrew Elphingstoun, Andrew
Ralstoun, Jon Steill youngest, Sir Mc̓ueill
Adam Gray, James Weir, Mr̓ and
Grahme, Mr̓ david Sharp + Rob͠r
Houstoun.

The glk day Convined w͠t the foirsds
members of faculte doctor Jon Colquhoune
at thir desyr du goe hiring The
foirsd invita͞on was red and he
conforme to the tennor yrof dosyred
to joyn w͠t them by advyes and
uyrwise with any whom he and the
faculty put sould dosyr to be assessor
to him Qlk invita͞on he dreland he
wes redy and willing to imbrace

only desyred that the articles afirmentionat
might be condescendit unto by the
sd faculty befor his acceptance and
making faith viz

**Articles proponned
by Doctor Colquhon
+ adhird unto.**

  followes the articles proponned
   to the faculty of Chirurgians
   in Glasgow by doctor Iohn
   Colquhon at his receptione grunto.

1 Imprimis yt the act for my call
be booked as it is now wordit or
at least in equivalent termes That
Iohn and my brethrine share in
the power of visitacne be declait
nor to be precarious or
depending upon the bare call of
the chirurgians But foundit upon
the express tennor of the sd gift
And be the necessities of some
phisicians concurrence enjoyned therin
(113) by his majestie But prejudice to
the chirurgians plea for excluding
phisicians as such till they be
called and acknowledged by the
Incorporatne ....

2 That ther be two at lust of my
own degree and progressioun called
up the same maner to be members
of the faculty and on of them
at lust a residentur in the town
who in caise of my necessarie
absenc may be visitor pro tempore
and qn a yur is exepyrd may
relieve me of the burding and be
Visitor for the yur insuing and
(if they think fitt) the uthir to be
residentur in the countrie unto
qom some poynts of the power of
visitaoun may be comittet for the
exerceis yeof and the facultie salb
think expedient And he to be
accomptabl to them yeaurut his
charg and the nominaoun of him
to be condrscendit on hiroft —

3 That in all matters dispinding upon
the gift the phisician visitor and
his brethren are to be determinators
and judgers conjunct wt the chirurgian
visitor and his brethren comun

concilio and y^t in caice of y^e
unanimous dissassent and prestacion
against any act as derogatorie or
prejudiciall to ther degrie the same
salb be ipso facto voyd & null. —

4 That in all courts to be holden and
acts to be made be the Chirurgian
Visitor and his brethrin depending
upon ther libertie is in brugh and
ther bris of dracourie the phicisians
are not to interest themselves. —

5 That respect be had to the degrie
and dignitie of phicisians especiallie
thos incorporat and to the phicisian
Visitor the uthir salb grant precedence
and his name first insert in all
acts bris & and y^t the Chirurgian
Visitor in name of his brethrin
take ane oathe to seik the honor
and advantadg of the phicisians
especiallie thos incorporat and to
doe nothing prejudiciall yeunto As
lykwyse the phicisian visitor sall
at his admission swein to seik

the good and wellfare of the chirurgians
and pharmacians incorporat and
to maintein and defend to his
power their just liberties and
priviledges.—

6 That yr be a select number of
Chirurgians and apothecaries pitched
upon by the prit chirurgian visitor
who sall have vott & sitt in court
wt the two visitors as sd is All of
them capable to exerceise some of the
articles of visitaoun contained in
the Kings gift and consequently to
be chosin visitor.—

7 That the phisician visitor sall
have power when things relating
to them in prticular sall requyr
to convocat the faculty And lykwyse
the Chirurgian visitor sall have power
to doe the same and the officers to
obey both conjunctlie or severallie.—

8 That all the errein aforesd articles
be sett doun in the book of the
sd faculty Ther to remain in extenso

ad futuram rei memoriam. —

sic sub̄ J Colhoun. —

(114) The facultie having hard the foirsd̄
articles red over to them did
willinglie accord yrunto. Only
dregrit this might be addit vi
Ane additionae that non of the phiecisians yr
article proponit by
the visitor & members servants sall be privilredgit or have
to the doctor — any power to medl wt Chirurgery
or pharmacie wt in brugh rscerpt
in caisrs of urerscilie for want of
Chirurgians and pharmacicians And
yr any assessor to be norat sale
cane the sam̄ hire'f by pluralilie
of vots at least by the facultie's
advyce The assessor being allwayro
on of the doctors dirgrie. —

Doctor Colquhouns To the qlk The sd doctor Johne
acceptas m — Colquhoune did condrserid And
and imediatlie yrff did acerpt
in and upon him the office of
phiecisian visitor conjunct wt the
Chirurgian visitor And he and
members of the sd faculty abor̄rit

440

did hine undr give ye gret & solem
oathes, viz the sd doctor to manta[in]
the just ryts and privilndges of
the sd incorporačn wi thr welfare
and the sds members to mantain
the honour and advantadg of the
sd phisician visitor and did take
uthir by the hand in farder
testimony of thr unanimous assent
to the premisse.

Doctor Hamilton
assessor for the citie
and doctor Wallace
for the countrie
Therft the sd doctor Being desyrit
by the sd Chirurgian visitor & his
brethrin to condrscend upon the
prson he aprehends fittet to be
his assessor to the nixt ordinar
tyme of electioun He did nominat
doctor Thomas Hamiltoun for the
brigh and doctor Michael Wallace
for the countrie Qlk being putt to
a vott by the sd faculty wes
unanimouslie assentit to and
approvin by thrm all and ordaines
doctor Thomas Hamilton to be
sent for imediatly to accept.

The Quorum
nominat to be
members of the
faculty

The sd day also doctor Jon Colquhoun
phisician visitor w the Chirurgian
visitor and his brethrein put did
condescend (in obedience to on of
the articles proposit by the sd doctor)
that the persones underwrein or
any nyne of them as a quorum
to be members of the faculty to
sitt and vott in court with the
sds two visitors as capable to
exercise all articles of visitatione
conteint in the kings gift and
consequently capable to be chosin
visitor viz John Hall late Baillie
and Bogill, Wm and Grahme, Wm
david Sharp & Charles Muat,
James Thomson, Andrew Elphingstoun
Jon Hall sone to the sd Jon Hall
late Baillie, daniel Broune, Jon
Robisone, Adam Gray, Rob Houstoun
George Lockhart, Andrew Ralstoune,
Evir McnNill, James Weir, Jon
Liddell & Jon Fleming.

The sd day Compt also doctor Thomas

442

doctor Hamiltons
acepta'on

Hamilton who accepted in and
upon him The office of being assessor
to the phicisians Visitor this ensuing
yeir and he w'. the Chirurgian
Visitor + his brethrein put made
faithe hine inde ut supra w'.
the phisitian visitor. _

(115)

Act for a new
booke. _

at the sd day ane new book
consisting of irvin quair of paper
and claspit to be bot by the
Chirurgian Visitor as the Record
book of the calling.
Thirdly the clerk is appoynted to
gor on w'. this same book for
recording ye acts + oyrs yeir till
the same be doon + endit. _

Hutchesons Hospitall the 21
of march 1673 yeirs. _
The 9th day conveend doctors Colquhoun
and Hamiltoun w'. Ard Bogill Chirurg
Visitor don Hall late bailler, W'.
david Sharp, Charles Linrot, And
brahms and don Hall yor chirurgian

Andrew Elphingstoun, Ro Houstoun, James
Weir, Evie McNeill, Andrew Ralstoun
don fleming & don diddells.—
At the 9th meeting the doctors declarit
that they judgit it convenient that
yr sould be ane phisitian imployit
for the west and for yt end doctor
Michael Wallace in Ayr being ay
put in toun sould be callit To
receive the power of visitaoune for
the shyre of Ayr including Kyll
Carrick & Cunghame Into the faculty
put condescendrd He being comptable
to them for his actions and for
the money yt sould be gott by all
licentiat persons and yt sould
have admission wt instanours
qrupon Wr david Sharp & Ard
Grahme wer sent for to invit him
to ther meeting who within a
short space comperit & having
hard the invitaoune given to doctor
Colquhoun red to him wt the Articles
propost & condescendrd to formnlly

booket declarit he was content to
accept wherupon they offered him a
commission wt certain instructions
for the sd shyre & a list of all
persons allready licentiat within
that bounds Reserving to themselfs
and yr successors liberty to call
and convein persons wtin the sd
shyre befor them not formerly licentiat
And to call him to ane accompt
for his actions and his intromissions
in caices any sall happin to be
wt comission The sd doctor Wallace
accepted & he & the faculty hine
inde gave yr aithes & he declarit
he sould be respeable to them
conforme to the instructions to be
delyvrit to him.—

The sd day James Robisone a
souldier being recommendit by the
Chirurgians of Egt to the faculty
for licentiating him to the exercise
of chirurgey wtin yr bounds The
faculty eft serious consideration yrof

(margin notes)
Doctor Wallace
admission

Act against
Robisone

denyed the his desyre and
ordained Baillie Hall ane of ye
number to wryt back ane ansr
to them negative to ye desyre and
him and in the interim discharges
him frae medling wt any pt of
the sd airt wt in thir bounds
untill he be tryed & reexamined of
his qualificaunrs._

Anent raising getts of horning The sd day ordaines the clerk to
raise thrie pair of lres of horning
at the visitors instance & he to
be payit yrfor by the collector And
for yt end yt he get out the gift,
Ratificaunrs & qt els is needfull
in order yrto._

17 aprylle 1673._
Convinned doctor Colquhoun, Ard
Bogle, Baillie Hall, Wm Ard Grahm,
david Sharp and Charles Miriat,
Andrew Ralstoun, James Thomsoun,
Jon liddell, Rot Houstoun, Evan
McneillE, James Weir, Jon fleming &

448

Adam Gray –

The sd day compt befor thrm John
Brown residenter in Pasley in
obedience to a charg givin to him

(116)
for practising sone pts of the
airts of medicine not being licentiat
And being reexamined by thrm anent
his skill in any of the sd airts
were found grosslie ignorant of all

Act anent Brown
And yrfor dischargit in all tyme
coming to medle wt any of the
sds airts ordaint to grant band
for yt effect under a penaltie –

The sd day ordaines the visitor

Act anent the clerks pay.
bose masters and any uthers goin
they please to meet wt the clerk for
taking his compt of his hand in
going to Edr and raising of brs
conform to a former act and to
draw a precept yrfor upon the
collector quho hereby they appoynt
to pay him –

Conveined in Hutchesons Hospitall
doctors Colquhoun + Hamilton, Ard
Bogill, Baillie Hall, Mr david Sharp
and Charles Muat, Andrew Ralstoun
Jon Hall yor Chirurgian, Andrew
Elphingstoun, Adam Gray, Ror Mc
nill Ror Houston, Jon fleming +
Jon diddell.—

Resc presentlie to Mr Th Smith The sd day compt befor them Mr
Thomas Smith indweller in glasgow
and gave in a supplicacion qrby
he desyred to be admitted to the
practise of pharmacie to oppin
veins and apply potentiall cauters
the faculty pnt taking his desyre
to yr consideracion ffinds it equitable
and yrfor ordeines him the say
following vz to make elxlet: dia=
cotholicon, pillula stomach: cum
gummi, stomach magisteij de
praseio trochisi elarab and ung:
de altheu and to make up thir
composiciouns betwixt and the first
of Junii next By the sight of Mr

Complaint against Alexr Wilson

david Sharp, Charles Muat, Jon Robison
and Wm and Gray or any two
of them -

The sd day Ther being complaints
givin agst Alexer Wilson garner in
glasgow for giving phisick & drogs
not licentiat & qrby doing such
skaith as sight be Ro: Marshell
maltman for applying to the now
deceist Robert Sharp his late spous
small things qrby her dratho wes
occasiond as he pretendit And the
said Alexr being conveened before
them answerd qrto and plainlie
confest yt he gave her plaintin
watter roots of comphrie and of
red roses wt some tumenting roots
and oils yt he gave her a handfull
of camovills to bath her feet in and
yt he desyrd her to sett her feet
to the fyre and to suffer as much
heat as shoe could Bot simplie
denyed yt ever he knew her wt
chyld -

It y{e} bring anoy{r} complaint ffor certain
aplica{cons} he had givin to Ion Crosbie
in gallowgait for the giu well qz he
did gek he dreyed.

It for aplica{cons} to W{m} Kirkbie, Ion
Hall carter & to Ro{b} Birknye & Ion
......

William Junds
discharged in
tyme coming
The faculty taking to y{e} considera{cons}
the small complaints w{t} his own
confession they all in on voce declare
that they find him guilty in
practising y{e} airte & y{r}for lyable in
a fyne gek they condescend to be
fourtie pounds & ordaines him to
grant band y{r}for pyable at
Whitsonday next. It to grant band
nevir to medle w{t} any p{ar}t of
medicin, chirurgry or pharmacey
in all tyme coming under the
pain of ane hundreth punds toties
quoties gek band is put in the box
and the former givin to the collector
to compt for.

(117) The sd day they ordain a pair of

Act anent instructions to doctor Wallace

bris of horning to be sent west to
doctor Wallace So be made use of
in that pñt comittie to his visitatione
It ordaines the visitor Baillie Hall &
Mr david Sharp to meet wt the
Clerk and to subscryve the instructions
yt are to be sent west to doctor
Wallace Qlk they approve of as
endor by the haill facultie —
It they Remitt to the Collector
damocks money wt Gilbert Wilsons
and Harpers fyne —

Act anent Jon fleming for miscarriadg

26 april 1673
It upon complaint maide for Jon
fleming his pñt miscarriadg befor
the faculty in reflecting on the
visitor they doe discharg him from
being a number of the faculty and
fra sitting or votting wt thim
during ye plesur and to pay
ane punde of fyne to the collector
and to crave the visitor & faculties
pardon for his transgression done
thereanent —

Hutchesons Hospitall
4 Junio 1673.

Conveenit ye doctor w the Chirurgian
visitor Baillie Hall Mr david Sharp,
Charles Murat, And Grahme w Rt
Houstoun, Jon Hall yor James Mou,
Adam Gray, Jon Liddell,—

Act for repratn of Wilsons band. The faculty put ordains the collector
to repeat Alexr Wilsons his band
for the 40 lib and to raise letie
yron and to put the same
to execucion.—

Act anent admission of Mr Thomas Smith The same day compt also Mr
Thomas Smith w the composituris
made be him at ye appoyntment
in ye last ordermt gifke Mr david
Sharp and And Grahme two of the
say masters appoynted for ye effect
declarit they saw the simples weighed
mixed and compounded qwh efter
the sam wes seen by the faculty
they wer satisfiet as being rightly
disprust And yrfor all in on voice
ffind him qualified for the exercise

or pharmacie and y[e] relates y[e]to
Bot refuses to admitt him to the
exercise of phlebotomie ventose
and potentiall cauters untill sik
tyme as it be sein by two or
mae of the chirurgians y[t] he can
practise certain p[ar]ts y[e]rof And quhe
dall be found qualifiet y[e]for They
declare they sall admitt to y[e]
p[ar]ts of chirurgy he sale be found
qualifiet w[ith]out any farder compositio[n]
then this p[rese]nt tyme q[uh]k they
condiscend to be fourtie punds &
this punds for the officers fiall
q[uh]k they ordains him to pay in
to the collector. —

Mudy his
diligence. The s[ai]d day James Mudy burse[r]
compl[eared] befor them at y[e] desyre and
gives ane account of his diligence
w[ith] the b[ur]s[ar] that the visitor had trusted
him w[ith] to charge in the countrie And
did produce befor them other b[ur]s w[ith]
ane receveings against twelve p[er]sons
living in the countries ffor q[uh]k they

ordain him for his paines and
expense upon finds &c. & ordaines
the elk. to subscryve a warrand
to the collector for y{e} end.—

fleming remittit to the Baillie

The s{d} day Ion fleming one of
y{e} number being warnit to
compeir befor them to pay his
fyne and give satisfaction conforme
in a former act Being callit Compt
not Therfor they Remitt him to
the Baillie for his fyne & approvis
the former act as to the rest.—

(118)

Hutchisons Hospitall
11 July 1673.—

Convened The Visitor doctor Colquhoun
and Hamiltoun. Ion Halls elder &
yo{r} Mr david Sharp James Thomsone,
Ion M{c}nride, R{t} Houstoun, Andrew
Ralstoun, James Weir, Adam Gray
and Ion Liddell.—

Doctor Bills answer for the Weik.—

The s{d} day The facultie taking
to their serious consideraciuns the
gift binding lying on doctor Wallace

454

by the late comission grantit to
him ffor the power of visitaone
in the west they judgit it convenient
yt he sould have ane assessor or
helper And yt doctor Bell at
Kilmarnock be writtin to by Jon
Hall late Baillie in yr names
To accept yrof And for yt end if
he come in to Glasgow & receive
his comission joyntly wt doctor
Wallace and instructions conforme
in respect they will send for doctor
Wallace his comission That both yr
names may be therin joyntly –

The 2d day the faculty put ordaines
that every fourtnight they have a
writing anent the affaires and
occurrences and that seivin of
thir number wt the visitor salbe
a quorum –

The 2d day they ordaine Robert
Houstoun to wryt to damook for the
money yt he to indew by band &
to get up the same fra the collector

and to grant a ticket for redelyvery
yrof on pay⟨r⟩ of the mony—

Hill bookit prentris The 2d day John Hill sone to Ro.
Hill in Meikle govvan is bookit
prentrise w⟨t⟩ Mr david Sharp for
sic yeirs ffrie his entrie g\[h\] was
sic at conforme to his indentor
sic daitit and has payi[t] to the
Collector fyve punds for his booking.—

Hutchesone Hospitall
25 Julii 1673.—

Compt doctor Colquhoun & Hamiltone, Son
Halls elder & yor Chirurgians, James
Thomsone, Mr Charles Lunat, And Grahme
and david Sharp, Ro. Houstoune, Eoir
Mc Neile, Adam Gray and James Weir.—

Kirkwoods Jarden admission The sd day Allan Kirkwood in darnlie
gave in a supplica'une graj̄ he desyrs
to be admittit Jarden To cure fractures
and simpl wounds in the flesh DLK
being considerd and he found qualifat.
They admitt him Jarder yrto And
ordaines him to pay Twelve pounds.

to the collector for his freedome fyne
and aughtein shillings scots pr annum
at lest to give band yerfor pyable at
Michaelmes niset, qlk band was
subt + givin to the collector –

doctor Bells
acceptane

The sd day Compt also doctor
Bryce Bell in obedience to the
faculties desyre quha being desyred
by the facultie to accept of the
office of visitacne joyntlie wt doctor
Wallace in aq for the wisterin
prtis did accept the sa upon him
and he and the facultie gave
ye auths hine inde ut supra –

22 August 1673 –

Conveind the Visitor John Hall late
baillie John Hall yr his sone, Mr
david Sharp James Thomsoun, Andrew
Ralstoun, Eon McNeile, Adam Gray
Mr Thos Smithe, Rot Houstoun, and
John Liddell –

Chart-Hall

The sd day ordaines ane charge of
horning to be givin to John Hall in

Pasley ffor setting up as a Chirurgian
licentiat w in the toun of Pasley
and setting out a signe & anoye
to don lang in Hamilton.—

Act anent
don How.
(119)

The 2d day complt, in Killbarchan
in obdience to a charg of horning
givin to him ffor bygain transgressions
contrar to his admission made in
maii 1654.— The faculty eft tryall
takin yrof assoilyies him yr frae
and declares him frie & ordaines
the charge to be takin back frae
him and cancellet and yr wrid
bris ordaines the clerk to retract
this act as a formall discharg to
him off all yt they can lay to
his charg preceding this dait
whrrupon he hes instantlie payit
to the collector ffor the use of
the poor twentie punds Scots
money.—

5 Sepr 1673.—

Convernd doctor Colquhoun The—

Chirurgian Visitor, Jon Hall late Bailie
Jon Hall yr his sone, Mr david
Sharp, Andrew Elphingstoun, James
Weir, Jon Robisone, Rot Houstoun, Adam
Gray and Jon Liddell..

Act anent
Andrew Ralstoun
his Compt —

The sd day the members of the
faculties put ordaines, Jon Hall
late bailie, Mr david Sharp, Charles
Muat, Jon Robisone and Andrew
Elphingstoun with the Visitor to
meit wt the relict of umqll Andrew
Ralston yr late Collector and take
in the compt of her hand and
if the same be found right they
are hirby impowered to discharg
her and the representers of the
defunct of his haill intromission
And ordaines the bonds & money
belonging to the faculty yt wer in
his hand the tyme of his dreise
to be given to the visitor who is
to compt yrfor to the faculties
untill they appoynt a new
collector.—

Act anent
lang his
admissioun

The sd day Compt befor them Lou
lang in hamiltoun in obedience
to a charg of a horning givin to
him at the instance of the
visitor ffor practising ye airts of
chirurgery inlicentiat and desyrit
to be admittit by them to the
practise yrof He always not medling
wt the practise of medicein To any
preson wtin the bounds of the phisitians
inspectioun and particularlie in
cronicall diseases qrto by his
admissioun he oblises himself under
the pain of fourtie pounds toties
quoties he sall be found to contravein
the same and the facultie did
ordaines him to pay in to the
chirurgien visitor fourtie pounds
Scots ffor his friedome fyne and
a rex dollor for the officers fiall
and to pay yearlie of qrin
compts thrittie shilling Scots
ilk year.—

11 Septr 1673.

Convened in the Chamber of Ard
Boyills Visitor doctor Colquhoun and
hamiltoun wt the sd Ard, Jon hall
late Baillie, Mr david Sharp, Charles
Murs and Ard Grahme, Jon Robisone
James Thomsone, Andrew Elphingstone
Jon Hall yr Ro— Houstoun, Mr Thomas
Smith, James Weir, Adam Gray
Wm Mc'nill & Jon diddell—

Jon Hall
fynd and
discharged—

The sd day Compeired befor ym Jon
Hall chirurgian in Pasley in
obedience to a charg of horning givin
to him for practising the arts of
medicin chirurgey & pharmacie
wt in thir bounds unlicentiat
and particularly for setting up in
Pasley and setting out a signe
thr of his airt—The facultie
thn callit for his testimonials
frae frae the ministers elder or
magistrats of the erale places
of his residence since he came
to this countrie or if he could

(120)

instruct by indentor & discharg
yt he wes taught Chirurgerie who
pduceit to them severall passes
from severall pairts in England
of aught or ten yeirs since thay
wer dateit Bot produceit nothing
of a testificat or testimoniall from
any place wt in this countrie –
The facultie pnt taking to ye
consideracne his presumption not
only to practise Chirurgerie conferred
be him unlicentiat Bot also to
sett out a signe of his sd airt
at Pasley wt out ye libertie thay
hairby fyne him in fourtie punds
Scots for the sd wrong and discharges
him frae the practise of any of
the sds airts for the future wt
in thir bounds untill he pduce
testificate frae the reseive places
of his residence conforme to the
tennor of ye gift and yt ye be
tryall takin of his qualificacnes
under the paine of fourtie pounds

toties quoties he contraverin this
act.—
The sd day ordaines Ro Houstoun
to wryt to darnock anent his
band & to report his answr the
nixt meeting.

Act anent
intrants in the
countrie to pay
30 S yeirly—
The sd day ordaines all yt
salb be admittit who liv in
the countrie to pay thrittie shillings
yeirly of yeter compts.—

17th Septr 1673.
Conveened in the Visitors Chamber
doctors Colquhoun and hamieltoune
wt the sd visitor don Hall late
Baillie, Mr david Sharp, Charles
Murat, Andrew Elphingstoune, don
Hall yor. Ro Houstoun, Adam
Gray and don Liddell.—

Admission
don drunroe.
Compt befor them don drunroe merh
in Crinock who desyrit to be
licentiat and admittit to the
practise of pharmacie wt in the
bounds the facultie yr tryall takin

of his qualificaciras y^r of dox admitt
and licentiat him to make and
sell comon oyles, emplast: de minio
emplast: de meliloturm simplex, ung:
de Egiptiacum, ung: de altheu, ung:
album, pulvis sanctus, and such lyke
composicurs conforme to the dispensacoune
and dois hireby discharg him frae
the practise of medicin & chirurgerie
w^t out the advyce of a graduat phisitian
or chirurgian under the pain of fourtie
pund scots totiis quoties And ordaines
him to pay tuentie pundis for his
friedome fyne and thrittie s yeirly
of quartar comptis._

18 Septr 1673._

Convened in the trade hospitale And
Bofill, Jon hall late baillie, M^r david
Sharp, Charles Murat, James Thomsone
Jon Robisoune, Ro^t Houstoun, Jon Steill
for Andrew Elphingstoun, Mr Thomas
Smith, Adam Gray, Ivir Mc Neill
Jon Liddell, James Braidwood. &

464

don hall barber.—

(131) The sd day The Members of faculties

Mr david Sharp Visitor.— put By pluralitie of votts nominat
and appoynt Mr david Sharp Visitor
for the yeir ensuing who hes givin
his aith de fideli administratione
as use is.—

Qiter Mrs The sd day The visitor did nominat
for him Archibald Bogill and
James Thomsone qptr mrs for the
ensuing yeir and the faculties
by pluralitie of votts electit Rot
Houstoun Mr Charles Umat and
Adam Gray qptr mrs for them
who also gave yr aithes as
use is.—

Rot Houstoun Collector The sd day by pluralitie of votts
electt Rot Houstoun Collector for
the yeir ensuing and don Hall
yor Chirurgian and don Liddell
box masters who all gave
ye aithes.—

Act for taking the Compt of Bogills hand & The sd day ordaines The compt
of moury of the late Collector

dreeist to be taken of the late
visitors hand and for y* end
ordaines a meeting this day
fyftein days and the same to be
given to the put collector.-

Clerk & Officer The sd day Ratifies the Clerks
admission & officer and continowes
the officer.-

13 octor 1673.-

Conveend in Hutchesons Hospitall
The visitor is doctors Colquhoun &
Hamiltoun, Jon Stall late bailtie
Ro Houstoun, Evir Mcneile, Jon
Stall y* chirurgian, James lies
Mr Thomas Smith and Jon
Stall barber.-

Act against raising caption ag* Stall prisons The sd day ordaines all presons
conteind in the exceequres of James
Mudy, Jon donald & Jon Yuille lyers
who have not compeired befor
them in obedience to the exceevir
charges of horning given to them
To be denunced And a caption

466

raiset agst them by the clerk who
is appoynted to give in his accompt
yrof to the collector and to
be payit.—

The sd day ordaines Baillie hall
Ro Stonstoun put collector and the
gfter masters to meet wt the
visitor and to take of the late
visitor his hand the money prtaining
to the calling aft he has gott fua
the deeris of the late collector And
having takin the compt of the
hand of his relict to discharge
the same and to report to the
faculty at yr next meeting.—
The sd day ordaines the collector
to get in a new charg.—
The sd day Baillie hall and
remanent members of the faculty
appointed by ane act daited the
6th of Sept last are ordained at
the next meeting to report to the
faculty ane compt of yr diligence
in arising of and Andrew Nelson

his compt of charg & discharg & q[uhat]
mony wes in his hand the tyme
of his decese & how they ruilt
y[e] affair w[t] his relict.—

18 Octor 1673.—

Conveened in Ard Bogills his Chamber
M[r] david Sharp Visitor, Baillie Hall
the 2d Ard Bogill, M[r] Charles Hucat
ho Stonstoun, Adam Gray, Jon
Liddell, Jon Hall y[e] chirurgian w[t]
doctor Hamiltoun.—

The 2d day Baillie Hall & remaneing
members appointed by the facultie
for taking in the compt of um[q]
Andrew Ralston y[e] late collector
relicts hand of his intromission
w[t] the @ rents, bands & u[the]rs
pirteing to the faculty w[t] ane
accompt of tha mony and bands
y[t] wes uplifted be Ard Bogills late
Visitor since the decese of thir late
collector by the faculties appointed
they all in on voice declared that

Collr Andrew
Ralston Compt of
introms dischargit.

they perusit the late Collector his
compt of intromissions And finds
the same to extend with the money
receivit by And Bogill To the somme
of ane hundreth nynteen thrie pund
sixtein schilling ten pennies Scots
money Qlk by the facultie appointment
were instantlie takin and givin to
Rt Houstoun ye late Collector And
he ordainit to compt yrfor And the
relief of said Andrew Ralston & his
representars dischargit of his intromissions
of any of the rents & uyrs perteining
to the facultie the tyme he was
ye collector.

Annent bands put
in the box and
some to be agreat.

The 2d day The facultie also receivit
up fra And Bogill ane obleisd[?] granted
be James Kerr in hamiltone. It
ane uyr be Jon Broun in paisley
and a third be Alexr Cobson in
Glasgow. That they sould not meddle
w Chirurgie & were put in the box
It they ordain Allan kirkwoods
band for twelve pounds & Thomas

Harper for eight pund & damooks
for twentie pund to be regrat And
for ye end the same wes drlyverid
to Rot Houstoun collector & he to
compt yefor And in regaird ye
Rot Houstoun receivit upon trustfie und Andrew Ralston the tyme
he wes collector damooks band
upon his granting to him
obleissment for redelyvring ye of
or then for pyt of the money

Houstoun dischargit ofhis obleius The facultie put doe discharg &
rescours the sd Rot Houstoun of the
sd obleissment in respect it wes
not retired or cancellit as Rot
alleggis and yt now the sd band
is in his hand as put
collector

Wilson dischargit The sd day the facultie ordaines
a discharg to be grantit to Alexr
Wilson of his fformer pund band
qlk wes payit to Ard Bogill yt the
arreris of then late collector & yt Ard
had comptd yefor

douglas muir — The 2d day The faculty did ordaines the Collector to pay to Mr douglas four punds Scots for service doon to the faculty in anno 1672 in executing of ye lres.—

Clerk & officers payit of th: fiale.. — It ordaines the collector to pay to Ro: Smellie thrie punds for his bygain fiale qlk wt the Clerks fiale were payit to Michaelmes last.—

29 octor 1673.—

Conveened in Ard Bogills his chamber The visitor wt doctor Hamilton, Baillie Hall the sd Ard Bogill, Anderw Elphingstone, Win Mcneill, Jon Hall yor chirurgian, Mr Charles Umat, Ro: Houstoun wt Jon Liddell.—

Coiuperin examined & dischargit. — The sd day Complt befor them Jon Couper in Lesmehago who being apprehendit & captione at ye instance ffor practising of the airts of medicin, chirurgrie & pharmacie unlicentiat did conveen the sam Bor drager to be admittit

by them to the practice of some
pñts of chirurgerie such as curing
of wounds, opening of veins & the
lyke. The members of the facultie
first did find it convenient to
re-examine him if he was qualified
yefor who after tryall were found
grosslie ignorant And yefor they
discharged him for the future fra
the practise of any of the sds
airts and ordaines him to grant
band yefor under the paine of ane
hundreth pund scots in case he
contraveen And to pay in to the
collector sxe punds scots for his
bygain fyne for the expenses of
raising trio. Qlk fyne were payit
and the band grantit & bothe
givin to the collector.

30 Octob 1673.
Conveend in Hutchesons hospitall
doctors Colquhon & hamilton w the
Visitor Baillie Stall, Mr Charles Unmot,

(23)

Ion Robirsoune, James Thomson, Ion
Hall ye Chirurgian, Rd Houstow, Mr
Thomas Smith.–

The sd day Compt befor them Mr
Andrew Hamiltoune in Killbryd for
practising tho art of medicin wt
in their bounds not having trie of
graduaone or licentiat by them
All being confessit the faculty
ordain him to grant band not
to medl wt the practise of medicin
in tyme coming untill he produce
befor them trie of graduaone under
tho paine of ane hundreth punds
Scots and ordaines him also to
pay to the Collector sex punds
Scots for expense of trie and the
collector to compt befor with the
band also given to him and he
dischargit of preceiding transgressione.

The sd day ordaines the Collector
to pay to Mart Low dochter to
umqll Ion Low ane of ye late
members three punds Scots for her

put supplie bring in grit
strait.—

**Caption to befor
to exxecun**
It ordaines the caption to be put
in execunn agst Mr   and Mr
Alexr dunlope and the caption to
be sent for frie don Kirk mssa by
the clerk.—

**lres to be sent
to seale ministers**
The sd day They also ordain
lres to be sent by the two
doctors and the visitor to Mr
Wedderburn in Kilmarnock. Mr
Oliphant at Strinhous & to Mr
Miller in Ochiltrie & to Mr Ross
in belshill To prohibit yn frie the
practise of medicine or

12 Nor 1673.—
Conveened in the trade hospitall
The visitor Baillie Hall. Mr Charles
Murat, And Bogill, don Robisone,
Andrew Elphingstoun, don Hall
yor chirurgian Adam Gray &
don Liddell
The sd day ther wre feucil a

474

doctor Bell
his diligene

bra frie doctor Bell to the faculties
agein wes inclose the lres of hom
he had sent him west wt ane
execuone agst sevill presons in
ye countrie contraveeners of ye
arts as ane acount of his
diligene ght wes givin to the
visitor.—

Soutters suspension

The sd day ordaines Baillie
Hall and the clerk to send
east & caus call the suspension
raisit be Mr Soutter agst them.—

4t decr 1673.—

Conveenit in the trad hospitall
Baillie Hall wt the visitor and
the two doctors Mr Charles bunar
Son Robisone Ro: Houstoun, Andrew
Elphingston, Son Hall yor chirurgian
Adam Gray, Son fleming and
Son Liddell.—

Anent Son donald

The sd day ordaines the collector
to gee to Son donald nurse & and
to require him either to give new

securitie for the money he is
indew to the facultie And in
respect his ca°nr is decessit) or
then to pay therewith And the
band given to the collector to
cause regrait & put to exerceme
in case of refusall -
The sd day Compeirit befor . the
faculties don Sutar in Hamilton
who having bein chargit w=
horning at y° instance for practising
of medicin w in y° bounds un=
licentiat not being graduat did
suspend the same And this day
confest himself to be in the
wrong for suspending the charg
given him and declarit he simplie
pay= yerfra and took to prive
the same to be cancellit brtait
and the begining of samin rasel
And remittit himself for bygain
transgressions in the faculties will
Who having taken the premises
to their serious considera°ne They

fyne him in ane hundretto punds
Scotts And to grant band not to
practise medicin wout the direction
of some phisitian is in thir bounds
under the pain of ane hundretto
punds tolies quoties And ordaines
a discharg to be granted to him
of the lres and Repones him to
his former admission & no farder
The facultie in respect of
Mr Sutar his apperance & confessing
his fault in dispending of them
and Remitting himself in ye
will for his fyne they give his
fyne to him upon payt of fourtie
punds Scotts to the collector for
the expense of lres and ordaines
the collector to discharge him
of his fyne upon payt ut
supra.—

12 xrem 1693
Hutchesons Hospitall
Conveend doctor Colquhon the Visitor

Baillie Hall, James Thomsone, Ro-
Houstoun, And Bogill, Wir Mc neill
Wr Th: Smith, James Weir & Jon
fleming.

Act anent
Hall

The faculta ordaines doctor Hamiltone
and Baillie Hall to speak to my
lord dundonald in answer to
ane lre sent be his lo: to them
anent Jon Hall sometyme in Pasley
And till yt tyme they supercide
any farder recenue agst him
in respect of the sd lre.

13 febru 1674

The sd day conveenie at Hutchesons
Hospitall doctor Colquhoun and
hamiltoun The Chirurgian Visitor
John Hall yor And Bogill late
Visitor, Jon Robison Ro- Houstoun
James Thomsoun, Wr Thomas Smith
James Weir, Adam Gray, Jon diddell
and Jon Hall barbour.

doctor Hamilton was receivit as
præses for this instant yeir who

478

accepted & made faith.

The sd day Gabriel Cunnighame was
admitted as officer for the sd year
who also gave his aith to obey
the visitor and faithfullie serve
the facultie.

The sd day Compt James Sayers
in douglas in obedience to a
charg of horning for practising
chirurgie wt in their bounds
unlicentiat who desyrit to be
admittit by the facultie to sie
pts of chirurgie as they could
eft tryall find him qualifiet. The
facultie eft tryall admittit to
the practise of chirurgie who
hes payit in to the collector threttie
erse punds Scots for his friedome
fyne and is ordainit to pay threttie
shilling yeirlie and who gave his
aith as use is.

19 febrie 1674
Convrnt in Ald Bogills chamber

doctor Hamilton & Colquhoun, Mr
david Sharp, don Robison, James
Thomsone, And bogill Mr And
krahine, Mr Charles Mucat, Rt
(125) Houstoun, don Bell yr chirurgian
Mr Thomas Smitte and James Weir
The 2d day Compl befor them
James Mutter in Stenhous in
obedience to a charg of horning
for practising the arts of
chirurgerie and pharmacie wt in
ther bounds wt licential who
desyrit to be admitted by them
yrto The faculter eft tryall admitted
him to sell drogs and to opin veines
at a phisitians direction allenarlie
and no farder And in caise he
transgress this his act of admission
he is ordainit to pay ffourtie punds
toties quoties who hes payit into
the Collector thrittie punds for
his friedoms fyne and is ordainit
to pay yirly thrittie shilling
who hes made faitte as

uer is:-

23 aprylle 1674:-

Conveenit in the trads hospitall
Baillie Neils, Mr david Sharp &
Charles Inneat, And Bogill, Mr
And Grahme, James Thomsone, Jon
Hall yor Chirurgiane, Ro Houstoun
Andrew Elphingstoun, James Weir
Jon diddell, James Braidwood and
Jon flening:-
The qlk day Compd befor them
William Bogill sone to Mr Bogill
mess who desyrit to be admittit
friman wt them as barbour as
he who servit prentise wt And
Bogill his master And to die
Arts of chirurgeria grts his sd
Master wes admittit who pduceit
his indentur wt a discharg yrof
upon the back bering him to have
servit eivine yeirs space and als
pduceit his burges ticket of this
brugh. The faculty but having takin

his dissyer to ther consideracun. They
admittit him to be friman as
barbour and perreworik maker and
qu they find him qualifit for
chirurgerie. They promise to admitt
him to die arts year as he sall
be found qualifit for ep: tryall
wt out farder payt. Thru the twelve
pund of friedome fyne qlk he hes
instantly payit to the collector
wt the three punds for the officers
ficals who hes made faitto as
ues. ie.

<table>
<tr><td>Act for bookiing
Grahame prentice
&</td><td>The sd day Robert Grahme is bookit
prentiss wt Jon Hall ane of the
pnt baillies who hes pdneit his
indentor and payit in to the
collector fyve punds.</td></tr>
<tr><td>Baxter prentice
&</td><td>The sd day Wm Baxter sone to Jon
Baxter in Kirpoch is also bookit
prentiss wt Ard Bogill for the space
of sevin yeirs frae his entrie qlk
wes at Whitsonday 1673 as barbour &
perreworikmaker who pdneit his indentor</td></tr>
</table>

482

and pyit in to the Collector fyve punds
and made faitht.

Huttons prenteis The sd day Wm Hutton is also bookit
prenteiss wt Ion ffleming barbour for
sevin yeirs space who also pyit in
to the collector fyve punds.

23 Junii 1674.

Conveint at the Trade hospitall Baillie
Hall, doctor Hamilton, Wr david Sharp
Visitor, And Bogill, Wr Charles Inneal,
Ion Robison, Rot Houstoun, Wr And
Grahame, Ewin Mcnrill, Ion diddell
+ Ion ffleming.

Robison + Stow
yor to be chargit. The sd day ordainis Thomas Robison
in Cauldwill Ion Stow yor in
Killbarchan to be chargit wt horning
ffor their practising the airts of
chirurgrie and pharmacie unlicenced
And to aprehend Gilbert Boill in
Mearns wt caption for the same
caus.

letteris givin to
doctor Bell. Ther wer also a pair of lris of horning
givin to doctor Bell to caus charg

the unlicentiat practitioners in
the west.—

18 Sepr 1674

(126) Conveened at the trads hospitall
don Hall pnt Baillie, Mr david
Sharp Visitor, Mr Charles Lunce and
Thomas Smith, James Thomsone, Andro
Elphingstone, don Hall yor, Wir Mc
neill, James Weir, don diddell, don
Hall barbor, don ffleming and James
Braidwood.—

Bands putt in the box The gR day The bands granted be
don Patersone in pasley, don Sutar
in Hamiltone and don Couper in
lesmehegou resceve are putt of
the faculties appointment in the box

Bojile Visitor The 2d day Archibald Bogill is by
pluralitie of votts nominated and
elected visitor for the year
ensuing.—

5r Octor 1674.—

Conveenit in the bill house Baillie

Hall, And Bogill, Mr david Sharp, Ro
Houstoun, James Thomsonne, Mr Thomas
Smith, Jon Hall yor, Jon Liddell,
William Bogill, James Braidwood and
Jon Heile barbour

Bogills acceptance The sd day And Bogill accepted upon
him the office of chirurgian visitor
for the year ensuing, who gave
his aith de fideli administratione
as user is

Visitor & masters to be chosen yearly The sd day The visitor & faculties
but enacted yt yr be soe getten
masters elected yearlie in tyme
coming g& this to be chosen
be the visitor and uther thrie
by the faculties

Masters chosen Lykwise the sd day The visitor nominats
Mr david Sharp, James Thomsonne
and Ro Houstoun getten masters for
the year ensuing And the faculties
by pluralitie of votts elects Mr Charles
Muat, Andrew Elphingstoun and
Mr Thomas Smith getten masters also
for the sd year who being put

accepted and made faith —

Box mr
Clerk —
Lykwes The bose masters are
continowed for the sd year
ensuing —

Act for Collectin:
It: Ratifies the Clerks Act of admission
Ordaines the Collector to pay to
the Officer thrie pund and
twentiefowshilling to the drimers
and sex pence to the beddels —

6 Nor 1674 —

Convened in Ard Bogills chamber
doctor Hamilton, Ard Bogill Visitor
Baillie Hall, don Robinsone, Mr
Charles Uniat and david Sharp
and James Thomsone —

John Robison yor
his ay presentie —
The sd day Compt befor them
don Robinsone yor late Sivilor to
Mr david Sharp who desyril to be
admittit frieman is ye facultie
as Chirurgian and pharmacian And
for ye end ought preserve to him
his The members of the facultie
pnt having taken his desyr to thir

consideratne fynd the sam equitable
and yr for præscryvit pilule de char̄o
cum agrario. confretio de alcariumsh
emplasti contra rupturam throschisei
de Cambo for his say in pharmacœ
and ordaines him to be examined
upon yt prt of the anatomie
concerning the heid, ears, nose and
eyrs and the diseases relative
yrto ad usum chirurgicum. And
anent his method in curing of
ulcers and fractures roetempore
upon the fystim dref nisel. And
ordaines him to have the forsd
composiones for his say in pharmacœ
redy against yr day. And Baillie
Hall, don Robisone and hir Thomas
Smith are nominated his say
masters.

<!-- margin note --> Ad-annul. collectin.
The sd day ordaines No Houstoun
collector to have his compt of charg
and discharg of the facultas names
redy against yr day.
dykeas yr is a recetne sent-in be

doctor bill agst srall untientiall
practitioners in the wrst qlk is givin
to the Clk to be kuipit till the
nrset meeting.—

Annnt Hall Ordaines don Hall in Pasley to be
warnit to the nrset meeting to
pduer his testificate from the srall
plaers of his residine conforme to
our act 11 Sept last.—

(127)   15 drerr 1674.
Convrned in the bill house doctor
Hamiltoune And Bogill, Visitor
don Hall & Baillie, hr Charles Hual
don Robirsoune, don Hall yor hr
Thomas Smith, Ro Houstoune, James
Wir, don diddall, James Braidwood
and Wm Bogill,

Houstoun continued The sd day continoure by pluralitia
Collector.— of votts Ro Houstoune, collector for
the yeir ensuing.—
The sd day the Collector ordained
to satisfie the Clk his bygain ficall
for the yeir preciding and als for

regra'ne of the lres of horning & raising
a caption yeupon extending   to
twelve pounds.

Admission
Jon Robison

The sd day Compt befor them Jon
Robison yor Chirurgian late Servitor
to Mr David Sharp in obediance
to ane former act of the facultie
in ther last sederunt And produced
upon the table befor them The
receive composicures ordered to be
made be him as his esy befor
his esy masters who being put
ireland they did see the sd
Jon Robison weigh the simples
and mixe the same orderlie And
after inspection taken by the haill
members of the facultie put of
the samine they did allow and
approve of each of the sds composure
made be him as being well dispos
and having examined him in
ther pryce upon the termes of the
airts both of pharmacie & chirurgerie
grunto he made perfyte answers.

They all in on voice declaret that
they found him able & sufficientlie
qualified both for the practise of
chirurgerie and pharmacie in the
severall pts yrof And did admitt
and receive him both as chirurgian
and pharmacian Having produceit
his burges and gild brother ticket
of this brugh Colie made faith as
use is And payed to the collector
for his friedome fyne twelve punds
scots and their punds for the
mens fialls.—

Admissioun Jhon Hall
in Paslay The 2d day Compt iror them the
aforseid Jhon Hall in Pasley and
pduceit ane Testimonialls frae dundie
w some burges tickets frae divers
brughs to the faculties and desyrit
to be admittit by them to the
practise of sevall pts of chirurgerie
The faculties taking his desyre to
ther consideracne does ordain him
first to be examined by some of
yr number and according as he

sall be found qualifiet To admitt him
and this they intimat to him
when the pleiers to pass his tryals
in order yrto the faculties sall
be conveened.-

The sd day Robert Houstoune Collector
gave in his compt of intromission
wt the faculties maiures from his
admission and that by charg &
discharg Qlk by the faculties wes
remittet to Ion Robisone elder to
revise and approve as he finds
just qlk being approven & subt by
him wes ordainit to be bookit and
he dischargit yrof Qlk compt is
as followes..

Charg for the yeir 1674.
Imprimis the Charger charges
himself wt the soumm of ane
hundreth nynten thrie pounds
seventein schilling ten pennies
recivit recivie be him fra
Ard Bogills who by the faculties

appointment receavid frae and
Andrew Ralston then late
collector his relict the money
uplifted by her and husband
pertaining to the facultie and
any money uplifted be him
y^e   fra ye late collector
dresis to the ellection of the
psnt collector. Say the soume of   193 – 17 – 10
It is the soume of sextein pund
threttein shillings four pennies
being a yeirs @rent uplifted
be him of the four hundreth
mark dew be Walter Broll
and his ca°ners. –   016 – 13 – 4
It Ten mark for a yeirs @rent
of Captain Rinnie his five
hundreth mark band – say   006 – 13 – 4
It ffyve mark for a yeirs @rent
of Griserl risbet ane hundreth
mark band – Say   003 – 6 – 8
It three pund sextein shilling
eight pennies being a yeir
and half a yeirs interest or

@rent of ane hundreth mirk
drw be don donald – Scay   003 – 16 – 8

(128) Item the @rent of twa hundreth
merks drw be william boill
by band for a yeir. Ten merks 006 – 13 – 4

The @rents uplifted for 1674

It a yeirs @rent uplifted frae
Walter Broek..   020 – 00 – 0

It a yeirs @rent frae Low
yor   008 – 00 – 0

It a yeir.. uplifted frae Crissell
nisbet is   004 – 00 – 0

It a yeir @rent frae Wm Boill is 008 – 00 – 0

Summa of the @rents is   077 – 03 – 4

Heirdome fynes and uyrs
It receivit dennoch's pell comne
with the bygain @rent extending
to twentie ane pund fyve shilling
Scots. It receivit don donald
his penell comne of 66 lib.13 S.
& It frae William Kirkwood
by band twelve punds. It
Thomas Harper his band for
8 lib. It Robert Herreis his

his precept upon a det of privile
and expense of pley 20 lib 12 S.
It receivit frae Mr. Andrus
Hamiltone 6 lib for expense
of lies. It frae don Soutar for
his fyne 12 lib. It frae James
Sayris for his friedome fyne
36 lib. It frae don Couper for
expense of lies 6 lib. It frae
Mr Bogill of friedome fyne
and officers fialls 15 lib. It
frae James Multer of friedome
fyne 30 lib. It of Ladvis Wilsone
his friedome fyne 5 lib. It frae
Arcl Bogill for booking his
prentais 5 lib. It frae Baillie
Hall his prentais 5 lib. It
frae don Fleming his prentais
5 lib.

      Summa is   253 – 01 – 4
      Uter compts is in brugh.
Mr Arcl Grahme frae the yeirs
1673 and 1674 twentie four shilling
Scots. It 36 S frae Iou dris for

72.73 and 1674. It 36S frae James
Watt for 72.73 and 74 yeirs. It
24S fr George Lokhart for 73
and 74. It 24S frae Andrew
Miller for 73 and 74. It 24 S
frae daniell broun for 73 &
74. It 9 tb frae Ro^r Henrie
for 15 yeirs at Michaelmas
last. It 7 tb 16S. frae James
frank for 13 yeirs at Michaelmas
last. It 5 tb 8S frae James
Wilsonn for 8 yeirs at Michaelmas
last. It ud frae Baillie Hall,
And Bogill, Ro^r david Sharp,
Charles Muncet, James Thomson
Ro^r Robison, Andrew Elphingsta^n
Ro^r Houston, don Hall yor
chirurgian, Wir h^r neill Ro^r
Thomas Smith, don fleming
James Braidwood, don liddell
James Weir & don Steell barbour
each of them 12S for 74 extending
to 9 tb 12S.
    Retur comptts Wout Burgh.

Soa Spruele 3 ttb for 72 : 73 and 74 at-
20 S p² ann. It be Soa Patsoro
14 ttb for 14 yeirs, at michaelmes
74 at 20 S p ann. It 4 ttb be
Mathew Miller for 71 : 72 : 73 : 74 at
20 S yeirly. It be Hew Hunter the
lyke. It 15 ttb be Thomas Robison
for fyftein yeirs. It 36 S be Ro-
Uuir in gorballs for 73 and 74
at 16 p annum. It 48 S be Soa
logan yor for 71 : 72 : 73 : 74 at 12 S
p ann. It 4 ttb be James Tobias
for 13 yeirs at michaelmes
at 20 S p ann. It 4 ttb 10 S be
Soa forein at 30 S p ann 72 : 73
and 1674. It 4 ttb 10 S be Mr
Thomas yor for 1672 : 73 & 74 at
30 S yeirly. It 24 S be Wm Simps
of dalrook for 73 and 74 at 12 S
p ann. It 40 S be Soa Lod for
2 yeirs at michaelmes 74 It
the lyke be Alexr Portar. It 30 S
be Soa dang in hamiltoun for
1674. It the lyke be Soa Annose

It the lyke be Mr Alexr dunlope
It the lyke by Gilbert Wilsone
It the lyke be don Contame. It
20S for don Crois for 1674
  Sua of optir compts wtin
  wt out bruch   £19 – 18 – 00
  Sua of the Charge is   644 – 00 – 6

    ffollowes the discharg
Item the compter recovers himselfe
wt the sowmes underwritt
givin to the prisons eftir
mentionat viz So Ro Smuller
officer 3 lib. It 4 lib to Wm douglas
nurser by order. It 3 lib to
Mart Cois by order. It 24S
to the deacon convriners
officer. It 24S by order to a
poor man. It 200 lib lent
to don Wallace by band. It
24S to ane uyr poor man
by order. It 6 lib 13S. 4d to
the deacon convriners hous
It 200 lib lent to the laird of

Corshill. It 3 lib for a hors hyre
to the ledy margers of montro
his buriall. It to the touns
drummer 24 S. It 6 S to the
kirk officer. It to Gabriell
Cunyghame for his officers fialls
5 lib. It to a poor man by
order 8 lib 4 S. It to the dracon
courrinus officer 24 S. It est be
the clk frat dou Coupar as a
pn[?] of the recpenss of recising
lris he wes cut by the faculltis
appointment 6 lib. It due be
flo harrie by precept 20 lib 3 S.
It be James Wilsoun of fredom
fyne 5 lib. It by Jh. Harper by
bond 8 lib.

Dittu compts win brugh.
It deus be lw and Grahm 24 S for
73 and 74. It be James Watt
for 3 yeir 36 S. It be Jou Ore
3 yeir 36 S. It be Jeorg Lokhart
36 S for 3 yeirs. It 24 S be Andrew
Miller for 2 yeirs. It be daniel

broun 24S for 2 yeir - It be Ro:
Harreis 9 lib for 15 yeir - It be James
frank 7 lib 16S for 13 yeir It be
James Wilsone 5 lib 8S for 9
yeirs -

    Orter compts W out breigh -
It draw be don Spruill 3 lib for 3 yeirs
It be don Patersone for ye allanerly
20S - It be Mathew Miller 4 lib
for 4 yeirs - It be Jeis Hunter
the lyke - It be Thomas Robison
15 lib for 15 yeirs - It be Ro: Muir
in garbells 16S for on yeir - It
be don logan on yeir 12S - It
be James Lobreas 13 lib for 13 yeir
It be don foster 4 lib 10S for 3
yeir - It be Wr Thomas yor the
lyke - It be damook 24S for 2
yeirs at 12S yeirly - It be don
Lod 40S for 2 yeirs - It be Alexer
Porter the lyke - It be don laing
30S for on yeir It be Wr alexer
dunlope the lyke - It be gilbert
wilson the lyke - It be don

Soutar the lyfr dt be don has
the lyfr dt givin to Mr Stirling
8 lib for his bygane fiale w^r
4 lib farder for expenss of raising
him to the faculteis by y^r order
attor q^t he gott frae lon Couper.

Suma of the discharg is   575 – 12 – 4
Reste in the compter hand
to ballance the acopt   068 – 08 – 2

This compt of charg + discharg is seen
and approven by me according to the
faculteis appointment.

    Sic subt^r John Robertsone

    Glasgow 22 March 1675
Conveened in And Boyills hous. The
visitor Baillie Hall, Ion Robertsone elder
and yor, Mr Charles Nisbet, James Thomson
Ion Hall yor chirurgian, Ro^t Houstoun,
Mr Thomas Smith, M^r david Sharp
James Weir.

The sd day Compt befor them James
Mortoun somtyma servitor to M^r
Patrick Arthour pharmacian in Edgr

Mortonis Remittee:— and produceit ane supplicacione qrby he cravit to be admitted to the practice of pharmacie and some pairts of Chirurgerie is in ther bounds And produceit to them ane lre of recommendatione in his favors frae the facultie at Edr to yt effect and his indentor betyt his sd mr and him dailtt 15 Junii 1670 for 4 yeirs space is a discharge yrof upon the back of the same The facultie efter taking the premisses to ther consideratione They judg it convenient That in regaird he his lalelie come frae his master Ther may be some competent tyme allowit him tryall anent his qualificatiouns in the sds airts and for yt end They allow him to appeir befor yin in thair nixt or qn he salb or redy.—

The sd day The trid of captione givin to the visitor.—

29 Apryle 1675.—

Conveinit at Ard Bogills his hous, The

visitor Mr Charles mcat. Jon Robisons
elder + yor Rot Houstoun, Mr Thomas Smith
James Weir, Wm Bogill + Jon Fleming.
The sd day the faculty put ordaines
a discharg to be drawon by the Clerk
and subt by the visitor to alexr Wilson
of his band + bis raisit yeupors.

17 Septr 1675.
Convenit at Hutchisons hospitall Bailie
Hall, the visitor, Mr david Sharp, Jon
Robisons elder + yor Andrew Elphingstoune
James Thomson Jon Halls yor chirurgian
Eoin mcneill, Mr Thomas Smith, James
Weir, James Braidwood, Wm Bogill, Jon
Fleming + Jon liddell + Jon Halls
barbor.
The sd day Rot houstoun collector payit
to the clerk his fiall for the yeir
preciding.
It the sd day Jon Fleming sone laull
to Jon Fleming mair burges of glasgow is
bookit prentise wt Jon Robisons yor
chirurgian.

Herbertson bookit — The sd day mathew Herbertson is bookit
prentise wt Mr Charles Miael conforme
to his indentor produceit who has payit
in to the collector ffyve punds of
booking money —

Anderson bookit — The sd day Charles Anderson sone to
david Anderson, cordoner is bookit
prentise wt Jon Jennings barbour and has
payit ffyve punds to the collector of
booking money —

Miael Visitor — The sd day Mr Charles Miael by pluralitie
of votts is nominated and elected
Chirurgian visitor for the year ensuing
who has givin his culto de fideli
administratione as use is — who did
nominat Mr david Sharp And Bogill
and James Thomsons ofteimrs for the
sd year And the faculties elected by
pluralitie of votts Jon Robison yor, Robt
Houstoun and James Wer ofteimrs who
all accepted in and upon them the
offices and made faithe —

Collector — The sd day The faculty by plurality
of votts nominats and elects Mr Thomas

503

Smitto Collector for the year ensuing and
Box mr. Jon Halt yor chirurgian + Wm Bogile Boxe
mr who all accepted and gave yr aithes
as use is..
The sd day Ratifies + approves the clerke
office and continowes the officer.

10 decr 1675..
Convenit at Hutchesons Hospitall..
The visitor Jon Halt late baillie James
Thomsone, Jon Thomsone elder + yor chirurgian
And Bogile, Mr david Sharp, Mr Thomas
Smitto, Wm mcnnee, Wm Bogile, Jon
liddell + Jon halt barbour..
Acts annent The sd day ordaines the collector to
Broks band. pay to thir officer fourtie eight
        shilling scots for to buy to him
        a pair of shoes..
        The sd day ordaines Walter Broks
        band to be givin to the clerk to
        regist and to cause raise lrs of
        horning yeron..
Harpers band The sd day Thomas harpers band
        givin to the clk to get in the band

draw be him.

Drumrss band The sd day Jon drumr his band given to the collector to uplift the money yr in continut.

Boils band The band granted be Wm Boils given to the visitor untill the frmrs of the decist doctor Hamiltons mrit granme and he to report to the nxst mrting.

Act for wryting to Sprule & myrs The horning and captions given to the visitor.

It the facultie ordains the visitor to

die wryt to James Sprule and Logyr in Paisley and to James Mortoun

die in Hamilton & to   Caruthers in Lanrick to come in & be admittit at the ordinar forms or dischargit frae the practice of any of the airts of chirurgrie or pharmacie.

Anent Barbors The sd day The facultie ordains yt if any prsons wt in the town & full barbors inlicentiat be them yt yr be aplicacion made to the visitor who is to goe to the magistrat and

complain of him to the end he may
ather retire it yow or desist in all
time yrof

(131) The sd day compt befor yow Jon Cox in

Coups admission

glasgow who desyrit he may be admittit
friemen for barborising and making
of perriwickes it in the toun who
faduct his burges ticket yrof The faculties
but does admitt him to barboris and
to make perriwicks and ordaines him
to pay fourtie punds Scots or give
band for so much yrof as he does
not prntly pay against hurstimes
nixt who hes payit thrie punds Scots
for the officers fiall and givin his aitt
as uss is

The sd day Wm Houstoune late Collector
to the faculties gave in the acompt
of his intromissions wt the faculties
muniers sine hallowmas 1674 by charg
and discharg Qlk the faculties but
ordained Jon Robisone Elder to pruse
and to subscryve his approbacne yrof
iff he find the same right and ordaines

the clk yrupon to book the sam an
to discharg the sd ld: of his sds
intromissions the tyme he wes
colleetor at the end of the sd compt
and subservs the sam in thir
names grof they approve as if sub̄
by themselfis. Qlk compt is as
followes.

Charg 1675.

Inprimis lying in the complers
hand as the ballance of the
yeirs acompt. 68 lib. 8s. 2d.
It received fra Jon Robison
for his pardons fyne & others
fiall 15 lib. It 12 lib as the
@rent of Jon Wallace 200 lib
frae Candlmes ½ to Candlmes
1675. It 20 lib for a yeirs @rent
of Walt Broū 500 mks band
It 4 lib for a yeirs @rent of
Jon Binnigs 200 mk. It 8 lib
for a yeirs @rent of Mr Boies
200 mk. It 12 for a yeirs @rent

drw be Corshill in Iuly last
of 300 mk. It 4 lib for a
yire Orent at Candlmes.
misel of Walter Colquhons 100
mks. It 8 lib be Thomas
Harper by band. It 20 lib
3S be Ro Harries by precept.
It 5 lib drw be Iames Wilson
of friedome fyne. It 5 lib for
booking Mr Charles mreat his
prentis. It the lyke for don
Robisons his prentis. It the
lyke for booking don fflemings
prentis.

    Sua of Orents & fynes   199 — 11 — 2
    Qtir compts id in brugh.
It Mr Ard Grahame 36S for 73:
74 & 75. It be John dira 2 lib
8S for 72:73:74 & 75. It the lyke
fra Iames Watt. It 36S be
georg Lokhart ffor 73:74 & 75.
It the lyke be Andrew Miller
It the lyke be daniel brown
It be Ro Harries 9 lib 12S for

16 yrs at Michaelmas last.
Dt by James Wilson 6 lib for
10 yrs at Michaelmas last
Dt 8 lib 8S by James frank for
14 yrs at Michaelmas. It
rest from Baillie Hall, And
Bogle, Mr david Sharp, Charles
Muat, James Thomsone, Jon
Robisone elder & yor Andres
Elphingston, Rbt houston, Jon
Hall yor, James Wrr, Mr
Thomas Smith, Rvir McNrile
Jon fleming, James Braidwood,
Jon Liddell & Jon Hall Barbour
each of them 12S for 7S
is 10 lib 4S.

          Swa of order compts is   46 — 04 — 0
          Order compts is out bright
Jon Spreul 4 lib for 4 yrs at
20S p ann. Dt by Jon Paterson
2 lib for 74 + 75. Dt 5 lib by Mathes
Miller for 5 yrs. Dt the lyke
by Hew Hunter. Dt 16 lib by
Thomas Robisone for 16 yrs dt

16S be the Moor in Gorballs for
75 & 24S be don Cogan for 74
and 75 at 12S pr ann. It 14 lib
be James Lobian mayr for
14 yeirs. It 6 lib be don foster
for 4 yeirs at 30S pr ann. It
the lyke be thos thomas yor
It 36S be dannoon at 12S pr
ann for 3 yeirs. It 3 lib be
don Lock for 3 yeirs. It the lyke
be alisor porter. It 3 lib be
don long at 30S yeirly for
2 yeirs. It 30S be don lennose
for 75. It 3 lib be thos alisor
dunlope for 2 yeirs. It the
lyke be Gilbert niltoun. It the
lyke be don Soulan. It 40S
be don stow for 74 and 75 at
20S pr ann.

Swa extendis to   83 - 06 - 0
Swa of the haill Charg is   329 - 01 - 2

followis the discharg
Imprimis the compter dischargis

himself w^t 6S payit to the
Kirk officer. It to the facultas
officer for those 48S It payit
to Walter Colquhoun upon
band 66 lib 13S 4d It to a poor
man by order 30S It to the
deacon conveiners house 6 lib
13S 4d. It to a poor man by
order 3 lib. It to anoyr poor
man by order 30S. It to
anoyr 12S. It to anoyr 30S
It to Wr and Grahme his
wyff by order 4 lib It to the
clk for his fialls for this yeir
75. 8 lib. It to his man 12S
It to facultas officer for his
fialls 3 lib for 75. It to a poor
man by order 30S It to the
deacon conveiners officer 24S.
It drw be Ror Henrie by
precept 20 lib 3S. It be Thom:
Harper by band 8 lib. It drw
by Walter Kirk a yeir arent
of his principal 20 lib. It be

gisel nisbet a yeris @rent of
his 100 mrk is 4 lib - It - 8 lib for
a yeris @rent of Jon Binnings
bairn of 200 mrk It the lyke
be Wm boill for a yeris @rent
of his 200 mrk - It - 4 lib be Walt
Colquhoun for a yeir at Candl-
nisel of his 100 mrk It - 12 lib
drew be Corshill as a yeirs
@rent of his 200 lib at July
last -

  Suma is   191 - 05 - 8

  Rettir compts is in brugh
Andrew be Mr Aird Grahme for 73 :
74 + 75 thrittie eres S - It be
James Watt 48 S for 4 yeirs - It
the lyke be Jon Airs - It the lyke
be george Lockhart - It 36 S be
Andrew Miller for 3 yeirs It
the lyke be daniel Broun -
It be Ro hennas 9 lib 12 S for
16 yeir at Michaelmas last
It be James ffrank 8 lib 8 S for
14 yeir - It be James Wilsonn

6 ℔ for the year –
  Sua extends to   36 – 12 – 0
Quarter compts w'out brugh
    drew be
John Sprewl 4 ℔ for 4 years at 20S
yearly – It be Jon Paterson 40S.
for two years. It be Mathew
Miller 5 ℔ for 5 years at
Michaelmas last – It be Andrew
Hunter the lyke – It be Thomas
Robinson 16 ℔ for 16 years – It be
Robt Muir in Corbells 16S for
7S. It be Jon Logane 24S for
2 years at 12S pr ann – It be James
Tobias 14 ℔ for 14 years – It be Jon
forler 6 ℔ for 4 years at 30S pr ann.
It the lyke be Wm Thomas young.
It be Dennock 1 ℔ 16S for 3 years
at 12S pr ann – It be Jon Coce
3 ℔ for 3 years – It be Alexe Porter
the lyke – It be Wm Alexr
dunlope 3 ℔ for 2 years at 30S
pr ann – It be gilbert Wilson
the lyke – It be Jon Louttan

the lyke. It be don stow 40S for
2 years at 20S pr ann. It be
don Cunnoe in grinok 30S
for 7S. It be don lang in
Hamilton 3tib for 2 years at
30S pr ann.

  Swa thing is   83 _ 06 _ 0
  Swa of the haill discharg   311 _ 03 _ 8

Swa yt ye rest drw be the compter to
balleine the accompt the just Somme
of srointein pounds fourtein Shilling ane
pennies deirs of k is instantlie given to
the rest collector.

In respect whereof and the foresd accompt
of Charg and discharg being approvin
and Subt by the sd don Robison the
faculter all in on voice sconer and
lempre dischargs the sd Ro Stonstoun
his airs and ssers of his haill
intromission had be him to any
of the monry or urinirs pertining
to thrm for both years he was thir
collector bzo of this and the former
yeir be thir fitte for 2182 and by

virtue of their former ordinance their
futo are sub by me Clk to
the sd faculter at yr comand —
Sic sub   W Stirling —

(/33)
                11 drcar 1675 —
Conveened the visitor Baillie Hall. Mr
david Sharp. Thomas Smith, Jon Robison
elder + yor. And Bogell, Jon Hall yor
Mr Houstonn —

The qlk day Robert Boyd shritor to
umghle doctor Hamiltonn. Compt and
gave in a supplicaon grby he craved
to be admittit to the practise of
some poynts of chirurgerie as they
sould find him qualifet, qlk
supplicaon being considerd And
thrupon he publictlie examined
befor them they admitt him to
oppin vrinrs, apply cauters and
vrutores and to cdir simple grrin
wounds and als to administer
clisters by our plisitians direction
in any prt is in the bounds comitt

to them except is in the brugh of
Glasgow wherein he is not to
practise any pairt of chirurgerie
gt sor untill he be admitted burges
of the sd brugh And gin he attaines
to mor knowledge and desyres to
be farder admittit they find it
just and equitabl that he be
re-examined and farder admittit
according to the knowledge litratur
and practise they sall find he
sall have then acquyred whois
fyne is remittit be the haill
members of faculta pnt for the
kyndnes showin by the sd doctor
Hamiltoun to the sd faculta qr
he was ane member and upon
his particular recommendatioun of
him to the faculta on his death
bed - who gave his oath as use is
The sd day compt also James
Sprule residentar at Pasley and
gave in a supplicatioun to you qlk
he desyrit to the practise of some

pts of chirurgrie and pharmacie
who being examined by them they
admitt him to the practise of
pharmacie and als to the ordinary
and comon pts of chirurgrie such
as opning of veines applying of
cauters and the lyke qr yr occurs
qrr necessitie therfor and ordaines
him to pay to the collector for
his friedome fyne thritie punds
scots and thrie punds for the
officers fiall qlk are instantlie payit
and ordaines him to pay thritie s
yeirlie q. qtr compt who gave
his aith as use is and is dischargit
to practise any thing of the sds
arts within this brughe untill
he be made burges therof.

At Archibald Bogills chamber
the 15 of decr 1675.
Conveened the visitor don hall late
Baillie, Mr david Sharp, And Bogill
don Robisones elder + yōr, Andrew

Elphingstoun, don Hall yor chirurgian
Mr Thomas Smith –

The sd day compt befor them John
Whyt in Pasley and gave in a
supplicacion qrby he desyrit to be
admittit frie w them to the
practise of pharmacie and sic
prts of chirurgerie as they sall
find him qualifiet for – Who eft-
tryall they admitt and licentiat
him to the making up of recit..
according to the phisitians ordor
and to sell drops and composicions
And farder to opin vrins by lancett
or loch lechers and applying of cautes
in caisis of necessitie in any prt
w in their bounds except the burgh
of glasgow wherin he is not
licentiat to practise till he be
admittit burges qrof And they do
hirby discharg him from vising
or making up of composicions w out
the advyce and assistance of ane
doctor on the place or to medl

beyond this his put admission
untill he farder tryd and found
qualifie by them And ordaines
him to pay to the collector fystie
punds scots of friedome fyne And
three pund for the officers fiace
(q[lk]s are instantlie payit) And als
to pay yeirly twenties s of qtr compt
and in caise of anie nixt admission
they declare he sall not be lyable
to pay any mor of fyne excep[t] be-
his good will + pleasor to them who
hes givin his aith as use is.—

(134)
Act anent Charles
Anderson and
Susanna Simson

The sd day also compt Isobell
Wilsone relict of u[mquhile] david Anderson
Cordoner in glasgo And gave in
a supplicatioun making mentioun
y[t] of hir sone Charles Andersones
being latelie bookit prenteis w[t]
Jon fleming barbour w[as] desseisit
hir love in consideraon of the
prenteis fie y[at] in obleist + som yet
payit to educat + bring up hir
sd sone and teach + instruct hi[m]

in his sd aint conforme to the
indentor betwixet ym yeaurent And
ye through his dece shortly apt
tho sd indentor his sd sone was
desolat of a master unles his
relict Susanna Morsone wold
take home some jurneyman to
instruct his sd sone sufficiuntley
And yefor eraved yr in respect of
the sd don filming his dece thos
might be fred of the obevissments
conttenet in the indentor for any
fit of the prentis fie unpayd
and hir conditions him & hir
sone fire to goe to some uthir
master or had as thoe sould
think resperdiunt Or uthirwaye
yr the sd Susanna Morson might
be obevist to take in to hir
house ane sufficiunt jurnyman
to teach and instruct his sd
sone sufficiuntley. Tho faculte
put taking tho sd supplicaoun
to thir sirious considraoue And

and having callit for the sd Susanna
and having sein the indentor
betsit hir sd wingt husband and
the sd Charles Andersone they find
it just and equitabl that shoe
take home the sd Charles and
intertein him as before the tyme
of his sd w^t masters lyff and
ordaines hir to take in a
suficient jurneyman by the sight
of the visitor and sic many of
his masters as he sall appoynt
who sall suficientlie teach and
instruct the sd prentis in the
airt of barborising conforme to the
sd w^t doline his own airt of
admission And to book the sd
jurneyman conforme to use and
wont of the sd facultie With
this expres certificaoun to the sd
Susanna that if shoe faillie in
doing yrof upon applicaoun or
complaint made by the sd Charles
or his mother to them yr ofuent

That they hereby declare the sd
Charles Anderson to be frie to
guy² hir in all tyme thereft as
if yᵉ had niver bein any indentor
pay² Remits all preires being put
consentit And yrupon took instruts
hine inde in the hands of mr
not publict undirsubscryvand clk
to the sd faculty And in farder
tokin yrof The sd descobels entut
hone putts hir sd sons wᵗ the
sd Susanna..

     sic subᵗ   Nᵗ Stirling was pbliet

       21 dcem 1675.-
Convend in Hutchsons hospitall
The visitor Baillie Hall, Mr david
Sharp, Jon Hall yor chirurgian
Jon Robison chirurgian elder + yor
Win mᶜneill, Nᵗ Houstoun,
Nᵗ Thomas Smith, James Warr and
William Bogill..
The sd day compt James Mortoun
in Hamiltoun and gave in a

supplica'ne Therby desyring to be
admittit to the practice of pharmacie
and small prts of chirurgerie who
ys tryall admitts him to the
practise of pharmacie And als to
open veins, apply cauters and
ventoses allanerlie and ye win
any prt of yr bounds except
ye brugh of Glesgow untill he be
admittit burges yrof And discharges
him frae all farder untill he be
farder tryed and admittit and
ordaines him to pay for his
friedome fyne ane hundreth merks
scots and thrie punds for the officiers
fiall who has instantly payit in
the sd thrie punds and givin bond
to the collector for the ane hundreth
merk and ordaines him to pay
yeirly thrittie shilling of qter comp
who hes maid faith as use is.—
The sd day ordaines the visitor &
collector to lend to the lairds of
Bangour and stonshiell ffour hundreth

Act for lending
of 400 mk to stonshiell
and Bangour..

mnk upon yr band gfk is now in
the collectors hand.-

24 Januii 1676.-
Conveand at Hutchsons Hospitall The
Visitor, Mr david Sharp and And
Grahame, Jon Halls yor and Jon
Robison yor chirurgians Rot Houstoun
James Weir, James Braidwood barbor
Jon diddell, Wm Bogill, Jon Top and
Jon Halls barbors.-
The gfk day complaint being made
agst Gabrial Cuninghime yr officer for
refusing to warn the faeultie at
comand of the visitor they dischargit
him of his office unles in thir jines
he confessit his fault + suld promise
not to comitt the lyke gfk he
accordinglie + yeupon was reponit.-
The sd day ordainis the Collector
to call for and tak in the money
drew be Walter Colquhoun and be
Walter Brok or wuresayes the sd Walter
Brok to give new securitie for his

money conforme to our former
act:—

Act for charging
hall¹ on
Parker
&
Snodgrass
The 2d day also ordaines
halthorne ane souldier in the
late disbandit companies to be
chargit w horning. And als James
Parker in glasgow ffor ye practising
of chirurgery w in ye bounds
inliberties:—

It ordaines Mr James Snodgrass in
Pasley & his mother to be chargit
w horning for practising medens:—

28 Janry 1676.

Conveind at Trads hospitall The
Visitor Baillie Hall, Mr david Sharp
don Robisons elder & yor And Bogill
don Hall yor Rot Houstoun, Mr
Thomas Smith, James Weir, Jon
diddell Wm Bogill barbor:—

Clauñe non pay⁰
of ¼ter compts:—
The 9th day ordaines the clerk by
the Visitor his sight & any too of
his appointment To retreit a list of
the non pay⁰ of the ¼ter compts:—

w^t in and w^t out brugh & to causer summon
y^m befor the compr court & to
draw a dit^l agst them for y^r
bygain aftir compt^r.

It ordainis Rot Herreis precept to be
givin to the clerk to raise horning
yron & to put the same to
execu°ne agst him..

It ordainis Walter Colquhounis band
to be taken out of the box & givin
to the clerk to raise horning yron
and to causer charge him yrwith..

It ordainis Walt Brok & his ca°ners
to be also chargit w^t horning.

The sd day Complt Ludovik Lyndsay
late servant in the laird of Blair
his company & gave in a supplica°ne
yrby desyring to be admittit by them
to oppin veins & the lyke and als
to barberise. Qlk being considred they
admitt him to barberise as a
comon barbor in polling of hride
and beards And als to oppin veins
by the sight of ane phisitian   or

chirurgian and ordaines him to pay
fourtie pounds of friedome fyne or
witherwayes to give band yr for pyable
at Michaelmes next wt Consent yrof
who gave his aith as use is._

28t Januar 1676

Act against Barbors transgressors and breakers of saboth

The sd day upon informatione givin
to the faculty that severall barbors
who are members yrof within this
brugh are prophaners of the sabath
by barborising of prsons yt day they
taking it to ther consideratne and
finding the same to be so gross a
sin and violatne and breach of
the saboth day Contrair to the
word of God and to all lawes both
humane and divyne that any soule
take upon them who are members
of ther Incorporatne & does sitt &
vote wt them to comitt the same
being in itself most scandelous as
it is a heily provoking sin they
all wt on consent doe hirby enact
that gif evir prson ether at first
incorporat wt them or who salbe

hairing be admittit as a member of
ther facultie sall presume to barborie
any person qr̃eof upon ane sabboth
day and he be conviel yrof in
pñer of the facultie sall for each
of the first and second faulties pay
in to the collector of the upsett
fountie fund scõs and upon refusall
to pay the sa to be declarit no
member of the facultie and his
act of admission cancellit and
delit lykeas if any sall happin
to be so gross as to be conviel a
third tyme of the foirsd sin They
dos herirby declair him no member
or yr sd facultie fra yr tyme furth
& if he had never bein admittit
and incapable at any tyme yrãft
to be readmittit and his act of
admission to be cancellit, scorit &
expungit furth of ther records as
a person unworthie of being incorporat
in any societie & much less to be
a member of ther facultie

(136)   28 of Apryll 1676..

Conveend at Hutchesons hospitall,
The visitor don Hall late Baillie
Mr david Sharp, And Grahme
And Bogill, don Robisone Elder &
yor Andrew Elphingstoun, James
Thomsone, don Hall yor chirurgian
don Liddell, Mr Thomas Smith ludovick
Lyndsay, Wm Bogill, don Sap..

The qlk day compt befor the faculty
Wm Cuming indweller in Glsgow
being cited to appeir ffor his
barborising wch in this bruгh not-
being burges yrof or licentiat by
thम who being challengd therfor
confessed the same But withall
declaird he was ignorant of thır
priviledg. The faculty eft consideraoun
yrof discharges him in tyme coming
to barborise wch in the brugh untib
he be made burges yrof undır the
paines of Twentie pund Scots quoties
he salb be found to transgres qlk
he was content by ane act undir

his hand to obliss himself to pay
to the facultie.

Act anent Don
Hall his tryalls

The sd day compt also Don Hall
sometyme chirurgian in Pasley who
desyrd to be admittd by the facultie
to the practise of Chirurgerie compleslie
and pertieularlie of fracturs dislocaons,
and opining of veines The facultie
efter having takin his desyre to
ther considraone ordaines Don Hall
late Baillie, Don Robisones elder & yor
Don Hall yor chirurgian wt Mr
David Sharp to meit on the first
or nynt dyrs of may nixt wt Mr
Ard Grahme & to examine him
upon his knowledg yrof and to
admitt him to sie pts of chirurgerie
as they sall find him qualifiet for
qlk admission they ratifie & approve
of as they find sufficientlie qualifiet.

Campbell bookit
prenteis.

The sd day Wm Campbell sone to
Don Campbell of parkhead of Rosneth
is bookit prenteis wt Mr Charles Mags
in his airt of pharmacie for fyve

yeiris space from his entrie qlk wes
the first of dcen last conforme to the
indentor past betwixt them daitit
18 Janii 1676 instant who has made
faith as use is & payit in to Mr
Thomas Smitte collector fyve pundis
Scots.

Act anent
qrter compts The sd day ordaines Baillie Hall, And
Bogill, Jon Robisone elder & yor to meit
wt the clk & to pruse the qrter
compts and to take some course
wt thos who are non pyt yeof.

Captain Binnies
band put in the box The sd day Captain Binnie his
band of corroboraone qlk wes in
clks hands put in the box.

lris of horning
gin to the Visitor The sd day the lris of horning &
captivis pertening to the faculties givn
to Mr Charles Miriot pnt Visitor to
lys in his hands for ye use.

Bangour and
Houshills band put
in the box The sd day also the band grantit
be Bangour & Houshill to the facul
bot blank in the creditors name for
four hundreth merks put in the
box.

the end of
its Booth

Ane list of the bands perteining
to the facultie and putts in
the boxe this 28 Aprile 1676 —

Imprimis ane Band of Captain Ion Binnies
for wr a band of coroboracne 200 mrk —
yron both in boxe. —

It ane band be Ion Wallace late
baillie and his carmrs to
them in boxe   300 mrk.

It a band be the laird of Corshill
and his carmrs for 200 lib
indts in the boxe   300 mrk

It a regrat extract of a band
be Walter Broß and his carmr
for 500 mrk givin to the clerk
to cause present   500 mrk

It a band be bangour and
Anshill for   400 mrk
put in the visitors hand..

It a band be Wm Boile + his
carmr for   200 mrk
put in the boxe ..

It ca band of the Harper for 8 lib
givin to the clerk feyie

It a band be James Mortoun in
Hamilton for   100 mrk
in the collectors hand.
It a band be don Gilhagie for
one hundreth mrk & his
caoures —   600 mrk.

At Ard Bogills Chamber
9 Maii 1676.
Conveened the Visitor Baillie Hall, don
Hall yor chirurgian, don Robisoune
elder & yor Mr david Sharp. Ard
brahme & Thomas Smith Ard &
Mr Bogill.

Act anent
don Hall giving
in band for his
removal out of ye
bounds at Ard don
dragie.

The sd day compt byor them don
Hall sometyme in Pasley who
declarit he was of intentioun shortly
to remove furth of this place & the
haill bounds committed to the inspec
of the faculties and for yt end were
content to grant band for his remova
furth yrof betuixt and the fyftein day
of Julii nixt under a penaltie. If
the faculties would desist fra medling

(137)

wt him till that tyme they taking
his dwayes & offer to yr consideracun
and the grit trouble he hes frequently
put them to grants his dwayes and
ordaines the clerk to draw a bond
of yt tenor with ane hundreth
pund of penaltie. qlk bond was putlie
drawn and subt by the sd domi
stall and put in the boxe.

The sd day Thomas Harpers bond of
eight punds givin to the visitor to
cause get in the money

Jt Thomas Trmills act and the recevung
under Andrew McKensies hand.

The sd day Wm Thomsone sone to umqle
Thomsone in garngibert is bookit
prentis wt Mr Charles Stuart in
pharmacie for fyve yeirs space fra
his entrie qlk is of the dait of his
Indentur being 13 dave 1676 instant who
hes maid faith and payit in to the
Collector fyve punds Scots.

The sd day the horning & caption
perteining to the facultie wt the recevung

534

...

ordaines the haills bygain great compts
of ungll andrew Miller to be also
scoril out of the charg—

At Trads Hospitall the
first of Junii 1676—

Conveint the Visitor Baillie Hall, Ard
Bogell, Mr david Sharp, Ion Robison
yor, Mr Th: Smith, Wm Bogill, Ion liddell
and Ion Hall barbor—

The sd day ordaines Susanna morrison
relict of Wm Ion fleming to be
warnit for booking her junry man—

Ordaines the fint and late Visitors with
the box nrs and clk to goe through
the roereenure & to caus demune all
yt are chargit & the clk to raise
a caption yron—

Ordaines Baillie Ion Wallace to be
spoken to anent Walt brok his money
for qlk heis cognne by the visitor &
if he satisfie not the drr to caus
put the crs to roereenure agst both
prinll & cauns—

At Hutchesons Hospitall
5 August 1696 —

Conveend the Visitor Baillie Hall
Mr david Sharp, Jon Hall yor, Jon
Robison yor, Rot Houstoun — Evin mc
uill —

(138) The 9th day Ordaines the band grantit
be James Mortoun to be regrat ansd
horning raisit yron & execent agst him
Ordaines Walter Brok and his cawoners
to be drunne in caise their money
be not payit against the 13 of this
instant the bris givin to the visitor.
Ordaines Rot Gray barbor to be warnit
to enter wt the facultie —
Ordaines Susanna Mortoun to be
warnit to book hir prinay man —
Ordaines Jon Saip ether to give band
for his freidome fyne or to pay the
samen in to the Collector —
Ordaines Alexr Wilson to be chargit
of new with horning for practising
chirurgrie contrair to his obleisment —
Ordaines the Visitor to wryt to the

laird of Corshill to make redy his
money against mertimes nixt –
Ordaines Jon Hall soutigin in
Pasley to be warnit to the nixt
meeting of the faculty –

At And Bogills chamber
15 August 1676 –

Conveened Baillie Hall And Bogill
late Visitor in absence of Mr Charles
Mead put Visitor, Mr david Sharp
Jon Robisoune elder & yor Rot Houstoun
Jon Hall yor chirurgian, Ludovie
Lindsay, Jon Liddell, Jon Sap –
Compt Byor them Jon Hall soutigin
in Pasley who desyrit of new again
to be admittit to the practise of
Chirurgrie and offerit himself to
ther tryall Whos desyer bring takin
to ther considnaeun and efter tryal
and examinaeun of his qualyieaeune
and knowledg They heirby admitt
him to the cure of simple wounds
qr thir is no loss of substance and

yͬ ther is nether nerves, arters or
tendents cutt and lyRevayrs to
open veines by a phisitians direction
and to apply ventosusrs, caulters &
loch leechrs. Allamrlia With this
expres provisioo that if it sall
be found yͭ he takrs any patient
under his cuir or in hand beyond
this his admissioo it sall in
yͭ caise be lisum to the visitor
for the tyme or to any chirurgian
bring a member of the faculee to
take the patient of his hand as
being a prison not only ignorant
but usurping also upon yͭ qͭo
he is not admittet and hes not
knowledg yͭof & farder that he
sall pays in to the collector for
the tyme twentie pundz. Sedͬ totis
quotis he sall be found to trans
this his admissioo And ordaines
him to grant band for yͭ effect And
whēn the faculee sall find yͭ he
hes acquyrd mor knowledg they

eft tryall are to admitt him to
ye farder they find him qualifiet
for in the sd airt and ordaines
him to pay in to the collector
fourtie punds scots for his friedome
fyne and thrie punds for the
officers fialls or then give band
and sufficient caune ye for it in
the toun pyrabe at Candlmes nixt
it @rent ye eft and ordaines
him to pay twelf s yeirly or
efter compts off the gtk he has
instantly pyit to Ard Bogill twentie
pund as a pt of his sd friedome
fyne and thrie pund for the officers
fiall who foluit his burges tikit
& maide faith as use is _

(139)

Hutchsons Hospitall
24 August 1676 befor noon _
Conveinit Ard Bogill in absence of
the pnt Visitor, dean Hall, late Baillie
Wr Ard Grahme, dean Robisone yor
dean Hall yor, Wr Thomas Smith,

540

Ro Houstoun, James Weir, Jon Liddell,
Jon Hall barbor & Jon Sap.

Annent lending out to Jon Gilhagie y 600 mks.

The 9th day ordaines the sex hundreth
merk lying in the collectors hands
to be lent to Jon Gilhagie as ple
and Thomas Bogill merchand as
his cauner who have grantit band
yyor being arrent frae Lombmess
last & given to the collector.

And Bogills chamber
the 2d day afternoon

Convened Baillie Hall, And Bogill
in place of the first visitor now
absent Mr David Sharp, And Grahme
Ro Houstoun, Jon Robisons yor Jon
Hall yor sone to the said Baillie
Hall, Jon Liddell, James Weir, Jon
Hall somtyme in pasley or gorballs.

Boille discharged and fyed.

Compt befor them Peter Boille in
Malletshuch who being apprehensit
& caption at the faculties instance
(grantit band for his appeirance this
day) for transgressing his act of

admission made in anno 1669 who
confest the same and yt he had
opnd veines and applyed clisters. The
facultie put taking tho premiss to thir
consideracone dos of new again prohibit
and discharg frō his medlling wt any
of the airts of chirurgery or pharmacie
beyond his former act of admission in
respect they find him not farder qualifye
then he was at that tyme and in
caise he contraveine ordaines the lres
& execucōne alredy raisit to stand in
force agst him Bot in respect of
his promise made no to medlle
farder in tyme coming then gf he
is admittet to practise they ordaines
him to pay in to the collector ffor
his bygane after compte and for the
expenss of raising lres they hawe
bein at the soume of Suntie merks
scots qlk wes instantly payit.

Hutchesons Hospitale
eleventh of Septr 1676.

Conveened the Visitor Baillie Hall, And
Bogill, Mr david Sharp & And Grahm
James Thomsone, Jon Hall yor sone
to Baillie Hall, Evir Mcneill, Thos
Houstoun, James Weir, Lodovik lyndsay
Jon liddell and Jon Sap.—

Acti anent
Mortoun's band
Ordaines the band grantit be James
Morton to be givin to the clk to
be regrat and he to raise his yron
and to caus charg him yrnt— the
same givin to the visitor—

anent charging
Jean West..
Ordaines the clk qn he goes wrst
to caus charg Jean West at the
place of Kirstoun for hir practising
unlicentiat in the countrie upon
complaint made of hir to the
facultie by Mr James Porter.—

Anent Hall
Ordaines Jon hall latelie admittit
to be warnit to grant band conform
to his act of admission and if
he refuse to certifie him yt thay
will cancell his act of admission—

Jon Craufurd fynie
and withdraft..
Compt befor them Jon Craufurd in
Korballs in obedience to a charg of

horning givin to him at the faculties
instance for practising medicein &
chirurgie is in ye boundis inlicentiat
Who confest yt he had givin to sralle
prsons recites for feveres and for
(40) wound not in this twelve moneth
or yeby and yt he uses to prserye
to such Juniper berries anat seedis
and syrup of roses and the lyke
The faculteis first taking to ye
consideraon his confession and
having examined him as to his
knowledg grof they fynd him
groslie ignorant and yefor not only
they fyne him in fowrtie punds Scots
for byganis transgression Bot also
ordaines to grant band never to
medle is practiss of medicein in
tyme coming gtk being refusit of
him The faculty ordaines him
to be drummed and the clk
to cause bring home a caption
agst him & any uyrs alredy drummed

Hutchesone Hospitall
the twentie two day of Sept 1676.

Conveened the visitor John Hall
late baillie, Mr david Sharp, And
Grahme and Thomas Smith, Jon
Robisone elder & yor, Jon Hall yor
chirurgian son to the sd Jon
Hall, Thos Houstoun, James Weir,
lodovik lindsay, Mr Bogill, Jon littill
Jon Hall barber, James Braidwood
Jon Hall in gorbells, James
Thomsone..

The sd day ther being a copie
of suspensione givin to the faculi
at the instance of Jon Crawfurd
in gorbells of a charg of horning
givin to him at ther instance ffor
his practising of medicin & in th
bounds the faculti first taking
the samin to yr consideratione tha
ordains the visitor for the tyme
to cause discuss the samin & he
to imploy both ane agent and
advocat in order yrto and to

satisfie them yefor gll sall be repayd
in to him be thir collector + for
persons to attend the discussing yrof
as sall be thought fitt.

The sd day ordaines Jon Crawfurd
in Kilmarnock a shoemaker ether
to be of new charge or to get the
former executors givin in be Andrew
McKersIe removit + to get frae him
any uther executors he hes and
tho elk is ordainit to get them +
to satisfie yefor.

The faculty considring the poor +
decayrd conditione of Rot Muir in
gorbells upon his supplicaçne givin
to them anent his povertie grby
he desyres to be frie and guyt of
payt of his yeir compts bygan +
in tyme coming they doe herby
discharg him of the sam both
for bygaines and in tyme coming
and ordaines the collector to cancell
his name out of his charg.

The sd day upon complaint maide

to the facultie That Alexr Wilsone
garner in glasgow hes transgressed
his obleisement in practising
chirurgerie contrair yrto They
thairfor ordaine his band to be
regrat and he chargit yrupon
for payt of the ane hundrith
punds of penaltie yrin content
the band givin to the clk yyor &
he to be satisfiet.

Warrt for paying
the clk for getting horne
his expens in raising
& captions.
Ordaines the collector to pay to the
clk for regrie of horning against
don Crauford in gorballs & the uyr
twa viz don fleming in grenok
and don Hamilton and in raising
captions yron agst them fyve punds
scots mony ffor qlk they ordaine
this his warrant.

Mr Ch: Inneat
continowed Visitor.
The 2d day By pluralitie of votts
they continow Mr Charles Inneat to
be Visitor for the yeir ensueing wh
being first accepted & made faitho
as use is.

Visitor continowed
The 2d day Mr Charles Inneat did

nominat & elect mr david Sharp, And
Bogill & James Thomsone after mrs
for him for the yeir ensuing.
And the facultie continowes Ror
Houstoun, Ion Robisone and James
Weir after mrs for the sd yeir.

Bose mrs.. Also continowes the bose mrs and
collector for the yeir ensuing &
the officers.

Mortons band.. The sd day James Mortons band
givin to the collector to get up
the money.

At the Trads Hospitall
the twentie day of Nor 1676.
Convened The Visitor Baillie Hall, mr
david Sharp, And Grahme, James
Thomsone, And Bogill, Ion Robisone Elder,
(141) Ivir McNeill, Ivir McNeill, James Weir,
Ror Houstoun, Ion Hall barbor,
Ion liddell, James Braidwood
Ion Lap.

about Ion Hall The sd day the facultie first ordaines
Ion Hall latelie in pasley to be

548

warnit to the nixst meeting for keeping
of ane servant yt practios in the
airt of chirurgerie and barborie.
To ansr qt they have to say to
his charg yr anent.—

Anent Robt Gray
Ordainis Robt Gray to be warnit wt
          to the nixst meeting.—

Anent the collector
his compt.
Ordainis Mr Thomas Smith collector
to be warnit to give in his compt
of charg and discharg wt his
intromission wt the meinis and
estat of the faculty the last yeir
against the twentie seventh day
of Nor instant.—

Anent dutiants
in tyme coming.
The sd day The faculty herby
ordainis and inacts that in all
tyme coming all persons who sall
herefter be admittit ether wt in or
without burgh sall pay ther entar
compts to the faculty frae the
tyme of yr admission yt is to
say they are to pay and be
lyble to the collector in name of
the faculty at the mucharlmes

court reset ensuing yr sd admission
for a year as if they had been
admittit a year preceiding notwithstanding
of the present practize in the
contrair –

At the Trads Hospitale
the twentie sevinth of Nor 1676 –

Conveened the visitor Baillie Hall,
Ard Bogill, James Thomsone, Jon
Robison yor chirurgian, James Weir,
Jon Hall yor chirurgian sone to
Baillie Hall, Mr Thomas Smith, Lodovik
Lindsay, Jon Liddell, Jon Hall
barbor, Wm Bogill –

The sd day Mr Thomas Smith gave
in his compt by charg & discharg
of his intromission wt the meinies
and retour of the faculties sine
hallowmes 1675 – The facultie ordaines
the visitor Ard Bogill & Jon Robisones
Elder & yor to meit wt the collector
and clk & to peruse the forsd
compt and revise the same & if

they dis the [Tre] ight to report to
the next meeting — The compt givin
in to the clk..

Gilhagies bond
put in the box
The 2d day the collector gave in
the bond grantit be don Gilhagie
and his cautioner to the faculty
for the ane hundreth mark and
put in the box.

Act anent discussing
of the suspension
raisit be Crawfurd
agst the faculty
The 2d day the visitor prsitit to
the faculty ane lre from don
Murshell lawyr in Edgr ye agent
qm they imployd for calling the
suspension raisit be don Crawford
agst the faculty ye charg of horning
givin to him for practising unlicentiat
Bring yt the suspensions wre
produced for stopping ane protesta...
The faculty judit it convenient that
the suspension be discust & minion
Hamilton advocat imployd yrin
And in order yeto. They took out
of ye box and gave to the visitor
to be sent in to the sd don
Murshell the lres of horning and

receawnrs yrof agst don Craufurd
togither wt ther gift + Ratificaoun
yrof frñ the late Parliat and
am dñt obtent at the visitor
of the faculter for the tyme ye
instane befor the lords and
ordainrs the visitor to get a recñt
yrof frñ the sd don Marshell.-
The faculter ordainrs that next
meeting to be this day fourtnight
being the 11 of dror next.-

At Hutchesons Hospitall
11 dror 1676.-

Conveend the visitor, Baillie Hall
Mr david Sharp, don Robisons elder
and yor, damrs Thomson, Ror
Houstoun, don Hall sone to the
sd Baillie Hall, damrs Weir, Weir
Mcneill, Mr Thomas Smith, don
Hall barbor, don liddell, Wm Bogill
and don Sap.-
The 9th day the Visitor pdueit ane
br frñ don Marshell wryt an

(42)

ger being a recit of ther richts
glk wer sent east to him in
order to the discussing of a
suspension agst don Crawfurd confor
to yr last act glk the members
of the faculty put ordains to
be laid in ther box untill ther
wrchts and richts be returned —

Anent any recits
for Crawfurd —

The sd day they ordains any recits
under don Crawfurds hand glk
comes to any of the pharmatians
for drogs to be givin to the visitor
to the end he may send the
same east to mak up a speciall
charg agst the sd don Crawfurd
acording yrunto. Ther wer severall
givin in to him glk wer ordred
to be sent east to the sd
don Marshels —

Anent a complaint
made be the visitor
agst Worth: Smith it
ther cousin thinge and
he recovfind yrfoae on
his confession —

The sd day ther wes complaint
made be the visitor that it in a
frio dayes bfor he had sent for
some of his wes and severall of the
faculty whom he suspected had

uents frae the sd Jon Craufurd, qlk
he demandit of purpose to send
the sam east to mak a speciall
charg agst the sd Jon Craufurd
conform to Jon Murshels his lre
at qlk tyme Mr Thomas Smith not
only refusit to give up this he
had Bot wt vilipending expressions
had abusit him And qlk he
remittit to the facultie who takin
it to yr serious considraoun having
hard and examinid the sd Mr
Thomas yeupon togither wt the
testimony of this frit wt the
Visitor and him being members
of the facultie they find him
guiltie of disobedience to the
Visitor and of sraa vilipending
expressions And therfor they ordain
the sd Mr Thomas (this having bein
the first fault) to crave the faculte
and particularlie the Visitor pardon
for his miscarriadg, qlk accordinglie
he did efter he had confest befor

them that he was then in passion
and yefor They quyt and assoilyies
him yefrae

At Ard Bogills hous
15 dber 1676..
Conveened the Visitor Baillie Hall
don Hall his sone Wr Ard Grahme
and Thomas Smith don Robisones
elder & yor, James Thomsone, Andrew
Elphingstoun, Rt Houstoun, James
Weir Wm Bogill, lodovik lyndsy and
don he is the deacon Conver..

Act for raising a caption.. The qlk day the faculty bot ordaines
the clerk to cause denunce theo
persons conteint in Andrew McKarsies
execuone & to regrat the same &
to bring home a caption agst them
and to give in his comptt therof
to the facultie and he to be
payit for regraone yrof & raising
of the caption..

Amut Alexr Wilson his trgait: The 2d day compt before them Alexr
Wilsone garner for having transgressit

555

his obleissement contenit in a band
grantit be him to the faculty
qrin he oblest himself not to
medB wt the airts of Chirurgery
medicin or pharmacie under the
pain of ane hundreth punds
scots of penaltie who confest the
saim and referrit himself to the
discretion of the facultie and
wt all desyrit to be admittit to
them frie to the exerceise of gt he
is abe to practise eft tryall they
taking his confession and desyris
to ther consideraone doe remitt
gt they intend to take from
him for his transgression untill
they have tryed his qualificaons
and for yt end ordaines him to
appeir befor them on the 29 of
this instant to be tryed & examined
The sd day Mr Thomas Smith Collecter
his last yeirs compt of chargis &
discharg wt the cruts and vmims
belonging to the facultie wes produceit

(143)

by the Visitor and thes ordainit by
ane former act to reexamin the
saim who reported they did find
the saim just whilk being considrit
by the sd faculty And they also
having perusit the same they
did Ratifie and approve yrof and
being ent by the prsons ordained
to revise the saim and ordaines
the saim to be bookit..

Act for deleting &
quytting scalk & ye
mimbers from payml of
yeir compts in tyme
coming.-

At thre taking to their consideraon
the long absene of georg lockhart ane
of yr mimbers out of this countrie
quby he hes not the benefit of the
exercise of his employment wt in
this place As als the poverty of her
And Grahme, daniell Brown, James
Watt, James dies and James Watsone
and ther dreayed condition they
doe ordain them to be free and
liberat of the payment of ther
efter compts in all tyme coming
and them to be scorit out of the
Collector charg except georg Lockhart

who is only ffird greg during his
absence furth of this countrie.—

  ffollowes Mr Thomas Smith his
  compt of intromission w^t
  the faculties merines frae
  d^{cer} 1675 to d^{cen} 1676 instant
  by charg and discharg.—

    Charg.—

Imprimis the compter charges
 himself is seventein punds
 seivintein shilling sex penies
 as the ballance of the
 compt made be Ro. Houstoun
 ye late collector and givin
 in to the collector indorsed 17—17—6
 ffreidome fynes and
  booking money.—

It dames Sprull his fyne and
 officers ficals 33 li It dames
 Mortons fyne and ficals 69 li
 13 S 4 d.— It don Whyt in paisley
 his fyne and ficals 53 li.—00.—00
 It lodovik lindsay his fyne

and fialls 43 lib:00:00 It don
Tapp barbour his fyne and
fialls the lyke It Peter Boill
his fyne 13 lib 6s. 8d. It don
Hall his fyne + fialls 42 lib
18s. It dauns Wilson resting
of his frisdoune fyne 5 lib
It Ard Campbell his bowking
money 5 lib. It Wm Thomson
his bowking money 5 lib.

Siua of fyns & bowking money 312 – 18 – 0

Soumes awand by band & arent

It don Wallacer his band of 300
mk wt arent frae Candlmes
1675 to Mert 76 indr   221 – 00 – 0

It Walt Broks band of 500 mk
wt arent to Lambmes 76 indr 363 – 6 – 8

It Crissell Misbrie band of 100 mk
wt arent frae Candles 75 to
Candl 76 indr   070 – 13 – 4

It don Binning band of 200 mk
wt 2 yeirs arent at Mert 76 indr 149 – 6 – 4

It Walt Colquhouns band of 100
mk wt fyve yeirs of a yeir

@rent inde   071 – 13 – 4

It- Ro- harris precept of 20 lib
38 + Thomas Harpers band
of 8 lib inde   028 – 03 – 0

It- Wm Boills band of 200 mk +
2 yris @rent yrof is   149 – 6 – 8

It- Corshills band of 300 mk +
2 yris + a half at merit
76 - inde   230 – 0 – 0

It of discount givin to the
compter farder   000 – 12 – 0

    Suma of bands + @rents 1384 – 01 – 8

    Detta complts wt in bugh.

It Mr And Grahme 4 yris in
2 lib 8S. It George Lokhart 5 yris
inde 3 lib. It be James Watt
the lyke. It be daniell Brown
4 yris. Inde 48S. It be James
Wilsone 11 yris inde 6 lib 12S
It be James lue 5 yris ind
3 lib. It be Ro- Merris 17 yris
inde 10 lib 4S. It be Andres
Miller 4 yris inde 48S It
be James frank 15 yris inde

9 lib. dt be Andrew Elphingston
for 76 12S_ dt be Baillie Hall
the Visitor. Mr Charles Muir
Mr david Sharp, And Bogill
don Robisons elder & yor_
don Hall yor chirurgian Rot
houstoun. James Weir Wm
McneiIl. Mr Thomas Smith
don Hall chirurgian barbor
James Bredwood, Mr Bogill
don liddell and James
Thomson each of yw haue
pyit in to the compter gk
is his own.

   Swa of qrtr compts win brgh 052_04_0
   Qrtr compts is out brgh
dt be don Sprewl elder 5 yris
at Michaelmes last inde
5 lib. dt be Matthew Miller
6 yris inde 6 lib. dt Rob min
in gorballs for 75 and 76 ink
40S dt be James Sobras 75
yris inde 15 lib. dt be Mr
Thomas yor 5 yris at 30S pr

(144)

ann inde 7 ℔ 10S It be don
Tod 4 yeirs at 20S pr ann
inde 4 ℔ It be Mr Alexr
dunlope at 30S yeirly for
3 yeirs space inde 4 ℔ 10S
It be don Lutou for 3 yeirs
at 30S pr ann inde 4 ℔
10S It don lennoxe for 75 &
76 inde 3 ℔ It be James Sayer
for 3 yeirs inde 4 ℔ 10S It be
James Mortone 76 inde 30S
It be James Spreul for 76
20S It be don Patson for
3 yeirs at 20S pr @ inde 3℔
It be Thomas Robison 1) yeirs
inde 1) ℔ It be don foster
for fyve yeirs at 30S pr ann
inde 7 ℔ 10S It be Gilbert
hrilcoun for 3 yeirs inde 4
℔ 10S It be don lang the
lyke It be James Hunter
the lyke It be don logane for
3 yeirs at 12S pr ann inde 36S
It be Wm Semple for 4 yeirs inde

48S. dt be Alexr Porter 4 yeirs
at 20S pr ann inde 4 ttb.
dt be don Stow 3 yeirs inde
3 ttb. dt be don Whyt for 16
yeir 20S. dt be Alexr Hunter
4 yeirs inde 4 ttb
  Suma of qrter comptis wout bngh 115 — 14 — 00
  Suva of the haull charg 1782 — 15 — 2

    followes the compting
      dischary
dt givin by order to the officer
for shois 48S. dt to a poor
woman in hospitall 18S
dt to Mr Anderson for warning
the calling 6S. dt to a poor
familie 2 ttb 18S. dt to a poor
man callit Inglis 18S. dt to
don dow Wochter 30S. dt to
the clirk for his fiaull 8 ttb
dt for expines of reparinis
of Walt brotis bound & raising
horning 4 ttb 4S. dt by order to
a poor man 13S 4d. dt for

raising lres & regra're of horning
agst Crawfurd & rest hos 5 ttb
dt giving to the deacon convnng
hous 10 mark — dt to the
officer by order 24S — dt to
don Marshell wrytt in Edgr
by order a exe dollar — dt
6S debursit to the post for
sending east ther gift — dt to
a poor man by order callit
Coptein Clark 12S dt for fyr
at Hutchsons Hospitalls 12S
dt givin by order qlk wes sent
to Edgr to discuss Crawfurds
suspensioun 20 ttb 18S dt lent
to make out of houshills brig
8 ttb 14S 8d.

    Suma is   69 – 19 – 04

ffirdome fynes unpayit
dt Archibald Campbell bowling
5 ttb — dt be Don Seip resting of
his fyne 29 ttb 13. 4. dt be Jauns
Mortoun 66 ttb 13S 4d w the
Rent — dt be Lodovik Lindsy

31 lib 2S 4D. It be don Hall chir:
barbor 20 tib. It be Somes
Wilsone 5 tib.

Swa is   157 – 09 – 0

Bands & Rents

It a band be don Gilhagie and
his ca'ners of 600 mks glR we
made up of Walt Bro'lls bond
and Walt lothers glR thuy
wer indris by bond Seay   400 – 00 – 0

It a band be Bangour and
houshils of 400 mk glR who
made up of Driserls mebtz
band & fridons fynes Seay   266 – 13 – 4

It don Wallace band of 300 mk
and Rent being 3 yeirs at
Mart: 76 mks   209 – 00 – 0

(45) It don Binnings band of 200 mk 133 – 6 – 8

It band of Corshills band for
300 mk and tio yeirs Rent
and a half at Mart 76 mks 230 – 00 – 0

It Rot Amies precept   020 – 03 – 0

It Wm Boills band of 200 mk + 2 yeirs R:: 149 – 06 – 8

Swa of bands   1408 – 09 – 8

Restan compts is in brugh
unpayit:-
It be Wor Ard Grahm to Michelmas
1676. 4 yeirs inde. 48S. It be Georg
Lokhart 5 yeirs inde 3 tib. It be
James Walt tho lyke. It be
James Lees the lyke. It be
James frank 15 yeirs inde
9 tib. It be Andrew Elphinstoun
for 1676 12S. It be Ro: Menzies
17 yeirs inde 10 tib 4S. It be
Andrew Miller 4 yeirs inde
2 tib 8S. It be James Wilsone
11 yeirs inde 6 tib 12S. It be
daniel Broun 4 yeirs inde
48S.

       Sua is   042 - 12 - 0
Restan compts is out brugh
       unpayit.
It be Jon Spreull Elder for 5 yeir
al-20S pr annu inde 5 tib. It
be Ro: Innin in gorballs tho
lyk for 2 yeirs inde 40S. It
be Jon Patson for 3 yeirs inde

3 lib don how for 76. 20S. Don
Whyt the lyke _ Lt be Math
huller the lyke _ Lt be James
Tobias for 15 yeirs inde 15 lib
Lt be don Sod 4 yeirs inde
4 lib. Lt be James Spreul
for 76 inde 20S Lt be Thomas
Robison 17 yeirs inde 17 lib _
Lt be Mr Thomas yor for 5
yeirs at 30S pr ann inde
7 lib 10S. Lt be don foster the
lyke. Lt be Mr Alexr dunlope
for 1676 inde 30S _ Lt be don
huniese the lyke _ Lt be James
hortoun the lyke _ Lt be don
Luter for 3 yeirs inde 4 lib
10S. Lt be James Layes the
lyke. Lt be Gilbert hrileong
the lyke. Lt be John long the
lyke _ Lt be James hunter
the lyke. Lt be James
logan for 3 yeirs at 12S
pr ann inde 36S. Lt be
Wm Simple for 4 yeirs

inde 48.

Summa of gdtr compts about
brugh unpayit retirds   96 – 04 – 0
Summa of the haill discharg is   1774 – 14 – 0
It in the Compters hand of money   0008 – 01 – 2
    qlk ballances (being in all) 1782 – 15 – 2
    the charg preceding retinding

Qlk accompt of charg and discharg
abovwin being seen & considrd were
approven & the compter exonered.

Thrid day of Junii 1677
     du Ard Bogill
Conveenit the Visitor Baillie Hall, Mr
david Sharp, Jon Robisons Elder & yor
Jon Hall sone to Baillie Hall Ard
Bogill, James Thomsone and James
Wm.

The qlk day compt James forrester
in the parish of Killmaronie in
obedience to a charg of a horning for
practing chirurgrie wtin ther bound
Who desyrit to be admittit by the
facultie to exe pr̃ts of chirurgrie as

he sould be fund qualifird yt tryall
and produce a testifical under the
hand of Mr Patrick Simpsone minister
at the sd Parish Kirk of his lyff &
convarne Who yf tryale wes found
qualifit for the practise thes pnts
yrof yt his father was formerly
admittet to vizt the curing of brokin
bons glks are not come through
the skrin and to cuir grin wounds
and to oppin the thrie veins of the
arme by adoyce of a phisician
Qrunto they hirby admitt him to
the practise yrof in any prt wt in
thir bounds except the citie of
Glasgow & suburbs yrof untill he

(146) be made burges yrof who has payed
in to the collector thrittie punds for
his admission and thrie punds for
his offiers fiall and ordains him
to pay yrily in name of qtr comple
thrittie shilling scots bging the first
yris payt at Michaelmes nixt who
hes made faith as use is.

The 2d day comprt also Thomas
Melvill srvitor to don Bels Provest
of Glasgow desyring to be licentiat
To barborise w[i]t[h]in the citie of Glasgow
The facultie p[rese]nt does at the requeist
and desyre of his said master
licentiat him to barborise and to
hang out basings w[i]thin the brugh
gratis w[i]t[h]out any pay[men]t ffor this his
admission paying yeirly the o[the]r
comp[en]ts as v[the]rs dois — Therr[efter] they
took his aith his aith de fideli
in respect they declare him a
member of the facultie —

At the facultie p[rese]nt ordaines don Hall
in Gorballs and Patrick Wilson farmer
in Glasgow to be warn[i]t to the[ir]
nixt meeting —

Hutchesons Hospitall
12 Julii 1677
Conveend the Visitor Baillie Hall, Jon
Robisons elder + yor daniel Broun, Jon
Hall yor chirurgian, James Weir,

(margin note: Admission Melvill barbor.)

(margin note: die)

(margin note: Ret agst Hall & Wilsone —)

570

ſon liddall, Evir Me'rvill, ſo
ſon ſap.—

Anent Baillie
Skills and Alexr
Tilſonne.—
The qlk day the viſitor ſ
lie frae david Baillie ſ
and ſamurs Skrills yor ſ
dreyn a ſupererdres ſ
miſet at qlk tyme They
inter ſt the faculty.—
The 2d day compt alexr
bring examind of his ſ
ſore found groslie ignorā
diſchargit in all tyme e
the practiſe both of chiru
pharmacie under the ſ
in his band and they
for his bygain tranſgreſſ
band put in the box.—

~Hall
lt they ordaine ſon hall
to be apprehndit ſt ca ſ
breach of his act of ad
his tʳo band givin to ſ

At and Bogills ch
9 febru 1677

Conveind the Visitor Baillie Hall &
his sone, Mr david Sharp, Jon
Robisones elder & yor, And Bogill,
Rot Houstoun, James Weir.

Complaint
agt Halls The 9th day comp't befor them Jon
Halls in gorballs somtymes residenter
in Pasley against whom ther being
a complaint givin in of his
transgressing frequentlie his act
of admission and for refusing to
grant bond in manner containd
in his sd act And mor
particularly for cutting of ane
camer of Mart Miller spous to
Richard Hall souldier in Coll:
Borthick company and yt als
about thrie weiks yrsst shoe did
Qlk he grantit And farder yt he
made applicacne to the Leg of on

Muir relict of
Shiells hammerman in gorballs
and yt shoe did shortly yrsst
Qlk also wes confest be him yt
he waited on her thrittie thrie

dayrs Bo^r allt he took advyce of
doctor Bell y^r anent and y^t he
wrs present w^t him at his first
applica'ns And farder for practising
and administrating of phisick &
frequent giving of vomiturs as
particularly giving phisick to and
Mr Kry hammerman. It confrst
y^t he had givin to the sd And
the syrup of pale rorrs w^t in tw
or thrie dayrs aft he had cooled
of a fevor. It confrst the giving

sie

him a dram wright of Cremar
tartar and ane scruple of
riobarb. It he confrst and grantit
giving vomiturs thrs thrttie yrir
past viz the infusion of antimony

(147)

or croins mrtalloid w^t sick. It
grantit cutting of srall canerrs
aftor the first condrserncht on
and such lyke.

2^k being considrrd by the sd faculty
As also the declarations of Baillir
Hall and of Jon Robisons eldar & y^{or}

Hall his Act. of
admirion amndit &
declair mlls.

who declarit That they being callit
to the sd Mart Muller anent the
cutting of her cancer and having
sein the same they found it not
saif to cutt it woul apparent
hisart of her lyf Wherupon they
left her togither w his own conffession
in thir presence of his applica'nes
made of severall cures and wyes
beyond his act of admission And
of his gross ignorane of thes airt
he practises They all in on voice
hairby declare his former act of
admission to be in all tyme coming
voyd and nule And he to be
proceedr againste as ane unlicentiat
persow and as if he had never
bein ane member of the faculty
and ther letis to be put in execu'ne
againste him qurevir he beis found
to medl w any of the airtis of
phisik or chururgery or pharmaci
w in the bounds.—
The sd day The nixt caption given

574

to the Visitor and be him to the
nurse² James Mudy.

Act for 10 tts to
Mr Ard Graham

It be pluralitie of votts ordaines
a warrand to be given to the
collector for his giving of Ten
pund scotts to Mr Ard Graham
his wyff in respect of their
povertie.

At Archibald Bogills Chamber
22 febry 1677.

Conveened the Visitor Baillie Hall, Mr
david Sharp and Ard Graham, Jon
Robisones elder & yor, Mr Thomas
Smith, James Thomsone, Wm
Bogill.

For Harris discharge
of his dett & after compts
& whichatties now
upon pmt to the collector
of 12 tts.

The qlk day compt befor them
Robert Harris chirurgian in
dumbartane Being chargit at ye
instance for bygaine after compts
he was indew to the faculty And
by a dett all qlk extendit to
fourtie three pund scotts qrof he
had payit formerly twentie pund

right shilling by vreut pducet and
allet he had drbursit in the
faculties service in anno 1659 at
glk tynu he was ane member
of the faculty residing at Glasgow
and pduceit ane acompt yrof glk
wold ballance the rest.—

The faculty takeing his alledgiance
togither w the compt pduceit be
him to thr consideracōn thry
all in on voice ordaines him to
pay in to the collector Twelve
pundo scots in satisfaction of the
sd dbt and of his bygan yrter
compts to Michaelmas nixt And
upon his pyt ordaines the collector
to grant him a vreit of the sd
12 lib in satisfaction of the sd debt
and of his yrter compts to Michaelmas
nixt and of all can be laid to his
charg for bygans preciding this
day glk wes instantly payit to
the collector & he grantit him a
discharg of this dait.—

Act for granting a discharg or assine of Colquhoun bond.—

The 2d day the faculty but ordaines the Visitor to grant ather a discharg to Walt Colquhoun and his cautrs of his ane hundreth merk bond or ane assine to the cautrs.—

Stirlings bond.

It ordaines the collector to lend to Mr Stirling ye clk sevin hundreth merk on bond and sufficient cautne.—

(148)

At Archibald Bogills Chamber
24 Maii 1677.—

Conveend the Visitor, Baillie Hall, Mr david Sharp, and Archibald Grahm and Thomas Smith, Andrew Elphingstoun John Hall yor chirurgian, Ro Houstoun James Weir, And Bogill, James Thomson John Robisoune yor Mr Bogill.—

Act for paying the agent the expenses of the caption.—

The elk day the members of the faculty but ordaines thar clerk to get frae John Murehead ye agent his accompt for expens of thar horning and raising thar last caption agt

don Crawfurd + uyrs wt a recit geof
under his hand and ordains the
clerk to pay him conforme and to
give him a rex dollar farder for
his paines and diligence in ye afairs
and prticular in attending the
discussing of don Crawfurds suspensi
agst thrm And ordaines the Collector
to repay the saim to the Clerk.—

Act for Baillie Hall
his repairing to
pay to attend the
calling of Crawfurds
suspension—
The 2d day They ordains Baillie
Hall ane of ther members To
repair to Edgr upon advertisement
frae ther agent for attending the
calling and discussing the suspension
raisit be don Crawfurd agst the
faculty.— And they prmitte to him
to take what prson he sall think
fitt to wait on him upon the
expense of the faculty And ordaines
the collector to repay to Baillie
Hall what expense he sall be
at ther for himself or to
advocats, clerks or ther servants
conforme to th accompt to be

givin in be him at his returne
which sall be allowit him in
the first end of this yeirs compt
and declars this pnt act to be
a sufficient warrand to him for
yt effect..

Act for 2 dollors
to the mess.

At they ordaine two rex dollors
to be givin to Iames Mundy mess
in pt of pymrnt for his paines
he was lattlie at in aprehending
of Iercuis prisons in the west Ait
this to be a sufficient warran
to the Collector for yt effect. And
the Visitor to get back the
caption..

At And Boyilis Chamber
26 Marii 1677..
Conveind the Visitor Mr david M
lon Robison, don Hall yor, Rot
Houstoun, Iames Weir, Iames
Bredwood and Wm Boyilis..

Iames dos
his comission

The gtk etc. Comprired befor the
Iames dos wryt in Edgr and gav

in a supplicacons desyring that in
respect of Mr Petir low his grandfayr
procuirer to the faculty of the gift
grantit be King James in anno 1599
to the Chirurgians of glezgow the
faculty did in consideracons gros
and for ther respect to him admitt
Jon low sone to the sd Mr Pet and
father to the supplicant a member
of the sd faculty ffor a benefit to
his children in anno 1636 And since
the sd Jon his father is now dicessed
they wold be plesit to confer the
same favor upon him 2Lk bring
considrd by the members of the
faculty put togither wt the act of
his fayrs admission in anno 1636
they for the same cause having
the same occuracons for his grandfather
first procuirer of ther gift of visitacons
and for the sd James his good
services doon and to be doon be
him to the faculty they hrby admit
the sd James friman w them and

to have the priviledg of a member
of ther faculty Who made faith
he use is –

(149)

At Archibald Bogill his Chamber
11 Junii 1677 –

Conveened the Visitor Baillie Hall,
Mr david Sharp, Andrew Elphingstoun
Jon Robisones elder & yor, Jon Hall
yor Ard Bogill, Rot Houstoun, James
Mr –

Act for the Visitor his borrowing 200 mk –

The qlk day The members of the facul
pnt finding it necesser That ther
be money raised for defraying of
the expense and incident charges
that Baillie Hall will be at in getting
that suspension raised agst them
be Jon Crawford discust before the
lords And yr being no money in
ther Collectors hands for doeing the
sam They ordain the visitor to
borrow upon the acompt of the call
the somme of Two hundreth merks
Qlk they declare sall be a debt

propertie belonging to the calling and
payeable be them out of the first
end of the money or debts due
to them als weill as if they had
bein all granters and subscrivers
of the bond to be grantit by the
visitor and this act to be a sufficient
warrand to the visitor for borrowing
the same.

The sd day Wm Stirling his bond
of 700 mk put in the boxe.

At Ard Bogills chamber
16 Junii 1677

Convened the Visitor Mr david Sharp
and Ard Grahme, don Robisone elder
and yor Andrew Elphingstoune, Ror
Houstoune, James Weir, don Hall yor
chirurgian, James Thomsone, Evir
Mcneill, don Hall barbor, don liddell
and John Sap.

The glk day The members of the
faculty put taking to ther serious
consideracon The grit necessitie they

have of a phisitian Visitor and the
loss they have sustained through
the want of a phisitian his
coneurrane (ffor the right and legale
exercise of the power of visita'ne
and uyr duties and priviledges
conteinit in the gift grantit by
King James of blessed memorie So
the nou's drecissit Mr Peter low.
and Robert Hamiltoun and their
successors) since the drecise of
doctors John Colquhoun + Thomas
Hamiltoun yt last phisilian Visitor.
And being sreuadrd and having
had the experient formerly of th
abilitie and good will of doctor
Bryce Bell now residentar in Glas
and who formerlie had the power
of visita'ne committit to him joyn
it doctor michaell Wallace for the
western shyrs did invit + earnesle
desyrs him to accept and take uy
him the office of visitor conjunct
wt the chirurgian visitor as fulle

fulie and honollie as the sd
doctors Colquhoun and Hamilton
did wt the Chirurgian Visitor pro
tempore And as Mr Rt Hamilton
did or might have doon wt Mr
Peter dow according to the first
intention and at procureing of the
sd gift And for yt end did nominat
Mr Archd Graham and John Hall yor
chirurgian two of yr number So
invit and represent this thir desyre
to him Who accordinglie came to
the meeting of the sd faculty and
accepted in and upon him the office
of phisitian visitor conjunct with the
Chirurgian Visitor And he wt the sd
Chirurgian Visitor and remanent
members of the faculty then present
did hine inde give ye girl and
solemn oaths viz The sd phisitian
Visitor To maintain the just rytts &
priviledges of the sd incorporation
and thir welfar And the sd
Chirurgian Visitor & remanent memb

(150)

abowin to mantain the honor and
advantadg of the sd phisitian visitor
And did take nyrs by the hand
in fardir testimony of thir assent
to the premiss.—

Act: for Regra°ne
of Capt Bunins band

The sd day the members of the
sd faculty taking to ye consideraone
the hasaint they are in of losing
that debt dew to them by Captain
Buny in respet of srall inystinents
and incumbrances on his land
yof the maills are assirit to them
for thir security And finding
themselves not sufficiently secured
through the sds inystinents gfR
in law will be prifrabb to ye
assenaone they ordaine his band of
coroboraone to be regrat and hornit
raisit yeupon and Baillie Hall is
is at put at Edgr ansint thir
affairs to cans charg him and put
the brie to secceone against him
untill he ather pay the money o
give them sufficint security therfor

58

Act for extracting
Doctor Bells admission
to be sent East.

It they ordain the Clerk to extract
doctor Bell act of admission as
phisitian visitor and send in the
doim to Edr to Baillie Hall To
the effect his name may be insert
in the Act of Suspension geh they
are seeking and is at put in
dependence And that his name
may be insert in the tres of horning
geh they are to cause joynt wt
the Chirurgian visitor.

At Hutchesons Hospitall
the 26 Junii 1677.

Conveend The phisitian and Chirurgian
Visitors Baillie Hall Jon Robisone yor
Jon Hall yor James Thomsone, Tho
Houstoun, James Weir, Lodovik Lyndsay
Wm Bogill, James Birdwood, Jon Liddell
Jon Hall barbor and Jon Tap.

Baillie Hall his report
of his diligence and his
Compt of disbursements.

The geh day Baillie Hall gave a report
of his diligence at Edr and produced
the double of his minuts of process before
the lords wt the two consultaions and

and his compt of disbursm...
to ane hundreth twentie
...se shillings eight pennies...
considrd by the members...
abовин they all in on v...
and approv'd both his com...
and his diligence And in...
was only ane hundreth...
by the visitor notwithstand...
imposerd by ane former a...
borrowit two hundreth m...
...gll ane hundreth pund
to Baillie Hall so y[t] the...
be daw to him twentie...
6s.8d They ordain the Co...
pay the same to him on...
first moneys he sall re...
this for his warrand.-

(151) the 2d day the members
first taking to their serious
the hasart of loss they m...
through Mr Thomas Smith...
Collector being dismiss'd...
by the loss of Rent-Co...

after conventicle they judg it convenient
that some of ye number may suplie
his place to official untill the ordinary
tyme of electing the Collector and
accordingly by pluralitie of votts nominate Houstoun ye late Collector to official
in his roome And ordaines the
Visitor and the sd Hor to goe to the
sd Mr Thomas Smith and get up frae
him what bonds or money is in
his hands pertening to the faculty
and to grant him a recit ye of untill
he make his accompt of his intromission
wt ther moneys qlk they ordain
to be doon wt all convenience And
then to intimat the same to him
at lest while he be frie to meet wt
them & give in his own accompt.
The sd day ordaines as of befor
Captain John Binny his band to be
regrat & he to be chargit wt horning
unles he either pay the money dew
be him or give sufficient securitie yrfor.

At Ard Bogills Chamber
3 Iulii 1677.

Conveend the Chirurgian Visit
Hall, Don Robisone yr Ard
Don Hall yr & divers uthers.

Act for a discharg to Crawfurd. The faculty finding by a
direct to the Visitor from
Marshell yr agent that
lords had scoped this a
suspensione agst Don Craig
untill they granted him
discharg of all by gain
preciding the twentie day
last. They therfoir ordaine
Visitor to subscryve a de
of yr aner & send the
lu to their agent.

At the Trads Hospitall
o August 677.

Conveend the Phisitian & C
Visitors Baillie Hall, Mr a
Sharp and and Grahme
Bogill, Don Robisone yr.

Thomsone, Don Hall yo[r], James Wm
Wir McNeill, Wm Bogill, lodovik
lindsay, don Hall barbor, don
liddall, don Tap.—

The det of suspensione
of two pair of new
lrs of horning graantie.
The 9th day The chirurgian visitor
pduced the det of suspensione agst
don Crawfurd 9th they obtenit
byfor the lords Together w[t] two
new pair of lrs of horning at
the faculties instance agst all
and sundrie sent to him
from y[e] agent at Edg[r], 9th the
faculty thinks fitt y[t] each of the
Visitors keip on, and the det
givin back to the Chirurgian
Visitor to caus put it in y[e]
box.—

Act for charging
small gouns
act
The 3d day they ordaine
Caruthers in . . . and James
Shiell in Lanrik and Mr James
Snodgrass in Pasley and don
Parker in glasgow To be chargit
w[t] horning ffor practising and
not licentiat.—

Act anent
Tape money

It They ordain don Lap to pay
in to Ro Stoustoun yͤ pticu-
collector what money he reste
drw of his friedome fyne and
upon his refusall ordaines the
clerk to give to the collector an
retreat of his act of admission
to the end he may be conveened
befor the magistrats or prosecu-
jyfor.—

Act anent Strangers.

It they ordaine that who evir
enters in the faculty being strangers
and salle be licentiat to use
either chirurgerie or pharmacie
salle pay in tyme coming of
friedome fyne ane hundrath

(153)

punds and if any prson bring
a Stranger salle enter barbor to
pay in to the boxe for the use
of the poor ane hundrath merk
and this Act the faculty declars
to be extendit only to strangers
who salle admittit is in the
citie of Glasgow allanerly—

59

At Archibald Bogills Chamber
22 August 1677.--

Conveind the phisitian & chirurgian
Visitors, Baillie Hall, Mr david Sharp
and Ard Grahme, Jon Robirsone yr
Andrew Elphingstone, Ard Bogill, Jon
Hall yr Ro Houstoun, James Wir-

Commissione
James Lockhart-- The qlk day Captain Samuel
Lockhart for futt residenter in
Lanrik gave in a supplicaoun
Drby he desyrit to be admittit by
them to the practise of chirurgerie
and pharmacie Qlk being considerit
by them togither wt his qualificaouns
qlk they found sufficient they
admitt him to the practise of
the sds airts in any place wt
in ther bounds and jurisdictioun
wt this express condition that
he futtly grant band to them
to pay ane hundreth punds scots
in caise he sett up wt in this
citie of glasgow - In respect they
gratis admitt him for the sait

of ther bounds q[ch] band was accordingly
granted be him and delyvrt to
the clrk wherupon he made
faith as use is.—

At Ard Bogills Chamber
18 Septr 1677.—

The q[ch] day Convrined doctor
Bell, Baillie Hall, Mr david Sharp
don Robisone eldr + yor, don
Hall yor chirurgian, Ard Bogills
dames Weir, Wm McnIele, Wm
Bogills, lodovik lindsay and John
liddell. The chirurgian Visitor
being absent.—

The sd day Compt befor them
david Baillie in lawrik in
obedience to a charg of a horning
givin to him as the faculties
for practising chirurgery and
pharmacie wt in ther bounds
unlicentiat. Who desyrit to be
admitted to the practise of the
sds airts as he who latelie exir

as prentice to Mr Campbell
pharmacian at Edgr who padnett
two missive letters yr annent qrof one
for his sd late master and the
uther for Samuel Heslie chirurgian
also in Edgr — Qlk being considered
by the sd faculty and they having
takin tryall of his qualifica'urs
in the sds airts they admitt him
to the practise of pharmacie in
all the prts yrof And als to opn
vains, apply cautars, loch leeches and
ventouses by the sight & advyce of
ane approvin phisician or experienced
chirurgian in any prt of the
boundars comittit to yr visita'un
Except the cities of glasgow and
anitorie yrof untill he be admittit
burges and gild brother yrof with
this express provision that he sall
not administer medicein or any
uyr prts of chirurgrey than this
abovwrittin upto he is admittit in
any prt of thar bounds wt out

the advyce of ane approvin phisitian
or liervе from the facultie in
all tyme coming And y[t] he pay
yeirlie of g[rei]t compt Thrittie
shilling scot[s] who hes givin his
band for ane hundreth merk of
pirdonie fyne and hes made
faith as use is —

Admission of
James Skelles —

The s[ai]d day Compt also James
Skelles in Dumfrik who also
desyrit to be admittet to the
practise of chirurgery & pharmacie
is in their bounds as he who
latelie servit drew Brown chirurgian
in Edg[burg] 2[th] being takin to their
serious consideratiu[n] and after
tryall of his qualificatio[n]es of the
s[ai]d airts they admitt him to the
practise of pharmacie in all the
p[ar]ts y[rof] And also to the practise
of chirurgerie in the s[ai]d p[ar]ts
y[rof] eft[er] mentionat viz[t] wounds
fracturs, ulcers, dislocatio[n]es and
some tumors in any p[ar]t of their

(53)

bounds except the citie of glasgow
and territorie yrof untill he made
burges and gild brother of the
sd brugh With this express provis.
That he in tyme comeing noewayes
administer medicine or medle w.
the cuirs undirwrin viz. makeing
use of the trepan in wounds of
the head, paracentisis, opning of
the empieum and sicklyke w. out
the advyce of ane phisician approvin
or experienced chirurgian — If eithr.
of them can be had with
conveniencie And y. he pay yeirly
of other compts thrittie shilling less
f. this nuarlaws who his given
band for ane hundreth mark
of friedome fyne and made
faith as use is —
The sd day y. was given in to
the Collector twelve pund, thrie
shilling four pennies for expense
of his all the satisfaction givin
to the nurse himself —

596

At Hutchesons Hospitall
the twenty fourth day
of Septr 1677 yeirs.—
Conveind Mr Charles Umat Chirurgian
Visitor, Baillie Hall, Jon Robison
elder, Mr Houstoun, Andrew
Elphingstoun, James Thomsone
And Bogle, Jon Hall yor chirurgian
Jon Menrice, Jon liddell, lodovick
lindsay, James Bredwood, James
low, James Merr Jon Jap, Wm
Bogill, Jon Hall barbor, Jon
Robisone yor & Mr david Sharpe.—

Mr Houstoun
Visitor
for yeir 1675.—

The sd dy The faculteie having
Conveind anent the election of
a Chirurgian visitor for the yeir
ensuing they be pluralitie of votts
nominat and elect Robert
Houstoun Chirurgian visitor for
the yeir ensuing who accepted
and gave his aitte de fideli
administratione as use is.—

Quin non the
sd yeir.—

The sd day The Chirurgian
Visitor nominat for him Mro

Charles Miuat, Jon Robison yo and
And Bogill gpter mrs for the year
ensuing.
And the faculty fint by plurality
of votts elect and nominat W
david Sharp, James Thomson
and Jon Hall yo chirurgian gpter
mrs for the calling who accepted
and made faitli as use is—

Collector

The 2d day they be plurality of
votts nominat and elrett James
Mein collector for the year ensuing
and Jon Liddell and Wm Bogill
bose mrs for the year ensuing
who accepted and gave ye aithes—

The agent
his compt—

The 2d day Jon Marshall wryt
in Edgr gave in his account of
his disbursements for yr affairs in
Edgr qlk is remittet to the
Chirurgian Visitor, Bailie Hall and
Mr Charles Miuat to revise and to
see him satisfiet yrfor—

Bailie a
Thrills bando—

The 4th day david Baillie and
James Thrills yr band in on for

yⁿ freedome fyne put in
dookham ass at the band of James
put in the bose..

Caption at the lds of Caption
to the visitor and
in the bose..

Mr Th Smith comp. The compt givin in be
Smith anent his intr
givin to the clerk..
The 2d day satyirs
the officer..

8 Octo 1677.
Conveened in, And Bogl
the Chirurgian Visitor,
Mr david Sharp, don Ro
And Rogell, James Weir
James Thomsone..

(154) The 9th day the memb
sic faculty put finding yᵉ
Hamilltons spous to de
sic Gordoun and
spous to Mr Walt Binn
does still practise med

and pharmacie medicentiall doe
thairfor ordain them to be
chargit w[t] horning...

13 no 1677..
Conveened in the Hospitall doctor
Bell w[t] the Chirurgian visitor
don Hall elder + y[e] chirurgians
don Robisons elder + y[e] M[r] david
Sharp, And Bogill, Rob M[c]neile
James Weir, James Thomson, W[m]
Bogill, don liddell..
The 9[t][h] day Compt don Campbell
in dursary who drayit to be
admittit to the practise of sic
parts of Chirurgie as he sall
be found qualifiet for and y[e]
in any pit of thir bounds who
yp[t] tryale they only admitt
him to practise the cure of
grein wounds brokin bons,
dislocao[n]ns, opning of veines and
placeing of cauters allanerly
and y[e] in any pit of thir

boundes except the citie
who hes maide fauttie
And givin bond for ffy
sectis as his fredome fy
by the members pre-
ordainit to pay yeirly
shilling yeirly of gpier
And is to pay farder
for officeris fieild   h
put in the boxe..

Anent Jon Crawfurd The sd day Compeired
Crawfurd in Kilmarnok
obedient to a chairge of
givin to him at the
instance ffor practising
of in this boundes comm
yr inspectioun who des
admittit be them Do t
of die pairtes of cliring
he said is found qual
who ff- tryale is adm
them To opin vrinos
canters allanerlie And
to grant band not to

gfk bond is put in the box and
he has payit Twentie punds Scots
for this his admission and
expense of his And is to pay
yeirly Thrittie shilling or after
complts and is to pay 3 lib of
officers fiells.—

At Hutchesons Hospitall
15 decr 1677.—

The qfk day Conveined the Chirurgian
Visitor, Jon Hallers Elder & yor
chirurgians, Mr Chares Lunai,
Jon Robisone yor, Ard Bogill, James
Weir, Mr Thomas Linlto and Jon
Hall barbour.—

Jon Cleland

The qfk day comperit befor them
John Cleland Chirurgian in Straven
in obedience to a charg of horning
givin to him at the faculties
instance for practising chirurgerie
& in thir bounds inlicentiat.
Who desyrit the faculties might
supersed any farder ssecen?ne agains

him for a months tyme or yrby
and he promittit it in yr tyme
he sould appeir befor them in
order to his tryall & admission
QlK being considret by them
they have continowed all farder
esieenone against him during
the tyme he desyrit and ordaines
him to appeir befor them about
the 13 day of Lanij nyxt in
order to his tryall.—

Binnies bond put in the box. The sd day Captain Binnies band
of corrobration qlk was formerly
in the clerks hands is put in
the box and he delyed till
Whitsonday nyxt.—

Act for 2 dollars to Mr And Grahme The sd day the members put takin
to ther consideration the sicknes
and powertie of Mr And Grahme
They find it necessar to suppeir
his present wants And yrfor ordaines
yr present collector to give him
tyne punds scotis shilling leris
money.—

The 2d day ordaines the Collector
James Weir to pay to the Clerk
his fiall for this yeir 1677 instant
for it was not payit by the
last Collector is 12s to his man
gk wes accordingly doon.

It ordaines him to pay to the
Officer his fiall for his shoes and
for his dayes fyars in all extending
to fyve pund fourtein shilling Scots.

Item Mr Thomas Smithe collector
the last yeir gave in his compt of
intromissions is the faculties names
sine the last compt on the gk all
money uplifted be Mr Houstoun as
he who was ordred to uplift in
his absence is also comptit be charg
and discharg gk wes sein, red
and approvin and ordained to
be bookit and is as followes.

The 2d day the faculty taking to
ther consideration the absence of James
Wilsone furth of ye bounds now of
a long tyme and the decreis of

James Frank and James Tobias they
ordains them to be score out of
the charg to be givin to the
collector the subsequent yeir And
not to be any articl of his charg
Together with Jon logan and loovrick
lindsay So that what is dew by
any of them To the faculty for
byganes they discharg the sam
and in tyme coming except
James wilson at his returne.
It they discharg Thomas Melvill
to be haurst in the Collectors charg
he not being ane member of
the faculty.
The Rigt of Ratification is the old
dit + the new dit of suspension
put in the box is Mr Th. Smitts
his compt this yeir.

    followis Mr Thomas Smitts
    his Compt of intromissions
    is the ffacultys moneys
    sine his last compt viz
    frae decr 1676 to decr instant

By Charg and discharg —

Charg
ffreedome fynes

Imprimis ye wes resting in
the Comptis hand at the
balance of the last yeirs accompt 008 _ 01 _ 02

It ei from Walt Broft as the
remainder of the expense
of his band and bris 007 _ 12 _ 00

It And Campbells booking money 005 _ 00 _ 00

It resting of Jon Sapp freedom fyne 029 _ 13 _ 04

It be James Mortoune 066 _ 13 _ 04

It be Lodi Lindsay 031 _ 02 _ 04

It be James fforrester 033 _ 00 _ 00

It be Jon Stell barber eh 020 _ 00 _ 00

It be Ja Wilsone 005 _ 00 _ 00

It be Jon Crawford in Killmannos
for his fyne and ficals 023 _ 00 _ 00

Summa is 229 _ 02 _ 2

Bands and Annutis —

Imp Jon Killiegiro band of borrowed
wt annut since Lambs 76 to
Mert 77 is 430 _ 00 _ 00

It Bangoure band of 400 mk wt
@rent sine Mart 75 to Mart 77 298 – 13 – 4
It Captain Binnings band for
200 mk wt a yeirs @rent at
Mart 77 is 141 – 06 – 8
It don Wallace band for 300 mk
wt 3 yeirs @rent is 209 – 00 – 0
It Corshills band of 300 mk wt
tuo yeirs and a half @rent 230 – 00 – 0
It No Armris precept 020 – 03 – 0
It Wm Boills band of 200 mk wt
3 yeirs @rent at Mart 77 inde 157 – 06 – 8
It a band be da Shiells & dawid
Baillie for 200 mk pyrable at
Mart last & wh inest 133 – 06 – 8
It rt from them of expenss of bis 012 – 00 – 0
It a band of 50 mk be don Campbell
in Luwrarie wt 3 tts dew for
offeirs fields 036 – 06 – 8
Summa is 1668 – 03 – 0

Wtin compts wtin the brigh
dring be da fronth for 16 yeirs at
12S per ann inde 09 – 12 – 0
It be Ard Elphingstoune 2 yeirs inde 01 – 04 – 0

It be Rot Henries for 18 yeirs inde   10 – 16 – 0
It tho grter comptes of this
underwrin viz Ion Hall elder
and yor. Rot david Sharp,
Charles Munat, Th: Smith, Ion
Robisons elder + yor, Ard boge
Rot Stonstoun, James Weir,
da bredwood, Iver McInnes,
Ioд lindsay, James Thomsone
don Hall barbour, Ion liddell
Ion Sap, Wm Bogil and Th:
Mulvill restend is to   11 – 08 – 0
            Summa is   033 – 00 – 0

        Grter comptes is out brigh
Imp be Ion Spreul elder for 6
yeirs at 20s pr ann inde   06 – 00 – 0
It be Sto Patson for 4 yeirs at
much: η   04 – 00 – 0
It be Ion Stow 2 yeirs inde 02 – 00 – 0
It Ion Whyt in Pasley 2 yeirs inde 03 – 00 – 0
It be Mathew Miller 2 yeirs inde 02 – 00 – 0
It be Ia Tobias 16 yeirs inde 16 – 00 – 0
It be Ion Lod 4 yeirs inde   04 – 00 – 0
It be James Spreul 2 yeirs inde 03 – 00 – 0

(156)

It- be Jh: Robison 18 yrs inde   18 _ 00 _ 0

It- be hir Jh. y' 6 yrs at-30S p ann   09 _ 00 _ 0

It- be Jon fhoster the lyke inde   09 _ 00 _ 0

It- be hir Alexr dunlope 2 yrs
at 30S.   03 _ 00 _ 0

It- be Jon Armore the lyke inde 03 _ 00 _ 0

It- be James Mortoun the lyke 03 _ 00 _ 0

It- be Jon Sutor 4 yrs at-30S.   06 _ 00 _ 0

It- be James Scyro the lyke   06 _ 00 _ 0

It- be Gilbert Neilsone the lyke inde 06 _ 00 _ 0

It- be Jon laug the lyke inde   06 _ 00 _ 0

It- be James hunter the lyke   06 _ 00 _ 0

It- be Jon logan 4 yrs at- 12S
p ann   02 _ 08 _ 0

It- Wm Simple of dounook 5
yrs inde   03 _ 00 _ 0

It- be Ja forestar in Killmacol.
1 yr at- 30S.   01 _ 10 _ 0

It- be hir Alexr Portar 1 yr
at- 20S.   01 _ 00 _ 0
_____
120 _ 18 _ 0

Suma of the haill Charge is   2051 _ 03 _ 2

ffollowes the discharg
disbursments

Imp to Cob: Cuninghame for
   fiall & tyrewayes by order   06 _ 02 _ 0
It to the Clerk his man by order 00 _ 12 _ 0
It to da hundy horsd at trall
   tyms by order   14 _ 08 _ 0
It given to John Marshall yr
   agent by order   01 _ 09 _ 0
It to Mr Ard Grahme by order 10 _ 00 _ 0
It to the clerk for raising his
   acc fr acompt of their agent 16 _ 09 _ 6
It to a poor man by order   00 _ 12 _ 0
It to the agent fr acompt of
   Mr Wm hamiltons man 01 _ 09 _ 0
It to the post for his the
   tyme of the discussing of
   Crawfurds suspension 01 _ 16 _ 0
It to Baillie Hall in pt of
   payt of his expence 24 _ 06 _ 8
It to the deacon conviner
   collector   08 _ 06 _ 8
It to master Gray fr order 00 _ 13 _ 4
It to the agent fr acompt ap 70 _ 00 _ 4

610

It to a poor man by order .... 00 _ 12 _ 0
It the dragon convines officer ...... 01 _ 04 _ 0
       Suma is   158 _ 00 _ 6

   freedome fynes & booking
   money unpayit. _
It Archibald Campbells bookingmony 05 _ 00 _ 0
It cists of Jon Saps fredom fyne   29 _ 13 _ 4
It br Lodovik Lyndsay is   31 _ 02 _ 4
It br Jon Ball eh: barbor is   20 _ 00 _ 0
It br James Wilsonne   05 _ 00 _ 0
It br Jon Crawfords officers fials 03 _ 00 _ 0
It br Jon Campbell his officers fials 03 _ 00 _ 0
       Suma is   96 _ 15 _ 8

(157)
   Bands is in the box
Imp Wm Stirlings band for 700 mk
  dewtie candle 77. is   466 _ 13 _ 4
It Jon Gilhagies for 600 mk is
  rent fra candle 76 to mert:
  77 mk   430 _ 00 _ 0
It Bowyours band of 400 mk
  is 2 yeirs rent at mert 77 is 298 _ 13 _ 4
It Capt Birnies band for 200 mk is 133 _ 06 _ 8
It yr is to be deducit of Rt Hms
  precept and of the compt for

order and aci   018 _ 19 _ 0

It Mr Boillo bond for 200 mk is
3 yeirs @ rent at Mert 77 inde 157 _ 06 _ 8

It resto unpayit of david Baillie
and dennes Skrilles yr bond
of 200 mk esay   100 _ 00 _ 0

It don Campbells bond for 50 mk 033 _ 06 _ 8

      Suma is   1638 _ 05 _ 8

The faculter is dew to the Sanders
for qch Mr Charles Murat gave
bond by act of the faculter
100 lib is @ rent sine cohrts
1677 and qk 100 lib wes given
to Baillie Hall to compent
his disbursements at Edgr

    Reten Compts win burgh unpayit
unp da ffrank 16 yeirs inde 09 _ 13 _ 0

It br da Thomsone on yeir inde 00 _ 12 _ 0

It br Th: Mirevill a yeir inde 00 _ 13 _ 0

      Suma is   10 _ 16 _ 0

    Reten Compts wout burgh unpayit
It br don Sprewl elder 6 yeirs
at 20s.   06 _ 00 _ 0

It br don Patson 4 yeirs at Mich 77 04 _ 00 _ 0

It don Stow 2 yrus indr .... 02 – 00 – 0
It br Mathais Miller the lyte 02 – 00 – 0
It br Iames Sobies 16 yrus indr 16 – 00 – 0
It br don Tod 4 yrus indr .... 04 – 00 – 0
It br Iames Sprius two yrus 02 – 00 – 0
It br Th: Robison on yrir indr 01 – 00 – 0
It br Alexr dunlope 2 yrus at 30S 03 – 00 – 0
It br don brumoe the lyte indr 03 – 00 – 0
It br Wm Th: yor 6 yrus at 30S indr 09 – 00 – 0
It br don ffoster the lyte 09 – 00 – 0
It br Iames Mortoun 2 yrus 03 – 00 – 0
It br don Soutar 4 yrus indr 06 – 00 – 0
It br Iames Sars the lyte indr 06 – 00 – 0
It br Will Wilson the lyte indr 06 – 00 – 0
It crsts of don long 2 yrus indr 03 – 00 – 0
It br Iames Mintar 4 yrus indr 06 – 00 – 0
It br da ffoster on yrir indr 07 – 10 – 0
It br Alex Porter 20S pr on yrir 01 – 00 – 0
It br don Sempe 5 yrus at 12S indr 03 – 00 – 0
It br don Logan 4 yrus at 12S indr 02 – 08 – 0
_____
Suma is 109 – 14 – 0
Suma of the hails discharg 2003 – 15 – 10
Rests to ballone the acompt 048 – 01 – 02
gftr is instantly givin to the Collector

James Weir who is to be chargit ye with
And the foirsd accompt of charg and
(158) discharg having bein sein, exd and
approvin as aforisd the facultie all
in on voice hirby resoluis and
simpre discharg the sd Mr Thomas
Smitto his airis &exers and oes
exers gin all effeirs of his sd intromissioun
wt that mureins and rent for bothe
precidings yeirs whrin he wes ther
collector Bi thir pntis sueto be elk
to the sd facultie at yr command.
      sic sut   Wr Stirling

At Hutchisons Hospitall
    15 Januij 1678.
Conveind The Phisitian and Chirurgian
Visitors, Jon Hall late baillie, Mrs
david Sharp and Charles Lunat
Jon Robisons elder & yor, Jon Hall
yor Chirurgian, Evin McNeill, Jon
Liddale, Loovik Lindsay and William
Rogiss.
The 9th day the Members of the

faculty put taking to them
the gul pomers their clerk
formerly act in their afou
juadgit it fitt ffor his rueo
in attendance ye upon I
his halls and w all be
of the preservaline of the
busines they hindy ord
all intrants in tyme
except thes who have
call serve as prentisse
bngh call the tyme of
pay in to the Clerk D
feots for their act of cidu
place of thritie shillin
payid to him and all
retracts to such who d
them And this act the
to continow during their
the sd day compt bef
of the faculty abone ho
Alexer thein late Servitor
Roderick chirurgian in
produ[c]it the indentor y

thrусd William and him with his
discharg on the back yr togither
with his burges and gild broy^r tickt
of this brugh And dsyrit to be
admittit (after tryall as use is) to
the practise of chirurgery and
pharmacie w^t in this brugh and
the haill uyr bounds as a member
of the facultie - Qlk being considrit
they preservs for his sey in pharmacie
pilula Rudii, pilula stomachica
cum gummi - Elect: diacatholicow,
Confectio alearnicho, Empl: drapalma
Empl: Eboeis lauri, ung. de althea,
syrop de althea familii With
veroehissi albi thasis To be made
and compound in pñce of the
chirurgian visitor, Baillie Hall
M^r david Sharp and Charles Stuart
don Robisons elder + yor or any
three of them against the last of
Jarie At-qlk tyme or at the next
meiting he is ordainit to give a
discourse as to the pills of the

hid contenuing and contenued and
farder to be examined upon severall
of chirurgery extempore ffor his tryall
in chirurgery.—

At Hutchesons Hospitall
the 5th March 1678.—
Conveened the Phisitian & chirurgian
Visitors, Don Hall late bailie Mr day
Sharp and Charles Maxwell, Don
Robissons elder & yor And Bogill
James Weir, Wm McNries Lodovick
Lindsay, Don Liddell and Wm Bogill
The 9th day Compeirit befor them
Mr Alexr Fraim to the Composures
made up be him By appointment
of the members of the faculty in
ther last ordenner Alko being sichted
by the members foirsd and ane
report given by the say no answrit
his dispensing yr of Qro they
declarit the Samin not to have ben
made Secundum artem The members
of the faculty above named notwith

Admission
Mr Alexr Fraim.

(159) grop ffor his incoradgment And in
hopes he will make his inthin
composi'ires better gn he setts up his
shope they admitts him to the
practis of pharmacie with this
qualifie - That they will order his
shop to be sichted and visited by
some of thir number as the visitors
and members ye order and as they
sall think convenient frae tyme
to tyme And accordinglie judge
the samin And having hard his
discourse gwitto they wer satisfied
and reexamined him upon the
sall prts of chirurgery they
notwithstanding of much lenitie
usit towards him ffind him not
sufficientlie qualifit And ye for
discharges him in all tymes coming
to medl witto any considerable
cures of chirurgery without the
concurrenc and assistanc of on
or two of the expertest chirurgians
of the citie At order and direction

of the visitor for the tyme, h
be found by the members
faculty for the tyme able
qualifiet to practise chirur
himself and ordaines him
in to the collector for this
in name of fredome fyne
hundreth punds Scots and
punds for the officers fiale
the collector is to be char
to pay yeirly his quin con
conforme as the rest of t
within this citie payes w
educit his burges and gild
tickit and his incid
as use is. —

the sd day Jon Adam
briag gave in bond daiti
for dresisting Also Anderu
of dolphingtoun the lyke
put in the bose. —

and grantit be
m Brown for
ising put in bose

At Hutchesonshospitall
4 Mau 1678.

Conveened the Chirurgian Visitor, John
Hall late Baillie, Jon Robisone elder
and yr, Mr Charles Umac, Jon Hall
yor chirurgian, James Weir, Jon
Mcnielo & Mr Alexr Thom

Jon Garner continowed

The 9th day Compt befor them John
Garner, merchand in Glasgow in
obedience to ther citatione for transgressing
ther acts formerlie maid agst him
And particularlie for making
gargarisons, syrups and uyr
composicions Qlk he denyed they
continow farder proceedor against
him untill some uyr dyet for farder
informacone yranent.

Rot Gray continowed

The sd day they licentiat Rot Gray
barber to hing out basings and to
barberise untill Lambmes nixt
Becaus 9th tyme if he enter not
they ordaine him to be fyned for
his former transgressions —

Act for 2 dollors to Mr Ard Grahme

It ordaines two rex dollors to be
givin by the collector to Mr
Ard Grahme in respect of his

put necessities and sicknes —

At Ard Bogills house —
19 Junii 1678

Conveened the Chirurgian Visitor, don
Hallers eldar and yor, Mr david Sharp
and Charles hunat, don Robisons
eldar & yor, Ard Bogilks, James Win
and Mr Alexr Lran —

Anent William Kelso —

The gth day complaint was givin be
William Kelso chirurgian in Ayr
and late Servitor to don Hall
late Baillie againes Mr James Stivin-
sones chirurgian also in Ayr ffor
taking our patient of his hand
in sua far as being imployit to
the cure of a broken leg and after
he had exponit and dressit the
samin according to method Being
necessarly callit out of the citie
of Ayr the sd Mr James did
(as it appeirs at the desyre of the
of the patient) untye the fractur
and dressit the samin himself

(160)

Althrough he his thrust the sd william
out of his imployment contrair to
ther acts and practise Qlks being
consdrd by the forisds members of
faculty put they (in respect both
painters are indicentiat to the
practise of chirurgry) find it not
convenirnt to mead yr witte ffind
therfor untill the sd Wm also
undirgoe his tryals in order to
his admissione witte them and
de facto or comittit Refuses to
come eite the rygt prtie befor
them And als jugit fitt that this
complaint be signifiet to the sd
Mr James Stivinson to the end
he may ether enter wt them or
desist frae any mc practise as
he will be amsrnabl to the
contrair .-

     At And Bozills house
     22 Julii 1678.
Concerned the phisitian & chirurgion

Visitors, John Hallis elder &
david Sharp and the Ch
John Robinsons elder & yo
Bogill, James Weir, Roin
Jon Liddels and Mr Bogill.

The 9th day Compeired
John Cowper in Irvinshego
to a charge of horning
him at the faculties in
transgressing one act h
him in Octor 1673 and
obervisment granted be
his appeirance upor the
a cert... day by paist
pain of two hundret
and her spreicicis if r
the aints of chirurgery
it in the bounds conu
villa'ns incalcul in
sprit in the ed obkwan
of the dail the 26 of th
and thereit in the 8o
and sessión upon the 2
last if k... Olk being

the sds Members with his answer
made yrto ingenuously confessing
the same togither wt his desyre to
be admittit by them to the practise
of die prts of chirurgey & pharmacie
as they sould find just after tryall.
They eftir matur deliberatione dois
not only recover and discharg him
of all fynes incurret by him for
bygain transgressions preceiding this
dait and of all bonds granted
be him yrfor and particularly of
the forsd obliesment wt all brts
and recencers yr followit yrupon
Bot also admitts him to the
opining of vrine oplyng cauters &
curing of grein wounds allanerly
by the advyce of our physitian
or chirurgian if he can be had
and als priviledges him to sell
drogs in any prt of yr bounds
outwith the citie of glasgow, With
this provision that he meddle not
with any vyr prts of chirurgey

or pharmacie than this aboverin
to qualifie and qto he is putly admitti
(161) under the pains of fourten punds
scots totic quoties he sall be convict
of transgressing hirof And of paying
or granting band payrabl agamrs
hirtimrs risel of fourten punds
to ther Collector in satisfaction
of the premise and paying yirly
thritti shilling to the Collector in
hame of quarter complo who hes
made faith as use is And
ordainies retracts hirof aut
by the phisitian or chirurian
Visitors witto the clerk to be givin
to him gn callit for who theirafti
give in bond for twentie aight
punds and payrd twelve punds
scots for qlk the Collector is to be
chargit nor qt he hes not pyit
a dollor to the collector for the
officers fiels till it be known
Whither the faculty doe exact
the same qlk acordingly is

ordainit to be exacte. —

Hutchesone Hospitall. —
24 Septr 1678. —

Convened Ro Houstoun phisit chirurgian
Visitor, Jon Hall late baillie, Mr
david Sharp and Charles Mueat,
Jon Robesounes elder & younger
Jon Hall yr chirurgian, James
Muir, Mr Alexr Frew, Jon McneIlle,
James Dow, James Braidwood,
Lodovick lindsay Wm Bogill, Jon
liddell, Jon Hall Barbour,
Jon Lap. —

Ro Houstoun   The gth day the members abovsd
continued Visitor   of the facultie of chirurgians,
takeing to yr consideraoun that
it be their ordinar tyme of election
of a chirurgian Visitor they in
pluralitie of votts continowis the
sd Robert Houstoune to be yr
Visitor for a yeir to come who
maie failto die was is. —

Qrmaster elected   The sd day he according to custome

nominate Mr Charles Muir, John
Robisone yor and Archibald Bogill
gptr mrs for a yeir to come And
the fried membris be plurality of
votis elects Mr david Sharp, James
Wair and Evir Mcneile gptr mrs
Iohn oils maer fruitteas wir is.—

Collector robe mrs
Wl the gptr continued

The sd day the members of the
sd facultie in on votes continuorse
James Wair to be thir Collector for
the yeir insuing and don liddell
and Wm Bogill boxe maisters Iohn
proctor maide fruitto and continows
Gabriel Cunyrighame ye officer.—

Officers fiaits kaiyis

Also they ordaine thir officers fiaitl
to be pyed by the Collector for
this yeir 1678.—

            Hutchesons Hospitall.
            22 Novr 1678.—
Conveenit the Chirurgeon Visitor, don
Steill laite bailla, don Robisone
yor, don Steill yor, James Wair,
Evir McneiIe, don liddell + divers igrs

62

Collector ordained
to call in byggain
arrets of Bangour
bond and sym.

The 9th day the members abovewritten of
the sd faculty Ordaines James
Weir their Collector to call for and
take in the byggain arrets of
Bangour and Mr Boill ye bonds
ressive and yt a letter be sent to
Stonehill for his giving new securitie
for both the debts yr wayes they
ordaines both bonds to be regrat
and also ordaines their sd Collector
to seik in all byggain arrets
of the haill remanent debts dew
to the faculty.

A Quorum of the
faculty nominat to
meet upon their affairs.

The sd day the forsd members
taking to ye consideratin the grit
troubl it is to all their members
of faculty in this city to meet
at all tymes upon ye affairs they
ordain the persons underwritten only
or any ffour of them to be a
quorum to witt the Chirurgians
Visitor for the tyme (being always ay
Jon Heale late bailleu, Mr david Sharp
and Charles Arnat, Jon Robertsons

alder and yor W: the Collector for
the tyme to meit and conveen
amongst the other compts and uther
concernes of the calling swa oft
as they salt find convenient for
the factories good and advantedg
and does hereby Ratifie & approve
all and sundrie other sederunt
qlk salt happen to be from tyme

(162) to tyme granent And ordaines the
clerk to record the same in this
ther regre to the end they sede-
reits and sederunts may be of als
full force as if yr war at ilk sederunt
a meiting of the haile facultie
or major pairt yrof.--

The sd day ordaines Ro: Gray band
to be wanint to enter at the next
meiting anywayes the certificatine
past against him in July last
to be put in execution.--

The sd day ordaines the Clerke
fialls for this yeir 1678 to be
payit him qlk were down

accordingly. —

At James Calt his house
the Twentie fyfth day of
March 1679. —

In prn̄ce of the Visitor and divrie
members of the facultie undr =
subscryve. —

The s̄d day the members of the
s̄d facultie pnt taking to their
serious consideracōns the prejudice
that may aryse through their
promiscuous admission of strangers
to practise Chirurgerie & pharmacie
within the citie of Glasgow And
y[e] by their gift from King James
of blessed memorie and Ratifica°ns
theroff they ar impowered to
make statuts for the comōn weill
of the lidges anent the saids
dietes. And for preventing yrof
for the future Statuted & ordained
lykeas they herby unanimously
statute and ordaine that no persons

or prsons qtsorvir Sals in any tyme
coming Be admittit to practise
ithir of the saids airts of chirurgery
and pharmacie is in the citie of
glasgow Bot such as ithir have servit
thir prenlisship witto ane fri
man or member of the faculty
for the tyme ffor the space of ffyv
yris conforme to the indentoin commun
form and have conforme yrto receiv
frea his master meit drink &
bedding is in his hous the
sd space or myr wayes be ane
friemans sone or married to ane
friemans dochter witto the qualy
allwayes sutable and reresan for
aithir of the sd airts Witto this
provision allwayes That it sals
be in the power of the magistrats
of glasgow for the tyme (in caiss
of dyfierence of qualefiid prsons
chirurgiens in the place) to call
on or mor were experimend in
the sds airts to revew in the

citie The intrants in yr case being allwayes subject to the tryalls of the faculty for yr qualificatiouns, and paying their friedome fynes, for the maintenance of thir poor according to thir acts and statutes. In witnes of the qlk putts this ... is ... of the hands of the members of the sd faculty day yeir and place foirsd.—

       Sic subr: Ro Houstoune
                     John Hall
                     Dod Lindsay
                     David Sharpe
                     J Hall
                     John Robertsoun
                     Alexr Fleem
                     James Muir
                     John Robertson
                     Charles Mouat
                     Tho Smitto
                     W Stirling no: subr for
Wm Mcluic because he cannot wryt.—

(163) The 2d day the members of faculty
present prohibits and discharges the
clk to book the admissione of William
Wallace in Paslay clk was doon in
dror last in respect of his non-
payment of ane hundrith merk
of freedome fyne imposit then upon
him it his own consent and of
the system funds money of expense
the faculty was at anent him
and ordaine thir lres to be serced
against him as a practiser in
the airt of Chirurgry unlicentiat.
The 2d day upon informatione givin
to them anent trades barbors it in
this citie thir transgressing ane of
thir acts in barborising upon the
lords day. They remitt the sarvin
to the tryale of the Visitor Bailli
Stalb, Mr Charles Unnot and don
Robinsons elden & yor and therupon
to call a meeting of the faculty
as they find occasion.
Item they ordain the sds Mr

Wallace in Paslay
his admissions
discharged -

Anent barborouin
on the Lords day

& Charles, don Robirsons elder & yor With
the clerk to draw up a new charg
to be givin to the put Collector.
It ordaines ane homing to be
sent to James Mutter for charging
of severall persons unlicenciat
practising in the countrie complained
of be him As giving ane obeissment
for redelivery yrof wt the succen'ms.
It ordaines ten marks Scots to be
givin by the Collector to the Relief
of wt Mr Ard Grahme and thrittie
shilling to the officer for his extraordinar paines.

At Auchrisons Hospitall
19 Maii 1679.

Conveened the Visitor Baillie Hall, Mr
david sharp and Charles Mutt, don
Robirsons elder & yor don Hall yor
chir: James Weir, lodovik lindsay &
Wm Bogill.

the qlk day ordaines the prisons
chargit to be drummen and the

clk to raise a caption yrupon.—

It ordaines the Collector to give to
the massr fform five dollors upon
giving in his soerenoure.—

Act for paying seto
yrielf by the cause
in the countrie.—

It ordaines in all tyme coming
that ilk prison that salb be hereafter
lierntlat in the countrie to pay to
ther Collector yrielf in name of
grtir evmpts thrie funds sevts attor
the small drivs to the clerk and
oficer at ther admissioro and that
the damin be inwrit in ther sd
admissioro.—

At James Galle Hovise
10 Octor 1679.—

Admissioro
John Adann.—

The ilk day don Adam in Eugletown
bridg is (upon his supplicaours) admitte
to opin vrinrs at the direction
of a plisitian allcanirj roeerpt in
cairrs of ureresitir And is ordeinit
to grant band not to practise fardir
under the pairnr of ofourtir pund
sevts totirs quotirs hir contravirus.—

and ^yr^upon to git up his old bond
Who hes payd Twentie merks of
fridome fyne to the Collector And is
to pay ^y{rly}^ Thrittie shilling in
name of ^yr^ compts and hes
oblcist himself nevir to practise
y^t^ in this citie And ^yr^upon made
faith.–

The 2^d^ day Mr Andrew Brown of
dolphingtoun is also admittit.–

(/64)
At Hutchesons Hospitall
The thrittie day of Octobr 1679.–

Convened the Visitor Ion Hall late
Baillie, Ion Robisone yor, Ion Hall
yor chirurgian, James Muir, Lodovick
Lindsay, Wm Bogill, Ion Lap.–

The 9th day The members of the
facultie takking to their consideration
That the ordinar tyme of election
of a visitor for the yeir ensuing
is now past They all in on voice
ffor cause Knowin to themselves
continow Robert Houstoun Visitor

untill the ordinar tyme of election
the next yeir Who made faith
as use is ..

The sd day continowes also the
same petimes and bose mrs
the sd spaces ..

Anent Iames Shiell
The sd day ordaines Iames Shiell
son tyme in danrick now in
Glasgow to be warnit to compeir
befor them for his practising
pharmacie wt in the citie of
glasgow the next day ..

Anent McS Gordoun
And als ordaines Mistris Gordoun
to be warnit for her practising
mediciniall ..

At George dunziells his hous
31 Octor 1679 ..

Conveened the Visitor Baillie Hall
mr david Sharp and Charles Mudie
Iohn Robesons elder and yor Iohn
Hall yor chirurgian and Iames
Thir ..

Anent the fellowes bond ..
The sd day They ordain Iohn

Gilhagies bond to be renewit w^t
new ca'ners and the prit band
givn to the Visitor for y^t end..

Also William Boill band and
Bangour are ordaint to be
renuwit and new sufficient
securitie for the money in their
hands or uyr wayes to be regrat
against them and both the bonds
givn to the visitor to that effect.

The sd day the members of the
faculty prit finding it necessar
and convenient that they consult
their Rights and priviledges ffor
preventing any debaits can be
raisit y^r anent. They ordaine
Baillie Hall to repair to Edgr for
consulting yrof and he to be
refoundit for his expense..

The sd day Compt bfor them
James Shiells (who formerly had
been licentiat by them when he
livd in Lanrick) ffor his practising
pharmacie w^t in the citie of

glasgow the members put f
convenant to prescryve to
for his cry in the sd a
emplost drapalma ung:
althea, confectio de alcear
tochissi de albi rosis, pi
aurea Balsum sulphuris
buithinatus and ordaines
visitor, Mr david Sharp,
Robison yor and don Hall
to see them dispensie. O
ordaines the sd daunes H
to have them in rediues
the first of Januarii next...

Mr [...] auchinya. The sd day Mr Gordoun
convenut byor them they
il necessar thir be discha
frae the practise of medcu
chirurgery And accordingly
ordered to desist ye prac
grant inn byfor or nyx
to be aprehindit & capon...

(165)   At Georg damgall his hou

13 Nov. 1679

Conveind the Visitor Baillie Hall
Jon Robisons elder and younger John
Hall yor and James Weir —

The glk day compeirit befor them
James Lin in Bagan wt in the
parochin of Balfron being apvrehendit
be virtue of lres of caption raisit
at ther instance for his practising
wt in the bounds comittit to ther
Visitacon The airts of Medicine and
Chirurgery medicentiall who confest
srverall curs of chirurgery and
particularly of the leg of Robert
Chapman mrst in glasgow, quhilk
being considrd by them with the
grit expruss he hes put them
to in raising and executing
lres against him they fyne
him in twentie punds Scots money
glk they ordaine to be payit in
to ther Collector for the use of
ye poor aftor his satisfeing the
clk and mrst or uyr wayrs

to be incarcerat untill th[e]
be payit and to grant bo[nd]
caone ffor his desisting fr[om]
practise of aither of the
airtis in all tyme comin[g]
the paine of ffourtie pund[s]
tolies quoties he sall con[e]

At the trads hospitall[s]
the 20 of Januar 1680.—
Conveind the Visitor Baillie
Mr Charles Umall and dav[id]
Jon Robisone yor Jon Bell
James Weir, Evin Mcniell a[nd]
loovick lindsay.—

Willie McnielL
bookit prenteise.—

The qlk day Willie McniellL
to the sd Evin McniellL is
as prenteis to Jhon Bell
Baillie in comune forma
produceit his indentor and
to the collectr onÿ ffoun[d]
yrfor, being a prenteis to
the uther ordinar small a[nd]
his indentor is of the s[ame]

day of   last by past
who made faith as use is.-

John Naismith   The sd day John Naismith sone
bookit prentise   to the desrist Mr James Naismith
lowtyne minister at Hamilton
is bookit prentise w Mr david
Sharp for fyve yeirs space frae his
entrie gk was

of the dait the 10 day of Octor 1679
who hes payit to the collector fyve
pundis Scots of booking money and
made faith as use is.-

James Bryce   The sd day James Bryce sone to
bookit prentise   Patrick Bryce maltman burges of
glasgow is bookit prentise w don
Robersone yor chirurgien ffor fyve
yeirs space frae his entrie gk
was at Candlemas 1679 conforme to
the indentor past betwixt them
thairanent dait the 16 day of
August 1679 who hes payit to the
collector of booking money fyve pundis
Scots and hes made faith as
use is.-

William Govan
bookit prentise.

The sd day William Govan son
to the decrist William Govan
    is bookit prentise wt
Robert Houstonne apothecairie for
fyve yeirs space frae his entrie
qlk wes at   conforme
to the indentor past betwixt them
thranent dateit the   day of
    1679 yeirs who has payit
to the collector fyve punds Scots
of booking money and made
faith as use is ..

Act for 2 dollers to
Mr Grahme and
1 doller to liddell &
12 s to the offic..

(166)

The sd day ordaines the Collector
to give to the relict of Mr
Archbald Grahm two full dollers
for supleing his present necessities —
It to give to don liddels barber
ane croe doller in respect of
his poverty — And twelve shilling
Scots to the deacon conviners offic
for warning the faculty —

Robs husband givin
to the Collector.

It the band grantit be Mr don
Hobo & his cacurr for his appering
befor the faculty upon the truth

of febru usuel undir a penalty
givin to the collector.

It They ordain John Tapp barbour
to be warnit to ther nixt
meeting for his allet Prophanour
and abuse of the lords day By
barborising thirupon and yeby
contravenuing the acts of the
faculty.

At Georg dainzielles hous
7 febru 1680.

Conveend the visitor Mr david
Sharp and Charles Unnat John
Hall yor, Jenuus Weir, John Robisou
yor Win mcnuill, Mr Alexr Fraim
and lodovik lindsay.

The sflk day Compt bfor them Mr
John Stobo in obediance to his bond
grantit to them for his appeira[nce]
Who dasyrd to be admittit (efter
tryalls) to the practise of phlebotomie
Whilk being considerd by them
and tryall takin of his qualificateus

therfor they admitt him to
phlibotomie by the advyce of ane
phisitian if ther be any upon
the place in any pairt of the
bounds except the citie of glasgow
and territorie therof And when
he acquyrs mor knowledge they
will farder admitt him ac-
tryall in the comone forme upon
payment as sall be modified
And in the meintyme they ordain
his bond for his appeirance befor
them to be redelyvrit to be
cancellit and him to grant new
bond that he sall not practise
in any tyme hireft beyond
his admission under the paine
of fourtie punds Scots he sall
be found to contravein And
ordaines him to pay to the
collector fourtie punds money
for his bygain transgressions
and his first admission or
to give the collector bond and

caºm therfor payrable at Whitsonday
nixt wt @rent therof- and to
pay yeirly of prtcompts thrittie
shilling who has made faith
as use is.-

Act for the giveine of this band. The sd day Ordaines the Clerk
to get up James the in bagain
his bond fra the Collector to
cause regrat and raise horning
yron and to cause execute the
Laan upon thir expense.-

Clks fiall pyd for 1679. The sd day the Clerks fiall for
the yeir 1679 last by past satisfie
and pyit to him by the collector.

(167)   At Georg drunzall his hous
                            8 March 1680.-

Conveind the visitor don Halls Calt
baillie wr Charles lunal, don
Robison yor, don dralls yor. Euir
Mcnrils, lodovik lindsay wr
Alexr Lran, don Lap.-

Mark Clifford admission The 9th day Compeird befor
them Mark Clifford in lanerik

in obedience to a charge of horning
givin him at y⁰ instance for
practising the airts of chirurgery
and pharmacie w⁰ in y⁰ bounds
underwritten Who desyrit to be
admitted be them to sie pairts
of chirurgerie and pharmacie as
after tryals he sould be found
qualifiet for — The members of the
facultie pⁿ⁰ having takin tryall
of his qualificaⁿⁿⁿ in the sds
airts they admitt him to thes
pairts of chirurgery after mentionat
allanerlie viz⁰ the curring of
wounds, fracturs, tumors, dislocatⁿⁿ
and incient allanerly and y⁰
in any pⁱⁱ of y⁰ bounds except
the cities of Glasgow and suburbs
yr⁰f And ordains him to grant
band not to practise any pairts
of chirurgery Nor thes aboverin
after he is presently admittit
Nor to medle w⁰ pharmacie in
respect of his ignorance yrof

under the pains of fourtie punds
toties quoties he salbe found to
contravern the same And ordaines
him to grant bond for ane hundereth
merks money of fridome fyne pyable
to the Visitor & collector against
Whitsonday nixt wt present yeaf-
glks they ordaine their Collector to
exacet only foure score merks in
caice of his pyt prensely against
the sd terme anyways to exacet
the bond – dykeis he hes instantlie
payit to the collector thrie pundes
Scots for oppens ficale and is ordained
to pay yeirly thrittie shilling Scots
in name of after compt who hes
made faith as usr is. –
The sd day the faculty pnt takeing
to their serious consideracens the
prejudice aryseing through the admissconn
of strangers promiscuouslie to the
practise of pharmacie they all in
ane voice hereby discharg any intrant
in the countrie To be herafft admitted

648

Annudon Sap..

to pharmacie is out preserving to
him ane sey in communi forma.
The sd day John Sap being upon
informa'n chalengit for breach of
the saboth in Barborising on the
lords day compeirit and denyet
the same upon his word of honesty
and credit and yerfor is quyt +
assailzied for by gaines and is all
of new injoynd y' he medle not
yerwitto nyr wayes thus will take
all in to thir considra'n and
proceed against him witts
severity.

At the trads hospitall
25 Maii 1680.

Conveend the Visitor Baillie Hall, hw
david Sharp and Charles Anae-
don Robinsons Elder + yor don Hall
yor James Win, Mr Thomas Smitto,
Win M'nrill, lodovik lindsay, Wm
Bogill, don liddall, don Sap.

The 9th day the bonds following we

Band givin to the
Colledur.

givin to the Collector viz Mr don Stobo
his bond, with Mark Cliffords, John
Campbell in dumbartane and
the laird of Stonhill. Qlks bonds
reciv the Collector is ordainit to
be put in exeren°ne.—

8) The sd day The members of the
Hall faculty put taking to ther consideration
yt That by ane former act John Hall
late baillie wes ordainit to goe to
Edr to consult ther Ryts and
priviledges for preventing mistaks or
debates They again Renew the sd
act and ordains him to repair
to Edr for yt effect with ther
richts following glk are instantly
givin to him viz King James his
charter wt a decreit of the lords
of Session thereupon The Ratifica°ne
of Parliament yrof with the
decreit of suspension obtenit against
don Crawfurd and uthirs And he
ordainit to report to them at his
returne wt ane acompt of his

expenss qlk is ordainit to be
satisfiet by the collector.

The sd day ther was complaint
givin in be the Barbors who are
a pendicles of the sd faculty –
againes John Or in glasgow for his
setting up w in the sd citie
unlicentiat Qlk being considrd be
them they licenciat him untill
the terme of Whitsonday nixt and
if beuvixt and then he doe not
enter w them as uthers he to
be dischargit fra then furth –

28 May 1680

Conveend the visitor Baillie Hall
Mr Charles Innat, John Hall yor
James Weir Wir Mcneill, Lodovick
Lindsay Wm Bogill –

The qlk day Compt befor them
Mark Clifford chirurgian in Lanerk
for payt of the ane hundreth
merk of friedome fyne contenit
in his band and in respect at

his admissione The members put
wer plesit to take the quantities
of his fyne to ther considera'ne
they having considrd his condi'ne
ordains the collector to exact only
fourtie punds therof and to delyvr
up to him his band who payit
the same w' the thrie punds to
the collector for officers fiall and
the clerk and officer ther dewes.

At georg dalziells house
3 Junii 1680.
Convend the Visitor Baillie Hall, Mr Charles
Muat, Jon Robisones elder and yor, Jon
Hall yor, James Weir, Mr Alexr Seam
lowith lindsay, Wm Bogill Jon liddell
James Birdwood, Jon Hall Barbour
and Jon Sap.
The sfR day ther wes a supplica'ne
givin in be Jon Or in glasgow making
mentione that of thes everale
weeks bygane he wes useing the
trade of Barborising within this citie

untill he wrs informed that he
wrs to be dischargt ffor doeing the
same w'out ther speciall licence
and he considring y't he wrs minor
and in a poor conditione and
y'rby unable and unfitt for entring
himself burges and gild brother
Whilk (y't his applica'ne to the dean
of gild and his brethrren) wre by
them superceided untill he wre
wer his majoritie and in a
capacitie for taking the burges
and gild brother aiths Humblie
desyrd That in regard of his wer
rela'ne to the now dreerist W'r
Pitter dow and the wyr ersone
forsd He might have the frie
exercise of his trade during ther
plesour and he in a better
condi'ne to enter w'th them. Qlk
bring takin to ther considera'ne
they graned the same and frie
libertie for exercise of his trade
and hinging out of his basings

untill he made burges of the
brugh, and then he is ordred to
(169) enter wth them during g^{lk} space.
They ordaine him to pay yeirly
to ther Collector for the use of
ther poor thir punds Scots and
upon production of his burges ticket
they will admitt him as they
doe uthirs.—

At Patrick Park his house
25 Junii 1680

Conveened the Visitor Baillie Hall,
david Sharp and Charles ...,
don Robisounes elder & yor, John
Hall yor, Evin M^cniele, James Weir,
Wm Bogill and don liddell.—

The g^{lk} day ther being a complaint
givin be the Visitor against John
liddell for his misbehavior towards
the visitor and abusing him wth
severall uyr members of the
faculty by his toring the faculty
put taking the same to ther

consideratione is his confessione yro
They herby discharg him of that
trust as a boxe master and for
yo end ordaines him to delyver
his key of the boxe to James
Weir the collector qlk wes accordingly
delyvred to him Also they dischay
him to compeir at any of
ther meettings untill they sie
his futur good behavior and
this to continow during ther
plesour

The qlk day Baillie Halls Reproduceit
the haill wryts and Richts belonging
to the faculty givin formerly to
him to consult ws at Edgr anent
ther priviledges conforme to ane
former act togither ws the queries
of the faculty givin in be him to
be adyset ws the answer yrto be
Sir John Cuninghame and Mr
McHamilton advocats ws some
privat instructions to the faculty
ffor secureing ther priviledges with

are unsub doubt of the act of the
town counsell in favor of Mr Henry
Marshell glk wer put in the bose
Togither wt his accompt of disbursements
to advocats agents and thir servants
wt the uyr incident charges extending
in haill to the somme of Thriescor aught pund sevin shilling
eight pennies scots money, glk
accopt being considrid they approve
yrof and ordaines the collector
to pay back the same to the sd
John Hall and ordaines the clk
to subscryve a warrand for yt
effect.—

As als they ordaines the collector to
and in to Edgr to John Marshall
thir ordinary agent Two esse dollors
farden and half a dollor to his
man for his extraordinar paines
and attendance on Baillie Hall at
Edgr anent the affaires of the faculty
and the clk to subscryve a warrand
to yt effect.—

Anent Hutchesons
Try

The sd day compeirit John Hutchesoune
apothecar in Irving in obedience to
a bond grantit be him to the
faculty ffor his appeirance befor them
upon the first day of Julie nixt
to come And craveit ane longer
dyet for his appeirance in order
to passing his tryall in pharmacie
efter his desyres to be admittit to.—
The members of the faculty efter
taking his desyre to ther consideratione
they grant him the second day of
August nixt to come conditionallie
that he sall that day come in
and by the sight of the visitor &
such moe of ther members as
sall be ther condescendit upon
He make the compositions following
(in order to his try for pharmacie)
viz pilula cochia minores ung:
dia pompholigos unple dia palma
and ellec: lenitivum syrwayre
they ordaine the bond & trie to
stand in full force.—

65

(170)

Act for extracting
the non payt & for
suuuing ym.—

The 2d day The members of the
faculty put ordaines the put Visitor
and Collector to extract and draw
out a list of the non payments
of after compts of thes persons
licentiat in the countrie and
cause summons them befor the
Comissar and ordaines the clerk
to calls and prsew them therfor
and the collector to pay the clk
the exspenses yrof.—

At Baillie Halls chops
15 July 1680

Conveened the Visitor Baillie Halls, Mr
david Sharp and Charles Umat,
John Robisone yor James Weir,
lodovik lindsay.—

Act for lending
1000 mk to Anderson
and his cautrs.—

The 9th day The collector informing
them that ther was ane thousand
murrke scots lying in his hands
of the poor money uplifted and
ingathrd be him And that it
wes necessar and convenient the

same be lent out upon good securitie
They ordains the same to be
lent out to William Andersone
merchand in Paisley as princ[ipa]ll
and Thomas Gilchrist and Walter
Blan merchands in Glasgow as
ca[utio]ners for him payeable at
Mertimes nixt w[i]t[h] rent frae this
dait and the Collector to receive
bond therfor.—

Hutchesones Hospitall

the twentie of Sept[embe]r 1680 yeirs

Convened Ro[bert] Houstoun ph[y]t visitor
Baillie Hall, M[aste]r david Sharp and
Charles Hunat, John Robisons elder
and younger, Jon Hall yo[unge]r, James
Weir, M[aste]r Alex[ande]r Tran, Lodovik Lindsay
James Birdwood and W[illia]m Bogill.—
The s[ai]d day the members of the
facultie ph[y]t taking to their considera[tioun]
that the ordiner tyme of their electing
a visitor for the yeir insuing is
now come Have by plurality of

votts nominated and elected Mr Charles
Minat to be visitor untill the
nixt ordinar tyme of election —
who being present accepted the
sd office in and upon him and
gave his aith de fideli administra‑
‑tione
as use is —

[margin: in Mr electio]
The sd day The visitor conforme to
custome nominats Mr David Sharp
and Robert Houstoun to be after
Mrs for the yeir ensuing And the
members of faculty elect be pluralitie
of votts don Robisone yor and don
Hall yor All geh accepted the office
in and upon them and made
faith as use is —

[margin: Collector.]
The sd day don Robisone yor is
electit and chosin collecter for the
yeir ensuing who accepted and
made faith as use is —

[margin: Box mr]
At they nominat and elect William
Bogill and Lodovik Lindsay box mr
for the yeir ensuing who also
accepted and made faith —

The lris of horning pertaining to the
faculty givin to the pnt visitor.

Wins Compt ordainit
to be rivisit.-

The sd day Jeames Weir last
Collector gave in his compt of Chearg
and discharg of his intromission
wt the faculties minnes thrs thrie
yeirs last. 2Lk the faculties pnt ordainit
to be rivisit and compaird wt the
book and if richt to be subt by

(171) the pnt and late Visitors Baillie
Hall, Jon Robisones elder & yor & the
clk or any thrie of them who
sall rivise the same & approve
therof And to be givin in to
the nixt Meeting to be bookit.-

At georg drinzeils his house
24 Septr 1680.-

Conveind The pnt Visitor Baillie Hall
John Robisone elder & yor John
Hall yor Jeames Weir, Lodovik Lindsay
Wm Bogile.-

The clk day John Robisone yor pnt
Collector art frae the persons following

frae each of them twelve shilling debts
in name of after compts vizt the
pnt visitor Baillie Hall, John Roberson,
elder, Mr david Sharp, John Hall yor
James Birdwood, Mr Alexr Tran, James
Weir, Lodwick Lindsay, Wm Bogill, and
Robert Houstoun and is to compt
for twelve shilling for himself ffor
the yeir 1680, qrof debursit at the
facultes order twe shilling to the
poor of the hospitals.—

Ane list of bonds given in to the pnt collector

The sd day James Weir late
Collector gave in the bonds following
to be put in the box or to be
givin to the pnt collector as the
faculty sall think fitt vizd ane
bond grantit be William Henderson
Mtr in pasley and his cautnrs
ffor ane thousand merk is ꝑvnt
frae the dait qrof It ane band
grantit be Mr Sterling and his
cautnrs ffor sevin hundreth merks
money — It Jon Campbell in
his bond ffor ffyftie merks is ꝑvnt

sine 11 Nov 1677 — It the bond grantit
be Mr John Stobo ffor ffourtein pound
tuolf shilling (grof a pairt is payd)
It the bond grantit be Wm Spalding
                for two hundreth punds
witho rent sine candlmes 1680
It John Gilhagie bond for sex
hundreth mark wt rent frae
Candlmes 1680 (glk is instantly givin
to the visitor to caus renew the
same) It John Couper his bond
for twentie aught pund glk wt
Jon Campbell + Mr Jon Stobo are
givin to the visitor to caus uplift
or caus put them in executione
the rest are put in the box —
It the obleissments following are
put in the box Ols Lennox live in
Bangour — John Adam in Auglistoun
brig — Mark Clifford in Lanrick —
Andrew Broun in Slapperfield —
Mr Jon Stobo, Henry Hamilton —
toun   Jon Couper in
and William Millar —

Act anent Andw Hunter getting a discharge

The sd day ordaines the pnt collector
to give to Andw Hunter in Kilmarnoth
a discharg of thrie yeirs pter compts
conforme to the recit grantit to
him be James Unidy mess?
who upliftd the same And glk
recit is givin to the Visitor to
call James Unidy to ane accompt
yror and als to discharg him
to Michell 1680 in respect ye is
ane yeir farder payit to the collector
by the clk in his name.

his compt givin in

The sd day the aforsd James
Weir late collector gave in his
accompt of charg and discharg
dualie revisit and subt conforme
to ane act in the former ordenant
clk the ffacultie ordaines to be bookt
and is as follows He having
payit in presently to John
Robinson yor ther pnt collector
the somme of twentie four pund
elevin shilling eight pennies as
the ballance of his accompt crest

(172)

the sd don is to be chargit.

followes the charg Inanes
Wir his Intromission frae
15 decr 1677 to the 17 of Septr
1680 instant.

Impris resting be Mr Thomas
Smitto last collector at receit
of mye charg on the 15 decr 1677 0048 _ 07 _ 2

It John Gilhagies bond wt Rent
frae Lambmes 1676 to Lambmes
1680 is   0496 _ 00 _ 0

It Wm Sterlings bond of 466 lib 13S
4d wt Rent frae Candl 1677 to
Lamb 1680 extends to   0564 _ 13 _ 4

It Bangours bond of 266 lib 13S 4d
wt Rent yry frae Mart 1675
to Lamb 1680 extends to   0342 _ 13 _ 4

It Wm Boills band of 133 lib 6S 8d wt
Rent yry frae Mart 1674 to
Lambmes 1680 extends to   0179 _ 06 _ 8

It Captain Binnies band of 133 lib
6S 8d wt Rent frae Mart 1677 to
Martimes 1680 is   0159 _ 06 _ 8

It resting of Innes Shrille and

david Baillie yr bond   0100 – 00 – 0

It is rest of @rrnt yrof   0003 – 10 – 0

It don Campbell his bond of
33 lib. 6s. 8d wt @rrnt since Mart
1677 to Whits 1680 extends to   0038 – 06 – 8

It indew be him for officers fialls   0003 – 00 – 0

It don Coupers bond for 40 lib attor
tho @rrnt   0040 – 00 – 0

It for his officers fialls   0003 – 00 – 0

It Mark Clifford bond of 100 mk
geh wre by order in a extending
of 28 of Undry wre by order
fast for payd of 43 lib both of
fredome fyne & officers fialls is   0043 – 00 – 0

It Mr John Stobo his bond of
40 lib wt the @rrnt yrof frae
Candl 1680 to Lamb yrof is   0041 – 04 – 0

It Lamre hrs band of 20 lib
attor @rrnt is   0020 – 00 – 0

It receivit frae Mr Spalding of
@rrnt 18 lib   0018 – 00 – 0

fredome fynis & booking mony

Impris Archibald Campbell booking
mony   005 – 00 – 0

It resting of Ion Sap his friedome
    fyne   029 – 13 – 4
It Ion Crawford in Kilmarnok
    his ffieers ffiale at his admission 003 – 00 – 0
It Mr Alexr Irain his friedome
    fyne and ffieers ffiale   103 – 00 – 0
It Anderw Browne unt for   006 – 00 – 0
It Douphingtons friedome fyne 022 – 08 – 0
It Ion Adam his friedome fyne 013 – 06 – 8
(173) It Ion Naismiths booking money 005 – 00 – 0
It Neill McNeill his booking money 005 – 00 – 0
It Wm Gowans booking money 005 – 00 – 0
It James Bryce booking money <u>005 – 00 – 0</u>
             Sua is   <u>199 – 08 – 0</u>
       Qrter compts is in brugh
       drw for Michalmes 1678
       1679 and 1680..
Imprus Ion Halls elder & yor
   Wr david Sharp & Charles
   Nuneit John Robissons elder
   and yor Ro Ironstounes elder
   and yor James Weir, Jorhe
   Neill Wr Thomas Smitto &
   Alexr Irain Ro James king

Birdwood, Jon Liddell, Jon Hall
barbor, Lodwick Lindsay, Wm
boyle, Jon Lap, Andrew Uplingstoun
and 16th Semple of Carnock
Being twentie in number
at 128 pr ann the sds this
yeir extends to   036 – 00 – 0

It mor indews by the sd Wm
Semple for 5 yeirs qrtercompt
preceiding Michaelmas 1677 vide 003 – 00 – 0
              Swa is   039 – 00 – 0

              Qrtercompts woud brugh
              dew by the preons ilk aprill:-
Amp: Jon Sprewle elder for 9 yeirs
    resting at Mich: 1680 it 20 S
    pr ann   009 – 00 – 0
Jon Patsone for 7 yeirs resting at
    Michal: 1680   007 – 00 – 0
Jon Stow for 5 yeirs resting at
    Michub: 1680   005 – 00 – 0
Mathew Miller 5 yeirs inde   005 – 00 – 0
John Lod 7 yeirs inde   007 – 00 – 0
James Sprewle 5 yeirs inde   005 – 00 – 0
Thomas Robinsone 4 yeirs inde   004 – 00 – 0

Mr Alexr dunlope erlick 5 yeirs
at 30s pr ann at Michael 1680   007 – 10 – 0
John dunmose 5 yeirs at 30s p@   007 – 10 – 0
Mr Thomas y⁵ 9 yeirs inde   013 – 10 – 0
James Mortoun 5 yeirs inde   007 – 10 – 0
James Sutar 7 yeirs inde   010 – 10 – 0
James Layrs the lyke   010 – 10 – 0
Allam Kirkwood the lyke   010 – 10 – 0
Gilbert Nrilsone 7 yeirs at 20s   007 – 00 – 0
James Lang 5 yeirs at 30s pr ann 007 – 10 – 0
James Mullar 7 yeirs is   010 – 10 – 0
James forrester 4 yeirs is   006 – 00 – 0
Mr Alexr Porter 4 yeirs at 20s   004 – 00 – 0
Jon Campbell 3 yeirs at 30s   004 – 10 – 0
Pet Boill 4 yeirs at 20s   004 – 00 – 0
Arij Hunter 4 yeirs   004 – 00 – 0
~~David~~ John Whyt 3 yeirs   003 – 00 – 0
David Bailli 3 yeirs at 30s   004 – 10 – 0
Jon Couper 3 yeirs   004 – 10 – 0
James Shirills 3 yeirs at 30s   004 – 10 – 0
Jon Crauford for 3 yeirs   004 – 10 – 0
                                  178 – 00 – 0
Suma totalis of the Charg   2576 – 15 – 10

discharg

John Gilhagies bond of 600 mks is @rent
   frae candl 1680 to lamb yeirs   412 — 00 — 0

It don Stirling his bond of 700 mk
   is @rent frae candl 1680 to lamb
   yeirs   480 — 13 — 4

It Captain Binnies band of 200 mk
   is @rent frae Whits 1680 to
   Mert yeirs   137 — 06 — 8

It don Campbells bond of 50 mk is
   @rent frae Mert 77 to Whits 80   038 — 06 — 8

It to him of officers fiall   003 — 00 — 0

It don Couperis bond of 28 lib altor
   @rent   028 — 00 — 0

It to him of officers fiall   003 — 00 — 0

It resting of Mr don Stobo his
   bond of 40 lib and @rent   020 — 12 — 0

It of resting of Ines band altor
   the @rent and expense   010 — 00 — 0

It Wm Spaldings bond of 200 tb
   is @rent frae Candll 1680 to
   lamb yeirs is   206 — 00 — 0

It Wm Androsons bond altor the @rent 666 — 13 — 4
                                      2105 — 12 — 0

ffriedome fynes and
booking money

Impr resting of John Sapps
ffriedome fyne   003 – 00 – 0
It don Crawford in Kilmarnock
his opens fiall   003 – 00 – 0
                             006 – 00 – 0

Later compts win brugh
Impr by Andrew Elphingstone for
Mich 78 and 79   001 – 04 – 0
It be Robt Armies the lyk   001 – 04 – 0
It be don diddell for 1679   000 – 12 – 0
It be the faculty for Mich: 1680 011 – 08 – 0
It be Wm Sempill of damock
for 8 yeirs inde   004 – 16 – 0
                             019 – 04 – 0

Later compts wout brugh
Imps be don Sprewl elder for
9 yeirs resting at Mich 1680 009 – 00 – 0
It be don Patsoune for 7 yeirs
at 20S pr ann is   007 – 00 – 0
It be don How for Mich 1680 001 – 00 – 0
It be Mathew Miller for 2 yeirs 002 – 00 – 0
It be don Lod for 7 yeirs   007 – 00 – 0

(175)

It Br James Sprual for 5 yeirs 005 — 00 — 0
It Br Thomas Robisons for 4 yeirs 004 — 00 — 0
It Br Mr Alex dunlops relict at
30S pr ann for 3 yeirs 004 — 10 — 0
It Br don Lennox the lyke 004 — 10 — 0
It Br Mr B yor at Mich 1680 007 — 14 — 0
It Br James Mortoun for 2 yeirs 003 — 00 — 0
It Br don Lulou for 2 yeirs 003 — 00 — 0
It Br James Sayrs 2 yeirs 003 — 00 — 0
It Br Gilbert Neilson for 2 yeirs
at 20S pr ann 002 — 00 — 0
It Br don Lang for 2 yeirs at 30S
pr ann 003 — 00 — 0
It Br Allan Kirkwood for 7 yeirs
at the lyke pr ann 010 — 10 — 0
It Br James Hunter the lyke 010 — 10 — 0
It Br James forrester 4 yeirs 006 — 00 — 0
It Br Mr Alex Porter 4 yeirs
at 20S pr ann 004 — 00 — 0
It Br don Campbell for 3 yeirs
at 30S pr ann 004 — 10 — 0
It Br don Crawford the lyke 004 — 10 — 0
It Br Peter Boyl 1 yeir at Mich 80 001 — 00 — 0
It Br Archd Hunter 4 yeirs

at 20s pr ann   004 – 10 – 0
It be don Whyt 3 yеirs   003 – 00 – 0
It be david Baillie 3 yеirs at
30s pr ann is   004 – 10 – 0
It be don Couper 3 yеirs   004 – 10 – 0
It be dames Shrill the lyke   004 – 10 – 0

disbursements
Imp to the clerk of fiells in
the compl yе yеirs   008 – 00 – 0
It to the officer   005 – 16 – 0
It to the clerks servant   000 – 12 – 0
It to don Hall yor for the
belrove of the relief of
rung livr and grahmе   005 – 16 – 0
It at a Meeting by order
givin to her   005 – 16 – 0
It to the poor of the hospitall 000 – 06 – 0
It to a poor man by the
deacons order   001 – 00 – 0
It to a distrest man by
his order   002 – 08 – 0
It to the deacon conviners hous 010 – 00 – 0
It to Rot Saunders by order   106 – 00 – 0

(76)

Itm by order to hir grahmes releif 005 – 16 – 0
Itm for regra'ne of Iohn Coupers
   bond in the booke of Counsell 001 – 13 – 4
Itm for horn: yeon 002 – 18 – 0
Itm to the post 000 – 04 – 0
Itm to the officer the tyme of election 005 – 16 – 0
Itm to the poor of the hospitall 000 – 06 – 0
Itm to the deacon convinar officer 001 – 04 – 0
Itm to Walt Grahm enrest on
   his lots for apprehanding
   Iohn Brown 006 – 15 – 0
Itm to Adam Porter by order 000 – 12 – 0
Itm to him by order 000 – 18 – 0
Itm to the officer by order 001 – 10 – 0
Itm to hir Ana grahms releif
   by order 006 – 13 – 4
Itm to a poor man by order 001 – 16 – 0
Itm to Iames Mundy four ? 001 – 12 – 0
Itm to Iames listoun for going to ? 001 – 00 – 0
Itm to the post 000 – 04 – 0
Itm to a messer for giving a
   charg of horning at ? 001 – 04 – 0
Itm to the 3 officers for taking
   down the french mans basings 000 – 18 – 0

It to the deacon conviners house

It to the kirk officer at a
    muiting in the bell hous

It to Allan Glen for a hors hyre

It to don Marshell for the capren

It to the officer

It to the deacon conviners officer

It by order to Mr ard Grahms relei

It to don liddell barbor

It to the deacon conviners officer

It to our officer by order

It to James Mindy messer

It to the deacon conviners officer

It to Baillie Hall by order

It to the clerk tuo yeirs fiall
    viz 1678 and 79

It to Baillie Hall for makin
    up his accompt

It to don Marshells this men

It to a poor man by order
    Suma of the haill dischar
    extends to

    Sua chary and discharg
    being compard Rests of

(177)

ballance in the Compters
hand 24 lib 11 s 2 d   0024 — 11 — 2

qlk was given to Johne Robissone yor
put collector And thairfor the sd
faculty all in on voice exoners
quy² clames and simpro discharges
the sd James Wir his aires and
exers of his sds intromissione
w the moneis and estate belonging
to them for the use of the poor
the sds thrie yeirs space And
hes ordainit me the Clk to the
sd faculty to subscryve ther pres
for them at day year and
place foirsd..
Sic sub   J Stirling Clk..

At Autchisons Hospitall
13 deer 1680 yeirs..
Conveend the visitor John Hall
late Baillie, Robt Houstoun, Jon
Robissoun elder, James Wir, Mr
Alexr Iran Wir McneILL, James
Braidwood, Jon Hall barbour etc..

Jon Sap..

Campbells band to be regrat —
The 9th day ordaines the band
grantit be Jon Campbell to the
facultie to be lookit out and
givin to the Clerk to be regrat
and lrs of horning raisit yrupon
and ordaines him also to be
summondit for his officers fiall..

Couper and Lod delet out of the charge —
Ordaines also Jon Couper in
lesmahegow and John Lod in
Killmarnock yr names to be
delet out of the charge in
respect they are both deceissit
poor.

Stobo and lrs band to be regrat.. —
Ordaines lw Jon Stobo his band
to be regrat and put to execuone
against him..
And als ordaines   lrs
band and lrs raisit against
him to be put to execuone..

Act for citing saids persons for yr compts. —
Ordaines the persons underwrin
ilk ane of them to be cited for
yr intercompts and fiall viz
Jon Crawfurd in Kilmarnock for

his officers fials and gter compts
fras his admission, Wo Herries in
Dumbartainr, Wm Simpl of damnork
don Spreule in pasley, don Patersone
yr, James Spreule yr, don How in
Killbarchon, Mathew Miller in
Killmarnok, Thomas Robissone in
Cauldwell, Wr Alexr dunlops relict
in Hamilton, don lennoce in
ginok, James Mortoun in
Hamiltonn, don luton yr, James
Lare in dorglas (nota James Wm
ingadges for him) Gilbert neilson
in Straven, don lang in Hamilton
Allan Kirkwood in darulie, James
Inttin in Strulions, James forse
in Kilmacolme, don Campbell for
his fials and gter comptt and
Peter Boile in Malletshugh, who
is also ordained to be chargit
for transgressing his admission
and don Whyt in pasley to be
also citid to the rest for his
bygain gter comptt and ordaines

the clerk to pursue them before the
Comr and take out a decreit agst
and he to be refundit by the
collector of the charges and
disbursements—

And als ordaines the sd dou Whyt
to be chargit wt horning—

Thomas yor delt
(178)
Ordaines Mr Thomas yor who was
given up as debitor to the faculty
in seventein pund fourtein
shilling to be delt in tyme
comeing out of the collectors
charge—

Ant forgiving to
wr and John relict gtt
Ordaines the Collector to give to
Mr Ard Grahames relict nyne
punds scots for her put supplie
and the clerk to grant warrand
yrfor and ordaines twelv shilling
scots to the officer for the fyre
furnishd at this meeting—

At Glasgow the twentie
fyst day of decr 1680
Conveend the Visitor, Bailie Stark

John Robirsones elder and yor, Rot=
Houstoun and James Weir. The
The 9th day Complt byor them
John Crawford sone to Mr Hew
Crawford Master at Cimnock
now residenten in pasley Who
dreyrd to be admittit to the
practise of pharmacie Which
being takin to ther considera°n
They ordain him to be tryed
and preseryves for his say
Benedm laxativa, empl: diathylon
cum gumii, ung diaphron tholigo
pil: cothar majores and ordains
the visitor and gom he sall
appoynt to sie the simples
msed and ordains the sd
son to appein this first day
of ffebru next to com yr witts.

At geore drunzisles hous
the 2d ffebru 1681.

Conveined the visitor Baillie Hall
Jon Robirsons elder & yor, Mr david

Sharp, Don Hall, yor chirurgian wt
Andrew Elphingstone.

The 9th day ordaines the Collector
to satisfie and pay to Baillie Hall
the sowme of fyve hundrith
merks scots for the expenss he
wes at in anno 1672 for procuring
the kingis ratifica'ne and the
elk to grant warrand yrfor.

Don Crawfurd admission

The 9th day Compt before them
the sd Don Crawfurd in obedience
to yr former act wt the composi'ns
therin mentionat Whilks they
find sufficiently compounded
And yrfor admits him to the
practice of pharmacie In any
pairt of yr bounds except the
citie of Glasgow So the qlk he
is not to be admitted except
wt the qualifica'nes content in
yr act of the date the 25 of March
1679 And ordaines him to pay
for this his admission to the
Collector for the use of the poor

the somme of ane hundreth mar
wt thrie punds for the yeires fiall
and to pay yeirly of qter compter
oyr thrie punds sebs...

Act anent the clerk... It ordaines the Clerk not to give
out the extract of any persons
admissiono untill they subscryve
the act of ther admissions...

Glasgow
fourth of March 1681.

Conveind Mr david Sharp, John
Robisones elder & yor, Robt Houstoun
Jon Hall yor chirurgian and
James Weir...

Mr James Stevinson try preseryve... The qlk compt befor them Mr
James Stevinson in Ayr who
desyre to be admittit to the
practise of chirurgerie & pharmacie
The sm being taken to thir
consideraon they ordain him
to be tryd and does preseryve
for his say in pharmacie Unge
diapalma: ung: diabasileon. Elect

Cutavum pilula cochias minoes
Trochissi albi chasis and ordaines
the simpls to be mixed in
(179) pnce of the visitor and whom
he sall appoynt at his returne
And Mr James ordainit to
appeir upon a lre from the
faculty or sooner wt his own
conveniencie And ordaines him
to have a discourse upon the
diseases of the heid for his
say in chirurgery.

Trads hospitall
2 Junii 1681.

Conveened the Visitor Bailler Hall
don Robisonis elder & yor, Mr
david Sharp, Mr Houstonne, don
Hall barbour, Wm Bogie & don
Lap barbor.

Act ordaining
seall persons to be
chargit wt horning

The slk day ordaines the persons
underwrin to be chargit wt
horning viz: Thomas Crumill in
blackwood. Edward Cristil in

Torboltoun, donat Chambers spons
to Alexr Montgomerie in Sandbed
of Kilmarnok, donat Bordland
in holmhead yrof, James Miller
in Milnheugh in the parish
of Blantyre

In the same parish wt dean
Blair spons to Mr Andrew Park
scholar at Kilwinning and the
clerk to receive the horning, to
caus charg yrm yr witts & to
returne to the faculty our
executor wt our accompt of
debursements in yt affair.

Mrs bond to be
put in execun Ordaines Mr & his caoner to
be charged for the remainder
of his bond.

The said day Compt Mr Stewart
in Kilmarnok who desyrd to
be admitted to the practis of
the pts of Chirurgy as he
could be found qualifie for
and produced his testifical unto
the ministers hand of the

parish as use is. The members
but taking his desyre to ther
consideraou̇n they ordaine him
to give a discourse befor them
of wounds & fractures in generall
and the methods of cures befor
he get the benefit of admission.

At Iron Church
19 July 1687.

Conveened the visitor Mr david
Menk, Jon Morrisoune elder and
yor Mr Houstoun, Jon Hall yor
James Wan, Mr Alexr Iron, lodovik
Lindsay, James Birdwood, Wm
Bogil and Jon Hall barbor.

The 9th day anent our suplicaou̇n
given in be Charles Andersoun
late visitor and prentices wt
the now deceassit Jon fleming
barbor and sine wt Susanna
Mordoun his relict whirby he
craves to be licentiat to cure
barborise and make perrewigs intill

his minority be expyred he having
servit the sd umof don perseuing
his late hir in that imployment
and after his deceis the sd
Susanna his relict during the
tyme of his prenteiship The
members of the faculty pairt-
taking his sd petition to their
considrac̃ne doe grant the same
and allowes him to cure,
barborise and make periwikes
during the tyme of his minority
and less age untill he be in
a conditione to enter wt the
faculty and admittit burges of
this brugh Upon payment of
three pounds scots yearly to the
collector Begining the first years
pyt yerof at Michaelmes 1682
nixt to come.

(180)
The said day anent the petitione
Admission
givin in be William McGie
Wm McGie
andrueller in Glasgow wherby
he craves to be admittit to the

pts of chirurgery as the faculty
sall find just and to euir &
barborise in respect he had
attendit a phisitian sevall years
and sine yt tyme had appleyit
himself to the opening of veins
and the lyke wt barborising the
members of the faculty above
mentionat taking his desyre to
their consideracon wt the reasons
assignit be him yrfor they doe
allow, licentiat and authorise
him the sd petitioner to open
veins and to barboris for no
farder And ordaines him to
grant band for thrittie punds
Scots for this his admission to
the Collector they having remittit
to him considerabe of of his
fredome fyne sould be in respect
of his being a phisitian sevall
years conceisting wt yr own
knowledg.

The sd day ordaines the Collector

to pay in to don diddell barbour
from arse dollars for his better
supplie and maintenance in his
put gill want and poverty.

At Glasgow
the 23 Septr 1681.

Convenud the Visitor Baillie Hall
Mr david Sharpe, don Robiesone
James Weir, lodowick lindsay &
don Bogills.

the 9th day compt Befor them
John Stow yor of drumptoun in
obediene to a charg of horning
formerly givin to him And of
ane obrisse also givin for his
appeirane befor the faculty for
his tryale Who dreyed to be
admittit to the practies of curing
simple wounds phlebotomie dislocationes
fractures and die uyr pits of
chirurgerie as he sould be found
qualifut for and als to be
authorisad be them to giv purgationes

by Linnes, Rhubarb and the lyke
Which being considerit be them &
he reexamined yerupon they heirby
admitt him To cure simpl wounds
and to practise phlebotomie by the
advyce of phisitians, ffractures qr ther
is no complicacone and to the
restoracone of dislocacones And they
dos heirby discharge him from
the practise of any Jarder pairts
qr chirurgerie and from the practise
qr medicine in any sort & discharge
from the practise of   qr chirurgerie
is in the citie of glasgow under
the pain of ane hundreth pound
Scots toties quoties conform to his
oblisst or act subt be him in
a paper apairt And ordaines
him to pay ane hundreth merks
Scots to the collector for this his
first admission or grant bond yerfor
And als to pay in pettie thrie
pounds for the glers fialls And
to pay yeirly thrinten shilling Scots

begining the first yeirs payt at
Michaelmas 1682 in name of
after compt conform to to subscription
of admission under his hand
of this dait..

(187)

At the Iron Church
24 Septr 1681..

Conveened the Visitor, Baillie Hall
Mr david Sharp, don Hall yor
chirurgian, Mr Allen Iron, &
Houstoun, James Muir, don Robison,
lodovik lindsay, don Hall barbor
James Birdwood, Mr Bogile and
Mr Inegis..

lodovik linday
electit Visitor.
The qlk day the Members of
the faculty put taking to ther
consideratiun that this is the
ordinary tyme of ther electing
a visitor for the yeir ensuing
have unanimously electit and
chosin lodovik linday Visitor for
the yeir ensuing who being put
acceptit in and upon him The

690

ld office and gave his aitte de
fideli administratione officii as
use is And he nominated &
electit to be after urs his Charles
Norvell & Ros Houstoun And the
Members put did nominat and
elect Jon Hall yor and James
Weir who being put also acceptit
and made faitto as use is and
did nominat and appoynt John
Hall yor chirurgian to be collector
for the yeir ensuing who als
being put acceptit and made
faitte And als they electit Wm
Bogill & Wm hiegie both urs who
acceptit and made faitto as
use is ..

They ordain the Cate Collector to
pay the officers fials for the bygane
yeir .

                 At George Drumzells hous
                    19 July 1682 .
Approvand the Visitor, Baillie Hall

Drumzin Collector &
box urs electit for
the yeir ensuing.

mr Charles Smeal and david Sharp
don Robisons Elder & yor: mr
Houstoune, don Hall yor chururgian.

the 9th day anent ane petition
givin in be Armour periwick
maker in glasgow wherby he
craves to be admittit be them
to the airt of barborising and
making of periwicks and as
a member of the faculty he
having produceit his burges and
gild broys ticket Whilk being
takin be the Members of the
faculty put to ther consideracons
they all in on voyce dos admit
him to barborise it in this brugh
and to the making of periwicks
and taking out his signe for
yr effect And to give band for
ane hundretto merks payzable
it in yeir and day to the collect
in nanne of the poor who hes
also payit thrie pounds to the
Collector in nanne of offecers fiales

Georg Armor
admittit barbor
& periwick maker..

and to pay yeirly his gelter comp[?]
conform as the rest of the members
of the faculty w[th]in this burgh
does who hirby obleiss himself
for y[e] effect and has made faith
as use is.—

The said day ordaines Jon Robisone
their late Collector to make his compt
of his intromission w[th] the means
of the poor of this s[ai]d faculty betwixt
and their next ordaines And
ordaines Mr david Sharp, Charles
Mowat and Jon Robisone elder to
revise the same and according as
they find it just to subscryve the
same as ratifiend by them and to
be produced to the next meeting in
order to a finall Ratificatioune & ordering
the same to be booked as followeth

By Charge & discharge
Sept[r] 20. 1680.—
Charge.—
Imps: He charges himselfe w[th]
John Bellzeas bond of six

hundreths markes is @ rent
from Candlemass 1880 To
Martinmass 1681 extends To   0442 – 00 – 0
It Wm Stirlings band of £ravine
hundreth merks is @ rent
from Candlemass 1880 to
Martinmass 1681 is   0515 – 13 – 4

Capitan Binnings band of 200
merks @ rent fra Whyt 1680
to Mart 1681 is   0145 – 06 – 8

Johne Campbells band of 50 mk
and 3 yeirs @ rent is   0041 – 06 – 8

The remainder of Mr Stobos band
being 20 lib 13S is @ rent fra
Whyt 1680 to Mart 1680 is   0022 – 06 – 8

Wm Spaldings band of 200 lib is
@ rent fra Candlemass 1680
to Mart 87 is   0221 – 00 – 0

Wm Hendersons band of 1000 mks
@ rent fra the 16 July 1880 to
the 15 Mr 1681 is   0720 – 00 – 0

Receaved fra Ja: Weir the ballance
of his compt   0024 – 11 – 2
    freedom fynes and

booking monye

Rcts of Johne Sapps friedome fyne	0003 – 00 – 0
Johne Crawfurd in pasley his	
friedome fyne	0066 – 13 – 4
It his officers fialt	0003 – 00 – 0
Johne Stores yor of dawntoune	
his friedome fyne	0066 – 13 – 4
His officers fialt	0003 – 00 – 0

Arter compts is in brughe.

Impr. Johne Hall, Mr dawid
Thorpe, Jon Harvie elder + yor
Mr Charles Mowat, Johne
Hall yor, Rt Houstoune, Johne
Hall barbor, dodowik lindsay
Mr Jho Smyth, James War
den Mc neile, Mr Alexer
Trann, Ja Beaidwood, Jon
Sapp at 12 S p annum is 0009 – 00 – 0

Arter compts is out brughe.

Impr: Rbt Hanes Rcts 3 yeirs	
at Martis 1681 is	0001 – 16 – 0
Johne Stores elder two yeir at Mart 81 is	0002 – 00 – 0
Jho Robertson in Caldwell five yeir	
at Mart 87 is	0005 – 00 – 0

Johne Sutan thrie yeires	0003 – 00 – 0
Mathow Miller thrie yeires	0003 – 00 – 0
Gilbert Neilsone thrie yeires	0003 – 00 – 0
Hughe Hunter fyve yeires	0005 – 00 – 0
Mr Semple of dalmok eight yeires	
at Miche 81	0004 – 16 – 0
Mr Alexr Porter in Britto 5 yeirs	
at Miche 81	0005 – 00 – 0
Johne Long in Hamilltoun 3 yeares	0004 – 10 – 0
James Hunter in Strihous 8 yeires	0012 – 00 – 0
John Whyt in Pasley four yeires	
at Mart 81	0004 – 00 – 0
James Mortoun in Hamilltoun 3 yeir	0004 – 10 – 0
James fforrester in Kilmacolm	
5 yeires	0007 – 10 – 0
Johne Adams at Inglistoun	
bridge two year	0003 – 00 – 0
Mr Johne Stobb two year	0003 – 00 – 0
Mark Clyford in Lanerk two year	0003 – 00 – 0
Johne Cradifoord in Pasley on year	0003 – 00 – 0

Discharge

Impr: The Compter discharges
himself wt don Gilhagis bate

of 600 mks wt @rent fra Cand:
1680 to Mart 1681 is   0442 – 00 – 0

Wm Stirlings band of 700 mks @rent
fra Cand 80.   0515 – 13 – 4

Capitan Binnings band of 200 mk
@rent fra Whyt 1680 to Mart 81. 0145 – 06 – 8

Jon Campbells bond of 50 mk + @rent 0022 – 08 – 0

Wm Spaldings band of 200 mks + @rent 0221 – 00 – 0

Wm Hendersons band of 1000 mks + @rent 0720 – 00 – 0

freidom fynes and
bookuig monye..

Anpr: Rests of John Lapps   0003 – 00 – 0

At Johne Crawfurds in Paisley 0066 – 13 – 4

his officer fiall   0003 – 00 – 0

Johne Stors yor of dauntours 0066 – 13 – 4

Qter compts wt in brughe
not payd..

Jon McNeill + Johne Lapp   0001 – 04 – 0

Qter compts wt out brughe
not payd.

Robert Harvie 3 yeirs al Mart 1681 0001 – 16 – 0

Johne Stow elder   0002 – 00 – 0

Thomas Robertson in Caldwell 0005 – 00 – 0

Johne Lutan   0003 – 00 – 0

Mathow Miller	0003 – 00 – 0
Gilbert Wilsonmyr[?]	0001 – 00 – 0
Hugh Hunter for 87	0001 – 00 – 0
Mr Semple	0004 – 16 – 0
(183) Mr Alexr Porter for 87	0001 – 00 – 0
John Laing for 87	0001 – 10 – 0
James Miller	0012 – 00 – 0
Johne Whyte	0004 – 00 – 0
James Morton[?]	0004 – 10 – 0
Johne Adam	0003 – 00 – 0
Mr Johne Stobo	0003 – 00 – 0
Mark Clifford	0003 – 00 – 0
Johne Clawford	0003 – 00 – 0

The Comptirs disbursements –

Impr givine to the poor of hutchisons hospitall	0000 – 06 – 0
To bal Cunynghame for a yeas fials	0005 – 00 – 0
To the deacon conveeners officer of fials	0001 – 04 – 0
To the conveeners hous	0010 – 00 – 0
To Mr Ard grahams wyfe of warrand 13 dea	0009 – 00 – 0

For fyr to the faculti in

hutchirsons hospitale	0000 – 12 – 0
To a weaver y{t} had his hous burnt	0002 – 16 – 0
To James dick bedell	0000 – 06 – 0
To James Muidie mess{r} for his pains	0003 – 00 – 0
To our distressed Chirurgians drufs	0002 – 18 – 0
To James dick bedell	0000 – 06 – 0
To John diddell for his daughters buriale	0011 – 12 – 0
To Patrick Park as Clerk	0001 – 00 – 0
To dodoviek for the drummers	0000 – 14 – 0
To Pat Park qn the Visitor was choysn	0001 – 08 – 0
To James dick for opening the Session hous	0000 – 06 – 0

3 Sep{r} 1684

Prntais Portafield. The sd day Alex{r} Porterfield is booked
prentais w{t} John Robisons for
fyve years from his entrie qlk
was at Lambmass last Conforme
to ther Indentour dated the sd
third day of Sep{r} 1684 –

28 Junii 1685 –

The sd day Johne Campbell sone
lanll to Robert Campbell Mer'd
burges of glasgow alias black Robert
is bookd prentice with Johne Hall
elder for the space of four yeares
from his entrie qlk wes at
Whytsonday last conforme to ther
indentors qlke are of the date of
thir prties and hes payd fourtie
shilling for his booking monye
attor clerk + officers dews.